The
CLOSEST POSSIBLE UNION

The

CLOSEST

POSSIBLE

UNION

JOANNA SCOTT

An Owl Book
Henry Holt and Company
New York

Henry Holt and Company, Inc.
Publishers since 1866
115 West 18th Street
New York, New York 10011

Henry Holt® is a registered
trademark of Henry Holt and Company, Inc.

Published in Canada by Fitzhenry & Whiteside Ltd.,
195 Allstate Parkway, Markham, Ontario L3R 4T8.

Library of Congress Cataloging-in-Publication Data
Scott, Joanna.
The closest possible union/
Joanna Scott.
p.   cm.
"An Owl book."
I. Title.
[PS3569.C636C58   1996]   96-44300
813'.54—dc20   CIP

ISBN 0-8050-3973-2

Henry Holt books are available for special promotions and
premiums. For details contact: Director, Special Markets.

First published in hardcover in 1988 by
Ticknor & Fields.

First Owl Book Edition—1996

Printed in the United States of America
All first editions are printed on acid-free paper. ∞

1   3   5   7   9   10   8   6   4   2

A portion of this book has appeared in *The Missouri
Review* in a slightly different form.

For Yvonne, Scotty, and the boys

Good people, how very far astray your childlike simplicity has led you! These attitudes of prayer conceal the most atrocious habits; these supplicating arms are lethal weapons; these fingers tell no rosaries, but help to exterminate the unfortunate passers-by.

J. H. Fabre, *Social Life in the Insect World*

HOW MANY SPECIES? Surely as many as there are stars in the heavens, from lice glued onto a strand of hair to powerful gnats that can pierce a man's boot, from aphid cows enslaved by ants to weevils napping comfortably inside curled poplar leaves. The library contains information on the most mysterious varieties, I shall not be bored. I doubt the captain has leisure to study his books — he is as tireless, as attentive as the harpy, our figurehead, that hideous, slack-breasted, bearded old maid who guides our ship.

My brother has asked me to bring him an ivory tooth, which, he explained, must be torn from a live elephant's jaw with my own hands because, he said, at the instant of the animal's death a brown mucus is secreted, the ivory forever marred. I am not sure how it is to be done; I will have a native help me. My sister has asked for gold. My dear mother wants only an honest account of my voyage day by day. She has met the captain herself, and she considers him a genteel, sophisticated man. She said I would learn much from him if I applied myself. I expect I will be full grown four months from now, when we've completed the voyage.

The sailors think they have signed on for a three-year whaling cruise. Only the captain, the chief mate, the surgeon, and myself know the truth. Though I am the youngest on board, I have been privileged both with the secret of our actual purpose and with a private berth directly across from the stateroom. I suppose it couldn't have been otherwise, since my father is the *Charles Beauchamp*'s primary financer. Papa has instructed the captain to make me into a gentleman, to spare nothing. The captain has a handsome, abundant beard and forbidding eyebrows that meet at a sharp diagonal — indeed, that seem a pair of locust wings implanted on his forehead. He takes his brandy at every meal, including breakfast. I am sure I shall like him very much.

That I was on an American Guineaman I knew, but whether I would ever wake from it I could not tell, so I struggled both to free myself from this confusion and to shake my shoulders loose from the talons of the harpy, that vile wooden bird studded with snails and barnacles. As she tried to pry me from my mother's arms, I heard my father's voice: "It will be morning soon." When I thrashed off my blanket I slipped further into the unyielding dark — time itself meant to torment, dangling me between yesterday and tomorrow.

My body has not yet adjusted to the dreadful rolling. I managed to set my feet upon the floor and stumble through the galley, up the companionway to the deck, but once there I did not reach the rail in time. Midway across I threw my arm around the ship's bell, collapsed to my knees, and retched while we slid over the quivering, aspic swells. I expected to find the pink lining of my stomach crumpled in a heap upon the planks. I hope it does not take long to earn favor with this element. I wiped my lips with my nightshirt cuff, then I leaned over the rail, invited the velvet wind to caress me, searched for constellations but there were none in the black-plated ceiling, looked for land and was comforted by a brownish crag windward, which I first mistook for my continent's shoreline but was, I realized, nothing but the cloud of a loitering squall.

In the sty built in the forecastle head half a dozen grunts

complained of their discomfort. The halyard rings clanked against the masts, the canvas snapped and fluttered, and I tried to flatten the lumpy waters with a command — *lie still!* — but of course I had no influence. So I peeled off my nightshirt, and, on my knees, with the smock wadded in my hands, the chill wind prickling my arms, I wiped the planks, erased all the gluey evidence of my seasickness, thinking my work remained unobserved, for I was fore and the midwatch sailors were nesting behind the binnacle. But when I stood I sensed an audience, I felt his gaze rudely scrape my naked shoulders, the curve of my rump, my spindly legs, and I wheeled around to find him there, a shadowy parcel in the foremast top, with his cigar stub like a pernicious yellow Cyclops eye. It was too dark to identify this sailor, but I am certain he could make out who I was, if not from my features, then from my size — by a forearm's length I am the shortest passenger on board. I did not wrench away, I could not. Only when he tossed the stub, tobacco sparks arcing in a slow, soundless descent to the sea, did he release me from his eyes. I flung my nightshirt off the port side into the ocean; it, too, was engulfed silently, like an angel following the outcast Lucifer to hell.

Today I have tried to single out this son of Neptune, hoping for a sign of recognition from him, for I mean to warn him not to spread an account of my lubber's sickness. But the crew wears a bland mask, indifferently shouldering the harness of this immense plough; none glance twice at me when I am among them.

The crew begins to suspect the true nature of our voyage. At the captain's order they broke out the hold today and discovered, to their surprise, a store of rice, farina, salt pork, and beef sufficient to maintain a crew twenty times their number. They pried open barrels meant for oil and found them filled with fresh water. They uncovered the pine boards that will serve as the floor. No one dares approach the captain, however — inquiry would be equal to mutiny in his eyes. How long we will keep up the sham of whaling I do not know, but still the warnings are called from aloft, the men rush to lower the boats and wait for the captain to send them over, but the command to proceed is never uttered, our captain merely stares toward the horizon as if he expected the sea mammoths to come willingly to us. I have spent the day spitting up my morning coffee, wandering thick-headed, completely useless. Tomorrow I shall ask to be assigned to a watch, regardless of my father's instructions, I shall build up my strength and show that I am capable, for aren't I my mother's pride, very nearly a man?

The hatch of chickens was transferred to the poop, sacks of rice and water casks were moved to the galley, and the sailors have begun to build a platform in the bilge. I overheard two men speaking eagerly of the Windward Coast and the "blackfish oil" that will be our cargo. The crew seems to approve unanimously of this change of plans, they know they will be paid generously and will be back in New London long before winter. Our purpose has not been formally announced, but the men need no explanation to make sense of the extra provisions in the hold and the floor being constructed to accommodate the merchandise. They are generally content and treat me kindly, demonstrating how to haul on the rigging and position the spars. Twice I was overtaken by a brief spell, and thankfully the sailors looked away when I vomited into a washing tub and tripped over a coil of chain cable. I have yet to act the part of a gentleman convincingly.

The captain's humor has improved now that he shares the truth of our destination with his men. After evening mess today he sent for me — I would have slicked my hair and made sure to wear my small peaked cap embroidered with the Company's house-flag had I anticipated the meeting. As it was, I proceeded in rather slovenly dress, my trousers stained with a dribble of soup, my fingernails packed with waxy tar, my cap nowhere to be found in the cramped half deck. I confess I expected a less than hospitable greeting from the man assigned to educate me. I expected a reprimand for my shortcomings, though they can't be helped.

His door was spattered with tiny, shallow pocks, rather like scars left by pitchfork prongs, and I rapped softly, hoping he wouldn't answer so I could return to my own berth. But from within came his gruff command to enter. I obeyed. Try as I might to achieve some semblance of control, I could not stop my hands from trembling. It seemed as if the captain's teak-paneled stateroom were a snug hollow carved in a block of ice, and I stood unclad in the glacial pocket — my fear was not emotion but a blue, penetrating light. He took no notice of my panic. A lamp swung from a beam above him so his face passed in and out of shadow. On his table was spread a navigation chart, the curling edges pinned flat to the blotter with glass weights, each containing a handful of guineas. A string of incense smoke rose from the mouth of a porcelain turtle. The captain sat stiffly, the brass chalice in his hand a gilded staff, the lamp an immense crown being lowered to his head.

His skin between his beard and brow had the texture of cloth, a coarse, red weave, and though his chest was expansive, his hips narrow, he had a protruding belly that made his otherwise admirable figure appear skewed, even faintly clownish in his brass-buttoned, double-breasted uniform. I stood across from him, waiting for his next direction, and since he said nothing as he scrutinized me, I forced myself to speak.

"Sir," I said, "you wished —" and he raised his cup, interrupting me with his toast: "To your mother, a rare enchantress."

My mother. His infidel's smirk insulted her. He fell silent

and I had no doubt he was privately calling forth her image. I would have liked to forget my place and lunge at him, my fingers clawed, teeth bared, smothering him with huge wings. But his interest had already shifted from the country behind us to the dark continent ahead. He said aloud, though clearly more to himself than to me, "They will eat you alive if they catch you," then shook his head as if to disperse the thought. He drank a great amount of brandy while I stood at the threshold, awaiting his pleasure. I forced myself to move a few paces toward him. He motioned me to come closer. I did so, reluctantly. He slipped his arm around my waist, positioned me in front of his table, set his cup down, and with the fingers of his free hand traced the jagged coastline of Africa from Cape Verde to the Congo River. He asked me how I would like to have my own little Negro. I told him I should like it very well. He asked me what I would do with my slave, and I said, "Sir, I shall care for him." And though he said, "Yes, to be sure," my response evidently was not sufficient.

He persisted. "And what will you feed him?"

"Giblets," I said, "to make him strong," for that is what Papa feeds our mastiff.

"And shall you make him work?"

"Very hard, sir," I replied.

"And how will you teach him to mind his young master?"

"With a whip, sir."

"And when will you flog him?"

"When he is lazy."

"And?"

"When he is sullen."

"And?"

"When he disobeys. Though I will not hurt him much."

At this the captain jerked his arm away and returned to his map, his tongue furrowing beneath his beard, rippling as the surface of a cocoon must when the butterfly inside awakens.

"When will we return to America?" I asked uneasily, for I had noticed that the captain's incense smelled like a woman's perfume, and I was thinking of my mother again.

But still he wished to question me further about my slave. "Of course you must not maim him," he said, massaging his temple to rub away his obvious displeasure. "But will you make him feel to the marrow? Will you make him tractable and God-fearing? I assure you of this: it is better to throw them into the sea than to encourage their impudence." With that he reached for his cup, drained it in a single gulp, and gestured with his elbow to a sea chest and a plugged flask full of brandy. I was not quick enough to do his bidding, and he cried out angrily, "Fetch me more drink, boy!"

The captain is a changeable man. Immediately upon quenching his thirst, he threw his arm around me again and indicated that I should sip from his cup. I am not partial to brandy but did not want to offend him, so I put the rim to my lips and pretended to swallow, though I took none of the brackish copper liquid into my mouth. I did not fool him — he tittered, pinched my cheek as if he were flirting with a chambermaid, and gave me leave to go. As I turned toward the door he said, "Thomas!" in a voice assuring me I would receive the flogging intended for my slave. Instead he said shortly, "I will expect you tomorrow night." That was all. He did not explain why he prefers me to the chief mate, to any of the crew, or even to his library. I suppose I should be honored, despite his toast to my mother's beauty. The captain's name is much esteemed at home. My brother shall be envious when he learns of my privileged position.

Tomorrow I will rise early and haul with the force of six men, and when I visit the captain he will acknowledge, "There's glory ahead for you, boy." I must rest now if I am to be strong through the day. Yet I do not think I will ever sleep again. With miles of water between me and the mainland, the sleep I am used to, the effortless sleep beneath blankets, within the timber and shingles of my home, seems only a disguise: my family, my neighbors, the people of my nation, assume they are safe in their sleep when in truth each of them is flung far out into oblivion at the moment he lets go of his senses. I shall not venture to the deck tonight, for I am certain I will see the pale, spineless forms of thousands of sleepers hovering just above the waves, soft white clouds of souls, like larvae, retaining their shape by inflating themselves with air. Even now, though the sea rips angrily beneath this Guineaman's keel, I can hear them sighing, pulsating, clinging to life, depending on air as I depend on this tallow and wick to illuminate the page. They will wake at dawn in their own beds, ignorant of the journey they have taken, but tomorrow I shall remember where I have been tonight. For I shall remain in the same place, floating, like the coins in the captain's glass paperweights.

Jack Carvee, the ship's cook, an ancient sea dog who hardly has wit enough to light the stove and boil water, discovered a crate of two hundred wooden spoons, and he laid thirty of them on the galley benches for noon mess. Poor Jack Carvee. The captain threatened to brand him with a knife and pour brine on his wounds if he ever felt compelled to make free with the contents of a crate again. I am finding it difficult to partake of the cook's preparations, though the men say our fare is better than the ordinary — we have fresh pork, pickled onions, and pudding, besides the usual salt horse and beans.

I opened my sister's gift today. She had made me promise to wait, indicating that I would appreciate the present when I had put a significant distance between myself and my home. My sister is only seven years old. I untied the ribbon and opened the box's lid to find a piece of fruit, a skull-shaped orange covered entirely in a fur of turquoise-flecked silver mold. She does not understand that perishables will turn rancid, she thinks an orange must remain as perfect as the fruit arranged seasonally in a bowl upon our dining room table. The spoiled orange would not have been such a disappointment if there were a single item on our menu to savor.

I grow frail instead of hardy. I climbed to the main crosstree this afternoon and pretended the southwesterly wind was lemonade. I sipped like a bee from a pistil. I shall climb to the platform whenever I have a chance: the sensation of riding aloft nourishes me, with the sun showering the sky with citrus colors, the water whispering, the air as warm as blood.

I went promptly to the captain's cabin this evening after supper. I knocked boldly this time, and though a puddle of light seeped through the crevice below the door, the captain did not answer. Perhaps he had fallen asleep over his navigation chart. I shall try again tomorrow.

I have found him, the sailor from the foremast top. I recognized him by the look he cast askance when I tried to work the lifts. He thinks that I am not as capable as I pretend and have no nautical ambition, doubtless he wonders why the captain ever permitted me to sign the ship's register. The men do not know I am an investor's son, and I shall not tell them. They may make up their own reasons to explain my presence on board this vessel. But I have identified the one who watched me scour the deck, naked, in as shameless a posture as a dog lapping paddock mud. I do not trust him; though he proves no sluggard and hurries to the lines when summoned, he stays aloof when his watch is at rest.

Today I slapped my cheeks to give them color, polished my shoes, slicked my hair with vegetable butter I took from the galley, and presented myself to the boatswain, Pharaoh, entreating him for some form of employment. He sent me to the bilge to oversee the progress of the deck. The space where we will store our cargo lies only a few feet under the forecastle, and every man except myself must crawl about on his hands and knees, while I needed merely to hunch my shoulders forward and keep my head low. Two weak lanterns provided just enough light so a man could distinguish between his thumb and the nail head. The sailors laying planks worked slowly, swaying with the motion of the ship as if they were supple aquatic weeds rooted to the ocean floor.

I hadn't been below for long when the chief mate called all hands. The clouds that had been trailing us since we left Montauk Point behind decided to attack, the front sheet of rain churned the water to a suds of whitecaps that spread toward our Guineaman with the ease and momentum of fire crossing an arid plain. The mate barked hysterical commands, to reef, to ply, to bind canvas to yard, but the wind had already filled the mainsail, the ship bowled and plunged, and the rigging rope slid through my hands, searing shreds of skin from my palm. I leaped backward, fumbling for a stay secured to the rail, my feet slid out from under me, and I held on to the shroud for dear life, hugging the prickly cord.

The squall passed as rapidly as it had overtaken us. I'm not sure when I met the eyes of the sailor, the rear man on the ropes — he had turned nearly full around to scan me as I huddled at the bottom of the shroud. I cringed against the prickling rain, against the foam cascading over the bulwarks, but most of all against this fellow's scorn, and only when the rain had passed and the gusts subsided did I realize he had no right to look at me that way — this secretive, beardless, ordinary sailor was insolent, that's all, he was insolent, and I knew him immediately for the midnight watchman.

A mast had been damaged by the winds so the ship's carpenter and three men set to mending the crack. Others were ordered aloft to inspect the sails, and the rest returned

to the lower hold to continue building the floor. The anonymous sailor, overlooked by the mate, spent the afternoon
idling at the lee rail, likely pondering some debt he has
left unpaid or some punishment he has narrowly escaped.
I hoped to ask the captain about the fellow, to inquire about
his name and station, for I intend to report him to my
father. But tonight the captain discouraged conversation.
Though he had me enter his suite and ordered me to stand
beside his chair, to refill his cup from the flask and the
flask from a bottle packed with straw inside the chest, he
had no use for my words. The captain seemed to be withering
in some intense, private grief. Perhaps he misses home as
much as I do, though he is an officer, and I only the son
of Charles Beauchamp.

It is apparent now why our captain rebuked Jack Carvee
for breaking open a sealed crate. Along with our provisions
in the hold there are goods for trading on the coast — tobacco, claret, gingham, five bales of cotton, dozens of darkie
low pipes and straw hats with red ribbon bands. It wasn't
these, though, that were forbidden — such articles are useless to a seaman, for he has his own tobacco and prefers
whiskey and rum to claret. But there proved to be a single
crate stashed below that the captain valued above the others.
Today he summoned two of the strongest sailors to follow
him, and a quarter of an hour later they emerged from
the lower deck, the men carrying a large, oblong pine box.
The ship's bell was rung and we assembled beneath a sky
saturated with brilliant topaz light reflecting off the sea,
off our hair, off the canvas, scalding my milk-white skin. I
prefer walls of mist surrounding us to this relentless heat.
Thankfully, enough of a breeze keeps up so we continue
southeast at a respectable clip.

The box was hoisted to a makeshift dais — three planks
laid across the tops of barrels. The surgeon climbed into

the small pulpit behind the deckhouses, and while the men crowded below him, caps in hands, the surgeon recited from a prayer volume, a leather-bound book that fit snugly in his palm: "The living know that they will die, but the dead know nothing." At the end of his short sermon he nodded vigorously, his jowls quivering like ripe pears hanging by a thread of stem, and the sailors tipped the contents of the crate into the sea. As the burlap sack tumbled out I understood — we were witnessing a sea burial, though the name of the deceased was not disclosed, the captain's interest never explained. Judging from the dimensions of the crude box and the bulk of the sack, we were saluting a near giant — why the body had been with us for an entire fortnight I could not say. The surgeon descended from his balcony, the men lifted down the casket and carried it below, and the rest of the crew dispersed. I managed to creep closer to the captain, who lingered by the rail, and together we searched the frothing eddy water. Of course the sea had already swallowed the sack. I don't think I would like to be dropped into the ocean, to disappear without even a wooden cross to mark my place and to announce my surname and the dates of my existence.

With balmy southern winds filling the sails, the tides have stopped sloshing about inside me, and I was grateful for the work when Pharaoh ordered me to help the cook move his kitchen to the firehearth on the upper deck, where, on an honest whaler, blubber would be diced and boiled. Later in the afternoon the messboy, Brian Piper, invited me to the tryworks to teach me how to make pudding. He has an unfortunate face, dotted with red pustules, scarred with white streaks like salt left behind by tears, and his hair hangs in a tattered veil over his eyes. While I watched him pulverize a stick of cinnamon with mortar and pestle I asked him what had been contained inside the captain's box. He laughed shrilly and said, "Why, maybe it was rotten pork, or maybe it was the captain's wives."

I didn't tell him that my father had given his name to the *Charles Beauchamp* and that the captain is a family friend. Instead I asked him, in jest, how many wives the captain had, how many could have been packed inside the crate.

"The sum total? There would have been eight, if there were any at all, Tom."

Of course I was skeptical. But I recalled the captain's insinuating toast. "Then where did he keep them?" I challenged.

"He used to maintain them in homes scattered round the world. But on this voyage he might have stashed them in the lower hold. And maybe Brian Piper saw them there, maybe he smelled them, a God-awful smell, and opened the box thinking we had left a porker to rot. But maybe it was a different kind of moldy meat. Just think of my consternation, Tom!" I suspected the messboy's candidness, and I told him how I'd descended to the hold myself and had seen no sign of lady passengers. He found me amusing, I don't know why. With a hideous leer he turned to me and said in a pinched, mocking falsetto, "Well, he brought them along, I assure thee."

Clearly he was abusing me, taking advantage of my credulity and innocence. I turned abruptly to leave and he said sharply, "Now it's possible we said goodbye to a sackful of ham and that this was just practice for the days ahead. But if that's the case, then you might investigate his wardrobe, if you've got the courage. You'll have to pilfer his key, for you must have noticed he keeps his cabinets locked. And tell me, Tom, why is the incense always burning in the captain's stateroom?" I kicked the iron door of the tryworks and asked him how the captain could have fit so many bodies into such a narrow casket. "We didn't say they were intact, did we?" challenged Piper, joyfully plunging his hands into the bucket of yellow pudding. So I left him.

At supper I did not bother to sample his pudding. And later I could not bring myself to visit the captain's quarters.

If tomorrow he wants an excuse for my absence, I shall tell him I assumed he wanted to be left in peace with the burden of his sorrow. He may punish me if he likes.

With the canvas taut and the ship steering well at eight knots, the captain was exceptionally amiable this morning. He monitored the compasses, scanned the horizon with a spyglass, and took the wheel while the helmsman retired for a smoke. In his smart blue uniform and sea boots he seemed irreproachable, and I regretted my unkind thoughts. I, too, remained fully clothed, my collar buttoned, my shoes cracked and brittle. No one but me appeared bothered by the heat. The men blustered about, throwing off their shoes and shirts, becoming increasingly raucous as the day wore on; I shrank away from them at messtime, for they took to pounding the benches, their thighs, their neighbor's sunburnt back when Jack Carvee kept them waiting for coffee. I don't entirely understand how power is distributed among the sailors. There are bosses and laborers, but the delineation among them seems derived from some mysterious criteria other than strength or wealth or comeliness — some men claim the upper hand and some defer. Jack Carvee must be fast to appease the hunger of these seamen. The carpenter, an able bagpiper, is obliged to entertain us hour after hour with his spirited melodies. And ever since we've passed into the tropics, the men have been searching for someone to sacrifice. This afternoon they eyed me, as chained dogs will watch a cat slinking freely along a path just beyond reach, so I returned to my half deck, where I remained for more than an hour, reclining upon my pallet, listening to the water sucking the keel and to an unlatched cabinet door lurching open and clapping shut. I could do nothing but wait, for mine seemed a warranted doom, I was obliged to pay for the crime. What crime? It did not matter: when a consensus is reached among sailors, doubt, protest, and contrary evidence have no meaning. A conviction might be arbitrary, but once it has been passed it shan't be retracted. For sailors seal themselves in a pride as resistant as any insect's shell.

There are insects even this far distance from shore, I have discovered. They ride along inside our sacks of cornmeal and flour. I should like to examine one more closely, though you may be sure I'll do the capturing and killing myself. I have seen the cruel methods of extermination among these men, the slow mangling of arthropods. While I was anticipating my own execution the sailors selected another victim. Who else but the midnight watchman? He has yet to strip off the bulky foul-weather togs, and he practically drowns inside the folds of cloth, his cap pulled low, his lips a delicate vermilion. He fancies himself superior, though he is the only greenhorn of the crew. And on board an ocean vessel, I have learned today, a greenhorn must undergo a rite of passage called a sea baptism: when a member of the crew passes into the Torrid Zone for the first time in his career, he must pay a tax, the amount fixed by a committee of sailors.

When I finally ventured from my burrow I found six men clustered in the stern while the boatswain sat upon the platform where just yesterday the captain's crate was mounted. Pharaoh had slung a blanket across his shoulders, and at his feet stood the watchman. I perceived that I had wandered into a trial, though I would have to wait until evening, when the messboy explained the intricate ritual to me, before I understood the nature of the watchman's crime. Pharaoh made some reference to a fee due; the watchman remained silent, though he didn't have to speak to show contempt. He had no patience for this artifice of court, but with five guards surrounding him he was forced to persist in his dissenter's role. Pharaoh cited the amount again and said, "I ask you one last time: will you pay?"

When the watchman did not respond Pharaoh sprang

to his feet, cast the blanket to the deck, and proclaimed that he, the magistrate, hereby sentenced this sailor, who refused to pass the line in an honorable fashion, to baptism by water. A murmur rippled among the men, Pharaoh lifted his hand to silence them. The rebel will be stripped, ordered Pharaoh, tied fast with a rope, hoisted over the port rail, and run three times under water. The watchman tried to wrench free, but one determined agent jerked his arm into a backward vise. Meanwhile, on the poop, the captain and the chief mate passed a spyglass between them.

I can't say what would have happened to the watchman had his punishment been carried through, I don't know how many keelhauled men have survived. But he was saved by fortune: the sailor riding the mizzentop called out a sail, the captain hailed urgently, "Where away?"

Since we are a slaving vessel and could be identified as such by any discerning authority who chanced to board and snoop around the hold, we are safest when we steer a solitary course and invite no contact with other ships. As the speck of sail approached, the captain consulted with his chief mate, and we waited for the mate to pass down the order. The captain decided to redirect southward. A convenient gust speeded us along our illegal course, we braced smartly and soon lost sight of the intruder. All hands were kept alert through the afternoon, and it seemed the interrupted baptism had been forgotten. I was sorry for it. I did not pity the midnight watchman and thought he deserved to suffer. Such dark, venomous eyes.

Through the rest of the day the bagpiper leaned against a bulkhead and squeezed his set of bladders, the cook fetched fresh water whenever a man called, and the watchman kept to his bunk. Only when we were having our evening coffee in the galley did he come out to gather the remnants of supper. Pharaoh and the others greeted him cordially, as if there had been nothing but brotherhood among them all along. I was seated next to the messboy. With a nudge he warned me to look sharp, for there would soon occur "a happening." I asked him what, and when it would take place, but he fell smugly silent, guarding his treasure of information. I don't know how the messboy can be certain of so many things.

The men themselves appeared unaware of the impending adventure — they talked quietly, as polite and harmless as any post-supper gathering of gentlemen, while the watchman settled at the edge of a bench and with his fingers scooped the dregs of cold kidney bean stew from the pot. I was certain the incident would involve both the watchman and the vengeful Pharaoh — no ocean storm will subside without a final, violent shudder. Someone called upon the carpenter to play, but other sailors protested, they preferred the muted sounds of weather and sea. A compromise was reached, they ordered the bagpiper to the pulpit, and soon the straining chords permeated the beams, muffled, overwhelmed at times by the hissing night waters. We spent a few minutes deep in thought, each man apparently serene, or at least resigned to this aqueous desert.

The event began with a small cloth parcel passed surreptitiously from sailor to sailor. If the messboy hadn't warned me, I would have been as surprised as our midnight watchman when, at a nod from Pharaoh, two sailors rose, and, moving rapidly, one seized the watchman by his elbows while the other, the bandy-legged but powerful sailor known as Yellow Will, cocked back his head, forcing his mouth open with his thumbs in the manner of a groom coercing a reluctant horse to take the bit. Though he looked as pathetic as anyone I'd ever seen, I still didn't pity him. Then Pharaoh stood, an inspiring, bloated shadow in the galley, with a lantern clamped on the wall behind him, so to me he was a solid, featureless gray boulder, haloed by light. He upturned the cloth bag and clapped one palm over the other to contain whatever had fallen free, raised his cupped hands before the watchman's nose, and said for us all to hear,

"You choose: shall it be baptism or shall it be communion? I tell you to choose one or the other." The watchman said nothing — I don't see how he could have managed more than a grunt with his head hinged backward at such an angle.

I think I would have chosen baptism. Unlucky man. Into his mouth was forced one live cockroach, nearly equal in size to my thumb. Down his moist gullet slid the uncooked intruder, into his intestines, seeping into his blood, to be pumped toward his heart, crunched inside his contracting ventricles, from there to infect his brain. He will never be free from the sensation, he will never forget, not even in sleep. I don't envy him his memories.

One of the sailors clamped his lips closed, Yellow Will continued to lash back his head in the crook of his arm. And then, abruptly, he stopped struggling against us. Stopped the spasms of resistance. We pressed in around him like a crowd around an epileptic once the fit has passed and the possessed man slowly regains control of himself. Someone leaned over and with his sleeve tenderly wiped his face, another man placed the cap back on the watchman's head. The bagpipes reached us from the distance, mewing that low, seductive siren's chord, inviting us to leave the ship, to come ashore, boys, come ashore. Then the sailors began preparing the rebel for a second course, though they couldn't unlock his jaw so easily this time. Having tasted once, he immediately stiffened, unwilling to open for another mouthful.

I am not sure when during the forced feeding the bagpiping was cut short, or at what moment the captain stepped into the galley. And how did he make his presence known? One by one the men turned from the spectacle to the silent specter, from the ring to the periphery. And like the skittish bugs they had hunted for this feast, they immediately retreated toward the walls, toward corners, shadows, crevices.

The watchman remained seated, a half-eaten, discarded fruit from which the sailors had withdrawn when a more powerful predator arrived. The captain surveyed us silently, and with the slightest gesture of his hand he ordered us out. One by one we climbed sheepishly up the companionway ladder.

I don't know what was said between the captain and the watchman when they were alone, and I don't know where the watchman sleeps, for the messboy claims he is not on deck, nor in his bunk, nor aloft in the crosstrees or the tops. "If a man is nowhere to be found on board a ship, it is more than certain that . . . ," the messboy proposed, but I refused to listen. Tonight I wrapped my head in the blanket that still smells of my cedar chest, and I pressed my face against the mattress so that no one could hear me whisper, "I want to go home, Mother, please come and take me home."

"Insects!" spat the captain tonight when I invited him to speak on the subject.

"So many variations, sir," I tried to suggest, "so many methods of adapting." But the captain, though his library is stocked with entomology, did not share my admiration.

"All are alike," he growled, "all gather in their vile clusters and gnaw slowly, steadily through a man's accomplishments. And never, never do they feel the satisfaction of replenishment. Compare the beetle to the swine: which of the two enjoys the draught following thirst, which appreciates the sun basking and fattening preceding death? The insect is too stupid to love pleasure. The insect is what a fool would produce had he the means to set a heart beating without God's help. The insect is nothing more than a skeleton with fluttering wings and hair-fine limbs, the insect defies our notion of life's worth. A finger severed from a hand would be classified an insect were it capable of digestion and reproduction — here, boy, here are insects plenty for you," and

with that he woke his hands from their usual dignified re-
straint and permitted his fingers to assault me, gently of
course, the captain only meant to tease, squeezing my kneecap, twisting my earlobe, prodding my belly. Perhaps I would
have found him amusing if we had been alone. But we
were all the while being observed by the watchman, whose
recent refuge, it turns out, has been the captain's suite.
The watchman's name is Peter Gray. The name is as decep-
tive as his costume.

"What will happen?" mocked the captain as I submitted
to his uninvited fondling. "Will we, too, give up meaning
and become nothing more than the shell protecting us?
Will humanity live in hives and sacrifice pleasure to function?
Will there be no secrets? Will we wear our skeletons on
the outside?"

And then, from the corner of the daybed, came a flat,
deliberate challenge: "You would not speak so glibly, Captain, had you ever seen two garden slugs embracing." This
from a common watchman, an ordinary sailor who has an
intimate knowledge of primitive species now. The captain
hushed his frolicking hands, turned to Peter Gray, and said
without any trace of resentment, "No, I never have seen
slugs in that position. Tell me what I've missed."

For the preceding twenty minutes I had remained sensitive
to the watchman's brooding presence, as one might be aware
of one's own reflection in a grand gilt-framed mirror placed
unobtrusively on a back wall. I had assumed that he was
to be for this captain what a Newfoundland dog might be
to a master on another ship: a pet, an entertainment, company, defense, and something warm and plush to look at
when a man is surrounded by acres of salt water. But my
captain's Newfoundland spoke with unaccountable audacity.
What reason had he to correct his master's opinion?

"Two garden slugs," said Peter Gray, leaning out from
the shadows where he had been brooding since the captain's
dismissive introduction, "two garden slugs on a moonlit ter-

race at summer's wane will hang by a thread of mucus attached to a fence post."

The captain laughed, insisting, "Go on, yes, go on," clearly finding a perverse delight in the description. I don't understand why the watchman wanted to persuade the captain to appreciate a life form so close in kind to a roach. Surely his insect left an aftertaste — he cannot have forgotten so soon.

"Two garden slugs will twist their supple, moist bodies around each other, pressing in continual spirals, reciprocating identical pleasures. Two garden slugs will link end to end, top to bottom, to form a braid, and each will implant its seed into the other. You see, each slug is masculine, each feminine."

My brother and I have often sat with my sister among a group of my father's acquaintances, we have seen the color rise in her face when they pursue a subject to the edge of decency, when they begin to snigger dryly, relax into their armchairs, and glance at her. My sister, though she is a child, must understand that they will continue their conversation the moment she has been excused from their company. In the captain's stateroom it was my turn to feel the pain of such exclusion.

The captain, even if he was impressed, refused to let Peter Gray pursue the mystery of the hermaphroditic snail. "All right," he grunted, "you've told enough, be silent now," and the watchman withdrew his face from the light, once again a proper dog, obedient, submissive, a lifeless plaster cast beneath the skylight, which had been shuttered before we left New London so that the only natural illumination in the room trickled in through the water closet portal.

While Peter Gray had orated for those few minutes, the captain had diminished in my eyes. He revealed himself to be less than the formidable, staunch, harrowing man whom I have feared: he showed that he is ignorant of science, he cares little for his library, he has not read the books and disdains insects simply because he has no knowledge of them. True, he is a brave officer and daily he grows fonder of me, but I am disappointed.

At any rate, the captain at once put the subject of entomology behind and pursued the topic that is his specialty: trafficking. He spoke in counterfeit, in lies, and gradually I perceived that Peter Gray might be the only passenger on board who still did not know our true purpose. Nothing is what it pretends to be, I am quickly learning, not the captain's claims nor the watchman's identity, not Pharaoh's title nor the messboy's information. When I return home I shall study to be a scientist, I shall devote myself to learning the patterns of nature, the impermeable laws, I shall trust again the continuity between yesterday and tomorrow. I wonder what my mother would say about the plots and deceptions.

"Let us speak of a more enlivening subject," suggested the captain as the ocean bulged and broke against the hull, the splash like a bucketful of water thrown on a flame and the captain's voice the hissing of doused embers. "Let us consider the treasures we will bring home in place of blubber and oil. I have been instructed by the Company to procure such items as ivory and indigo, gold dust and tortoise shell. Young Tom, if we gather seventy-five ostrich plumes, you shall have the seventy-sixth. And Peter Gray, you may keep the dried, cured skin of the first snake we catch. The continent abounds in reptiles — serpents, lizards, crocodiles — they are much valued as curiosities and are easily flayed. Or perhaps, Peter Gray, you would want another sort of skin, one less abrasive, more becoming, a cheap, handsome robe that would reach to your ankles, covering your legs, Peter Gray."

"I need nothing beyond what I wear upon me now or have packed in my duffel," replied the watchman, who, obscured by the suite's gloom, seemed merely the fragments of a man, a stain of a shadow on the muckish surface of a

pond. He didn't understand that there will be only one
type of skin in our cargo.

"Palm oil for you, Peter Gray, so you may anoint yourself
and strut naked before the admiring crew. I shall reward
you both if you perform to your credit. Tom, the other
day I offered you a young hippopotamus. The rivers are
full of them, you shall have *two* if you like, you can chain
them to the mast and perch on their backs. But it will be
up to you to keep them alive, you must observe their habits
and feed them yams, grapes, and grain accordingly. And
you, Peter Gray, shall have the hide of an adult, along with
the skull. And the teeth, if they are intact and fair. Bad
teeth are worth nothing, but good ones, unchipped, are
valued more than ivory. The closer their resemblance to
human teeth, the higher the price a dentist will pay. Curious
monkeys and baboons are found in great quantity, but we
want only a few to occupy the men during the passage home.
We shall trade trifles for ox horns, for coffee, minerals,
and goatskins, we shall barter for beeswax and, Peter Gray,
I will leave it to you to strain the honey, we have brought
along a large iron kettle for that service. But you must take
care in the process — the cook will teach you how — for I
like my honey pure, and solid beeswax will bring twenty-
five cents a pound. And if any man captures that most exquisite of African beasts, the camelopard, and brings the patch-
work beauty safely on board, I shall pay him a bonus of
ten dollars. So what say you, Tom and Peter Gray, my two
loyal friends — will you stick with me and show the other
men what courage means?"

I was glad he kept my influence hidden from the watchman, but I had no wish to fool Peter Gray; the crew had
punished him severely enough. So I said nothing, neither
did Peter Gray, and into the captain's narrow suite with its
fine mahogany bookcases and wardrobe seeped the sound
of water sloshing against the hull, and that music was our

doom. We were the rotten produce contained in the crate thrown overboard yesterday, sinking fathoms into the ocean canyon, into a narrow, bottomless cleft. Until the captain spoke, as abruptly as the squirting noise of a harp string breaking: "Tom!"

"Sir?"

"I want you to explain to Peter Gray."

"Explain?" I knew what he was demanding, I tried to stall.

"I have enumerated several types of beasts and birds, but I think Peter Gray would appreciate a statement of general intent."

I looked from the bearded officer to the unfortunate watchman, I struggled to describe our cargo. "We want to collect," I said, twisting the knuckles of one hand against the glass pane of the bookcase, "such things that are dear and yet can be easily transported!" I exclaimed, so to my own ears the words seemed to fold into one another, my speech was nonsense. But the captain only clapped his heavy paws upon my shoulders and called me a sly Tom Fool. Then he had me pour and serve the brandy — to himself, to the watchman, to me. Nothing is what it seems. I will be glad to be finished with this journey.

The captain watched me, making certain I ingested the liquor, not just one portion but two. "Rare beasts, colorful birds," he kept murmuring, the phlegm collecting in his throat so his laughter seemed a death rattle. "Young Tom, imbibe," he ordered yet a third time and rose from his chair, steadying himself against the table. "My man, prepare yourself. Tonight is a night for discovery. You shall see how we may become whatever we wish."

As soon as I return home I'll follow the trail leading across my father's fields and into the grove, I'll find the lichen-carpeted eggshell boulder that sits half buried in the woods, I shall climb to the summit, wrap my arms and legs around the rock, and cling. It is not our Guineaman careening beneath my feet, the turbulence is not in the depths but in the globe itself. I cannot say how long I shall be able to hold on.

The captain approached the watchman, fumbled for his hand, and jerked him to his feet. I could have reached out and touched the sleeve of his pea jacket. Peter Gray stood as if he were being outfitted by his tailor, but the captain did not prim, tuck, sew together the sailor's clothing, no, he unpeeled the outfit, as I might have done to my sister's ruined orange instead of throwing it overboard. Who knows? Inside the rind the nectar might have been sweet, the segments unspoiled.

Off came the checkered Highland cap, revealing the roughly shorn hair as black as stale blood, as fine as corn silk. Off came the jacket, like a snake's dried integument. The captain bundled one shirt sleeve, stretching out the sailor's lank arm as if he meant to snap it in two. The flesh was the shade of damp, clotted sand, and blue veins dribbled like tidewater seaweed over the knot at the wrist. Peter Gray kept his eyes focused on me, as if I were the one being revealed. The captain opened the shirt from chin to waist, button by button, he lifted the neck of the tight-fitting flannel chemise beneath, and in a single, deft movement he ripped the material and opened the flaps like skin pulled away from a deep incision. Peter Gray disappeared. I wished that I had gone with him.

The captain said, "Young Tom, you doubt what you see? Come closer, then." I did not move. The captain took my hand and placed it directly upon the breast of the creature who stood in place of Peter Gray. I was surprised, yes, but not by her contours; I was surprised to find her surface so smooth, polished, like maple candy, though the heat was oppressive and the multiple layers of her disguise must have been stifling. I wished I had refused to handle her — it was as if I had reached for a goat's tit and found it made of porcelain. Of all senses touch is the most discomforting, yet how evasive it remains when we try to remember the texture of an object, to revive the sensation in our mind.

The captain takes great license. "As soon as he is fairly at sea, a commander will push his men to their limit and beyond," the messboy had warned me at the outset of our voyage. There is no chance for desertion. I wanted to clutch her as I would have clutched the boulder on my father's land. She was the ship's own harpy, with dark, unblinking eyes and an insatiable appetite. She despised me though I was merely a pawn on the captain's board. I do not know why the captain used us in this fashion, why he stripped us in each other's presence, Peter Gray of her identity and me of my innocence.

I needed no further urging, I knew what had to be done. "Miss," I heard myself say, "please understand. We are a slaver. Yes, this is just what we are." Her neck resembled a raw, skinned chicken leg, taut, more muscular than I'd imagined any female could be beneath the collar of a frock. The captain was right. Fingers would turn into insects, chewing dispassionately, were they ever independent from the hand. My fingers would have been segmented, glistening worms upon her naked breast. But I made my hand lifeless. It was blowing a mere fret of a wind above, yet inside the captain's chamber the walls were about to give way, the pressure of the deeps would explode upon us. There is only one true direction: a slow, irreversible sinking. We are an American Guineaman, traveling east.

Then the captain separated us, he swept my arm away as if he'd just caught Peter Gray and me in the midst of the illicit act. She snapped alert and shielded herself, not demurely, no, she had an inspiring savageness as she locked her elbows between the cleavage of her bosom, braced her hands around her throat. The captain did not try to replace my fingers with his, instead he reversed the inquiry, wrenched apart her stiffened arms, impatiently buttoned and wrapped the model back into an unkempt Peter Gray, setting the cap on her head while she remained as indifferent as a great trunk being carved and painted into ugly godheads.

"Tom, she's a surprise to both of us, I assure you. I wouldn't have accepted command of this ship if I'd known we were nothing but a hen frigate. A woman brings disgrace and disaster at sea. But now we've found her among us, what can we do? Why, we make the best of our lot. Have you ever known a lady, Tom? Have you ever been stirred by the mere sight of her? We'll teach you how to love before we teach you anything else. Romance. There is no subject more important to a young gentleman's education than romance." I don't care if the captain is a family friend — Peter Gray must think the captain rude, and so do I. "And you, will you be handy, ready to do work as before? Wake up, Peter Gray. I ask you, will you continue in our service now that you know our purpose?"

Though she was clothed in her disguise again I saw it coiled in her eyes — an unalterable, contained fury that I had earlier mistaken for scorn. I do not know how she has been able to lie among the sailors all these days. Even when the men pinioned Peter Gray, they mistook her body for a boy's. I cannot say how she was capable of deceiving us so thoroughly. And I do not like to consider what the crew will do to her if they discover the truth.

Thankfully, the captain perceives the danger. He has promised to give Peter Gray his own custom-built gimbaled bed in the sleeping cabin, and he instructed me to keep the discovery to myself. He said we shall amuse one another, the three of us, during the balmy evenings on our voyage to the coast of Africa. But he did not allow me to linger tonight — he ordered me from his stateroom, and I was eager to go. Peter Gray can fend for herself, she is capable. After I pushed the door closed behind me I hesitated in the passageway, and I heard the captain taunt: "You will be useful in laundering my socks, Peter Gray." He shall try to tame her. I doubt he will succeed.

Hot unto suffocation. I shall never again return to sea. I would like to escape this hold, dissolve into the sultry night, and leave my father's Guineaman behind forever. Yet I continue to dream. I know that if I wander above I will face leeward, and I will sense it behind me, approaching as soundlessly as a lizard scaling a rock — indeed, its membrane will appear translucent scales of gray, dry, cool to touch. How would I know touch when I will do nothing but turn around and stare at it? A great wall of water cresting over the windward rail, a wave one hundred feet high, not a violent roller on the verge of breaking but a grotesque living vertebrate, cloaked in a reptile's hide. Motionless. Our Guineaman will lose all momentum, we will slide backward into the cavity.

I try to tell myself that my premonition is spurred by this entire change of life, but explanation does no good. Green, the wave will be, as green as the tea she brought me tonight. She slipped into my quarters without greeting, without warning, she entered as silently as a slow deluge of mud. I didn't hear the door open or her feet sliding across the plank. I lay face toward the beams, picking at the caulking in the cracks, and I cannot say how long she stood there, but suddenly, as on that recent midnight, I felt my audience's gaze. It was as though I had been struck blind, so acute did my other senses grow. I didn't want to look at her — of course she left me without choice. I twisted round to see her teeth flashing, her eyes as black as the night sea.

"Peter Gray." I uttered the name to assure myself I could still identify this charlatan, classify her, label her, so she would be destined to remain Peter Gray, to be the one name, none other. In one hand she gripped a metal cup tinted a mottled lemony color by my lantern. In her other hand

she held a saucer. She set both plate and cup upon the
floor, stepped back, and withdrew. This was no vision. Green
tea and biscuit with soft butter. I would have liked to leave
them there, the tea to evaporate, the lard to dribble off
the saucer and seep through the keel into the sea. I would
have liked to ignore her gift for she had no right to tempt
me. But the fragrance drew me to the center of the berth.
The rim was warm to my lips, the green tea sweetened
with molasses — the most exquisite luxury I have known
since we sailed.

Her tea and biscuits strengthened me, and I lost the desire
to sleep. Instead, I carried a handful of buttery crumbs to
the deck, where the swine snored obscenely beneath the
grating, the hens cackled, the men slept with their blankets
tangled in their arms. I strode regally from stern to bow,
challenging the sea to rise; but she remained at bay, afraid
of me now that I was her equal. The men on watch had
made a nest with spare canvas between the deckhouses;
only the helmsman at the binnacle kept our ship on course.
Nothing to fear. We had light air, cat's paws of wind, we
continued south-southeast across glassy water.

I threw the crumbs over the lee rail and watched them
disperse like seeds off a dandelion head. Suddenly there
appeared first one and then another fleeting billow of gray,
two stormy petrels plummeting out of the night, sweeping
for the biscuit. But they arrived too late, and I was sorry
for them. They skimmed the slick surface, arced upward,
flew side by side around the rectangles of canvas, and I
lost sight of them. The men have their own names for the
petrels — Mother Carey's chickens, they call them, I don't
know why. They say each bird is the soul of a dead sailor.
Such superstitions are passed among the crew.

Here I am and here I must stay. Today I crushed my day's
allowance of bread, soaked the hard nuggets of dough in

water, folded in slivers of salt pork, added a spoonful of lard, and gave the preparation to the messboy to bake. And while I waited for my souse, Brian Piper tried to frighten me with this: "Then you mustn't dismiss the facts, lad, you mustn't object if the account has a quality of the fantastic, for I only repeat what I've heard with my own ears. And it isn't just a morsel of tavern gossip, the embellishments added simply for flavor. No, it's word for word with no room left for a messboy's lies.

"Now listen to me because I'm about to begin. But first you'll want to know how I became acquainted with the captain, how I found myself, one day, hanging on to a broken plank, drifting somewhere in the North Atlantic. I was cold, alone, beset with grief, and a peculiar numbness began to creep from my fingers up my arms, I was growing drowsy, Tom, I knew I didn't have much time left, when suddenly I saw a boat approaching, and standing on the wales was our own old man. I was dazzled by the sight. Well, I say this is what a lady sees when she meets the captain. Perfectly carried away, no matter what other plans she's got. Our old man, you must have noticed by now, has patience about as short as this fingernail. When a girl confessed her love for him he would take her hand and lead the innocent darling down the back stairs of her father's house, he'd help her into a borrowed carriage, drive to a local customs house where he was sure to have a friend, and there, with a contract, a few biblical words, and a scurrilous chap enticed off the street as witness, make sacred the union. They'd sit down to the nuptial feast of champagne, sausage, tobacco, and a few fine chocolates, and then off they'd fly to the bridal suite on board the captain's ship. The captain's bride would never set eyes on her homeland again.

"A sea captain has a globe to crisscross, Tom, and his heart may stray as far as his vessel. When our old man grew bored with a lady, he put her aside and went out and found another. But he kept them well provided, for it wouldn't do to have his women complaining to their friends. A captain had best maintain a respectable profile all around if he wants to guarantee a fanfare welcome. So he lavished his wives with jewels, with robes and ribbons. And each one thought she was the banquet's centerpiece, a roasted porker's head on a silver platter, garnished with olives, leeks, and truffles, an apple in her mouth. When the ladies felt a chill coming on, the captain sent them a coat like the one a German king ordered for his precious daughter, a coat made from the hides of every furred species from the wilderness of her favorite country. When the wives complained of loneliness, he supplied them with dozens of blackamoors. Whatever spice, scent, or fabric they wanted, he found it for them. But even our captain might accidentally mix together ingredients that will make havoc in the gut.

"So it was that at the height of his popularity he kept eight dames in as many cities. Wonderful, you must think, that a sea officer could keep so many ladies gay, their beds always prepared for his unannounced arrival in the middle of the night. But Tom, our captain is a calculating master, don't you know, and he understood the appetites of his brides as sure as he judges the talents of his crew. Since he could not entertain them all at once, he gave them each occupations to distract them during their long, solitary days. He gave them pens so they could record the slightest fluctuations of emotion, he had elaborate flower gardens planted outside their bedroom windows, he hired dressmakers, and the women had only to stand straight as a roasting spit while the finest damask was fitted to their bodies.

"Aye, Tom, you'll find out soon enough: a woman's confidence depends upon the reflection in her lover's eye, she will be seeking her own image in the pools of his affection. Here's one proven way to nourish a lady — with your admiring eye, Tom, don't you forget. But mind you, never repeat the captain's mistakes or you'll come out as poorly as he — the prime of his life, and he's got nothing to show.

"Now listen to this: once and only once I, Brian Piper, principal messboy, was called upon to ride out with the whalemen, they being short a hand, and after two or three conquests I found it to be such an easy sport that I grew cocksure and boldly smashed the head of a large and impetuous cow. Well, I succeeded in denting her forehead, but still she bore down upon us, foaming and gnashing, she rammed our boat and stove us in. Wouldn't you know but my ankles were tangled in the harpoon line, such is my luck, and when she dove into the deeps she carried me with her. You don't need to hear the rest, it's enough to see that I survived. But I offer this experience to compare with the captain's own. He took a terrible risk, like as not he was set on being damned. He brought his newest wife to his Pisan home, snuck her up the back staircase, convinced her that the astonishment of the servants when they met her in the bedroom would be worth the effort. He mounted the bride while, in the parlor directly below, his first wife, a beauty in her own right, I'm told, stood motionless as the seamstress measured her waist and the dressmaker unfolded squares of colorful silk.

"The captain knew no shame, Tom, though my heart sickens to admit it. He used up two women, he drenched the bed with the fluids of a most reprehensible love, just imagine, and in the pitch of joy, without any sense of discretion, he bellowed. That, Tom, was a death knell. Downstairs the good woman heard the noise and realized her man had come home. She abandoned her pedestal, dropped her sequined shawl, and rushed up the back flight of stairs.

"Our captain had been keen enough to fasten the bolt on the bedroom door. In the middle of his lovemaking he heard his first wife calling out to him, rattling the latch, demanding to be admitted. Well, Tom, the pair uncoupled hastily, the captain pulled on his nightdress and gave his newest spouse a helpless nibble. But she had already devised her own disappearance. A lady's wit is fast, Tom, you will find this to be ever true. She can plot her escape in the time it takes a flame to singe a moth's wing. And so the captain's new wife fixed her eyes upon the empty sea chest pushed against the wall. She stuffed her garments beneath the mattress, hopped stark naked across the room, and climbed inside the chest. You see, it was nothing but a game to her. She didn't have to tell the captain to shut the lid, to lock the chest and hide the key beneath a starfish on the mantel. When he lifted the bolt on the bedroom door his first wife flung herself into her husband's arms and begged him to declare his love for her.

" 'My dear,' he said, 'I was dreaming that you were big with child and they took you away from me. I ran down a corridor; beneath my feet was a picture, your face, lovely, your face beneath my boots. The marble doors on either side were locked, and from within each room I heard you weeping.' Aye, the captain is an artificer, Tom, no one can beat him for that. He comforted the woman with that false dream, he tricked her into thinking his love for her accounted for the moan she had heard. So she plumped the pillow, smoothed the sheets, and stayed until his eyes grew heavy. Then she kissed his lips and left him.

"As soon as our master heard the latch click he stood up quick and hurried to the mantel. What was his excuse? He wasn't sure. He unlocked the chest and discovered . . . well, Tom, he thought his lady was affecting sleep, as he had done before his other wife. He reproached her, but she wouldn't answer, not for a dollar or a hundred dollars. He pulled her arm, and when he released it her body fell back into the chest. Why, the body was a corpse, the sleep, death. The lady must have known that she wouldn't last long inside the drawer, but she didn't shout for air — she preferred death to life as the captain's harlot. Even our old man couldn't contain a sob. And the other wife, what about her? She'd stationed herself just outside the door, where she meant to remain through the afternoon, warding off haines and criminals. The wife heard her husband and a second time she rushed to his aid.

"The scene when she entered the bedroom . . . think of it, Tom: our master on his knees, bent over a bluing body. She approached her husband, looked over his shoulder at the naked bosom in the sea chest, displayed like a golden cast of Helen's tit, aye, the dead have a strange beauty. Through the hour the wedded couple mourned while downstairs the household began to rouse. The servants prepared tea, gardeners beat the branches of olive trees, and the dressmaker — the *dressmaker*, Tom — made a sketch of a pink satin gown.

"Finally the captain stood, and without a word he left the room; wearing only his nightshirt, he walked down the stairs and out of the house. Sort of like the emperor, Tom, the one in the tale. And that good woman, what do you think she did? Shriek in despair? Fling open the window and cry for help? Not at all. She wanted only to protect the captain's name. She didn't know the exact circumstances of the unlucky accident, but she convinced herself that the captain was as unlucky as the woman in the chest.

"Think of it: the wife surely touched her fingers to the chilled, raw meat, the rotund, padded waist, the immense breasts. She decided she would have to dispose of the corpse. Pisa had been her home for two years, and her home was full of fresh flowers, china, and silk. Silk. Even this good woman had not remained indifferent to the plush, soft texture of fine cloth. *Vanity*, Tom. What could the dame do but apply to the dressmaker himself? He was her closest friend in this foreign land — his technique seemed to her masterly, aye, his accuracy perfect.

"So she summoned the signore upstairs, pushed the door closed, and asked if for a quantity of money he would keep a secret. He noted the lady's distress, heard out her proposition. As soon as she raised the sea chest lid and revealed the sight, he saw how simple it would be to take advantage of this young woman for whom he had lusted throughout the days of travail, the endless fittings. She begged him, 'Please do me this kindness: carry her away from here, bury her in the hills, and I will show you gratitude with gold.' The dressmaker's reply? He traced the corpse's jaw with the point of his scissors, then he turned and curled his fingers beneath the chin of the captain's first wife. You may be sure that no one else had ever dared trespass onto the captain's property. But this fox knew how to snap up a tidbit. At first she pushed away his hand, she tried to force him from the room. Too late, Tom. In broken English he managed to convey that he would go directly to the authorities if she wasn't quick to submit.

"On the same bed where it had all begun, with the corpse as witness, the dressmaker took possession of the captain's wife. Imagine it, imagine the ravished woman staring at the ceiling as the dressmaker belted his trousers again, wrapped the husband's shame in the satin spread, and carried the cadaver out to deal with it properly. He stuffed the corpse into a barrow, covered her with straw, and once outside the city, slit her throat and wedged her behind a boulder in a grotto. Then he returned to the captain's home, where he found the wife still curled on the sheet, and with the insolence bred from familiarity, as they say, he blackmailed her with the guilt of two crimes: murder and adultery. No port in the civilized world would admit a man whose wife had assassinated a whore and taken her dressmaker into her bed. The captain would be condemned to drift in exile back and forth across the sea, never touching land. And what of his wife? Why, his wife would be sentenced to hang by the neck.

"Later that night — now listen to this, Tom — later that night the wife received word that the captain's ship had sailed, and that same night the dressmaker joined the wife in bed again. The next day, and on and on, they continued to face each other, he taking advantage by lowering the top line of her bodice, adorning her in festoons of ribbons, she fixing her eyes not upon the cloth but upon the window, the west, the mosaic sea.

"I can't help but wax eloquent, Tom, when there's a lady concerned, especially when the story is as sad as this. So the spring gave way to a lovely summer, and one day the lady decided she had had enough. Who can say what influenced her? Who knows what provokes transformations in a woman's soul? A mystery to me why one night she was helpless, splayed upon the bed, the next night she was a murderer.

"She hid the dagger beneath the pillow, and when the dressmaker climbed atop her she plunged the knife into his back. Don't let the vision invade your dreams tonight, Tom, don't you think about the dressmaker when the blade punctured his lung and the thick blood dripped from his mouth like mud from a flooded bog onto the lady's pallid face. And what did she do then? Why, the same as her husband had done. Wearing nothing but her dressing gown and the night's shadow, she left the house and entered the city, she followed his course through the streets, aiming straight for the harbor. But you may be sure no ship was waiting. So she continued walking, the water lapping around her ankles, her knees, her tender thighs, the gown clinging like withered skin to bone. She hadn't a keel constructed to float, don't you see.

"Now Tom, that's the end, and look here, your souse is past done, black as a bull's turd. We've got no more time to waste dallying. Take your food and leave me. There are tasks wanting attention. And don't you report what Brian Piper has said to you tonight. It's a secret you must keep to yourself, or we'll both be a sorry case. Go promptly, now, and on the morrow I'll boil you some duff, and maybe if you stay out of my way I'll add a second chapter to the first."

Obediently, I left him, but as I walked away from the

tryworks stove I mumbled weakly, so he might or might not hear, "Brian Piper, you can be sure I don't believe a word you say."

First: it is certain that the Africans captured by warring tribes would be destroyed; some would be hung, others buried alive in the resinous pitch of coal tar, others boiled in huge cauldrons, others bound in chains and cast into the sea, others flayed, others pressed to death beneath huge slabs of granite, others beaten about their private parts, then tied and abandoned on a barren plain to be eaten alive by ants and vultures. Such is the fate of native prisoners who are not fortunate enough to be deported to the West.

Second: the quality of life on the plantation is, in general, an improvement over life in the jungles and deserts of their home continent. They have two meals a day to sustain them, they have shelter, they have trousers instead of loincloth, they have salt. A planter pays a high price per head, and you may be sure it is in his interest to take good care of his property.

Third: they are provided with graveyard plots close enough to the slave quarters so that the living may tend the burial sites, ensuring that the deceased are not soon forgotten amidst a tangle of sumac and bracken.

Fourth: they are baptized.

Long ago it was when I would scramble into my mother's lap and announce, "Today I learned . . ." Mother, tonight I learned — are you listening? — I learned that a bee's tongue has three divisions, enabling it to suck nectar from the deep throat of a columbine blossom. I learned that the shell of an insect begins as a milky liquid secreted from glands in the soft white larva. I learned that insects may be reborn as many as twenty times and that some species swim a short way into the sea to shed their skeletons. A fantastic prospect, this: to rid yourself of your outer casing while floating in the surf.

The captain scorned insects for their redundant behavior. But Peter Gray maintained that we cannot match their talent for disguise, and our revulsion to them stems from envy. Indeed, she would have us look to insects instead of to our own history for a guide. The primary difference, she said, between an insect and a man is not that one has language and the other only instinct, not that one evolves less rapidly, but that one has the ambition to cross from continent to continent, while the other respects the boundaries of the land. The ocean traveler must adapt both to seasons and to unfamiliar worlds, he must rediscover how to survive, he must discard old knowledge and learn through accident, deduction, and coincidence how to cultivate a foreign soil. Or, if others have arrived before him, he must either serve the inhabitants or overpower them. Not so for the insect, which is designed to change with the land where it is born rather than adapt to an unfamiliar climate. True, there are fishermen who will swear to have seen swarms of sawflies hundreds of miles out at sea. Peter Gray herself has walked on beaches where the flies could be scooped up in shovels, so immense were their numbers. But she claimed there is no proof that the sawfly or any other insect has ever independently crossed from one continent to another. The displacement of the bug, she contended, accounts for the world's incurable, consuming diseases. Insects without the means to cross the ocean have easy access now — parasites cling to a sailor, hide in his cargo, ride in his matted hair or nestle in the flesh beneath his toenails, carve intricate tunnels in his loaves of bread. Thus the continents mingle. These days insects regularly make the middle passage or the journey round the Horn, follow the Trades or the Gulf Stream without returning home or dissolving into the sea. It is no exaggeration to say that a single flea in a ship's bilge is more dangerous than an entire stock of ammunition.

A migrating insect is no novelty, admitted Peter Gray. Consider locusts, dragonflies, ground beetles. But although they journey to the edges of the land, they will not press beyond. Certainly, she said, insects wander far distances, impelled by a scarcity of food or a change in climate. Brazilian cabbage flies will continue day after day without ever settling, feeding, or copulating, only to reach the ocean and drown. Yes, she said, insects migrate, that's clear. But an insect carried on board a ship breeds only destruction. Peter Gray should know.

I wonder what she thinks of me. She directed her argument toward the captain but repeatedly she glanced across the table as if she expected me to comment, to interrupt, to agree with her. What her eyes expressed I cannot say. She has an interest in me, obviously. I should not like to be alone with her. But then I should not want to be Peter Gray, alone with the captain in his stateroom.

Jack Carvee slaughtered one of the swine today. At first I mistook the sound for the cry of some strange sea bird tangled in the rigging. Tonight the captain, Peter Gray, and I enjoyed a banquet of fresh pork and claret, along with a crock of pea soup, which the captain ordered boiled to the consistency of pine sap.

The messboy delivered the tray laden with food to the captain's suite, but he was not invited to enter, so I carried our supper into the room, knocking the door shut with my heel to make certain the messboy did not spy the soundless, flickering dances of the lemon candles, the smoke rising from the porcelain turtle, the silver arranged upon the table, the fine Belgian crystal. The captain stood over Peter Gray, swaying slightly to keep his balance as the ship listed. When he was satisfied with her empty bowl he took his place at the head of the oak table and ate methodically, slowly, continuously, listening to Peter Gray speak of the danger of sea commerce and the consequence of insects.

After the meal the captain enjoyed his pipe, Peter Gray a plump cigar, and then, instead of giving me leave to go, the captain asked me to accompany him on deck. We left Peter Gray reclining against the wardrobe, her head tilted back, her eyes closed, oblivious beneath the canopy of smoke. She plays the part of an uninterested, satisfied gentleman more convincingly than I ever will.

I followed the captain to the helm, where he spoke with the steerer about our course, then we walked forward, just the two of us, past the men on dogwatch and the crew dispersed in groups, playing poker or having a smoke. Despite my doubts about the captain, I was proud to have been selected as his escort on this fine, if windless, tropical evening, with the rising moon nearly full, a heavy, bald ornament. But suddenly, though the ship was motionless, the claret swelled inside me. I stumbled, groped for the rail, and found instead the captain's hand. He did not pull away, he did not thrust me from him, scorning me as another man might. He held my hand, his flesh like a warm poultice, healing me. So we remained in open view for any sailor who happened to rise and glance in our direction.

How different this scene must have been from that of a seasick boy on his knees, mopping up his own vomit. Though the captain has peculiar habits, I shall stand by him — a melancholy man with such a wellspring of compassion may be excused for his mistakes. After all, with my home so far behind, no one but the captain has reason to look after me; as long as he is my guardian I don't want to probe.

But he has chosen to take me deep into his confidence. Tonight he turned to me, his face made purplish-white by the moon, and whispered, "We must find him."

I said, "Please, sir?" for I did not understand his reference.

In a barely audible voice he said, "Haven't you asked yourself, Tom, why she has come along?"

There is only one she. And the reason why had not occurred to me. She frightens me, yes, she challenges, and she entertains, that has been enough, I do not need explanations. So I replied, "For the fun of it, sir, that's what I thought. The thrill of a sea voyage. She's not like other girls."

"But she is, Tom, more than you know. And there's someone on board who is the reciprocator of her affections. You must find him for me, Tom, that's your job. Locate the other fellow on this ship who knows the secret of Peter Gray."

He wiped a fleck of saliva from the corner of his mouth. And then the heavens sent an omen, a weak gasp of wind, the inert mainsail went taut, rustled, fell slack again. The captain, immediately preoccupied with the promise of renewed momentum, hurried back toward the wheel. I curled my arms beneath a short piece of planking bolted to the ship's side, pressed my thin chest against the rail, and leaned over, dangling my feet a few inches above the deck, as if I, too, could have plunged head first toward the water and veered away with my stormy petrel mate. I thought of a woman strolling at the ocean's edge on a beach marked with dark crescents, the bluffs fissured with red veins. A woman, utterly alone, sinking to her waist in a morass of dying sawflies.

Well, Jack Carvee could not restrain himself and opened a cask of grog meant to celebrate our arrival at the coast. A little bit of spirit can unbalance an entire crew. The cook must have started tasting a short time after breakfast, for it wasn't yet noon when I heard in my half-deck quarters a dreadful babble, not unlike the agony of a pig beneath the blade.

So far I have been treated like a first-class passenger, dining with the captain and joining the watch only when I felt compelled, but this morning the chief mate found me daydreaming in the galley and he ordered me to scrub the bunk boards in his berth, which he shares with the surgeon and is adjacent to mine. When I heard Jack Carvee singing I gladly put down my bucket and brush and went to see what was about. I found the saturated old man at the try-works, stirring a pot of horse bean soup, celebrating his delirium. "In a jungle round a barracoon," he sang, "you'll never see the sun, but when the vultures soar you know the daylight's nearly come . . ."

There were already half a dozen men assembled by the firehearth, some playfully poking Jack Carvee's ribs, tugging his straggling beard, while others were outraged — perhaps they envied him his oblivion or despised him for wasting a fraction of their rum. Yellow Will himself took charge of the matter, dragging the cook away from his stove and calling to the chief mate, "Sir, not just a trifle this time, sir. He's been into the grog, he's nearly emptied the entire cask."

Meanwhile, Jack Carvee smiled wanly at his prosecutor and sang, "Then once you've done your plundering, stacked your booty in the hold, tread backward through the swelter to the empty glade, pluck the final mango, strip the kernel of its meat," or some version of this, I couldn't understand him word for word. The chief mate gestured to Yellow Will and approached the helm to confer with the captain, who had not deigned to show any interest in the uprising. But after a brief exchange the mate stepped to the quarterdeck and spoke privately with Yellow Will while behind them two men held Jack Carvee fast. I heard one sailor suggest the cat, some men called for bamboo, while others laughed and clamored, "Let the fellow be!" The cook, though, was fearless, chanting lustily, "Be sure to give your sweet a show of your affection, tell her, Love, one wish, that's all, just one, is yours inside this mango pit." The discipline was not meant to be severe, but Yellow Will executed it with vengeance. He marched Jack Carvee over to the washing tub, forced him to his knees, and pushed his head into the water. The cook's voice, trundling on with "So waste no vagaries, Lady . . . ," was abruptly cut off, replaced by Yellow Will's malevolence: "You want a drink, you'll have it!"

The stinking, greasy suds splattered as if a hot coal had been dropped in, our cook struggled but Yellow Will kept him immersed. The carpenter, who had remained aft to oil a block and stay, finally cried out, "That's enough, man!" an act of courage that roused the rest of the crew, and their voices rose: "Release him, Will, by God, don't keep him under any longer!" Indeed, Jack Carvee's body had relaxed completely, like a deflated mainsail. But not until the command "Avant!" was shouted by Pharaoh, stationed in a crosstree, did Yellow Will oblige us. He lifted the cook from the wash water and let his body slump onto the deck. I thought for certain he was dead. His skin above his whiskers was the color of February slush, his lips the same mud hue of his eyelids.

Piper approached him and whispered, "Jack Carvee?" squeezing the cook's slack, fleshy, bloodless cheeks between his hands, the same hands that had so rudely kneaded the vat of pudding. "Jack Carvee, are you among us?" the messboy demanded, his voice rising in pitch. I suppose he must have grown fond of the cook during the long hours of victual preparation. A sailor nudged the drenched man's leg, and with that Jack Carvee groaned, rolled on his side, and spit out the grog, the suds and sea water, coughed up such a great amount I couldn't believe he had anything remaining inside him. When he was done heaving the messboy and two sailors gathered him into their arms, lifted the empty sack of a man, and struggled across the deck. Yellow Will called after them, "Mind you, the captain says he's to have no sip of water. Not a spoonful."

A sailor beside me muttered so low that only I could

overhear, "But he's our cook." I would have liked to think at least one man on board was brave enough to protest publicly against the order.

We draw no dead water, no foaming malt eddy trails aft. The weather teases us with occasional light airs that snap and ripple the canvas, dissipating after giving us a gentle shove forward. Pharaoh has made it my job to look after the time, so at every half hour I must stop whatever I am doing and ring the ship's bell, and now the men, seeing that I am no longer such a special commodity, send me to fetch marlinespikes and grease pots and whatever else they might require during the course of a day. I have hardly a spare moment to climb the pulpit, to gaze west, toward home, to wonder if Papa has caught my brother chewing a tobacco plug or if my little sister has been practicing scales on the piano or if my mother thinks of me as often as I think of her.

I cannot say for certain where my loyalties lie. I would like to weld myself to the captain's side and obey him unthinkingly. Yet I must continue to think, to consider, to judge and secretly condemn him. I would like to feel only the boundless love the messboy attributes to the captain's wives, I would rather be driven by pure devotion than tormented by these ambivalences. Our cook is suffering. The captain has no pity.

Why does cruelty breed and flourish in some men and not in others? And what has cruelty to do with power? I think they are of one species, the impulses fertilize each other like those procreating slugs Peter Gray is wont to describe. What would Peter Gray have to say about Jack Carvee's punishment? For three days she has not shown herself on deck. I am not entirely guileless, I can see that she uses the captain as ruthlessly as he uses her, for what purpose I don't know. I doubt she would bother to put in a kind word for the cook. Two slugs at summer's wane. I shall not consider their monstrous offspring.

The smokejack extending from the hearth is so clotted with soot that from time to time a chunk the size of a walnut dislodged and splashed into the soup. The messboy took no notice. He divided his attention between the stove and the drowsing cook, who was propped on an overturned scotch pan, his shirttails knotted around a cabinet handle to keep him from tumbling to the deck. Occasionally, the messboy would admonish the man: "It's a bitch's life and you do no good regretting it." As far as I knew he had not given Jack Carvee any water, but he enlisted me to mop the sleeping man's brow with a rag soaked in vinegar, he said now we've crucified him we might as well follow the script. And though by himself he had to prepare pork pie and soup for thirty, the messboy found a few minutes to make the duff he had promised me yesterday.

I am almost sorry to have tasted it once — duff is a dear item on board a Guineaman. I shall teach our cook at home to make the loaf, which comes out looking like a brick of salt and is simply a few handfuls of flour, sugar, and dried apple moistened with water and boiled down until it turns as heavy as lead. I broke the piece in two, pocketing half for the night. The other piece I gripped in my left hand, and when I wasn't drawing the vinegar rag across Jack Carvee's forehead I brought the duff to my lips, sliding my tongue back and forth across the ragged surface, swilling the juices inside my mouth, making my duff last for as long as the messboy spoke.

"Now listen, because I'm going to give you some food for reflection, and it makes no matter whether or not you believe me. It's the truth, and Brian Piper knows it's the truth as surely as he knows the Pope won't be inviting him to tea on Whitsun Day.

"Understand, Tom, gossip fits snug in a sailor's pocket, and soon every Mediterranean saloon was abuzz with the scandal — one of the captain's wives had been found mauled in the hills outside of Pisa, and the body of another wife had washed ashore. Somehow the story slipped past the harbor, wound through back streets and alleys, tapped on doors. And so it was that four of the captain's wives gathered in his Marseille house and made a remarkable pact.

"Hush, Tom, try to imagine: the blinds are drawn, the candles lit, there is plenty of the best wine. The hostess pours water over the hands of her guests, and then she carries from the kitchen dishes that have been weeks in preparation. A feast, Tom, you and I will never see the likes of it: a rabbit stew powdered with red coriander, inlaid with pomegranate seeds and fried almonds, white beans in a thick syrup of honey and milk, a hen seasoned with sage and glazed with the yolk of its own last egg, pork pie decorated with prunes and pine nuts, a pheasant cooked in a broth of cabbage and marrow, a jelly made from calves' feet simmered in wine. The women eat silently — what could they say, Tom, since the existence of each denies the existence of the others?

"When they are through with all the various courses the hostess provides water and they wash their hands a second time. Then they empty their glasses and into each they drop a pearl. They've come to the last bottle. The hostess shakes powder from an envelope into the wine and pours a libation for the household god. She sets the drugged drink upon the mantel and fills the glasses of her guests. Returning to her chair, she raises a trembling hand, announcing, 'Thus we are free.'

"Tom, it will be woven into a gruesome tapestry someday, you may be sure. The hostess drinks, two wives follow, and one by one three blanched pearls rattle around the concave crystal bottom, rolling to a halt at the top of the glass stem. A candle flame is doused by a gasp, a chair is flung against the china cabinet, shattering the doors. Don't ask me to linger at this party: fire burns, that's the formula, you don't need me explaining how paper shrivels, turns a bruised black, and dissolves into the air.

"But one lady remains, a red-haired, excitable beauty — her turn has come to drink. She stands, places her glass upon the mantel beside the libation, and says to the hostess, who is coiled on the floor, quivering, clutching her knees, 'Your death only disgusts me.' So this was her intention all along, to accompany the three wives to the threshold and then to abandon them. While they claw at their skin, the little red-haired matron rushes out into the streets and skirts round the corner, her heels striking cobblestone, the clatter growing fainter, Tom, fainter, until the night is sovereign once again.

"The bodies were found by a servant the next morning. And though the arsenic in the wine glasses on the mantel was easy to identify, the servant made up her own version of the slaughter. She insisted that the bruises and scratches on the women could only have been made by the sharp talons of carrion birds — a great flock of winged creatures flew in and flew out through the front door, the maid believed. And you know, Tom, I think our captain himself would prefer to blame birds. Watch how he surveys the sky, watch his face puckering when he spots an albatross gliding innocently overhead. I expect he doesn't want to believe that his wives chose their manner of quitting.

"But Tom, I say, Tom! Look to Jack Carvee, you've been neglecting the man. What good are you if you can't attend to this simple matter, you'll let a drowning man sink rather than throw him a line, that's the way you are, Tom, you won't do what you're told. What will happen to us if we lose our Jack Carvee? Be off, then, pest, take your duff and leave the rag. I'll revive him, see if I don't. Be off, I said!"

True, I hadn't been applying the vinegar assiduously —

the messboy had kept me distracted. Yet he is able to put his tales aside when he pleases, as if the words were tobacco ash or breadcrumbs to be tossed overboard and never missed. I don't know what to believe. I would have liked to follow the captain's red-haired wife through the streets, to catch up to her and ask if Piper's story had any truth in it. Instead, I drew the other half of duff from my trouser pocket, and after placing it carefully on the cook's lap, I returned to my berth.

This evening, lying alone in my berth, I conjured Peter Gray. Do not ask me to be more precise — when all light but the faint moon diced by the portal has been cut off and a boy knows only the sluggish rolling of his quarters, he cannot be expected to distinguish between experience and dream. And I do not think the difference matters. If, while on board a Guineaman, a boy imagines voices, and one of them — a resonant, assured, calculating voice — suddenly addresses him out loud, how can the boy decide whether the sound is another's or he himself is an unwitting ventriloquist? I suppose a man who covets a woman and then wins her does not care if she belongs to his fantasy, as long as he continues to believe.

She had slipped inside my half deck and was crouching so close to me I could have reached over and pried open her mouth as Yellow Will had done. I wanted to demand, *Tell me who you are.* But before I could speak she asked, "Tom, are you eager to see Africa?" It wasn't any of her business. Had I ever attended a slave scramble? Had I ever seen traders pricing Africans just off the boat according to size, age, and sex? I said nothing. I did not let her suspect the limits of my experience. She asked if I would like to hear a story about a famous mulatto man named Quince, the son of a Boston sea captain and an African princess. I did not care to have another story told — this voyage has been wasted with legends of sea captains, I have spent too many hours trespassing in other lives and have not been attending to my own education, which is my purpose here, education.

I finally managed to mutter gracelessly, "I wish you would go away," for I needed my rest, a boy who stays awake at night listening to a disembodied voice will be useless on a Guineaman. But Peter Gray of my dreams persisted with a compulsion that seemed to have its source in some secret, pressing shame. Or in a grave premonition. Maybe she is spurred doubly, by private guilt and some clairvoyant insight that her end draws near. I had no choice but to indulge her.

Locate the other fellow on this ship who knows the secret of Peter Gray — the captain charged me to investigate. But as long as I remain ignorant she is secure. I would not like to betray her. I want to believe that this mulatto man of whom she spoke has nothing to do with Peter Gray, that he was merely her excuse for conversation, as a perfectly round stone is enough of a reason for a lively game.

"If you, Tom," she persisted, "had been born an heir to an African throne, and if you had been stolen in your first month of life from your mother's arms, taken by your father from your homeland to America, there educated by a private Creole tutor and then left destitute, at the age of fourteen, by your father's death, you might very well be lying in a berth on a ship bound east."

I did not want to take part in her speculations. Still, I saw her purpose — she meant to remind me of my advantages, the privileges of name and property. So I said, "If I were this half-blooded boy, then I would not have been invited to the captain's stateroom, I would not have shared his meals, I would not have been introduced to the actual Peter Gray. Likely I would have thrown that green tea at you the first time you intruded here."

"On the contrary," she said, "the captain would have already singled you out from the crew and enlisted you as his companion. You see, the color of your skin and your poverty make you every sailor's prey, so you would have to show absolute loyalty to whoever promised to protect you. You would be bound to your guardian, completely dependent. And you would be thankful for my attention. But I do not mean to include myself on this voyage. I am telling you a story about a man named Quince.

"If you were returning to your homeland, leaving behind all that was familiar — the brownstone cellar where your bed was arranged in the corner; a Creole tutor who nurtured in you not simply an ambition for learning but a potent rage as well; half-brothers and -sisters who considered your rank equal to that of a household cat and who pulled, patted, kicked you accordingly — if you had left all this behind and were determined to find your mother, whose language you did not even know, then you might be somewhat melancholy as you lie in the darkness. The journey east means profit for every other man on board. Why not for you? The direction only diminishes the value of your life — the years in North America slough off one by one as you leave her coast behind. What good would all your education be to you in Africa? What use could you find for any of your books? Your father raised you to be his servant, now your father is dead. I ask you, Tom, to imagine yourself in Quince's place. He was your age when he made his way back to Africa."

Some urgency in her voice, some hint of her desperate need to make me understand this Quince, compelled me to participate in the masquerade. "Explain to me," she said, "what it is like to be a boy who is a stranger, yes, nothing else — a stranger in his father's house, a stranger to his own people."

I began, tentatively at first, then more assuredly as the drama took hold: "Well, I should be listening carefully to the water sloshing against the hull, for you know that sound can tell you whatever you wish to hear, or it can speak of the things you fear most. If I were a bastard son I think I should want reassurance tonight. I would want to hear in the sea a promise of good fortune. You say I am next in line for a throne? Then I will no longer feed on scraps of pork tossed to me from the table, I will no longer suffer the polar nights in my father's basement or waste hours studying books about the past. I am going to make myself anew, I may go where I please. You say I am a stranger? What an immense relief it is to be free from my father's service, to have no responsibility, no attachments. There is heritage to consider, of course, the shade of my skin. There's no escaping that. But aren't I traveling east, where my breeding will secure for me the highest title possible for a man? *King*. I will be king."

I was proud of my performance and thought it a proper moment for Peter Gray to light the lamp and reveal herself. I would have liked to hear her praise my eloquence. But still she remained only a shadow and the vapor of a voice.

"You don't know the customs of your people, Quince," she said, and I wondered whether she had forgotten that this dialogue referred to nothing. "How would you rule if you don't know the customs of your people?"

"I should think," I said carefully, "that I could learn. My mother would help me. Besides, I am a stranger wherever I go, so my people will excuse my mistakes. And perhaps my tutor's influence won't prove entirely worthless, perhaps I can use my training."

"How?" Her word leaped out of the darkness. "How would you use your education? Would you join the missionary effort?"

I said I had no interest in converting savages.

"Then would you build a library and import your books?"

I said I would be too busy learning the native language and did not have patience to teach English to brutes.

"Then would you, Tom, pursue your training in commerce? Surely your tutor gave you some knowledge of liabilities and loans, exports and investments."

I admitted that I had some skill in business. "I think I will like being a merchant," I ventured, and here I meant to refer to my own future, but Peter Gray assumed I was still posturing as Quince.

"A merchant — exactly! An overlord ruling the coast. A man merchant, Quince! This is the plan you devise on your journey to Africa: you will claim the throne, you will conquer your neighbors, and then you will build a marketplace where you can collect and trade your slaves. You, the son of a sea captain and grandson of a native king — you will be a man merchant.

"You spent fourteen years in a white man's basement, your father despised you because you were his shame, yet he needed you because the memory of her, your mother, both plagued and comforted him. He had enjoyed her as we may enjoy the unique quilted pattern of a spectacular dawn, knowing that the colors will never be repeated. She had been sent to the sea captain's bed by her own father, as tribute; she was fifteen, such a lithe, ripe beauty, and when she fled the next morning no one could track her, for her feet left no impressions in the earth. Your father had wanted to purchase the girl, but he was told that he would never see her again, no one could survive the island jungle overnight, or so the natives maintained, and three days later they brought to the captain, as proof, a gold-thread tassel torn from the girl's shawl.

"So the sea captain left the village, sailed up the Bonny River to inland barracoons, collected his cargo, fell ill with pox, recovered, and nearly a year later returned to the island. He found her in the thatched receiving hut, perched on top of an empty barrel that had been discarded by another ship. A barrel still fragrant with witch hazel, a coveted, magical panacea. She raised her eyes impertinently, scanned the captain as if it were her privilege to appraise *him*, then looked

down at you, Quince, the infant in her lap. African prince.
She did not struggle to keep her son when your father
snatched you away — perhaps she had intended that he take
you, perhaps she thought that though you had the rights
of a native sovereign, your skin was polluted by the white
man's blood, and in order for that blood to nourish instead
of poison, you had to understand intimately the white man's
mind. The captain stole you to punish the girl who had
fled him, and he kept you as a memento of that single
night of love. He cultivated you, made you suffer for your
mother's scorn; he meant to train you to be his educated
boy, the captain's cultured nigger. The only gift you ever
received from him was a barrel of witch hazel on your fourteenth birthday. He ordered you to sponge yourself before
you climbed the basement stairs, he said that since he could
not hear you approaching from the sound of your step,
which was panther-soft just like your mother's, he wanted
to be able to smell you.

"And then he died. At Thanksgiving dinner. You were
standing behind him, waiting to clear his plate and carry
in the cook's rice pudding. You saw his shoulders brace
against the spasm; he tried to rise and collapsed to the
floor.

"He left his widow, sons, and daughters with a secure
fortune. He left you with nothing. Except thirty-seven gal-
lons of witch hazel. So you were compelled to bathe, but
not out of respect for your dead father — you felt no respect,
not even hate, nothing but indifference toward him — you
washed with witch hazel because you had a vague idea that
it was your distinction, as much an ornament as the frayed
gold tassel brought to you by the sea captain's youngest
daughter on the morning when you departed the basement
forever.

"The day after your father's funeral you gathered your
belongings in a flour sack and pushed the barrel out ahead
of you along the street. 'Stop, Quince!' the child cried, 'take

me with you!' You did not turn, said nothing when she caught up to you and feebly tried to help you maneuver the cask. She was seven, half your age. For years she had studied you, mutely, obsessively, she was the only member of the captain's family who had never dared to taunt you. You didn't mistake her harmlessness for compassion, though — it was clear she felt afraid, afraid of her father's captive, entranced but frightened. Who were you? You had no history, no surname. You could not know that after years of watching you she had come to love you. Not a sibling's love, no, and not an admiring curiosity — she had given up the hope of solving you. Yet it was a possessive love, as a boy who finds a grackle frozen in a pond's crust will return day after day as long as winter holds out, staring at the bird trapped in the milky ice, unwilling to share his secret with anyone. So she followed you the day you left. She respected your silence and did not utter a word as she walked beside you. Indeed, her love depended on this silence, as the boy's love for the frozen bird depends upon the ice. But your bond was fragile, temporary. When her mother called shrilly from the door, the girl knew that her brother must go on without her. She helped push the barrel over the slight incline and trotted to keep up as it clattered downhill. She did not ask you where you meant to go. A second time her mother hailed, and the girl tucked a white lace handkerchief into the pocket of your overcoat. She did not stay to watch you unfold the cloth containing the gold tassel, a present from her father. It was the only thing of value the child had to give away. Her mother called again, and the girl spoke hastily, the last words she would say to her brother: 'I've forgotten my hat.' Then she fled, never once looking back at you.

"But she could not forget you — rather, increasingly the sea captain's daughter brooded upon your absence. For seven years she couldn't be sure whether you were alive or dead. Sometimes she mistook a winter birch for you, an imploring skeleton on a distant ridge; once, wandering through a churchyard, she thought she had located your tombstone — *Quince,* she read, then, bending closer, reading carefully, *Quiet reigns* . . . As she approached her fourteenth birthday she realized that she could not rest until she had found either you or your grave. So she left home to look for you; in her passionate ignorance she had faith that her persistence would be rewarded. Whether it took one year or twenty she would find you. She went to live with an aunt in New Bedford, and there she searched newspapers and ship registers, she grew into a woman, waiting for an opportunity to go after you. If only she could have foreseen how she would waste her youth pining away, if only she could have convinced herself that you were dead. It's a terrible curse, such a desperate —"

"Stop!" I cried, as if I meant to repeat, "Stop, take me with you." Instead: "Stop! Say nothing more!" Didn't Peter Gray understand? I must tell the captain everything. Was it instinct compelling me to interrupt, did I sense that with the next sentence she would confide the awful truth that this story of Quince was her own? Had she stowed away on the *Charles Beauchamp* in order to recover her own father's bastard son? Or was this story so close to my own that I had become the mulatto and I could not stand to hear how others had suffered for love of me?

I did not order her to go; I merely said in an exhausted, throttled whimper, "Please, I want to be alone."

She rose then. I could make out the vague outline of her head less than an arm's length from me, though she might as well have been in paradise, I in hell, so far away did she seem. On board a ship space has nothing to do with an actual inch. Since everything is cramped, compacted, distance must be measured by a revised scale — though Peter Gray stood close to the surface of my skin she was nowhere near my soul, which had withdrawn, retreating to its deepest, secret haven.

I should like someone to assure me that Peter Gray came to my quarters tonight, someone to agree when I say, *We are floating upon almost nothing* — for this is what I believe, and I would like to prove it to be true. Perhaps men keep slaves not merely as field hands and servants but as witnesses. I understand much better now: a man needs a double. A man needs a double who will confirm what he suspects. But I fear a slave would not suffice. There's only one person I could trust. I am certain that if I demanded the truth from Peter Gray she would tell me. I cannot say the same for the captain or the messboy. Peter Gray would tell me who she is. Yet were she to disclose her name and purpose I would have no choice but to pass on the information. So I won't inquire about her part in the story of the mulatto, and I won't ask her to explain what this man merchant has to do with me.

Papa, you cannot have forgotten that famous cargo, the shipload of mutineer slaves, the ones who overthrew the pirate crew midway between Guadeloupe and New Orleans. The Negroes had got hold of rifles, knives, and spears stashed in the hold, and once they had deposed the sailors they were left to navigate the schooner alone. They determined that if they directed the bowsprit toward the rising sun they would eventually reach the African coast, they did not realize that at night the ship ploughed north; on overcast, squally days they were blown west. After two months at sea they sighted land, and thinking it was Africa, they sent a few of their men to swim from ship to beach.

But they weren't in Africa at all, were they, Papa? They had sailed to Long Island. These slaves — do you recall? — these slaves were rounded up by the sheriff, but they couldn't be sold as slaves, since they had been procured by the American crew unlawfully, and since they were contraband without an owner no one knew what to do with them. So they sent the Negroes to a New Haven jail, and this is where we saw them, a dozen and more to each cell. You had come to negotiate, you wanted to raise money on behalf of the Africans and have them shipped back to their homeland because, you argued, in every business an equilibrium must be maintained, goods that can't be sold should be returned.

How many days since I have adequately slept? For what fraction of eternity have we been hauling the lines, bracing against the gale? When did I last strike the bell to mark the passing hour, the change of watch, teatime, or supper? While we were still floating in Paddy's Hurricane (this is a sailor's term for no wind at all) we seemed to have no purpose, the sea rippled away from our ship in even spokes, like the collection of silver feathers that my sister used to arrange on her bedroom floor. Yes, just so: the still water was patterned with radiating lines, like my sister's feathers, like strings extending from a web's inner circle. She wastes her youth making useless designs. For nearly a week the panorama surrounding our Guineaman was as unchanging as my sister's floor. Feathers.

But then the wind gusted without warning, I do not recall what night Pharaoh's rude voice intruded into my dreams, rousing all hands from our warm bunks into the drenching rain. The ship pitched like mad and it did not matter whether we kept our topsails reefed or furled, for we had no jurisdiction over the wind, no control over our balance. A dull, black banner had been stretched between the sky and the sea, so we could not tell if dawn had ever broken, the divisions between night and day could not be distinguished.

When the clouds finally spit their last foul juices and withdrew, I stood surrounded by the broken seas as I had once stood in my sister's bedroom, alone, after I'd opened the windows and invited in December's fury. Feathers. I do not know how many feathers my sister had gathered, how many afternoons she had spent weaving her gauzy net. But I know that the bewilderment I felt as I stood in the midst of my destruction, the windows shut again, the feathers scattered, is exactly what I felt when the storm finally rolled on and left us in peace.

How long did we wrestle with the halyards, pretending that strength, skill, and courage would save us when it was only luck that mattered? How many choruses of "Old Whiskey Bill" did the men sing? The captain said we were blown south-southeast, propelled directly along our course. During the storm he stood by the bowsprit, gripping the stay as if it were reins, as if bridled to the *Charles Beauchamp* were seven whales, seven powerful steeds. He will see that we reach our destination. I think I understand what skills a captain should possess. To master the sea he must have the relentless momentum of a fish. Water is the most accommodating element, so easily displaced, and the captain must command his ship accordingly, trusting that the ocean will oblige the intrusion, he must keep his vessel surging forward and never glance behind. Water erases all signs of passage. I fear the influence of Peter Gray — our captain is easily distracted. And what shall happen to our Guineaman if the captain lingers in yesterday?

How many yesterdays lie between this ship and my home? How long would I survive if a comber swept me over the rail? I am the smallest here, I would be the first to perish. The captain seems to have forgotten that he was assigned to make me a gentleman, he allowed me to be assigned to the vilest of tasks. Today, when I was finally able to sit down with a cup of coffee sweetened with molasses and a biscuit that was fairly edible once it had been soaked in the steaming liquid, Pharaoh took it upon himself to cut short my rest, summoning me with "Up you go! Give us proof you're a nimble monkey, a quick blue monkey. Up to the yard with you," and he slung over my shoulder a heavy rope. I was forced to climb the ratline with this reptile carcass, the huge bowline that was to be pulled through a block and tackle at the masthead and through another block at the far end of the yard. I think the boatswain selected me for this task because I, of all the crew, am the one whose absence would matter least. I've been labeled Blue Monkey. Now I regret not establishing my importance at the start of this voyage; I am a prince trapped in a beggar's disguise, and you may be sure no man would believe me if I insisted that I am his superior. They consider me nothing but a blank slate to fill with numbers, with tallies, advice and insult, brought aboard this Guineaman to become an accomplished seafarer. An apprentice, like a young surgeon who must probe and slice the dead before he is licensed to work upon the living.

I had already satisfied my curiosity: I had climbed to the mizzentop and explored the lower hold, yet I had never ventured out on a yard. At least I knew to trust the shroud ropes and not the ratlines, so I reached the crosstree easily, but midway along the treacherous branch I lost the courage to go farther, I stopped, clung with my knees, and waited for the next swell to dislodge me. Sailors congregated below, staring as silently as a jury after the verdict, guilty, has been passed. Indeed, I might have been standing on the top rung of a ladder, wearing a hangman's noose instead of a bowline loop. All those upturned faces were waiting somberly for me to fall — they wanted entertainment and did not care if their show involved the sacrifice of a mere boy. I saw the gleaming eyes of that skunk Yellow Will, I saw Pharaoh with one arm slung around the mast, as if he meant to shake me loose. Though I could barely hold on to the yard I had no desire to provide my audience with their spectacle. I dragged myself to the narrow tip, managed to thread the bowline through the iron block, and wormed backward to the mast.

By the time I reached the deck the crew had dispersed, even Pharaoh was occupied aft of the deckhouses, and no one had remained to say, *A job well done*. I suppose this is one of the hard lessons to be learned — a sailor earns no praise for his efforts, his only reward is his spared life, and if he wants a compliment he must mutter it himself. More than once I have overheard a conversation between a man and no one. "Who could do it better?" a sailor will ask himself. "Standing our course and who's responsible, let them tell you different, you know what's what."

Before I boarded the *Charles Beauchamp* I assumed the crew would be like so many brothers to me, in such close quarters for such a length of time I thought surely we would grow intimate. On the contrary, I'm more alone than ever before. I am not exceedingly fond of the messboy but I keep returning to him for lack of anyone better. I shall never let Peter Gray suspect how I crave her company; I want nothing to do with Pharaoh, Yellow Will, and their assembly; the carpenter is reticent, not easily approached; the surgeon is always busy measuring serums, counting pills; and the captain has lost interest in my education. So I have the messboy for company. The messboy and Jack Carvee. An inimical pair. I cannot tell whether the messboy wants to nurse the cook back to health so that he may return to his indolent habits or whether he feels a sincere compassion for the broken man.

I do not think Jack Carvee will ever regain his senses — daily the infection of madness spreads through him, he has begun to make impossible requests. It seems he lost a sweetheart to disease many years ago, he still carries dirt from her grave. Now he's decided he wants her back, he wants his love made whole again and in his arms, he says he'll starve himself if whoever stole his girl doesn't return her in a snap.

The messboy has had some success in persuading the cook to take a bit of food in moments when he's not entirely staggered by his sorrow. This morning, after Jack Carvee broke a biscuit with his teeth, his appetite returned in a

fury. I thought he'd next be devouring his own hand, so
voraciously did he chew. And when he had finished his
ration he demanded a cord of licorice, which of course wasn't
to be found on board. "Licorice," he cried, "or I'll rip out
my heart!" So the messboy bent over, cut the leather tongue
from his own shoe, and said, "Here's your licorice, man,
now make it last."

As I leaned against the hearthbrick and watched Jack
Carvee savor the cracked leather I couldn't help but wonder
if this was every sailor's fate. The potable spirits contained
in casks and the spirits inhabiting a ship's hull have a similar
effect: they give a false satisfaction. The drunken sot and
the seabound man think they are blessed, as simply as this,
blessed with security, blessed with a direction. It's no coincidence that a storm at sea and liquor in the blood cause a
man to erupt in foolish songs.

But every fool knows they aren't to be mixed, every fool
but our cook knows these two types of spirits must be kept
separate. Poor Jack Carvee. His imagination won't be staved,
he's acquired a principal horror and no matter what we
do or say he remains confused. He hadn't been chewing
the leather tongue for long before he let it fall from his
mouth and he recoiled, shrank back against the brick, and
said, "Why do they want to plague me? Take him away
from here, I beg you!"

The messboy did not bother to look up from the slab of
salt pork he was dicing, did not bother to ask Jack Carvee
what he saw, did not bother trying to persuade the man
that his horror was only a hallucination. The cook might
have said, *Please oblige me by standing on one foot,* so calmly
did the messboy reply, "As you wish, Jack. It's gone, you
needn't worry anymore." The crazed man hesitated, seemed
to struggle with the messboy's pronouncement, looked at
me with swollen, terrified eyes for verification. Didn't I say
all men need a double? But I wanted merely to know what
had frightened our cook.

"What is it you see?" I asked, plunging him back into his delirium. Now he's irretrievable, and I'm to blame.

"Why do they bring that Mandingo here to frighten me? I know them, they're going to let it loose, why do they want to set the black dog on me when I've done nothing? Take it away, I beg you, I've done nothing." No Mandingo man was aboard, and I told him so, yet he wouldn't hear me, he just insisted that whoever tied the monster to the bulwarks meant to set him loose upon the cook, he would be mauled and no sailor would raise a hand to help him. "I'm going to die," he said, and wouldn't be convinced otherwise.

I passed my hand before his eyes, I tried to bring him to by touching his head, I tried to reason, arguing that if there were indeed a black man leashed to the bulwarks I should be able to see him. I said I could see the deck, the bell, the canvas of the *Charles Beauchamp*, I could see the cook and the messboy, I could see water on either side, but I saw no Mandingo. "How about you," I demanded of the messboy. "Do you see any black man?"

He turned from the butcher board, cutlass raised as if he intended to behead me, and said, "Tom!"

"Yes?"

"Vanish!"

Was I, then, the illusion, and the black man as much in the world as the severed leather tongue? Vanish. Such is my worth on board this Guineaman.

"I just wanted to . . . ," I began, and fell silent. "Take it away from me," Jack Carvee implored, pressing his hands together, rocking back and forth like an ancient, sorrowing widow. I did not want to cause more injury; I became the wisp of the dream the messboy had bade me to be, I climbed through the hatchway and disappeared into the belly of the ship.

Jack Carvee, I demand you return and explain who you were! I say come back!

Me, lad? Why, I was born a pawn on the eastern seaboard, apprenticed to a ship's cook before I could take my first communion, I never learned to read or write, which was a great regret to me, for a man who spends his prime years on the water collects valuable legends and comes into contact with an assortment of sea villains, a vast array. I have known the best and worst of the lot, I've been along on the fastest Gulf Stream runs, life on board can be so pleasant when the weather is soft and the lazaret stocked with exotic delicacies.

But when there's nothing, only wretched beef and a three-pound loaf to last a week, a sailor grows haggard and mean, he'll blame the cook for the riot in his belly, he'll kick and pummel when his cook ladles out cold soup, he'll tie his cook to a mizzen shroud and flog him first with his trousers up, then with his trousers down for having snatched a cup of the captain's fine Madeira. I've been fed leather for licorice, they've tormented me with black beasts, doused me in washing suds, it's true, I've been handled cruelly, but I can't say I blame the men who have abused me. They've got to endure such suffering, and make no mistake, they don't choose this life for the sake of adventure. It's usually money responsible, the lack of, or sometimes it's a woman who debilitates them, so they register a false name and board a ship, never once looking behind as they climb the gangway.

I've seen them come up one after another, always with the same sodden look of forgetfulness, for they don't dare remember where they've been, what they're leaving. But if you catch one on a tropical night when the swells are fetching slow, if you let him pull a crate beside the hearth and you pretend to be holding court with your lentils and broth, then he just might fill his pipe with wood shavings, a few tobacco leaves, and out will drift the many chapters of his life. He'll tell you how in the old days a whole tribe of Negroes could be bought with a few yards of calico, he'll tell you how he's seen their teeth filed to sharp points, like a set of daggers in their mouth, and them wearing nothing but a band of blue cloth around their waist, dancing deep into the night inside their barracoons, their feet hardly moving, swaying back and forth like the stalks of cane they'd soon be hacking. He'll tell you of Africans who never saw America, for they were found in the hold, sleeping in a puddle of blood, strings of gut leaking out their hindquarters. They were cured the same way we cure a biscuit infected with maggot, by throwing it overboard. He'll tell you how he once saw a boy open his mouth and instead of gibberish out came a worm, plump as a sailor's forearm. There's no end to the collection a cook will gather, he thinks he's heard the worst and then another man arrives and does the last one up.

But if anyone would trouble to ask his cook, *What about you?* he'll be found to contain his own recollections, which he'll confide, if pressed. He'll tell you how the girl he meant to marry was taken by fever two days from port, he'll tell you how, when he wrapped her in burlap and weighted her with marlinespikes, she wouldn't remain below: seven times I dumped her in the ocean, seven times she rose to the surface, looking like a bloated fish carcass. Not until I carried her to a remote northern corner of the country and carved her a hole in the frostbit soil did she concede to stay down. I took the liberty of pinching a bit of frozen clay, for there's nothing like dirt from his lady's grave to preserve a man from drowning — it was only a crumble in my pocket at the end, but during my forty years at sea, though I took a few baths in the icy water, I didn't sink. I sometimes wondered if God had a plan for me, a special assignment that would account for my luck. I've ridden *Teaser, Loyal Sam, Witch of the Waves,* but I was always somewhere else when my barque caught fire or smashed upon the rocks. Well, it seems my good fortune has finally been used up. I think how all the time I was expecting a reward for my efforts and what do I have to show?

The boys don't yet understand what they're losing when they're losing me. Who will look through the hearth grate for the blue flame that indicates an impending blow? Who will be able to forecast the weather by watching how readily a tea kettle sings, how quick the dough expands? Sailors search for warning in the mackerel skies, but a cook reads the signs around him — if the fire sputters he knows to watch for a veering wind, and if the smoke drops to the sea instead of rising he'll expect a calm; if a pig carries a straw in its mouth there will be a storm by evening, and if the chickens eat during a rain it means the sky won't show a patch of blue for at least three days. But maybe predictions are only an annoyance to a man, for though he may carve the cross out of the air with his knife, though he may say a prayer and drop the blade overboard, he won't discourage the one catastrophe that's got his name. Though he may take a live cat and tie it to a spit revolving slow over a bed of coals — and I've seen it done, I've heard the unnatural cry a roasting cat will make — though a man may offer any sort of sacrifice in an effort to quell the storm, the gesture means nothing once the weather has its mind made up. There's no refusing the invitation from the other world. So a man may as well go out adorned in all his pride.

If I could do it over I wouldn't have let myself end in blood, in shock, uttering bestial sounds, no, I would have gone out singing a thanks-be-to-all, for though the ocean can be severe she has relinquished a few odd treasures, the best of which, I'll never forget, was a swan who visited me once when I was just a boy, trolling for my breakfast. I saw that grandmother approach my dory, a magnificent, gossamer bird, marsh weed dripping from her beak, she paddled slowly across the glassy inlet and when we were floating side by side she turned her head, pretending to ignore me. But I knew just what she wanted. Before she drifted away I reached out and patted that ancient madam on the neck, and I say now it was the greatest thing by far I ever did.

In other words, we've lost Jack Carvee. So suddenly. Again the surgeon mounted the balcony, the crew assembled aft, and again I did not reach the rail in time to see the water swallow the burlap bag. We are taught that the earth is founded upon wisdom, the heavens upon understanding, that just as the clouds drop dew God fills the ocean basins with his secrets. Maybe in another world dew is a blessing; on the *Charles Beauchamp* the dew is poison and has caused the accidental death of our cook. Do I dare call him lucky?

The carpenter found him at dawn, sprawled across the hog sty grating, completely naked, speckled with tiny wounds that had already formed thin scabs, like the first skin of ice over shallow puddles. At the dead hour when he left his berth any member of the crew would have helped him to a mug of fresh water, but Jack Carvee was determined to obtain his refreshment without offending the captain. In his confusion he devised an ingenious plan: instead of drinking fresh water from a cup he would lick the moisture from the bars of the sty. Once he had dragged himself to the upper deck he lacked the strength to return. So the hogs feasted upon our cook.

The surgeon turned a bench into an infirmary bed for Jack Carvee's last hours, and I requested permission to visit him. But the man laid out in the forecastle wasn't our cook anymore, he was bitten and scratched beyond recognition, and the surgeon had shaved his head so Jack Carvee resembled a wigless doll left out in the rain.

He swallowed his last sip of water this afternoon. I would not like to have the captain's conscience. But I have my own portion of guilt, for I referred to our cook as Poor

Jack Carvee, and I have since found out that in the seaman's language "poor" before a man's name means "dead." I cursed Jack Carvee. Dead Jack Carvee. Who was he? The ocean has erased the answers in the man, we have only the riddle now. The cause of death will be recorded as "decrepitude" in the captain's journal because, according to the surgeon, a younger man would have survived the punishment.

What wisdom, what understanding, what knowledge, would drag a man to the sty and leave him there? There is no justice on a slaver, no way to atone. A boy had best stay put in that narrow quadrant bounded by commands and prohibitions, he had best do what he is told and never try to claim his liberty, for a rebel on a slaver has no chance — if the crew doesn't abuse him, then the captain will, and if the captain misses, then the swine will do the damage. It makes no difference who you are because once you've broken a rule you're everyone's quarry: they will eat you alive if they catch you.

The seas are fretful today, the spindles of foam revolve in slow motion, then crack with surprising force against our hull. When we make our way across the deck we must push through the cobwebs of moisture, so dense is this sponge, and when we go below our faces are wrinkled with salt. I have washed my uniform, and until it dries I wear my blue serge pants and a cotton shirt, so nothing but my size, my shoes, and the Company insignia on my cap distinguish me from the ordinary sailors. Pharaoh has directed me to clean and trim the lamps, and when I am not watching the clock I am rushing to the binnacle with a lit match or dusting the galley lanterns with a square of flannel. Only when Pharaoh turns the ship over to the chief mate and retires from the watch do I have a chance to relax, and then I seek out Brian Piper, who has suffered the greatest loss among us.

The messboy doesn't have time to banter anymore. I would like to be of use to him but he assigns me only to the most insignificant tasks, boiling coffee or washing the carving knives. And when he grows weary of me he turns to Jack Carvee, summoning the apparition with a greeting. The messboy has a child's perception of the world: within this fog Jack Carvee is not dead but only dozing, and the meat is not salt horse but lamb and black prunes in a pastry shell, and into the pot of soup the messboy casts a fistful of violets, into his pudding he'll stir ripe cherries and gooseberries, peaches, almonds, borage leaves. A game without consequence, for the messboy relishes these tastes that don't exist, and he is comforted by the presence of the dead.

"Right enough, friend," I have heard him counsel. "Sleep, and you'll gulp long draughts from a bucket. Dream, and forget your withered tongue, the ash filling your throat, your aching limbs. Tom, hand me a spoon and don't you step on Jack Carvee's toes, he's earned his rest" — rattling on, addressing the nothing that has replaced our cook, speaking with grand authority, no sign of sorrow, no hesitation, as if it were in his power not only to declare but to revise the truth. I know better than to trespass into his private world and rob him of his black men, his exotic spices and companions. So I'll concede, *Yes, Jack Carvee has returned*, and I'll leave it to the messboy to decide what we shall do with the specter.

"Blue Monkey, lie still," he ordered, straightening my arm, extracting my finger from my mouth. Neither light nor sound travels as rapidly as a boy's thoughts when he is rudely dangled over the chasm between midnight and dawn. "Blue Monkey, I say lie still!"

I knew what it was: the harpy had come for me, I could feel the shriveled dry lobes of her breasts brushing against my cheek, her porcupine beard scratching my lips, I could even taste the filthy metal quills as she forced my arms to my side. *She means to devour me,* I thought, for everyone knows that harpies suffer from an insatiable appetite. *Let go, or I'll scream!* But since I was still half asleep I had no control over my voice, as though in that moment between sleep and waking I had forgotten the very language of my body.

Then, even before I had drawn a breath, I understood that the intruder was no fantastic creature. With the thimble-ful of moonlight spilling through my portal I could examine the wingless form; in the fragment of a second before my reason returned to me I thought, *This must be a dream,* a dream in which I was Peter Gray on a gimbaled bed, and the captain had come to bugger me.

But then, fully awake, I no longer confused myself with another, and the voice commanding me to lie still belonged not to the captain but — I don't like to admit it — to the messboy. The messboy. I realized with a start what was hap-pening. I yelped, he smothered my face in the bunched-up blanket and whispered urgently, "Tom, I'm not going to hurt you, it's just I've had a scare, a terrible fright. I can't tell you, no, don't ask, but Tom, I need your company, so hush, lie still," which I was compelled to do whether I chose to or not, with the blanket covering my mouth, the messboy pinning me to the bed. I could feel him trembling as he said, "Monkey, just hold on to me." In such intimate contact I was forced to share his fear; we tumbled together, yes, this was the reason for his panic. He had felt the clouds collapse beneath his feet.

I tried to push the dead weight off, but he merely buried his face in my shoulder and said, "Lie still, I tell you to lie still!" When he was certain that I would not wrestle against him, he relaxed his hold. I had little compassion. The mess-boy was a less inimitable foe than any harpy or sea captain, but in such close proximity he disgusted me. Pimpled, stink-ing of pork fat, he doesn't comprehend how he is related to his looking-glass reflection. I have watched him stir soup with his right hand, cup the left beneath his nose, blow, and catch a gob of mucus in his palm.

I see more clearly what Jack Carvee and the messboy had in common: swift fantasies, imagination so powerful that they thought they could make the world over according to their specifications. But it seems this quivering, whimpering puppy sharing my berth had stayed too long in the other world. Was it a black man giving him this fright? If I could draw an explanation from him, if I agreed to listen to his account, let him describe the vision that had shaken him so, if I treated him with a delicate tolerance, pretended to believe in his Mandingos, then he might leave me in peace. So I inquired gently, "What did you see?" and prepared to indulge him.

"Will you hold on to me, Tom, warm my fingers?"

"If you release my arm, I will. Now answer me: are there monsters out there? Or have you seen a dead man come to life?"

"Not a man. Not death," he said, gripping my hands in his. "A monster? Aye, it was awful. But no, it was beautiful. Beauty — she's enough to drive a fellow mad. Tom, are you listening to me? Are you listening closely?" To please him I raised my head so my ear was flush against his lips, and though he spoke in the faintest whisper his voice surged into me, as the ocean would if my portal window ever shattered.

"Tom, I've seen a lady!"

I was prepared for black men, for Jack Carvee, for unicorns, Hydras, sea serpents, or any other vision born in Piper's mind. I was not prepared for Peter Gray. In this lawless, floating state I have discovered that I recoil from the living and prefer ghosts. The messboy has caught sight of a woman.

"That's impossible!"

"But I saw her, Tom, standing at the starboard rail."

"What about the men on watch?" I charged. "Did they see her too?"

"They were all asleep, Tom, abaft of the wheel, and the dame, she had a blanket wrapped around her, draped over her head, and I would have thought she was one of the crew up for a breath of air. But she let the blanket fall to the deck, and there she stood in all her natural glory, thoroughly soaked, glistening like Caribbean coral. She must have heard me draw in my breath because she turned her head and stared at me, cast a spell upon my tongue, I couldn't call out."

"She saw you looking at her, then?" I didn't understand why she had left the captain's stateroom, I couldn't imagine what had prompted her to take this foolish risk.

"She did as good as turn toward me, but she looked right through, like she could see the Azores between my ribs."

"Piper," I said hoarsely, "you're exhausted, doing the work of two men. You've been confused by a dream. Listen — you sleep in my berth and I'll stand guard by the firehearth."

"I won't let you go above alone, Tom. She's waiting there."

"Waiting, you say? For whom?"

"Why, she's waiting for the captain."

"Enough of your lies!" I burst out, pummeling him in a fury, which only served to bring his rank body over me again, flattening me as he urged, "Lie still, Blue Monkey."

"How do you know what she wants?" I demanded. Instead of answering directly he released me and told me to get dressed, and he sat on the edge of my bunk with his knees up, his hands tucked tightly behind his calves. "How do you know?" I repeated weakly, fumbling for my trousers. I could only try to extract information from him, it was useless to insist anymore that Peter Gray did not exist. But the messboy refused to reply.

When I'd secured the belt around my waist, he led the way out of my chamber and up through the companionway. At the top stair he gripped my arm and muttered, "She must have heard us coming. But she'll be back, take my word."

The spray from a feeble swell brushed against my face like strands of hair as we traced a serpentine course around the bulwarks and hatchcombs and the coils of rope left out to trip a man in the dark. Without a word the messboy began to sort spoons and arrange cups in a row across the butcher block. I wondered why he had brought me to the galley at all; with light enough from the moon to cast a shadow, he didn't need me hovering beside him.

Finally he replied, as if my question had only then been asked, "It wasn't just any lady, Tom," he whispered, and I pretended interest in the minute fissures of a brick. "It was," and while I silently supplied the name — Peter Gray — the messboy said, "one of the captain's wives."

Of course: they'd been wedded, he had made her his bride. *And you, Brian Piper, you are the captain's confidant,* I thought, though I did not speak my suspicion aloud.

"And she's stuck between the realms. I mean, Tom, she's neither entirely dead nor living. You see, this milky lamb left the world by accident. Now she wants to say a proper goodbye before she takes leave once and for all."

"Tell me what you know," I insisted as it became clear to me that the messboy had confused Peter Gray with one of his imaginary characters. He shed the last remnants of fear, gloating now before his eager audience.

"You keep your eyes open. The next time she appears you leap upon her and see if she is made of flesh and bone. And I'll tell you what I know." He paused, a lengthy pause to let me know that the ensuing tale required some reflection, and I pretended interest to encourage him, glad to hear him stray so widely from the truth.

"Now I have already told you some shocking things, Tom, and I aim to tell you more. With the comforts of home behind, it's time for you to learn about the crimes of men, now or never is what I say. But first you've got to tell Brian Piper how many wives he has chronicled so far."

I counted to myself on my fingers, my thumb and forefinger for the pair in Italy, three more — or was it four? — in Marseille. And did the sum include the redhead who survived the banquet? I opened my fist to begin the count over again, and Piper exclaimed, "Five is exactly right, Tom, you're a good listener and you make my effort worth the trouble. So now we move on to number six."

Who was not Peter Gray. The messboy did not know about Peter Gray.

"How many girls, Tom, would rise from the sea at midnight? How many girls would volunteer to wander the deck of a slaver? Hear me out, then you decide whether Piper belongs in a madhouse.

"It was another seashore town in France where the captain's sixth wife preferred to settle, a child bride and still a child when she learned that her marriage was not valid. Flat-chested, her nose an oily red, her hair strung in two tight-woven braids — she had an advantage, Tom, though she couldn't know it. She was foolish as they come and worried no further than to the end of the hour. When the other wives learned the truth, they filled their cups with death. Or walked into the sea. But this dame, the youngest, didn't understand what she had lost, she had no sense of her destiny, and after hearing that she had no husband she said to herself, *Then I'm free to go.*

"Flight, Tom. A girl commits herself to flight and there's no holding her back. She'll make haste and leave everything behind, she'll rush ahead with such speed that like a seedpod in a battering wind she'll break apart, splinter into a thousand pieces. I don't think you need Brian Piper to tell you that the wicked survivor of that fatal feast was responsible. She stopped in uninvited to squeal to the little lass about the captain's misdeeds. A quarter of an hour later this young sprite wrapped a scarf around her head, filled a purse with gold, and left her new marriage. She jaunted at a fast clip, hurried west, through the narrow streets, until she reached an old, untended churchyard. And as she stood panting beneath a towering willow, the leaves scratching her face like fingers of gypsy children gathering round, she saw in the cemetery grove ahead — no burning bush, no apparition of the Virgin — she saw, Tom, a magnificent balloon, a great tangerine bubble attached to a small wooden boat. Now she didn't care to consider whether this vehicle had an owner — to her it was nothing but a timely gift from heaven. And if the silk balloon did not belong to her, then, well, she belonged to it. Don't ask me how she knew the method of that machine, Tom. It was extraordinary from beginning to end. She clambered into the dory, untied the drag ropes, twisted open the nozzle, and in a moment she was airborne. The balloon had risen to the treetops before three men in laboratory coats appeared below, shouting and cursing, throwing rocks at this young innocent, who meant no wrong, who thought she was merely doing what was expected. And like those tropical girls who drop bags of perfume on your head when you pass below their window, minding your business (and it's been done to me, Brian Piper himself was once baptized with a bag of love on a South Sea isle, believe it or not), the captain's wife dropped her sack of gold over the edge of the boat. With this portion of ballast jettisoned the balloon swooped upward and disappeared into the clouds.

"You're looking skeptical, Tom. You're thinking to yourself, Piper's pressed too far this time. But you've got to know that Piper has no need to fib, the world's too marvelous to tamper with, and if I'm leaving out some of the hows and wherefores it's because I want to tell it all to you as straight as I can.

"I don't claim to know what she was thinking as she surfaced from the clouds into the brilliant, empty blue, I don't

know what passed through her head as she bobbed in her
dinghy, and I can't tell you what went wrong. Maybe it
was a gust of wind that loosened the rip panel, maybe the
sun spit out a spark, maybe the angry hand of God tore
open the silk hide. Or did the girl herself yank the valve
cord in a frantic effort to return to earth? Does it even
matter? We know for sure that she attempted to regain
her equilibrium, because sandbags were found scattered in
the fields miles around. As the vehicle dove toward the land
below, the girl flung out all the bags, cast off the oars, heaved
the extra weight over the side until no free ballast remained.
Maybe she thought faith would save her. Maybe she didn't
pray at all.

"It reminds me of my own fast descent from a mizzen
yard once, years ago, when I was called upon to furl the
royal, and as I fell I didn't think about God or the hereafter
like I should have done, instead I was thinking how nice it
would be to be buried up to my neck in warm sand. But
that's by the bye, Tom. The fact is that as the shrinking
balloon descended through the clouds the girl threw herself
over the rail. They say even as she plunged she disintegrated;
her fingertips, her hair, and her patent leather shoes broke
off her body, she dissolved into ever smaller particles until
she was nothing but a swirl of dust. Not enough of her
intact to disturb the surface of the lake directly below. The
vehicle itself crashed in the mossy bank a few feet from
the water's edge. But do you want to hear the real miracle?
You won't believe me, but I'll tell you anyway: in the dory
were found six glass bottles containing specimens, Tom,
specimens intended for the laboratory. Fetuses, they were.
Six unborn piglets, six pieces of raw pork preserved in salt
water. And out of these bottles stacked beneath the bench,
not a single one was shattered."

"Then she's haunting us!" I cried, eager to bolster this
fantasy that was so wrong. "The captain's wife, she's joined
the crew."

"And I gazed upon her myself tonight."

As he remembered the ghost his jaw dropped, the amazement resurged, his mouth hung open, and I could see the barnacles of paste coating his tongue, I could see the chocolate surfaces of broken teeth, indeed, the oval between his lips seemed an incomparably spacious, secure cavern. *Is there room for me, Brian Piper? I won't be much trouble, you'll forget I'm there.* Like a gadfly that will live and breed inside a woman's lip, I'll take refuge in the messboy's mouth, his unreal world, I'll nestle between a molar and his cheek, lodging snugly until we are sailing round Montauk Point.

Becalmed again today. I rode in the crosstree from noon to dusk, descending to ring the bell at every half hour, scrambling up the shroud again to watch the light pave strips with cobblestones, then crust the water with gold and then with blood. I have seen — no one knows what I have seen this evening — but I am convinced now that I must abandon this rotting carcass of a ship. The *Charles Beauchamp* has no soul and we are simply parasites, taking our nourishment from a cadaver. The sailors mend canvas, grease the steering gear, and putty beams, thinking nothing has changed. *Go on, trod up and down this Guineaman's spine, drape the ship in colorful garments, point the harpy east.* Fools. Blinded by the sea's manteau of light, they don't understand that their vessel is steadily decaying beneath their feet. But I understand. And like the captain's Ariel, I will leap out of the boat, I will go down unencumbered.

Papa, if you lose your youngest son tonight, remember this: he still had hope of seeing his family again even as he sank. Let people slander me, let them say Tom abandoned ship without permission, but Papa, know that your son was lost trying to defy death. And if you have any doubts about his courage, then you must locate a girl named Peter Gray, she will assure you I played a hero's part to the last.

This is my plan: at supper I will slip a message beneath her dollop of sea pie. I'll be prompt to pour the captain's brandy, and I'll ask him to show me our latitude on his chart in order to distract him while Peter Gray draws the greasy paper across the plate and slips it into her pocket. In my note I'll instruct her to meet me at the bell as soon as the captain falls into a stupor. From the stateroom I'll go straight to the lower hold and collect the necessary articles — a ten-pound loaf of bread, half a wheel of cheese, a cask of water — and these I'll load into a whaleboat. We'll use a hammock for a sail, a spoon for a rudder. While I wait for Peter Gray I'll watch the new moon worming to the sky's summit, and just when it seems I'll have to make my escape alone, she'll arrive wearing her sailor togs, her hands thrust into the deep pockets of her trousers.

I don't think she'll need much persuasion once I inform her that the messboy has been spreading rumors that the *Charles Beauchamp* is a hen frigate. She'll scramble ahead of me into the boat, and I'll follow her, pushing away from the ship, dipping the oars soundlessly. We'll skate across the surface until the Guineaman's bulk has disappeared from view. What shall we say to each other? I think we will ride quietly. I will break a piece from the hard loaf for Peter Gray, the moonlight will be her melted butter, the breeze a delicate claret. At sunrise I'll pull the hammock sail taut and we'll let the morning wind determine our course, then we'll clear the bottom of the boat, spread a potato sack, and lie together. The only sound will be the water ripping gently as we pass, soon there will be nothing to hear at all. It doesn't take long for a man to become deaf to a changeless, drumming beat. Peter Gray and I will sail into oblivion, and when the sun hangs directly above we'll take off our clothes and tie a canopy of shirts across the oar locks. In the muted light my senses will return, I'll listen to her breath seeping through the tissue of her lungs, I'll see myself reflected twice in her eyes, and finally I will touch her, yes, she'll let me discover her. I will explore the secrets of her body, the smells hidden in the crevices of her shoulders, beneath her breasts, her groin.

By the time this message reaches you, Papa, you may exchange the words "I will" with "I did." I will have Peter Gray, I will know a man's pleasure. You may be proud of your son, he was quick to learn from the captain's example. And when after two weeks at sea the supply of water is nearly depleted, remember that your son acted bravely. The last ounces of fresh water could be stretched over three days if there were two of us, nearly a week for a solitary passenger. So I'll lower myself into the ocean when Peter Gray is asleep, the cold will crawl up my ankles, my thighs, I'll hold my breath and swim underwater, and when I emerge a faint smoke will be rising from the surface like steam off the snow-covered mansard roofs at home. I'll grow numb to the chill so tell Mother not to worry — I will not suffer much.

And what will become of Peter Gray? If the boat capsizes in a squall, she'll hug the empty water cask, and when the storm passes she'll crawl into the barrel, draw the lid closed, and float for days, lulled into a dreamless slumber. She won't even wake when the surf shoulders the barrel upon its crest and flings her onto the sand. Three days she'll sleep inside the beached cask, until the dogs arrive to paw, whine, growl at the container. A lonely child collecting shells will wonder what has attracted the hounds. He'll pry open the lid, and Peter Gray will be born a second time. The boy will jostle her awake and ask her if it's true what they say about seashore jinnees — can she grant him a wish, just one uncomplicated wish?

It seems the ocean does not find Jack Carvee to its liking, for the duffel containing the man refuses to sink, the corpse continues to float behind our lagging ship. It must be the clay from his lady's grave that buoys him to the surface — this, and the fact that we neglected to tie sinkers to his sack. The crew has not bothered to scan the water, they do not suspect that the dead man loiters astern. But I have seen him. So tonight I have resolved to flee with Peter Gray from this watery grave.

"Every king must have a fetish," she said, straddling the chair, propping her chin over the back arch as she pierced the sea pie with the prongs of her fork, stabbing a cipher in the meat, a message only she could read. If only she had pushed the congealed mass half an inch across the dish. But she toyed with the food without dislodging it, so my note remained unread. Our escape will be postponed until I can find a sure method of communicating with her.

Peter Gray has more experience than I thought. At supper she proved knowledgeable about the history of trafficking, she made reference to the Company of Royal Adventurers, and she could tell us of the most recent voyages of pirate slavers. She understands the industry as intimately as she knows the habits of insects — she could name which "factories" along the coast were most productive when the trade flourished, how many slaves were shipped out annually. And as she held a match to her cigar she hinted at the atrocities: "A fetish, Tom, is not simply a good luck charm. The king's power depends upon his fetish, and the spirit inside an idol must be tended with the utmost care and reverence."

I said, "It sounds like nothing but a pagan superstition."

"Yet if the people stop believing, if they no longer fear a king's fetish, then the king is doomed."

"I presume," interrupted the captain, his eyes shining a molasses brown, the color of his brandy, "that a fetish must be fed. It must be adequately nourished. Tom, if you were king, what would you serve your fetish for lunch?"

"Giblets," I said, which provoked the captain to his rude hilarity; his mirth depends upon a scapegoat, someone to play the fool. He thinks I've been born to amuse him. Tonight I appreciated Peter Gray's austere, serious air — I've come to prefer a monastery to burlesque, a granite-columned edifice with simple pavilions, herb gardens, and apple trees to the captain's traveling show.

"Not just any kind of giblets, I'm afraid," he chuckled, motioning Peter Gray to resume. But she deferred to him, and he eagerly continued the description. "A king must make sacrifices to a fetish. If he wants to be renowned for strength, he'll feed his fetish warriors; if he wants to engender children, he'll feed pregnant women to the spirit."

"Captain," I interrupted, "if you know about these kings, then perhaps you've heard of a certain gentleman mulatto on an island in the Gulf of Guinea; they say he is the most powerful man merchant of all." I glanced at Peter Gray to see if she approved of my inquiry, but she kept her eyes lowered.

"A gentleman, you say? A nigger tyrant, you mean — at every full moon he slays four hundred prisoners, there's a gentleman for you! Shall I tell you how the king visits his barracoons on the day of the sacrifice and divides his prisoners into two groups — those to be sold and those to be slaughtered? Do you want to hear the truth about your gentleman, Tom?" He pointed his finger at me as if to counter some objection I had raised. "And don't think he preserves the worthiest for the market, no, the king's fetish always has first priority; you may be sure he'll offer the finest of the harvest to his dark angel."

"Then you've attended his fetish ceremony?" asked Peter Gray, loosening the grit beneath her fingernails with a quill pen.

"I've dined on mutton and palm wine with his majesty while hundreds of heads were stacked at our feet."

"His majesty?" she asked, with artful nonchalance.

"The toughest broker in the business."

"Is his name Quince?" I demanded.

"Quince? Why, yes, his majesty Quince, that's right, like marmalade." Peter Gray, did you hear? This is Quince, the captain himself has met your man merchant. Here was a strange, unexpected coincidence.

"Then you know him?" I pressed.

"I've sat beside him while handsome boys were led onto the torchlit stage, Tom. I've watched the priest lay hands upon a lad's head and chant the consecrating hymns. I've watched the executioner take a step forward and with a sword behead the prisoner in a single stroke."

Was Peter Gray surprised to hear that the same mulatto, baptized and educated in America, has ruled over this bloody ceremony? "His majesty never flinched, never twitched, or even scratched his shin during the butchery." Was Peter Gray shocked that the captain had met her Quince? It should have pained her to hear him tell it. But now, as I reflect upon the evening, I am convinced that she snared our captain, enticed him to speak on the subject of fetishes and kings. She must have suspected that the captain was familiar with this man merchant, this royal bastard, perhaps all along she has known we are a slaver bound for the Guinea Coast. The captain dined with Quince while hundreds of heads rolled across the stage. The man merchant of Peter Gray's account is the captain's associate, they have broken bread together, drunk great quantities of palm wine. Not only has the king been host to the captain in the past but will do so again. We sail toward Quince's kingdom.

"So you mean to return?" I said urgently.

"He's got the finest crop on the continent. I'd be a fool not to do business with that devil. So prepare yourselves, my young friends — you're used to the violence occurring behind the curtains, you hear about horrors in soliloquies, in headlines and history books. But soon you will be watching the actual event. If you've got the courage, Tom, I advise you to put out your eyes with a marlinespike, and you, lady, I'll snip off your ears if you want me to, for once you've been an audience at a fetish ceremony you'll be forced to join ranks with the vilest outcasts. The memory, simply the memory, will be your debilitating injury. You'll be consigned to float between the continents, never able to return home or to purge your head of the screams. The king's fetish will protect your ship, you won't even be permitted to drown bravely in shoaling waters, no, you'll suffer exile into your old age, my little friends, and the only country you'll have is the one inside yourself. There's no spot on earth where you'll belong. So I tell you to start founding your solitary nation now. You want evidence of the effects? Isn't your captain proof enough? Come, consider me, be as harsh and unforgiving as you like. For I cannot help what I've become. Consider me."

The captain had driven himself to this powerful lament. I don't know whether to hate him for his threats or to pity him. He has promised to give us a memory that will alter us forever. And this, a memory, is just what Peter Gray has set out to recover.

Nobody comes to my quarters, nobody crawls into my bed. I have spent much of the evening staring out my eye slit of a window. This sky reminds me of a deserted beach I wandered long ago, I do not remember the season or why I was alone, but I can tell you just how the stranded starfish were arranged: there must have been hundreds of them scattered across the wet sand like so many constellations, and I could trace Little Bear, Castor and Pollux, Orion's belt. I think if I had to thank Providence for something I would thank it for my portal. Without the thin blue light trickling in I would be prey to superstition. There is nothing like the combination of water and darkness to drive a boy mad, for you know a dream grows out of proportion on board a slaver, just as moss flourishes in crevices of a broken stump.

I must try to stay awake or he will seize me. His majesty,
I mean. Quince. The captain and Peter Gray have conspired
against me, they plague me with talk of this mulatto and
now I can't rid myself of him. He will appear to me if I let
myself sleep, he will take me as his captive, bind my wrists,
and thrust me into the prison yard, the barracoon. And at
the next full moon I will be lucky if he selects me as a
slave instead of a sacrifice. Yes, I shall not mind being a
slave, I will be grateful if he spares my life, and I will do
whatever I must to indulge him, to keep him tranquil.

No outrage and no familiarity — this, my father told me,
should be every owner's dictum. Papa took me woodcock
shooting the day before I left for the coast, and he tried
to explain to me the complex bond between an owner and
his property. I will make sure I don't provoke Quince either
to anger or to compassion. Never give a master the chance
to single you out, for if he notes your differences he will
be sure to find fault. And remember that your condition
does not merit complaint. You will join the lampreys in
the fishpond if it's a struggle for liberty you choose, but I
will kneel at Quince's feet, I will walk before him in the
jungle and clear the path of boulders and nettle, I will boil
his rice, pluck his fowl, tend his crops. *Spare me,* I'll beg,
one voice among many in the barracoon, all of us making
the identical plea — *spare me* — as Quince strolls between
the rows of prisoners and points his finger at those who
will be slain to feed his spirit.

Quince. See how he haunts me, though I remain alert.
I must concentrate on tracing the Southern Cross in the
sky. There is nothing to fear. My father will purchase
me if I ever fall into Quince's hands, Papa will give me
a pileus cap, turn me three times round, strike me with
the broad side of a knife, and say the words *liber esto.* No,
I have nothing to fear from Quince, African king, bastard
mulatto.

·   ·   ·

Well, I have changed my mind and will not be hurrying off this Guineaman. I admit I enjoy the minor comforts, the warmth of a wool blanket, the vague scent of my mother still clinging to it. Besides, Jack Carvee has finally deserted us. The messboy says last night he saw the cook crawl from his sack and stand upright, bobbing like a petrel; he swears he saw Jack Carvee lift a hand as if to wave farewell, then turn and walk toward the horizon. But in place of Jack Carvee we have other persistent followers, ones with less patience and sharper teeth. No, I'm not so eager to test the shark-infested waters.

The messboy forfeits sleep so he can spy upon the captain's wife. He remained in the galley through the night, hoping to catch another glimpse of her, but instead of seeing a woman he saw our cook's transcendent soul, or so he maintains. "Farewell, Jack Carvee!" I heard him shout. We were at the cusp of dawn when I was woken by the messboy's voice, and since he has no friend but me on board I decided I must do what I could to help him. For I expected the messboy was finally acknowledging the loss of Jack Carvee, I thought at last he'd recognized what he couldn't control. But when I found him on deck, looking like a shade himself in the tropical orange light of the new day, he was in a giddy mood. He had witnessed a miracle and wanted to boast of his luck.

"If you'd stayed up with the moon, Tom, you'd have seen our cook, you'd have seen him walk over the water. Away Jack Carvee went, but first he waved goodbye to me, and that's the truth."

So it seems there will be no sorrow for the messboy; the dead constitute a treasure to him, a glorious mystery, and he considers his visions a fortunate talent. In this exultant fit the messboy bade me to stay with him, he prepared a pot of coffee and continued to cluck about the sight of Jack Carvee walking across the water, Jack Carvee resurrected, Jack Carvee saluting to the *Charles Beauchamp*.

So I watched the inky darkness fade, helped the messboy set out breakfast, and afterward watched the carpenter knot leather tails and wool to the sounding line. The carpenter, a polite but skittish sort with a thin, parted beard, has his own technique of navigation. He made me promise to keep his method a secret from the rest of the crew, who would be sure to ridicule him. The carpenter does not simply drop the line over the rail, does not simply note the water mark to measure the fathoms — he has to touch his tongue to the lead bar once it's been dragged on the bottom, he claims the taste of the ocean is a more precise indicator than any compass. And I've seen proof of his abilities; this morning he licked the sounding lead, raised his brows, perplexed, tasted again, and muttered, "A body south-southeast, wrapped in dangerous waters." His assessment differed from the charts, but since the carpenter's predictions have always been reliable, the captain rerouted us to avoid the shoals.

Toward noon the island that does not exist on any map appeared, a dromedary's hump in the distance, and then, as if the animal had clambered up, the island rose, yes, it seemed to stand and then to grow immense before our eyes while the sea boiled treacherously around it. The men left off whatever they were doing and gathered at the lee rail to look at the marble cliffs, the waterfalls glimmering like veins of liquid pewter. Only the carpenter and I know that this island has a rancid taste. I am glad we made a wide arc around it, though I heard the men grumbling; some of them think this island was the Land of Promise, and now they've been deprived of the opportunity to see the famous apples that are always ripe, to bathe in the springs, to eat the white bread that blossoms like cotton. I do not think the island would have welcomed us kindly — the omens have been multiplying lately, what with Jack Carvee and the sharks. Perhaps we are sailing along the rim of hell.

Of course the messboy has his own explanation. He says we've mistaken a giant fish for an island. He says by tomorrow the fish will have swum away, so we won't be able to plot this island on our map. He told me that this fish wants only to catch its own tail in its mouth but can't because of its wide girth, and so the waters are turbulent as it waggles helplessly beneath the surface.

"We should pity the fish," the messboy proposed.

His lies have begun to irritate me. I snapped at him, "I think you are merely describing yourself," and walked away. I wonder if he shall ever speak with me again.

Thirty fathoms below us. Breeze from the southeast. Spoonfuls of quicklime sprinkled through the lower decks. Bow painted white.

The men have removed all traces of our identity, smearing paint over the name *Charles Beauchamp,* and the captain and I packed every scrap of paper that could link the Company to us, every card, map, magazine, or cloth — except for my hat — into a crate. Though the crew hadn't been summoned to witness the burial, each man stopped what he was doing when the captain and I heaved the box over the rail. Goodbye *Charles Beauchamp.* The jagged fins in our wake disappeared as the sharks dove to examine the paper feast. "And now," the captain whispered to me, the waters swirling below us, the clanking and knocking of the crew momentarily silenced, "we are nobody."

After checking to see that the canvas hood over the binnacle sufficiently veiled the lanterns, the captain walked forward to the stove, dipped a ladle into the soup, held the steaming liquid under his nose, then directed the messboy to bring our suppers promptly. I kept my chin down while the captain spoke, but as I followed him away from the galley I turned to glance at the messboy and our eyes met. I expected to see Piper redden with indignation, but it seemed he had forgotten my insult, he merely looked eagerly at me, forming exaggerated shapes with his purple lips to convey his message soundlessly. I do not know what he tried to tell me, I do not care. What good is a fellow who has no sense of himself? He is just like that fish, struggling to bite his tail, submerged in his imagination, and if we went ashore and built a fire on his back I suppose he would not notice.

Nearly forty days we have been sailing. I realize now that I have been carried along two divergent courses, I have been traveling toward Quince and the horrors of Africa, and I have been drawn closer to the murky center of the messboy's fancy. Shall I ever meet the romancer of the messboy's tales? I do not think so — that captain is only Piper's hypothesis, and I am too incredulous to believe such a fantastic biography. But I am convinced by the converging accounts of the man merchant. Indeed, at supper there was a moment when the captain seemed to have been replaced by Quince.

Peter Gray had already retired to her gimbaled bed in the night cabin, a dark closet with a coffin's dimensions, but though she closed her door I knew she would be carefully following our conversation. I tried to ask the proper questions, steering the captain back toward the topic of kings and fetishes. I did not need to pour his brandy tonight — he gripped his flask in his right hand and every two or three sips he'd replenish his own cup. Through most of the evening he showed no signs of the influence, his hand remained steady when he pointed to the fleck of ink that was an island barracoon, his voice wasn't at all soggy with emotion.

At first the captain was preoccupied with navigation and studied his charts silently. When I inquired about our cargo — how many did he mean to take, what ages would they be — he did not reply. But when I spoke the name Quince he stiffened, glaring as if I'd referred to a crime the captain himself had committed. Had he forgotten our earlier conversation? After swallowing a great amount of brandy he brightened, leaned across the table, roughly mussed my hair, and said in a low, conspiratorial voice, "You see, Tom, the blacks all around owe him money; he has a usurer's authority." He spoke with pride, as if he were the tyrant. "He dresses in cloaks woven from mango leaves, fringed with colorful cotton threads. His table is furnished with the best silver and crystal." He pressed the tip of his tongue between his teeth, and I couldn't help but feel that Quince was an obscene joke. "His English is flawless, and he's extended his thatched hut with terraces and stucco verandas, he's planted pumpkin and the vines wind around the palace, magnificent tentacles, Tom, and the immense fan leaves of the palms provide shade. When he's not smoking his opium pipe he's chewing the bark of a sweet lime tree, cleaning his teeth with the twig. You'll see, he's the comeliest, wealthiest devil you'll ever meet. A gentleman. But let's hope he doesn't include you on his menu, pray he doesn't take a liking to your figure and order you to be boiled and minced. We're all on our own once we set foot on his majesty's terrain, we're taking a terrible risk doing business with this wicked, pitiless *mallata*, but I'm expecting that since he's favored me in the past, he will do so again."

Another swig from his cup and the captain fixed his eyes on me, staring, testing my forbearance. There is evil ahead. Only a matter of days before we meet. I will try to gain courage in this short interval — I will drink the barley water meant for the sick, I will sleep from dusk to dawn, storing up my strength.

"Tom, pretend to esteem him, don't bother trying to influence him with your rank. But if you think you see his appetite awakening, if you think he's starting to appraise the quality of your flesh, beware. And if he has the women sew a scarlet patch upon your shirt, you'll know what he intends. We're putting our heads between the jaws of a wolf, Tom, a foul-smelling, rabid wolf. Yes, I covet his sleek pelt. But I warn you, when you feel his breath on the back of your neck, his fingers tickling your hindquarters, don't flinch. Wait until you have a promising chance to escape."

Why must everyone on board this slaver tease me with the tragedies of other lives and warn me to prepare for my own assassination? I wanted to prove to the captain that I would not buckle beneath any man merchant, so I managed to rise to my feet, though his eyes were a burden, and I bowed slightly. As I looked at him the captain seemed to shrink, diminished by his collaborator's shadow. He stared into the depths of his cup, and I did not wait to be dismissed.

Instead of immediately retiring I wandered to the deck and searched until I found Sirius in the sky, a lovely, comforting jewel. With my face turned upward I bumped my shin against a hatchcomb, stumbled backward, and fell over a coil of rope. From the darkness behind the mizzenmast I heard men burst into laughter, I was sure that they were laughing at me. But as long as I have the stars for company I do not need respect from other men. I think I shall try to unlearn the knowledge I have gained on this ship, I shall erase my education just as we have obscured our name.

I do not understand what inspires us. Who will tell me why we've chosen Quince's island as our destination, trafficking as our job, who will tell me why we don't simply keep to our own parcel of land, cultivating and harvesting, breeding and burying each other? Who will tell me why we can't follow the example of the sexton beetle, that ingenious bearer of the dead? There is some information accumulated on this voyage that I don't want to forget — perhaps when I am at home again I can persuade Papa to buy the captain's library for me. And if my father wants me to defend the worth of the books, I shall refer him to the passage on the sexton beetle, for this has been my best lesson in survival.

If we learned the sexton's trade we wouldn't need any other profit. Like the sexton we could use death to our advantage. He flies through the dark, and when he smells a mole decaying he alights in the garden, flips over on his back, and wedges his body beneath the carcass. He pushes upward with his legs, wiggling the cadaver forward while his wife clears the path of stones and twigs. When they reach the sandy soil they scratch a pit for the animal and bury it, that's right, they bury the corpse. Then they line a side tunnel with the cadaver's fur and wait quietly for their eggs to hatch, feeding upon the body, gorging upon the rotting flesh. Later they will share chewed mouthfuls with their little grubs until the young ones grow robust, and when nothing but bones remain of the carcass the beetle family wastes no time tunneling to the surface.

That's all there is to it: find a mole's corpse in the garden, claim it as yours. You see, if we could learn to need only the spiritless bodies we wouldn't have to hunt human souls.

But for now we must be either captive or captor, aligned or imprisoned to kings. The captain and Peter Gray have an interest in Quince. And with a potent magic his majesty lures us ever closer — everyone on board this Guineaman must suffer to meet him. He signals to the harpy, our figure-head, she drags us east. The captain has tried to convince me to fear Quince, and Peter Gray would like me to serve as understudy for this bastard king. I would rather have nothing to do with him.

As I searched the constellations tonight and thought of home, I could hear the echo of my father's voice. "Treat a nigger like a nigger," he had said to me that morning we went woodcock shooting. Treat a nigger like a nigger. When I am standing face to face with his majesty Quince I must remember this.

2

AFRICA. In the middle of the night the harpy shrieked, I felt a witch's cloying hand around my ankle, and when I sat up to catch my breath I saw a frieze of landscape in the heat lightning. I convinced myself that the Windward Coast was only another unnatural vision and willed it away by shutting my eyes. But at dawn I looked out my portal to see the sun rising from behind the distant concave rim of the continent.

Later that morning, while we coasted offshore in the pounded copper waters, before this rancid, gusting wind overtook us, the messboy woke me and demanded that I come see the flock following in our wake. Sea birds, I supposed he meant. I knew he wouldn't leave me alone until I obliged, so I dragged myself from my berth and went up to see the strange birds myself, I stood at the rail and watched as one after another rose from the water, then dropped and disappeared. The messboy explained that these creatures were a band of fallen angels trying futilely to return to heaven, he said if I could observe a specimen closely I would see it had the legs and head of a tiny blue man with wings instead of arms. Since I could offer no better explanation I said nothing. For nearly an hour we watched the creatures flinging themselves up, flying forward for thirty yards, and then falling exhausted into the sea.

I had grown bored and was about to return to my berth when one of Brian Piper's little blue men made a desperate leap and landed on the aft deck of our Guineaman. He was about ten inches in length, with a white stripe on his belly and blue fins instead of angel wings. I thought the messboy would accept the evidence and stoically endure the humiliation when the crew ordered him to fricassee the fallen angel, but he never altered his opinion. Even as he scaled and chopped the fish he let me know what a blue man portended: a blue man in a ship's wake augurs a storm, a blue man on board means there will soon be prisoners in the bilge, and a blue man fried and eaten will drive a sailor mad.

At supper last night I had no choice but to eat a portion of the flying fish, since the captain insisted that Peter Gray and I savor the thin, buttery fillet. I noticed that he took nothing from his own plate — he is satisfied with brandy, tobacco, a few wooden biscuits. Now the typhoon winds might not be an unusual occurrence for this area of the world, and the blue men have nothing to do with the blackfish oil we mean to collect, but I cannot help but wonder if I feel insanity tugging. Instead of Sly Tom Fool to the captain I shall be Tom o' Bedlam, fettered with Negroes in the hold.

I admit I am inclined toward superstition, if there's no other explanation offered. The messboy says he's seen a dead girl pondering the water, he means to catch her, and he says once we've trapped her we must do a variety of tests to find out whether she's en route to heaven or to hell. Well, I have gone ahead and studied Peter Gray on my own, made a few careful observations, and if I shared them with the messboy he'd surely conclude that Peter Gray should be burned at the stake.

We do not need a spyglass to see the forested shore, where at this moment black men are being hunted. At noon today, beneath an ominous sepia sky, the captain and a crew of four, including Pharaoh, Yellow Will, a sailor named Mr. Benjamin, and the surgeon, embarked for land in a whale-

boat. They took a few articles of trade — flint, rum, calico —
so I supposed they meant to offer the first "dash," or token,
to the natives. I was glad the captain hadn't asked me to
come along, since I don't feel strong enough yet to stand
unflinchingly before a man merchant.

The whaleboat was swallowed and spit up between oily
furrows, and after it had passed over the foaming neck of
a sandbar I wasted no time scuttling to the stateroom. I
knocked softly and held my ear against the door. Hearing
nothing, I rapped again impatiently. When the door opened
I wanted to shout triumphantly, *We're here!* but I suspected
that the coast of Africa held a different sort of promise
for Peter Gray than it did for me. Besides, I'd come to
perform an experiment, I wanted to apply the messboy's
proof.

At first she wouldn't permit me to enter the captain's
quarters. I lodged my foot inside the door and murmured,
"You never finished telling me the story of Quince. I want
to hear the end." I surprised myself, so firmly did I insist,
but when she released the door handle and I stumbled into
the room, I saw she wasn't impressed at all; she merely
swiped her arm through the air to clear away the smoke
above her cigar stub.

"There is no end," she said, turning away from me, and
I reminded myself that I had to be prepared for any sort
of grim discovery. "It's the kind of story that goes round
and round." She sat in the captain's chair, tapped her finger
against the compass on the chart — the instrument had been
placed over the interior of Africa, that barren cavity between
the coasts, a dead land. The desert. I looked at Peter Gray
and wondered if the sands of Africa would seep from a
puncture in her hand, for this is the test I meant to carry
out. Would she bleed? A witch does not bleed.

"Besides," she said, pointing her finger at me, "I can't
tell a story without complete cooperation."

I ran my palm over the dusty glass pane of the bookcase.

When I had acted Quince the last time I didn't realize how thoroughly brutal he was, but now that I knew him better and knew that perhaps as soon as tomorrow he would be deciding whether to spare me or eat me, I had no desire to play the role. A man can't be expected to imagine himself as his own assassin. The captain has suggested that Quince prefers young, delicate boys, and insisted we are all obligated — for mercenary reasons — to kneel before the mulatto. *Don't try to escape,* he has warned, for it's clear I won't be able to run fast or far enough. And I don't have to wear fetters in order to call myself a slave — the captain said we need only witness a fetish ceremony, and memory will be our pitiless master.

But today Peter Gray required an actor for her play, and since I was compelled to find out the quality of her blood, I had to follow her directions. "We left Quince on his voyage to Africa," I said softly — already I had begun to devise the method of the test. "And I was wondering what became of him when he finally reached his homeland."

"Tom, he's hidden from me now. I know what he set out to claim — a throne, a fortune — but what exactly he's become, we've got only instinct and hearsay to rely upon."

"And witnesses," I ventured, "like our captain."

"Like our captain, who confuses the event with an account he's read in the pages of a book."

"But the captain doesn't read those kinds of books," I objected. "He couldn't be mistaken."

"The captain is an old man, he's got an old man's appetite for yarns, and he takes an old man's delight in frightening a boy." So she has assumed the captain exaggerated when he described the horrors of the fetish sacrifice. But I am certain the captain wouldn't lie to me about his past transactions with this powerful king — too much is at stake. He has contracted his soul to the mulatto. Why else would the captain concede to return and do business with a man whom he clearly fears?

"You said yourself: every king has a fetish."

"That's so. But if you inherited a fetish, would you agree to follow custom? Or would you alter the rules and allow a few substitutions?"

"I suppose," I said, "I would try to persuade my spirit to accept an analogous offering, one that did not include a human corpse."

"Because you've got a gentle disposition."

I've slapped my sister and brother more than once, but I've always made some sort of reparation, brought them gumdrops, chocolate, strung a rope swing from a branch.

"And you would sooner puncture a hole in your barrel of witch hazel than take the life of an innocent man."

"We left him on the voyage east . . ."

"Tom, listen, you must promise to keep a secret."

"I promise nothing!" I exclaimed, and to hinder her from speaking further I began, "It will be raining the day I steal away from the ship in a whaleboat. I'll let the surf wash me onto the beach and immediately I'll collapse to my knees, for you know this is my true home, I have been away fourteen years but the island will recognize me and welcome me back." Summoning all that I could remember from my guide to Africa, I said, "When I raise my head, my lips and brows coated with wet sand, I'll find myself surrounded by Negro girls dressed in stiff crinoline skirts, naked from the waist up, each carrying on her head a convex wooden dish stacked with oranges and coconuts. I will ask them to take me to their queen. Of course they won't understand, so I will pantomime my wish and hold a sprig of seaweed over one girl's head, I shall make them understand I mean a crown. They will lead me, then, into the jungle, covering their mouths, muffling their laughter as I roll my cask of witch hazel over slippery roots that seep rust-colored blood. They will take me to the same thatched hut where my father had stolen me from my mother's arms. I will pass through the sheet of rain water into the windowless room, I will kneel upon the earthen floor behind my barrel, and offer this, the witch hazel, as a gift to my mother."

Peter Gray turned a paperweight over in her hands. "You see, Tom," she said, "the story goes in circles."

I thought of the messboy's giant fish, the one trying to catch its tail in its mouth. Then I remembered why I was here: would she bleed? "My mother will recognize me immediately," I persisted. "The rains will magically cease in the evening, and we'll set my mother's hut ablaze, the same hut where I was taken from her arms, where she had remained fourteen years, waiting for me to return. In the light from the quivering stalks of flames my people will make me their king."

"And your mother?"

I imagined: "My mother will have the eyes of a sarcophagus mask, sockets without their jewels, so the ovals will give the impression that she is both ancient and immortal, and she'll wear around her something that might have been a bed sheet once, a cotton toga embroidered with visages of kings, and her head will be shaven, her skull painted with gold dust." I spoke with absolute conviction now, as if in a dream.

"And the language?"

"My mother will teach me; she will prattle endlessly until the words begin to have meaning, she will instruct me in the customs of the tribe, she'll tell me all I need to know about our gods and the sacrifices necessary."

"And your fetish?"

"She will send me to the burial ground, a beach where corpses are brought to be strewn with leaves and left for the tide to carry away. I will wade among the skeletons scattered like wreckage from a huge schooner, I will search through the bones that have been polished by sea water before they were washed back ashore, and I will find my grandfather. I don't know how I'll be able to identify his skull, but I will. Trapped by the tail between his teeth will be a small salamander, alive, an incandescent creamy yellow, no larger than my thumb. I will shatter my grandfather's jaw to free the salamander, and it will dart out of my hands and bury itself in the sand. As I walk away I'll glance over my shoulder and see the slight ripple in the beach behind me. This is my fetish."

"And you will feed it?"

"I will feed it only — only the young of zebras. Half white, half black. My fetish will be pleased with this delicacy."

"And how will you grow rich?"

I paused. "I must send my warriors to the mainland to gather wild herds. If the men are forced into battle with local tribes, and if they take prisoners, I cannot stop them. And if they bring their prisoners back to my island, I shall be obliged to dispose of them."

"Trade them to the slavers?"

"Exchange them for claret, tobacco, six dozen darkie low pipes. And silk for my mother's gowns." I stopped to reflect and found myself thinking of those mutineer slaves who sailed to Long Island. "Of course I wouldn't send my prisoners of war away without giving them reason to hope. In the hold of every slaver I do business with I'll stash rifles and harpoons. Just before my captives are led from the barracoons I'll tell them what they must do to seize control of the ship. And then I shall let fate take over."

I hooked my forefingers together and cracked my knuckles, delighted with myself. I thought I had given a fine performance of Quince and wanted to hear Peter Gray's opinion. But she said nothing, and I watched as she raised the captain's paperweight and struck it down upon the chart, she clapped it down a second time with greater force, as if it were a mussel shell she meant to smash, making such a dreadful knocking I was sure one of the crew would rush in to see what beast had been set loose in the captain's stateroom. But no man came to investigate.

So I pressed on without her encouragement. "Of course,

to satisfy my fetish," I said, "I'd have to draw human blood
at every ceremony." I had maneuvered adroitly, and now
I would find out whether or not Peter Gray was unnatural.
"As the full moon rose, I would summon the virgins of
my tribe . . ."

I stalked Peter Gray, ambling around the corner of the
table, and into my hand I slipped a shark's tooth that had
been displayed upon the bookcase. For a fleeting moment,
with the fang hidden in my fist, I became a lustful, magnificent captain, greedily circling his latest wife. Would she
bleed?

"Naked, slick with a coating of palm oil, they would parade
toward the platform where a fetish priest waits for them,
gripping his sacrificial blade. One by one they would mount
the steps . . ." I had reached her side, and suddenly I was
holding her wrist in my hand again, the coarse skin, the
tangle of veins. I would not let myself meet her eyes. "The
priest would lift the knife, sing the incantations." I squeezed
the tooth between my fingers. A mere puncture I intended,
a pinprick, just enough to draw a drop of blood.

But I shall have to find another way to test Peter Gray.
For when I tried to pierce her she didn't flinch or yank
her hand away. She simply laughed, a loud, bawdy, ridiculing
guffaw.

"Poor Tom," she said while my arm remained suspended
in the air. "First you need to find a virgin." She would have
no part in my show. I flung the tooth against the wardrobe,
but Peter Gray rose, caught my sleeve, and pulled me sharply
against her, wedging me between her insulated body and
the table, the map of Africa spread before me as it was
the day the captain first called me to attend him.

"You've been wondering about me, Tom? Why I'm here,
why I'm keeping the old man company? But I don't think
you want to hear what I have to say. You're a naïve boy
and I wouldn't want to change that." I fixed my eyes upon
the tabletop and noticed that the captain's glass orb was

splintered with hairline cracks, the guineas floating inside could hardly be seen behind the milky fissures.

With her long, angular body, she had to dip her knees in order to bring her mouth to mine, and she twisted me round awkwardly, her hip knot pressed against my belly. Her lips felt like the wet sand I had so recently imagined, and when our teeth clicked I thought for an instant of the skeletons being dragged by the sluggish surf on Quince's island. I am ashamed of the impure passion that overpowered me: at once I despised and desired her. I have never before felt a girl's tongue exploring inside my mouth, tracing the brackets of my lips, and all the while the ship seemed to fall away beneath us, as if a boulder we'd been rocking side to side had finally been dislodged.

We wrenched apart when a sailor on the morning watch rang the hour, Peter Gray studied me with a furtive, mocking look while the five bells announced my panic. In the ensuing silence I grew embarrassed and tried to affect an indifferent manner, staring at the floor. I was grateful when she finally spoke.

"We won't know what he's done until we find him," she said, tousling my hair to remind me of her superiority. "We can't pretend to understand him until we see him for ourselves." She had returned to the subject of Quince, as if there had been no interruption, assuring me, "But you've got a lively imagination, Tom, you're more convincing than the captain." I wasn't certain what she meant. Did she think my version of the fetish ceremony was more accurate than the captain's account? Peter Gray uses me to steer her through the enigma of Quince, she tries to manipulate me with kisses. I am more easily swayed than I expected. Peter Gray will prove a traitor, but I also know that she may trust me — I will never be the one to disclose her secrets.

She assured me that I was an agreeable lad. A child, she was suggesting. Ignorant, with a gentle disposition. At that I turned from her, she didn't try to restrain me. I strode around the table and bid her an icy goodbye as I crossed the threshold.

From the stateroom I would have gone directly to my berth, but I heard a sudden uproar above and feared that Peter Gray and I had somehow caused the disturbance on deck. I found the messboy stoking the firehearth, ignoring the activity around him. He explained to me that an English naval vessel had been sighted, and though legally only an American ship may take possession of an American slaver the captain had left strict orders to retreat immediately if any sail approached. So the men were winding the anchor chain, unfurling the sails. Within a quarter of an hour the canvas popped with well-timed gusts, and we easily outpaced that English schooner, left her to slide backward over the horizon. We have left our captain behind, too, temporarily; it won't be safe to return to the same anchorage for a number of days. Peter Gray will have the stateroom to herself. I almost feel inclined to visit her tomorrow. Our destinies have converged, she'll be asking for favors and I won't so adamantly resist. After all, she didn't bleed. "Poor Tom" she had called me, cursing me.

"But Mother," I protested one day, "listen to this," and I read aloud from my slate, upon which I had copied: *There shall never be any Bond Slavery, Villeinage, or Captivity amongst us.* My mother quickly wiped away the Massachusetts law with a cheesecloth she'd been using to strain boiled raspberries, staining my board with seeds and purple dye. She prowled once around the kitchen, peering under the table and behind the closet door — a precaution against my sister, who is inclined to eavesdrop. Then she asked in a hoarse, reluctant whisper, "But if they sell themselves?"

While we were breakfasting in the galley the sound of the wind changed, I cannot say exactly how, but the alteration was pronounced enough to cause every sailor to lower his fork and stare at the beams overhead.

"That's a waterwind," said the carpenter as he rose from the bench. In a few minutes we heard him blowing a bagpipe jig, and shortly after the rain began, all at once, like a burst of applause, the skies clamoring, *Bravo, carpenter, bravo,* to the rigadoon chords. The chief mate came through, drenched, muttering about this cursed quadrant of the world, and when he had left his berth again, wearing oilskins now, still with the same embittered, impotent expression, one of the men threw a biscuit, which glanced off the mate's hollow cheek, struck the wall, and rolled against his boot. He remained motionless a full minute or more, then he picked up the bread and whipped it furiously, blindly, and since I happened to be in its path the catapulting biscuit struck directly upon my throat apple. It felt not so much like a blow, more like someone had pinched my tongue from the inside of my gullet. The mate didn't bother to apologize — he ordered all hands above as he staggered along toward the rear companionway, like a drunkard who imagines himself a prince.

Sailors gathered round me and began pumping my arms, slapping me on the back, combing my hair from my forehead with their tarry fingers, cooing with soft urgency, "Blue Monkey, are you hurt? Take a breath, a deep breath. Little Monkey, open your eyes, watch this." One of the men placed a biscuit on the table and brought the anvil of his fist down, smashing the dough into a hundred pieces. I understood what he meant. I found myself giggling, sputtering and giggling; the sailors can't be as malevolent as I had assumed. With the captain gone it seems I've lately become their prize, and all day they've been bringing me such things as shoelaces and tobacco pipes, as if I were truly a blue monkey, a rare, valuable specimen, and they hoped to domesticate me with trinkets.

The downpour continues to batter this Guineaman, the

waves threaten to capsize us. We don't have sufficient ballast, our stern sinks deeper into the water without our captain as a dead weight in the bow, and the sailors grow increasingly churlish without a capable officer to intimidate them. The chief mate has no authority. Even the sea birds, the gulls, boobies, others I can't identify, strut insolently about the deck or perch in pairs along the rail, huddling against the rain. The African sky does not breathe, this storm is a continual, furious exhalation. We will break apart if we drift for long off the coast, we will unravel like a worsted scarf snagged on a boulder in the rapids. Well, I am glad to have some purpose, to be able to draw the men's attention away from the weather, to distract them until we can return for the captain. I still don't know which sailor aimed the biscuit at the chief mate; each man appears equally guilty, equally repentant and eager to comfort. They have distributed the crime among them. A dozen hands threw that single biscuit, a dozen men take turns visiting me, stroking the welt on my neck, a dozen suitors covet my affection.

In 1637 a group of Pequot warriors attacked the peaceful colonists of Fairfield, Connecticut, burning their houses, murdering their children, staining the soil with blood. While the mothers wept, the fathers armed themselves with muskets, axes, and pitchforks, and they pursued the Pequots into the forest. The savages blended into the dusk beneath the deciduous arcade, they melted into sugar maples, into mottled elms and birches until they were absorbed entirely by the shadows. But the pilgrims kept running crazily through the wilderness, and soon they found themselves sinking to their knees in the mud, stumbling over warts of skunk cabbage, hacking not at Indians but at thin, webbed vines, and once at a pair of pheasants that burst from a clump of fern. The colonists surged forward though they followed no track, they stampeded aimlessly, not in pursuit anymore but away from the debacle behind, blundering on until they heard the harrowing cry, voices chorusing one word, a single word in our own language: "Halt!"

The colonists shrank back against the command and collapsed into one another. Their mindless rage faltered as the swamp rose up against them. From all sides the trees descended, the screams assaulting even before the arrows flew. But suddenly the white men sprang to action and began to fight with a trapped beast's frenzy, stabbing at shadows, hurling their axes toward the splashing water, shooting the voices. Their bullets pierced the voices of the Pequots, shattering the war cries, the terrifying gibberish. Somehow they destroyed the sounds before the substance. And after the voices were defeated the bodies of the Indians were easily slaughtered.

The pilgrims looked blankly upon the bodies lying face down in the swamp water. The battle had lasted only minutes but the men remained for over an hour in the midst of their victory, reciting a simple thanks-be-to-God for the miracle. Finally, when actual twilight obscured the scene, they dragged themselves farther into the swamp, and in the last shreds of light, instead of returning to their own village, they found a ridge of dry ground — the Pequot trail. They trudged with the habitual fatigue of men who have walked back and forth, season after season, between their families and unyielding fields. They walked for miles, tracing the trail in the moonlight, until they spied the fires of the Pequot camp.

Fifteen boys and two women were taken captive by the Fairfield colonists that night. In the summer of 1637 a ship named *Desire* sailed to Providence Isle in the West Indies, where seventeen Pequot prisoners were traded for cotton, tobacco, and Negroes fresh from Africa. The Negroes were sold in Boston the following year, and *Desire* became the first American-built vessel used to transport slaves.

Must a boy know the Lord before he calls for help? Must he praise God before he knows Him? Will he come to know God through praising Him? Might he mistakenly pray to another in His stead?

Their eyes, their appetite. What do they want from me? Why must they look at me that way?

I suppose it was all the sugary trifles baked by my mother, the eggnog, the conversation around the dining table that served to make my rest uneasy. I can recall my gradual descent into the dream as I drowsily compared my discomfort to a traveler's first days away from land, attributing the intestinal turbulence to rough ocean waters. Though I'd never boarded any vessel larger than a two-log raft I could see this ship in detail — the whaleboats hanging from davits, the hatchcombs, the bunks, the cogs in the beams, the crudely carved teeth of our figurehead, a harpy with her mouth yawning, her breasts hanging, her claws snagging sea birds that flew near our prow.

I do not know why I had ever come aboard this doomed vessel, but in my dream I pass in an instant from the first day to the fiftieth, and instead of the gray, foaming waters of our own coast the foreign seas are as thick as my mother's corncake batter, so that a man who finds the close quarters of the ship intolerable may lower himself over the rail and stand upon the surface, even walk away if he chooses, until he appears nothing but a blanched almond dropped into a bowl.

In this dream a rumor has begun circulating on board, something about an island to the east full of otters that excrete nuggets of gold. With clubs, a couple of demijohns of fresh water, and sacks of salt beef and biscuits, the crew, including the officers, leave the ship in search of these fantastic creatures. I watch them drop into the mush and trudge toward the horizon, but not a man among them invites me along — I am small for my age, too small to be noticed or to be of any use on a hunt. So I brace myself against the solitude. At first I am content to wander the abandoned ship, napping for an hour or so on the cushion of folded sails in the deckhouse cabinet or exploring the bilge with an oil lamp, testing the comfort of the bunks in the hold, searching through the galley crates, the barrels, and the cabinets of this *Flying Dutchman* until I realize they've left me with nothing at all to eat or drink. I rush to the rail but the men either have sunk into the ocean or have already slipped over the horizon. I scramble frantically through the lower deck and find a few crumbs beneath the galley benches but no water. I decide to break into the captain's quarters, certain that he'd have a stash of delicacies in his sea chest.

I prepare to smash my foot through the door when it opens of its own accord. The room I enter is adorned with chandeliers, gilded molding on the mantel, gold hearthbrick; the ceiling is impossibly high, and worn tapestries hang on the walls.

Then I see someone in a rocking chair. I don't know how I can tell she is a woman, for she has her back to me and armor completely disguises her shape. The armor — this is the most extraordinary thing — has been woven from the dried shells of June beetles, with a Medusa helmet of dead centipedes knotted together. I don't remain long in this Erebus. I take a step backward, another step, I push the door closed when suddenly an arm reaches from behind me, the hand slides along my sleeve and grabs my wrist. The fingers are slippery and I easily twist free, but before I have the opportunity to run another arm clamps around my neck. Then there are more hands, hundreds of hands pawing me, unbuttoning my jacket, tearing my shirt, pulling off my shoes, my trousers, and I cry out, "Who are you?" as if identifying them would somehow diminish their power.

One of the molesters responds by lashing his handkerchief over my eyes, and they drag me from the captain's suite to my own berth, they throw me upon the pallet and a man straddles me, another presses my head into the blanket, suffocating me, while spidery fingers grease me with lard from ankle to chin, gently squeezing my member, fifty tongues lick the ridge of my spine, coarse oxen tongues dissolve my salt skin, and then they stuff tinder between my buttocks — I can smell the kerosene, I know what they mean to do. They set a candle flame to the frayed twigs. Bodies press against me, vying for the closest position now that I've become the Guineaman's furnace.

When the fire has burned out the men cover me entirely with the blankets and slip quietly away. I remain buried, smoldering, waiting for the dream to end. Finally I tear off the handkerchief and free my head and neck from the woolen husk. I test the broken machine that is my body, bending my fingers, tickling the raw surface of my skin with a pen's quill. Oh, how terribly I want to believe, within this dream, that I am dreaming, but the moonshaft through my cursed portal reveals the cornmeal puddles left behind by the men, my own crew. I can't deny it. They did not find the Island of the Otters; instead they found me.

In the next moment I have returned to the beginning, I am wandering the abandoned Guineaman again, searching for food. But now I know what to expect — I know what I will find when I enter the captain's stateroom, and I know what the men will do to me. So I live in perpetual fear. This is the point of any nightmare I dread most — believing that I can never again open my eyes.

"I've brought you a special slop, Tom, all afternoon I've been boiling our best pork with some salt fish — it's a slabber sauce lively enough to blacken your gut. I cheated, Tom, I used a week's worth of cayenne pepper, and now we've got none for tomorrow. Monkey, savor this stew, I'm giving you first rights because I heard you talking in your sleep last night, and I see how you're troubling yourself over nothing when you should be standing on deck, your head turned up, gargling with raindrops. Because after six weeks at sea fresh water at this latitude is tarter than the finest cider. Eat, Monkey, then come with me and taste the rain. And if we're lucky we'll hear an inspiring song — not the bagpipes and not the chorus led by Yellow Will. Not the tempest and not the ocean. No, it's music from a nearby island, an island called the Paradise of Birds. Anyone who overhears the birds can't help but weep, which is why I want you with me. We're going to spy upon the ghost of the captain's wife tonight, we're going to see if the song brings tears to her eyes. If she listens to the birds without any sign of sorrow, we'll know she is a witch. Because witches cannot cry.

"Eat, I say, or you'll insult me, and then ready yourself for the show: you'll see her, too, through your own tears. I won't predict what we'll discover tonight. Eat, or I'll make you clean the deck with your tongue, I'll have you licking up splinters and brine if you don't finish my good slabber stew. And don't you waste away pitying yourself — we're tracing the Windward Coast of Africa, and we've nearly steered on top the Paradise of Birds. Tom, someday you'll appreciate your travels. Such a pup you are, and such adventures you've already collected. You'd better learn to take advantage of the novelties, for a man is treasured for the tales he's stocked. I promise you: an adventure well recited will win you at least one invitation, and maybe more, maybe someday you'll return from a long voyage to find your people parading in the streets, shouting and dancing, wearing feather robes, carrying pigs on poles. They'll have a magnificent feast in your honor, Tom, if you can entertain them with a few lively eyewitness accounts. Follow my example — don't dwell on the inconveniences but stay attentive to all that's wonderful and strange, and you'll be everyone's favorite, an admired, oft-requested guest. Follow my example, and when you're my age, nineteen or twenty . . .

"Let me think: on the calendar it falls in the middle of the month, in the almanac the moon is supposed to be lit three quarters. I don't know the exact date, but I remember it's located in the middle, between a half moon and a full, between last week and next, maybe between yesterday and tomorrow. Today, then. Today must be my bloody birthday! I've turned twenty, Tom, today is my birthday. We've got reason to celebrate now! So let's go above, let's introduce ourselves to the captain's wife and dance with her. There's a rare music in the air tonight, the night Piper turns twenty. My birthday. Fancy that."

Today we returned to the same coordinates where the whaleboat had been launched, we cast our anchor and awaited the captain. Just as I was crossing the deck to ring in noon the whaleboat pierced the curtain of rain and slid into view. We saw Pharaoh and Mr. Benjamin at the oars, Yellow Will, the surgeon, and a stranger idle in the stern, but not until the boat was directly below did we see the captain lying on a mattress of palm leaves and faggots. A sailor beside me exclaimed, "They've brought him back dead!" but right then the surgeon leaned over to wipe the corpse's face, and the captain raised his bandaged head, scanned the rounded bow and the huge curved ribs of the *Charles Beauchamp*, and said in a loud, irritated voice, "Why didn't you tell me?" I suppose he had been asleep and the ship caught him by surprise.

With the captain on board again the sailors have stopped watching me with starved eyes. I walk invisibly among them. They are variously employed about the ship, knotting strands of rope together, greasing the masts, checking the stays. I am left out of their confidences, I don't know the subject of their whispering that can be heard in each quadrant, above and below. Besides hauling in the captain, his expedition crew, and a Virginian missionary found on shore, the men have brought aboard a secret, a lewd and astonishing secret, which they pass between themselves like the handful of cockroaches they once collected for Peter Gray's dessert. The mystery has something to do with the captain.

I am glad he has returned, even if he remains all day and all night in his stateroom. Perhaps he is ill with fever. Perhaps he is amusing himself with Peter Gray, making up for the time lost. I only know that the captain has lit a stick of incense, for the aroma has drifted across the passage and into my berth — a redolent perfume, so tart, so comforting that I can nearly forget where I am. It doesn't take much effort to imagine myself at my mother's satinwood table, to linger among her powders and scents, her pewter hand mirrors and combs, Mother's room, where I might dare to smear lilac fragrance behind my ears and spend the afternoon in the meadow, wandering not alone but with my double because the scent will divide me, I'll become two halves, neither entirely a daughter nor a son. A strange sensation — to be cleaved in two by perfume. And when I grow tired of the fragrance I shall strip entirely and stretch upon the pebbles of a shallow creek and let the cold, silky water make me whole again.

Mother, do you think the captain burns incense because it reminds him of you? Forgive me for wondering, but your Tom has been corrupted by Piper's lies, by Peter Gray's seduction, by the captain's example; your Tom won't speak ingenuously ever again.

Reverend Theodore, the missionary man brought from Dahomey, should turn his attention away from the east and work at converting the heathens on this Guineaman. He is a nervous, shrill-voiced preacher, his baggy skin nearly pigmentless, bleached by the tropical sun. As a younger man he must have been rotund, but I suppose the equatorial

climate will wear anyone to bone, especially such a determined missionary man as he, dedicated to teaching the natives about divine consolation. He hadn't been among us
for an hour before he found an appropriate roost in the
pulpit, where so far only funeral sermons have been delivered. He does not suspect we are a slaver. He is concerned
only with the salvation of souls. The men ignore him, but
I found myself attracted to this orator, who carries on as if
a congregation of a thousand knelt at his feet.

"Grow, jungle!" he shrieked, leaning his wasted body so
far over the pulpit's rail that he practically tumbled into
the water. "Grow, poison trees, bamboo and tangled vines,
hide from our eyes the blood spilled by cruel superstition.
Monster Satan, you rule over this savage world, but not
for long, no, not for long. Weep, Africa, you who do not
know the author of your being. Weep, you who have no
hope of immortality, no faith."

He had been gesturing toward the shore, the swamps,
the hills barely visible through the mist, but suddenly he
pivoted and thrust a finger directly at me, his only audience.
"Tell it!" he said, and I thought, *He wants to hear me confess
my filthiest secrets.* I was his trophy, impaled by his finger,
pinned to the bulkhead. He screamed again, "Tell it, tell
it!" and as I faced my accuser I said to myself, *If he insists,
I shall lie.*

Then he spread his arms as if to embrace the entire ship's
population. "Drunkards striving to cover your sin as the
thicket covers the dead, have you no voice? Revelers, de-
bauchers, and murderers, raise your bloodstained hands and
tell it! Speak, vulture, of the putrefying flesh that nourishes
you. Speak, reptile and vermin, of the nameless dead. Tell
it, unburied bones, and the Lord will hear and look with
pity upon this fallen Jericho. Children, have you no voice,
no story? Tell it, I say, and be blessed. Sing, land of gold
and desolation . . ."

It soon became clear that this missionary man was not

indicting me in particular, and as his sermon was neither entertaining nor persuasive I crept off, locking my fingers together to keep them from trembling. He had been on the verge of penetrating my secrets, forcing his way into my private world. A man so passionately incensed is not easy to stop.

Tell it, Captain: "The instructions being to proceed to the northern coast of the Gulf of Guinea, to stop at the usual place and announce our purpose to the local headman, I selected my ablest sailors and with all possible dispatch we launched the whaleboat. The requirement being to take soundings along the way, determining how close we might bring the ship. The warning: to be prepared for a show of hostility, keeping armament upon our bodies. The command: to continue despite intimidation. No sooner had we steered over the treacherous bar and beached our vessel than we were surrounded by a horde of fishmen. One, an interpreter among them, commanded us to put down our guns and come peacefully. Having dealt with the fishmen of Dahomey before, I knew they could be pacified with worthless baubles. I signaled to my crew to disarm, and I extended a string of colorful glass beads, which one savage accepted gratefully. But then they relieved us of all our clothes as well, bound our wrists with crude braids of bamboo, and marched us in this humiliating state across the sands. As I passed into the jungle I felt a sharp blow against the back of my head. I remember no more."

Tell it, Missionary Man: "At dawn I breakfast on monkey stew, prepared the night before by my servant, reheated by myself. Then I gather the necessary articles — my robes, my water pitcher, my holy book — and I make my way through the mud and heavy rain to the rivulet where native girls are already laundering their European cloth, staining flat rocks with running indigo and saffron. I take my place at the base of the waterfall, which serves as my baptismal font. I wait for a pagan to step forward and accept Christ as his Savior. I search the banks for the first soul who will come to beg redemption. I wait until my own toes extend into knobbed roots, binding me to the mud, moist green nubs erupt upon my arms, thickening, spurting fringed leaves. My holy book soon lies hidden inside the tendrils. I wait while the washerwomen collect their garments and return to the village. I watch the serpent gliding along a ledge beside my knee, I watch the brown, glinting cord stretch toward me, I watch him wind around my legs. Against the demon king I can do nothing. I wait, and the serpent wraps me in his coil. Then the reptile is gone, in his place only an unbreakable, spiraling vine. I wait until the day darkens, and then I hear the sound of gravel dislodged by light feet. Through the blur of rain I see my servant descending a path beside the waterfall. He has brought the cutlass. He will hack away the vegetation and free me. So far he is my only convert. But someday another member of the tribe will step forward into the cascade, and then others will follow. I will Christianize this village, I shall not die until my work has been completed. I have been spared from atrocity, I am blessed, indestructible, and someday these inhabitants will accept the gift I bring them."

Tell it, Piper, tell me what you've learned: "Think of it, Tom. All around you are chattering baboons, parakeets, ostriches, zebras, camelopards, porcupines, panthers, and niggers, but you can't catch a glimpse of any of them because the jungle keeps them hidden, all you see on either side are the trees, unless it's raining, and then all you see are smears of green. It's not the novelty of this world that makes the exploration dangerous — for all that, you and I could do as well lying in a hammock and reading a book. But the jungle produces a peculiar kind of impairment, Tom. You'll hear birds that will make you think a dame is being beaten nearby, you'll hear a low grinding and you won't know whether it's rock against rock or teeth against bone because the interior won't reveal the instruments or the musicians.

"So the change is not simply a change of place. But the change occurs always and only when a man and the jungle are newly acquainted. Think of it: you've still got the faculty of sight, but your understanding of the natural world doesn't pertain now that your eyes and ears have stopped agreeing. I have seen weaker men surrender to jungle fever, they give up their bodies to some tropical disease in order to acquire a reasonable explanation for the delirium. But remember, Tom, the sensation precedes the illness, it's a dislocation somewhere inside a man's head. And there's no possibility of preparing yourself — there's nothing you can do except to stay on board your ship, which is exactly what Brian Piper plans to do.

"These are mysteries that torment a man through his ears, so come close to me, make yourself useful and scrub the frying pan. I'm taking a risk, don't you know. The men love you for your innocence, Tom, and they don't want you spoiled. But I say innocence is only a handicap at sea.

"To be sure, the crew were treated tolerably well by the fishmen; they were given an old tarpaulin and sequestered in a hut. But the captain, he was cracked on the back of his head by a club. The Dahomans locked an iron collar around his neck and tied him to a tree. No one can say for sure what happened — the hut where our men were kept had no window, and the captain was insensible and the niggers made no sound at all. Later, the surgeon tried piecing together the evidence, and he figured this: that the captain, unconscious all the while, had been tortured by the villagers. When he was dragged into the hut, his hair a bloody mess, his face chalk white, he must have looked a fine monster in that death mask. I suppose he was lucky that the fishmen didn't borrow his head and hang it from a branch. According to the surgeon, the captain was covered with flecks of blood, as if he'd been mauled by mosquitoes and scorpions, which the sailors still generally believe — that the fishmen fed our captain to the insects.

"But the missionary who came around later in the evening says insects weren't responsible at all. He says the children of the village should be blamed. *Children,* Tom. It seems the men had left the captain chained to a tree while they had a palaver about his fate, and the children had crept closer to the heap of flesh, no doubt he was the color of buttermilk, and the children must have thought at first that their fathers had tied up a cadaver. I expect one of the bolder ones leaned over the captain and placed a grimy finger in his mouth. I can't say whether curiosity or cruelty inspired them to do it, Tom, but they treated the captain as if he were a witch doctor's dummy, they poked him with their fingers and toes, they gathered bramble and pressed the thorns into his flesh. Just children, Tom. They didn't often have the opportunity to explore a white man. They might have tugged at him, pummeled him with their little knuckles, and said in their own tongue, "Mister, wake up," for they would see he wasn't dead at all, only dozing. A naked captain sleeping in the mud — now here was a rare treat. You've surely heard of that traveler named Gulliver, who was threaded to pegs in the ground and immobilized while legions of miniature men marched back and forth over his body. Tom, this is one of the primary terrors of barbaric lands: to be overwhelmed by miniatures, by children and Lilliputians, to be bound fast while they snoop about.

"The missionary says he convinced the tribe to release our men. I don't know what lies he told, what promises he made. I doubt the Africans listened to his threats of damnation and perpetual suffering — maybe they meant to demonstrate their strength and intended all along to release our crew. The fishmen of Dahomey are acquiring a reputation. I say we turn about and point our bowsprit toward America, Tom. We may have rifles and ammunition, but the Africans have the land itself, and Brian Piper knows that there's nothing to compare with a thorn bush in the arms of a child. I ask you, our Guineaman's own little monkey, how do we prepare a defense against such a crusade?"

How do we defend ourselves? Why, we do just as the children urge: we must wake up. I am grateful to the messboy for relating what he's overheard. Now I'm fonder of the captain than ever before. While he was in Dahomey dreaming of thorns, I dreamed of fire. Piper thinks we should quit our job and give up our hope of prosperity. If he had any common sense he would understand that the captain will never be dissuaded, especially not now, after Africa has greeted him so rudely. He will find someone to punish. I pity his next host.

We've washed the lower hold with vinegar, divided the calico into four-yard pieces, we've counted the straw hats, the beads and brass wire, tobacco pipes, two-gallon kegs of rum. For three days we've been navigating like a distempered dog, cruising south at night, into the center of the gulf, turning about and loping in the opposite direction during the day; in the distance, halfway between our ship and the thin band of the coast, I can see a forested blemish, and I don't need anyone to explain that the island is an Island of Promise where our cargo even now is crowded in barracoons, awaiting us.

Reverend Theodore has finally understood that we are a pirate slaver, and he wanders bow to stern, begging sailors to toss him into the sea. From time to time he pounds upon the captain's door. Of course the captain does not allow him to enter the stateroom, does not even reply, and the feeble preacher collapses to his knees, beating the planks with his fists.

He says he's not asking for an impossible favor, only to be belched out of this belly. He apologizes to heaven for temporarily deserting his work in order to accompany the sailors — he came aboard the *Charles Beauchamp* hoping to find other holy men who spoke his language, who would share in the sacrament. A missionary's loneliness must become intolerable, no matter how often he converses with God. Well, he shall have plenty of company in the days to come. Now that he knows what we're after, I am sure he will not be allowed to return to his village.

The captain has sufficiently revived, though he still sports his bandages, wound in a turban around his head. Wherever he goes the missionary man trails him, imploring, "Send me back, I beg you to send me back," and the captain has taken to brandishing a marlinespike when he can't stand the missionary's whining any longer.

I've tried to approach the captain myself, but he doesn't acknowledge me or meet my eyes, and I won't be caught shuffling after him like a Chinaman's wife. I suppose he has ample cause to detest boys. Soon we shall be visiting the barracoons, and the captain may decide I'm worth as much as and no more than a bale of tobacco. He may exchange me for a couple of slaves, and I'll become Quince's property. My future depends upon regaining the captain's favor. What can I do to influence him, what shall I say? He needs neither my pity nor my wealth, I don't have the artfulness to impress him with my service, I don't have the wit to entertain him with my conversation.

I could tell the captain what I know about Peter Gray, what I have deduced from the games we played while the captain was away. I could tell him about Peter Gray's personal interest in the gentleman mulatto. But haven't I sworn in these pages that I'll never be the one who betrays her? Peter Gray is pursuing Quince. The captain depends on me to discover her purpose here, and I depend on the captain's affection. What do I owe to Peter Gray? *She has come after the mulatto* — I might whisper exactly this in the captain's ear. I could tell him how she has tried to seduce me, how she is using the captain and crew of this Guineaman, my papa's Guineaman, in order to reach her own bastard brother. What she intends to do when she finds him I cannot say. But the captain will surely expect me to know.

"Sir, she intends to leave us behind."

"She intends?"

"To leave us behind and join the mulatto."

"To remain in Africa?"

"By his side." Understand, sir (of course I did not say this), she values us as she might prize a reliable mule. We're carrying Peter Gray to her new home. So you'll have to do without a lady in your compartment on the return trip, for we're going to lose Peter Gray, sir, she'll disappear as soon as she's set loose upon the sand. We've transported her from continent to continent, now we might as well begin growing accustomed to her absence. She's been preparing for exile, and that's as much as I know. Admit it, Captain, we mean nothing to her. And next time you possess her, whisper farewell for me, wish her the best of luck.

"Unless, sir, you choose to detain her."

"Who's there? I say, who's there?"

"It's only me, Reverend Theodore, Tom is my name. Piper — he's our only cook now that we've lost Jack Carvee — Piper sent me down here with a nugget of dough, it may not be sufficient to fill up the hollow in your stomach but at least it will sharpen your teeth. And look here, I've brought you a candle, maybe you'd like me to light it. Reverend Theodore, sir, you're not relegated to the bilge, you know, the captain doesn't mind you ambling above as long as you stay out of his way. It's not the most suitable time to be presenting your case — the captain isn't ordinarily as brusque as he's been these last days. But he's had a trauma, and now he's got the business of trade to attend to. Still, he won't mind you — in fact, he's been asking after you, and we've had to tell him that the Reverend Theodore has retired for eternity, those were your own words to the carpenter, if he reported correctly. Retired for eternity. But there just won't be room for you in these catacombs once we've collected the cargo, so you might as well give up your vigil — all due respect, sir — and come above. You could give us a Sunday sermon. The men would benefit from your severity, and Piper has promised to slaughter a hog for Sabbath mess. Are you listening? We're grateful to you for looking after our captain and crew, and I'm sorry we can't send you back to Africa, but I assure you, sir, you'll be treated like a gentleman — we're providing you with a free passage to America. And maybe you could do us the service of communicating between the sailors and the blacks, you could be our linguist. I promise that you'll be paid generously.

"Sir, Reverend Theodore, have you heard a word I've said? You haven't lost your senses, have you? Cloistering yourself in the interior of this dry pod won't do you any good. But you heard me climbing through the hatch, you asked, 'Who's there?' so I know you've still got your faculties intact. Have a chew of biscuit, sir, and you'll improve." I dipped the candlestick into the glass chimney of my own lamp and held the flame close to his face.

A pitiful sight. He was squatting, lopsided, his clasped hands hanging between his knees, his head bowed over the yoke of his white collar. His skin was the same consistency as the vanilla tallow, his three-day beard just dust upon the wax. I felt oddly inclined to rub his cheek, to mold the excess flesh into the dark pockets beneath his eyes. He must have spent the entire night in the bilge. This morning when he didn't appear on deck we nearly concluded that he'd thrown himself to the sharks. But the carpenter finally found him here. The missionary man won't be persuaded to resurrect, he's assigned himself to the tomb beneath our feet, he's doing penance for abandoning his flock.

"Reverend Theodore, I've brought you a flask of the captain's brandy. I knew he'd want you to have it, now take a nip, sir, and I expect you'll find your appetite returning."

But he wouldn't move, and in the unnatural light, in that absurd posture, he looked like an idiot's sketch of a sphinx. His eyes showed no emotion, his haunches protruded, his skin seemed about to slough off from so many months of languishing with dysentery and ague.

"I wish you would take some nourishment, and then come above. The rain has slackened, and the men are busy with the arrangements, so no one will bother you."

I waited, but I might as well have been speaking to a stone effigy, a monument to *the Reverend Theodore lost in Africa the Year of Our Lord after a lifetime of selfless dedication to* . . . Rot, it's nothing but rot, I thought, what they inscribe about you when you're gone.

I gave up trying to cheer him. I had an important question to ask this crazed missionary man. "Sir, Reverend? Have a chew, I'll wait for you to swallow. No? Then I'd like to ask you about something that's been a late distraction: I'm not certain what he wants with me — he's African, my destiny, I've never met him, but I have an intuition, if I may call it that, an intuition — this mulatto, I wanted to know if you've heard of him. Quince, they call him Quince, like the fruit."

Before I could spring clear from this soldier of God he was clutching my shoulders, pressing his fingernails through my shirt, shaking me violently. I dropped the candle, which conveniently extinguished as it rolled away from my foot, and I managed to maintain a grip on the metal loop handle of my lantern so I did not incinerate the *Charles Beauchamp*. But I had clearly provoked the good reverend. For a moment I couldn't distinguish whether he was compelled by joy or

horror to embrace me in this manner. I learned soon enough
that I might as well have flung my own excrement at him,
so disgusted was he by a mere name.

The missionary man quickly exhausted himself, collapsed
to his knees, and covered his face with his fingers, inordi-
nately soft and plump appendages, souvenirs of a more
prosperous time.

"I didn't mean to make you miserable, sir." He had caught
me by surprise, but I was unharmed. I tried delicately to
pursue the subject. "Please, then, what do you know of him?"
How long would it be kept from me? Must I wait for the
earth to revolve as many times as it has since my birth?
Could I be certain of nothing until I met Quince myself?

"Blasphemer. Infidel. Glutton." The water sloshed against
the keel, beating insistently, an impatient fist against a door.
"I see now." A short, bitter laugh escaped from the missionary man. "I understand. Amid the changing scenes, I remain
your opponent. In vain, devil, you have tried to mislead
me. But I have found you, I have discovered you where I
least expected — inside a child. Come to me, boy, give me
the lamp and let me look at you. Don't be afraid. You're
under his influence, intoxicated by treachery and deceit,
but I've arrived in time to help you. You want me to describe
him? What do you imagine him to be? A Gargantua holding
a fish spear in his right hand, the head of a victim in his
left? Think again, boy, think of an ancient, bald woman,
so corpulent she must be lifted from her chair by two servants. Paint her the color of baked clay, give her a man's
aspect, clothe her in Turkish drawers, and you have a mold
for the monster king. King, pah! The devil is a mere viceroy,
a deputy, he maintains a monarch's harem, a regiment of
women. He arms them with machetes and muskets, dresses
them in tunics, parades them through his village and forbids
all men save himself to gaze upon them. Yet he has buried
himself alive, entombed himself inside four hundred pounds
of flesh."

"Tell me, then," I said urgently, believing every word of his unlikely description. "Is it true what they say? Does he sacrifice prisoners to his fetish?"

"Child, I have seen for myself the lake of human blood. I have seen the devil's own canoe tethered to the bank."

"He paddles about in a lake of blood?"

"While lagoons off Dahomey are filling with silt, the lake deepens. The devil's lake deepens." And with this his voice dropped to an incoherent mumbling, he had lost interest in me for the moment so I left him his biscuit and brandy and I departed. I am sorry, now, for uttering the name; the reverend has transferred his purpose from the jungles of Africa to me, the Guineaman's own blue monkey, and my terror has only been intensified. No longer innocent, no longer hopeful. I would submit to you, dear missionary man, if your magic could return me, transform me into the boy I once was.

Between Ouidah and the Gold Coast, between Little Popo and Grand Popo, beyond the Quittah Lagoon, and north of the Volta River slave traders maintain illegal outposts, protected against the British navy by the native tribes. With the exchange imminent, the messboy has forgotten the dangers. He has promised to buy me an article of worship, an idol three inches high, glossed with oil, inlaid with precious stones. He tells me I had better not watch what the women drop into their clay pots; as long as I don't know the ingredients I'll eat heartily, he says, and I'll consider the taste ambrosia. He promises to inebriate me with palm wine. I haven't told the messboy that we intend to barter with only one man merchant, I haven't told him our point of destination is an island, not one of the smuggling factories on the coast. And I don't bother to ask him about the mulatto Quince, for I don't care to hear yet another version of this multifarious grotesque. So I pretend to look forward to handling the trinkets, admiring the novelties, savoring the spices of Africa. Piper has regained his convivial attitude and thinks only of the treasures awaiting us.

The captain, too, is thinking of the days to come. He stands in the pulpit and points his spyglass toward the island — with his turban and telescope he looks as if he could be calling prayer from a minaret. When I grow bored with Piper I wander aft, stationing myself at the captain's knees, and from time to time he reaches down and affectionately snaps his fingers against my Company cap, imitating the gentle clatter of rain. He is fond of me again, since I have proved a capable spy. I know he has not forgotten the evening he gripped my hand while we surveyed the watery oblivion before and behind us. He is grateful for my services, and I'm certain to receive a favorable report from him.

I wonder when he intends to parley with Quince. Already he has taken the precaution of locking his stateroom door from the outside, ensuring that Peter Gray won't wander and the missionary man won't trespass. But without access to the captain's library I have difficulty occupying myself. We float at the edge of a terrible mystery, a mystery to be used to our advantage, according to the captain, or to be conquered, in Reverend Theodore's opinion, or to be recovered, if you are Peter Gray. I only hope the mystery doesn't notice me.

Africans, just like the illustrations in the book my brother gave me on my fourteenth birthday. Africans, swathed about the loins with blue cloth. Six African brokers and their interpreter, all armed with rifles, gathered around the bell, conferring with the captain, arguing the terms: rum and gunpowder for men-slaves, tobacco for boys, calico and salt for women. I don't dare interrupt them to ring in the half hour — as long as they are on board time has stopped. The crew scans the water for masts of military cruisers, the mess-

boy prepares a stew with dried shrimp and sweet potato
brought by our visitors, the carpenter pumps his bagpipes,
and the missionary man trumpets his own lament, pacing
the deck, banging his fist upon a scotch pan as he passes
the tryworks block. The *Charles Beauchamp* has gone raving —
Piper's angels did indeed infect us, and while the captain
and surgeon bargain with the Africans, we are left to our
own wanton freedoms. The sailors saunter about, virile and
rude; I stay clear of them. From an unobtrusive position
along the rail I watch as the Africans gesticulate angrily,
the interpreter translates, and the captain shakes his head.
I had expected to be included when the terms were being
arranged, the captain assured me that I would be introduced
to the man merchant Quince. When will I attend the fetish
sacrifice? When will I see his palace and pavilions, his harem
and Amazons, his barracoons, his lake of blood? The exchange takes place without me.

Dear Papa, have you ever met a Captain Homans? Do you
know how he eluded the British patrols? Surely you've heard
of his slaving brig, the *Brillante,* and the extra weight he
once added to his anchors. A cunning, resilient bandit, you'd
agree. Maybe you've even met him yourself, maybe you've
dined with him at a public house and listened to him chronicle his ingenious escape, thus:

"Indeed, maritime law stipulates that a vessel cannot be
captured without evidence on board, whether she's outfitted
for whiskey or slaves. And it's a just law, for what court
can fairly prove a captain's intention before the hold has
been filled? Besides, why must I be a victim to changeable
popular opinion? I was a respectable trader thirty years back,
now I'm a pirate, a criminal, because the public's sympathies
have shifted. No, I don't regret the choices I've made, I'd
do over what's behind; put me in command of the *Brillante*
again, give me a cargo of suitable bulk, let the British navy

bear down upon me, and before the cruisers are within calling distance cloak me in darkness. I'll show you that Captain Homans won't be easily snared. If you build a labyrinth around me I'll find a way out, if you name my crime I'll prove my innocence. I'm clever and quick, but most importantly I know how to use the rules to my advantage, and if it weren't for the salt water in my blood I'd have chosen courtroom gavels over barometers and compasses, if it weren't for the sea's attraction I'd have chosen law, but as it is I'm a captain and a smuggler, I do what I must to retain command. So if an English schooner tries to catch me when I've got six hundred darkies packed in the hold, and if you give me the benefit of a moonless night before the cruisers can immobilize me entirely, I'll arrange my cargo in rows against the rail, I'll weave a single rope through the loops of their handcuffs and through the links in the anchor chain, and I'll do just as I did once before, I'll order the anchor cast."

One after another, six hundred bodies strung on a chain cable. Had you heard of Captain Homans, Papa, and how the English did not find a single African on board his brig the next morning? Did you know we would be visiting his cemetery? We've cast our own anchor and rock sleepily in the mist, our nest secured on rubbery ocean boughs. We enjoy the security of night, and the men tell and retell the story of the famous Captain Homans. He does not belong to lore or fiction. Although he has returned home his trail remains: the aqueous lamps illuminate six hundred corpses, the perennial *Brillante* continues to sail the middle passage. And hecatombs of slaves float just beneath the surface of the dark water. Our Guineaman is surrounded by corpses, some supine, their eyes like shells knotted to long stalks of seaweed, and some prone, their bodies crowded together, fathers with their arms slung around children, sisters with their fingers intertwined. I see only what is visible. I haven't dreamed these corpses — they are history's inscription, dumped by a slaver before us. The bodies won't simply disappear. One hundred years from now the ocean will turn an unnatural hue after sunset, a strange phosphorescence illuminating from the deeps, and sailors will observe, as I observe, the unburied dead from centuries past: Captain Homans's profit.

All lights are prohibited except the lanterns beneath the binnacle hood. Even the moon remains veiled by a band of equatorial mist, yes, the captain has ordered the moon extinguished. We are close enough to the island now to hear the breakers splitting against the rocks. It must be long after midnight, but I doubt a single sailor on this Guineaman gives a thought to sleep. The Africans and their interpreter have long since departed in their canoe, the captain remains on the poop, and the chief mate oversees the parceling of our commodities — crates are lugged one by one to the upper deck, I hear the men grunting and cursing as they struggle with their loads through the hatchway. I wonder what sort of insect societies have taken up residence in the bric-a-brac, I wonder what changes our North American bugs will make in Africa.

At any moment the captain may send for me, and since the business depends on haste and secrecy he won't soon forgive me if I delay. So I lie in my berth with my shoes on, my collar buttoned, my bladder uncomfortably full. Like a circus panther I have no sense of the world outside my cage, I know only that the whip and fire hoop are imminent. When I will be summoned I cannot say.

I suppose it is enough to know that I am not the only passenger consigned to this awful isolation. Peter Gray has told me about a girl who has no purpose in life other than to find her father's bastard son, a girl who has devoted her prime years to an absence, burning as Echo burned, fretting, pining, wasting away until her bones turn to ash and only her voice remains. And now, because of me, she will never meet her mulatto, while I may soon be served as his holiday dessert. I am the traitor, the one who has obstructed the reunion between Peter Gray and her demon king.

I would visit her, but I don't dare leave my berth for fear of meeting the missionary man, whose own voice penetrates with the brittle draft: "Mothers sell their sons, and still the wild jessamine blooms . . ." An annoying crier of corruption, he has unwittingly convinced the men that a slaver is a savior, they think they have come to rescue the blacks from themselves. I suppose it makes no difference how the sailors justify the trade, as long as they do what is required. As far as I am concerned, it doesn't matter why we transport slaves, trafficking is full of danger and lately it seems we would have more success building a tower to heaven. The ambition to exchange human flesh for tobacco involves so many hardships, and I'm not certain I'll agree when we're through that the profit is worth the investment.

I hope the blacks come quietly and have it over. I've seen for myself how they scorn barricades and manacles, I looked upon those mutineer slaves distributed ten to a cell. I shudder to recall how the New Haven jail was silent, all but for my father's footsteps and my own heels clacking the aisle boards, and in the shafts of sunlight particles of dust swirled like swarming gnats, and the smell of moldering hay was a delicious fragrance compared to the odor emanating from one hundred unwashed bodies. But neither the smell nor the close quarters made the mutineer blacks despair, no, they formed such a union — I've never seen anything to compare with it — ten pairs of hands protruded through the metal bars above the door of each cell, every hand clasped another, and on either side of the grill fingers stretched to meet the closest neighbor in the adjacent cell. One hundred pairs of hands, and though I couldn't see their faces and they made no sound, I found myself sinking into this illusion:

my father and I had been thrust into the middle of a children's game, the blacks might as well have been chanting *ashes, ashes,* circling us, so taunting was their silence, and I knew — though I didn't admit this to my father — I knew that no matter how fiercely we threw ourselves against the circle, no matter how desperately we tried to wrench apart their hands, the ring could not be broken.

Gone, Mother, gone are the beads, the gingham umbrellas, the calico rolls, the velvets, the cashmere shawls, gone, Papa, the bales of tobacco, the extra kegs of rum, the pipes and straw hats, gone, the bulk of powder, the firearms. Our sails are bunted, the main chains taut, and the last of the native couriers has loaded his canoe and disappeared into the mist, such a dense steam, a glutinous secretion from the nearby larva of land. The captain assures us that the fog is a blessing.

He sent for me this afternoon. I found him alone at the binnacle, laying out a row of playing cards, challenging himself to a game of solitaire. So smug, so confident he's grown of late, you'd think a fortune teller had assured him of our safety and success.

He instructed me to spend the night in his stateroom, to keep Peter Gray occupied. *Occupied* — that was his word, accompanied by a playful punch, a jovial rub against my jaw.

An entire night alone with Peter Gray, and the captain indicated I may handle her as I please. I tried to pretend gratitude for the assignment, but truly I'd rather sleep in my own half deck. Peter Gray must perceive by now that I revealed her secret interest in the mulatto, she will find a way to revenge the betrayal, with guile or magic she will punish me, and how the captain will groan with laughter when he sees my bruises. I have no choice but to appear in his quarters this evening. He trusts me with his key, but he made me promise to open the door to no one, regardless of the sounds I hear tonight. Above all I must keep Peter Gray inside, and though she will certainly try to coax the key from me I must close my ears to her demands.

He asked if I understood the importance of this task, and I nodded. He wanted to know when I would open the door, and I muttered, "Only upon hearing your permission, sir."

He slid a card along the binnacle case, aligning the edge with the compass needle beneath the glass, and he demanded, "What will you do to pass the hours, Tom?"

I replied, "That will depend."

He grinned, likely envisioning the mismatched pair, a beardless greenhorn spending the night with Peter Gray, that saucy Amazon. Thankfully he didn't persist in the interrogation, he merely dropped the key into my shirt pocket and said, "Until tomorrow, Tom."

So I wasn't obliged to explain: *Captain, it will depend upon whether or not she can recite the Lord's Prayer.* For a witch cannot recite it.

She did not speak to me about emancipation, economics, the Rights of Man, vendettas, war, mulattoes, sea captains, slave factories, fly pupas, or fetishes, she did not try to enlist me in her staged biography nor question me about my own history, and at first she showed no interest in the key to the stateroom door. A small hooded lantern provided faint illumination, a sepia light that seemed to exude from Peter Gray's face. I waited for her to glance up, but she ignored me.

"What are you doing to the captain's chart?" I asked, though the activity was obvious enough, and since she didn't feel compelled to answer I stood listening to the mist, the sky melting, moisture dripping off the yards in an uneven plock-plocking that would go on through the night, long after the sound of tearing paper had ceased. Finally I demanded, "Why are you doing that to the captain's chart?" but her only explanation was to continue ripping a narrow ribbon from the map, following a latitude line, then plucking squares off the strip. Nearly two thirds of the chart had already been shredded, the pieces scattered about the table and floor. I wondered whether this was part of some insidious spell or whether she meant to use Penelope's strategy and bide time by unraveling the clues. I decided that the days of confinement had driven her quite mad, and were it not for my strict orders I would have left Peter Gray to indulge herself alone. But I was obligated to attend to her.

Perhaps I should have envied her absorption with the nonsensical task. While the men worked frantically to prepare for the load of blackfish oil, Peter Gray remained as serene as a sea in the doldrums, unflustered by the chafing cries that would soon be heard. Even after the Negroes had begun to board, Peter Gray continued to tear the map into ever smaller pieces, as calmly as the captain had arranged the playing cards for solitaire, all attention invested in the meaningless act, no thought to the changes occurring above, as if the soul were paralyzed, the body mechanically carrying on without fear or desire; all the while our Guineaman gorged upon the blacks, Peter Gray destroyed the chart, shredding slowly, persistently, like an old woman darning stockings while revolution rages in the courtyard.

I don't know if the captain depends upon that map to mark our route back to South America. Perhaps we will let the vagaries of the wind determine our course. Or we could follow the sun, like those mutineer slaves. Maybe we are destined to float for decades, drinking rain water that collects in hammocks and eating flying fish that leap upon the deck. My mother won't recognize the beggar who taps the parlor window on a winter night thirty years from now, for I will have silver whiskers, my beard will reach to my knees, and my face will be as brown as a Moor's. My mother would have long ago stopped grieving for me, so I shan't disturb her, I must not identify myself as the son lost at sea, no, it would be best to creep away without an introduction — *Mother, your dead son has come home* — best not to tamper with the past.

Peter Gray has learned this lesson and likely she wishes she had never donned a pea jacket and gone hunting for her kin. Her whole enterprise has accomplished nothing, she has sailed thousands of miles and now she'll never set foot on Quince's island. If I were Peter Gray I would not want to consider the hours wasted. But I am Tom, at the opposite end of the deal, I've profited from this exhausting night though I admit my gains are less than I had hoped. And though I've not been fed to cannibals and our cargo is guaranteed to fetch an admirable sum at the slave market scramble in Brazil, I must suffer the consequences of my mistakes. I confess I gave in to curiosity when I should have kept my eyes closed, and I cannot forget what I have seen. Perhaps the captain exaggerated his account of the fetish celebrations, but he spoke accurately enough when he predicted the impact of Africa upon an untried boy. I will be plagued by these visions. Mother, whether we meet again in three months or three decades you will not recognize your son. He might as well have been replaced by a stranger — now I must relearn myself, I will have to return again and again to the abominable events of the night when the *Charles Beauchamp* began to clank with chains and the sky sprayed a mist fine as pollen.

The captain had instructed me to remain in his quarters no matter what mysterious sounds I heard. I had known we were preparing to receive the blacks, but I did not suspect they would be brought surreptitiously on board by native Kroomen in skiffs during the night; the captain deceived me, promising that I would tour Quince's barracoons, drink his palm wine, watch the fetish sacrifice. The babble of the Negroes themselves revealed to me that I'd been tricked, but by then I was too saturated with a contrary emotion to resent my treatment — even before the voices reached us in the stateroom Peter Gray had carpeted the floor with scraps of paper, and I was on her lap. I'm not certain how I arrived in this location. When she indicated the available seat I hadn't known how to respond.

I stammered, "What do you mean to do with me?" staring not into her eyes but at the cleft below her nostrils, the tender, buttery rift of flesh above her lip.

"Tom," she finally said, "let's pretend we've just met."

She couldn't have offered a more agreeable proposal — I wanted to ignore how I was even then the captain's agent. As I balanced upon her thigh I felt my fear diminishing, I thought I wouldn't mind touching her breast again, if she'd permit me, and I dismissed my trifling resentments. I allowed her to unknot the drawstring of my trousers, to unbutton my shirt, I let her use me as she had used the captain's chart, as absorbed in the activity of undressing me as she had been ripping the latitude strips. But when I tried to insert my hand beneath her pea jacket she wouldn't have me, and when I moved to give her teeth a polishing with my tongue as she'd once done for me, she turned her face away. So I sucked her earlobe and buried my nose in her matted hair and tried to locate her body beneath her togs. Soon she was standing before me, lifting my foot as if she meant to scrape my shoe with a hoof-pick, she tugged my trousers and edged a fingernail along the curve of my protruding pelvis bone, leaving a faint fissure of red upon my flesh. By then I was in a hot fury and hardly noticed the strange jangling and cries from the deck; the anguish from without didn't interest me.

She pushed my legs apart and began to fondle me in the most tender fashion, kneeling before me, and with her head ducked I couldn't gauge her countenance, but she had a shameless appetite, that was an incontestable fact: young Tom didn't disgust her. She might have been praising heaven, a voiceless grace, or she might have been invoking, yes, more likely she was beseeching God for aid in the project. With her tongue she moistened the colored threads of my veins, with her lips she molded me, and when I began to shake convulsively she clutched my hips, belting me to the mahogany chair like a bowl on a potter's wheel. Her head rotated gently on the pivot of her neck, the tufts of hair brushed my abdomen as softly as sprigs of lavender. My skin strained to split, to release my soul, it seemed that in the next moment the membrane in my pores would have to burst, blood would spurt in all directions, flecking the bookcase, the wardrobe, Peter Gray's impassive face.

I did not know what would be left of me when she was through. My fear crawled down my throat, pricked my chest, made my bones ache and my breath wheeze. I don't exaggerate when I describe the emotion, which was as furious as the North Atlantic surf, and my body, as powerless as a clam dredged from the sand, tossed by the waves, as insignificant as a quahog dashed about, then spit out on the beach, my shell clamped shut, squirting my own juices into her mouth, a clam that had wanted merely to be left alone, buried in its private sand bed. She swallowed me whole. And then she wrapped me in the cruelest embrace I have ever known — with the vigorous pressure of her arms she conveyed to me that the intimacy meant nothing to her.

I hardly had strength left to nod my head forward. I slid off the chair and sprawled upon the rug, and from the floor I watched her bite the tip of a Havana and spit out the wrapper. She dipped a quill into the chimney of the lantern and held the smoldering sprig to the cigar. The messboy has told me that a witch's cat carries fire in its tail — I reminded myself that I meant to hear Peter Gray recite the Lord's Prayer. The cigar's glow stained her nose with a coppery disc as she stood smoking and meditating, her gaze fixed upon me.

"Have the dead risen, do you think?" I joked weakly, gesturing toward the ceiling. I couldn't distinguish between the voices, the clanging of iron, the sea clapping the hull; I still didn't comprehend what the noises signified.

"Tom," she said, and if I'd considered it I could have predicted what she intended to request: "Will you give me the key?" There was no resisting Peter Gray. I motioned with my toe toward the crumpled shirt and watched her search the breast pocket.

After she had gone I remained inert on the woolly tundra of the captain's rug, perhaps I even dozed, though the clamor on deck had risen to a tremendous volume. When I finally sat up my perspiring body was dotted from foot to neck with pieces of the captain's chart. So I began to peel off the confetti — it was my turn to proceed with mechanical intensity, alive but indifferent, I pinched the tiny squares of the Guinea Coast and placed them carefully beside me, still ignoring the clamor above, as if the sounds were merely a violent storm and I trusted completely the talents of my navigator, the insulation of the cabin. Hours I must have spent removing the map from my drenched skin while the greatest drama of this voyage, the loading of slaves, was performed over my head. My reason returned proportionately to the growing pile of the shredded chart. I recalled — the profligate mistress, the consummation, my orders, the key.

Unable to stand without staggering, I balanced against the bookcase to pull on my trousers, I pressed my shoulder against the glass and found myself thinking of mayflies — with Negroes climbing over the rail, I thought of mayflies, clouds of them hovering above putrid swamp pools, thousands of tiny insects gamboling in ecstasy, a twenty-minute lifespan, no time for sorrow. Surely Peter Gray had read about mayflies during her endless confinement. I wondered what else besides books she had opened while she was alone in the captain's stateroom. Had she searched his sea chest, read his journal? Had she looked through his desk drawers? And what about his wardrobe? I wondered how many changes of dress hung inside.

Tonight he hadn't bothered to secure the padlock on the handle as he usually did. Inside I found the expected items — two smart double-breasted blue uniforms, one in which to receive visitors on board and one to wear at functions on land, a pair of waterproof boots, an umbrella, a pistol, along with such odds and ends as empty pint bottles, spools of thread, a dented brass kettle, colored neckcloths and white linen handkerchiefs, which smelled of the captain's incense. There was nothing unordinary here, nothing that would prove or disprove Piper's tales. But I continued to rummage through the wardrobe, turning the pockets of his trousers inside out, digging in his boots.

I noticed then a small oval frame the size of a goose egg hanging on the inside of the door. The face was poorly defined with watercolors, the skin a strange orange tint, lips dark red, nearly black, the yellow hair falling about the shoulders. Sometimes when my mother came to give me a good night kiss her hair would be unfastened from its topknot, and the strands would feel like mites scuttling across my forehead. The woman in this portrait might have been beautiful, but it was difficult to tell from the crude rendering. A better painter would have shaped the nostrils with delicate lines and highlighted the ridge of the cheekbones and certainly wouldn't have curled the lips into such a sly and vulgar smile. Yes, the painter had been quite unfair to his subject; I doubted whether my own mother's beauty would have survived the rough treatment.

Disappointed to find nothing of interest among the captain's property, I was about to close the door when something in the wardrobe caught my eye — wedged in the corner was a pile of rags, dust rags, old handkerchiefs, innocent enough, but when I moved to let in more light I saw those rags were brown, discolored. Not just stained rags but blood-stained rags. Impulsively, I grabbed them in my fist, felt a small, hard nugget hidden inside the folds, and knew at once that I had found what I was looking for. When I shook the rags a plain gold band clattered onto the floor.

I stared at the ring as though it were the remains of something that had once been alive, I stared until my vision blurred. The stateroom furnishings appeared glazed, warped, on the point of melting as I stumbled toward the water closet, clutching the rags in one hand and the gold ring in the other. Before I could ask myself what I was doing, I had forced open the portal and dropped the evidence into the sea. The ring disappeared, but the rags dipped and fluttered like stormy petrels before they, too, were sucked into the darkness. Neither my family nor anyone else would ever know what I had found in the captain's wardrobe. I would never tell. This is what it means to be a gentleman.

Searching the gray, wrinkled water surrounding the ship, I thought of the funeral service for the anonymous corpse early on this voyage east. The surgeon's sermon: *the living know that they will die.* I wondered what a nineteen-minute-old mayfly knows. And Peter Gray — I wondered if she had managed to unlock the wardrobe and had left it open for my benefit. I comprehended fully: every story told, every experience recalled, and impossible history recited were true, as true as the wedding band that I had thrown away, as true as the fact that the hands I held before my eyes belonged to me, as true as the two-ton cargo, blackfish oil, boarding on the leeward side of the *Charles Beauchamp* while I cowered in a water closet.

I ran through the deserted hold and saw, jutting between the hatch and the night sky, two naked, scrawny legs, a child's dimpled rump. I rushed back to the rear companion-

way and climbed up to the open air, my fingers already
curled around the column of air, an emptiness I wanted —
in my confused rage — to fill with the captain's neck. But
at the top of the stairs I stopped. Brian Piper was right
about Africa, the jungle disguises the sources of sound. Was
the riotous laughter coming from the current swilling against
our hull? The cries from the remaining swine in the sty?
The groaning from the wind? Judging from the noise I
thought there must have been one hundred Africans already
on board, but I could count, as yet, only two dozen, all
naked, with a wooden spoon tied about their necks and a
silky mist clinging to their skin, glimmering, incandescent
sheets, so in the darkness the bodies seemed tenuous, amor-
phous, on the verge of dissolving, even the children, and
there were children even smaller than me. Captain Homans's
profit, dredged from the sea. And still more were being
sent from the canoes up ladders hung over the ship's railing,
like marauders over parapets, but our men squelched any
protest, threatening with their machetes and guns. Oh, they
were impressively fierce, our men, nudging musket barrels
against the clavicles of young girls. I knew I had better
stay scarce — anyone wandering the quarterdeck without a
weapon would be shackled and transported to South America
and there traded for a fair sum of money. I knew the danger,
I understood how this night erased identity — the only way
a fellow could distinguish himself was by brandishing blade
or gun. So I grabbed a ratline and heaved myself aloft over
the heads of the crew and the Africans, I climbed with a
blue monkey's agility, keeping my eyes focused below, and
I reached the crosstree before I even noticed her. Without
a word Peter Gray shifted to make room upon the precarious
platform.

We sat side by side, watching the bodies multiply below
us. Steamy daylight replaced the night and for hours we
said nothing, though her deep inhalations and my short,
urgent gasps constituted a dialogue full of meaning. When-

ever my elbow brushed against her I jerked away, for it seemed to me that touch was reprehensible, the human form nothing but a demijohn of foul water and blood.

The sailors worked through the dead of night like the thieves they were, dragging in the booty that in six weeks' time we will hawk in Brazil. I watched as the blacks were manacled about the ankles and chained to ringbolts on the deck, I stared at the exposed breasts, the pubic mops, the penises, I watched when once in a while a small rebellion broke out among a group of slaves, they shrieked and strained futilely against their chains but a sailor would remind them: a sharp blow with the broad end of a knife against the bare buttocks, a stinging welt was sufficient to keep them docile.

Extra canoes nosed against the ship and the sailors hauled up supplies for the journey home. Pharaoh called out the articles while Yellow Will inspected: fresh water, rice, a bag of yams, a poultry coop with half a dozen guinea fowl inside, tea, a few indigenous curiosities — monkey skins, clubs, tortoise shells, straw matting. The loading was carried out with exceptional ease. No military patrols closed in upon us, and we suffered only one significant loss.

He was the last to climb the rope ladder and the only black man not put in irons, the only one clad in a loin swathe, balancing a straw hat like a china plate upon his head. In the instant before the fight broke out I studied this African, and though I felt an immediate recognition I did not have time to name this misproportioned, light-skinned man. He was of a dwarfish stature with ripe, muscular legs, as if a small boy were wrapped around each shin — not at all what I expected. No sooner had he thrown both legs over the rail and extended a hand in greeting than the nearest sailor sprang upon him. The African collapsed beneath the brute and others leaped upon them — Pharaoh, Yellow Will — they pulled him to his feet and Yellow Will deftly whipped a cutlass through the air, slicing the African's hamstrings. He shrieked just once, an inhuman sound, more like the note produced when horsehair scrapes a loose gut string. The captain instantly slapped Will and denounced him, shouting, "Fool, you idiot! You bloody idiot! Now he's worthless and you're to blame."

I was glad to see Yellow Will receive his due. But the captain has no sympathy for anyone. He surveyed the crippled man, who crouched with his back against the gunwale and his palms clamped against his wounds. Then the captain uttered the most ruthless direction I have heard in the course of my apprenticeship: "Throw him over," were his words. The men lifted the injured black as if hauling a canvas coffin bag, and they dropped him into the sea. I could see the wake of blood that indicated he was swimming beneath the surface, the choppy, copper-colored stain upon the water flowing like hot spilled wax toward the shore. And while the last of the African Kroomen struggled to untie the ropes securing their canoe to the ladder, the chief mate ordered the sails hoisted and the pin holding the anchor chain cut.

I was astonished, then, to find myself clutching Peter Gray. It seems she had attempted to leap off the platform and follow the African into the eight-fathom water, and I had thrown my arms around her neck, hooking my foot through the ratline so we wouldn't tumble off together. A moment earlier she had been as motionless as the mast, now she was trembling. I wanted to remind her that a slaver's crosstree was no place for a girl. She didn't try the suicide again. She merely pressed her fists against her eyes, and I wish I had done the same. Instead I tightened my embrace and looked back toward the sea. The Kroomen finally managed to free their craft, but before they could rescue the wounded black the trail pointing shoreward stopped and the streak began to widen and fade.

I would like to say that I was horrified, but in truth I relished an ugly, craven relief, for I knew that the murdered African had been Quince, the same, the one who would have devoured me if he ever had the chance. When Peter Gray groaned I exhaled gratefully, finally releasing the heavy burden of fear. *Throw him over* — the order might as well have been given by me. As we pulled off I watched the streak widen and fade until I could see it no more.

3

"AN ESPECIALLY LOVELY CARGO," the captain has announced, "without excess or defect."

Sailors threw together crude kennels on deck that will serve as our shelter during the middle passage, and the surgeon led slaves in pairs from the hold to be thoroughly sanitized. I remained all afternoon upon the mizzentop, watching as each African was unshackled from his counterpart and brought to a medical bench, where the surgeon inspected every detail of anatomy, from the crescents of toenails to the pink underlining of eyelids. If the African was female the surgeon pinched each nipple and listened with his stethoscope to her abdomen and crouched in order to investigate her pubis. The surgeon himself is a squat, bulky, humorless man, and he didn't speak at all during the examinations, though if one of the slaves happened to be stricken with a sea stomach and lost his last meal of boiled rice on the planks, the surgeon would take the opportunity to make a note in his journal. When he was through with them the slaves were brought to a wash basin and a sailor scrubbed their shaved scalps with sand, after which a tablespoon of palm oil was dribbled over each shoulder, and the blacks were encouraged to anoint themselves. They rubbed voluptuously, tenderly, as if caressing the bodies of lovers, indeed, young and old seemed to find this bath a welcome deliverance, and the few crew members standing by regarded them with lascivious grins.

Never have I seen anything to compare with the sight of this brief ecstasy, as the blacks were granted a last moment of freedom before being manacled again and returned to the tombs. The men-slaves remain entirely naked; the women have been given burlap sacks to wear as skirts. I try to avoid distinguishing individuals — throughout this entire middle passage I am determined to see the bodies as a single blurred mass, a distant thundercloud, a cartographer's blot. I wish the cries from below would cease.

With Papa's cargo aboard I am the Company watchdog and have a certain authority as a manager if not as a sailor. I shall make sure that the Company's interests are respected, and I must watch for negligence and mishandling; who else on board this slaver can claim rights of possession? The captain is a mere transporter, he has contracted to steer this Guineaman from continent to continent, but you won't find his signature on the deed to the *Charles Beauchamp,* the captain's surname has no significance while my own has made this voyage possible. I am my father's son and share his responsibility. I don't want the scramble at the slave market in Brazil delayed — I have heard of the fattening farms where living skeletons right off the ships are nourished, plumped, and groomed before being sold, but I don't want to waste an extra month in South America; I am eager to return home, my sea chest heavy with gold. I'll dole out the captain's commission myself so he may buy new loves to replace the ones he buried at sea.

At least he's got a substitute. Just as Piper said of the wife's apparition — *she waits for the captain* — Peter Gray waits impatiently for the meeting, anxious to be dismissed from this realm into the next. But she won't beg a kiss from her protector. She paces her cage, eager to dine, to suck blood from the raw chop, she means to devour the captain before taking leave. From the crosstree perch she watched the men dispose of her half-brother, who turned out to be not quite the handsome gentleman that she remembered, nor the gargantuan tyrant of the missionary's description, and not nearly as impressive as the captain's version. Peter Gray has lost her purpose in life. Now she waits for a chance to revenge him. I know what she intends. As she passed into the captain's stateroom she turned, handed me the keys so I could lock her inside, and I found myself nodding, mutely pledging secrecy as I glanced at the floor to avoid her eyes — such eyes, the same carnivorous, yellow, lashless slivers I've seen on bull terriers just before they are unleashed.

The missionary man remained in the pulpit during the activity, and not until the blacks had been stored below did he erupt: "Pestilence, mourning, and famine!" he crowed as the men hammered, the chief mate rattled orders, and the carpenter piped a tune for this confused libretto. With Africa no longer in sight the reverend trilled hysterically, "See what you have done, Captain He-goat!" This, the first public insult aimed at our commander, abruptly silenced the hammers and bagpipes, only the groaning of the slaves below could be heard during the missionary's potent pause, and I found myself sidling toward a bulkhead to avoid being caught in their midst when the captain retaliated.

"You have eyes in your horns, cunning prince — you prosper, but not forever, no, you shall die by fire, He-goat!"

I expected the captain to call for a pistol or simply to puncture the reverend's heart with his handspike. The reverend himself seemed to be prepared for an execution — he had thrust out his chin, offering his collared throat — but the captain remained at the windward rail with his back toward the pulpit, gazing west, and though every sailor expected a casualty, our captain merely combed his fingers through his beard and grumbled, "Don't waste your voice, man!"

The missionary continued to point his condemning finger. He has acquired a remarkable power, and the captain endures him as he might tolerate his own blackmailer. I doubt that both men will survive the middle passage. Before we reach South America one of these dark angels will likely be dropped into the sea.

Set the topsails, break her out, and we're coming home, Mother, our course west by north under a pasty russet sky, with the men smart on deck, not a loafer in the crew, all of them stepping lightly, as if the very planks of this Guinea-man were live coals. But I know that the men work vigorously not out of a sense of duty but because they take joy in free motion now that they have the Africans as an example of the alternative, seventy-plus men, women, and children in the dark, restricted levels below.

I am not sorry that I never set foot on the African continent. I feel as if I had explored the land thoroughly, for all morning I have listened to Piper speak of huge silk cottons, of mangrove seeds three feet long, of purple butterflies with a wingspan as wide as a raven's. I'll tell my family everything the messboy has told me, for my knowledge is as rich as Piper's fanciful account, I'm familiar with the jungles, villages, and barracoons of Piper's Africa, an imaginary world, perhaps, but at least I have explored this land and no fetish priest sprang out from behind a bush, no man merchant caught me wandering through Piper's Africa. I didn't mind following the messboy deep into this safe interior.

An amiable lad, Brian Piper, he's not upset that we weren't sent ashore, for he has acquired a couple of novelties to conciliate him: this morning, while breakfast simmered on the stove, Piper darted from poop to bow, back and forth with a fly net in hand. The gray moth he pursued teased him endlessly, alighting upon the bulwarks, fluttering its splotched wings in the breeze, flying off just before the net descended. Finally the moth made the mistake of landing

in a small puddle of molasses on the galley block, and now
Piper has a fine native specimen all to himself. He put the
moth in a jar, and he intends to display it in a glass medal
strung on a gold chain when we return to America. I have
spent most of the day examining the whiskers, the velvety
wings, the pinpoint eyes of the insect. I envy Piper his catch.

His other new possession is a lemon, which he found
among the provisions brought by the Kroomen. When he
made an incision in the rind he discovered a second, smaller
lemon contained completely in the outer skin, like an egg
inside an egg, an entire lemon perfectly intact. He offered
this impregnated fruit to me but I refused it — I would
rather have the gray moth.

So far the slaves have been fed boiled rice or cassava,
and the messboy must stand on a crate in order to reach
within the great cisterns. I have not seen the blacks since
they were sent below, but I can hear their voices, as constant
and irrepressible as my own troubled thoughts. I doubt they
understand what we mean to do with them, likely they expect
to be thrown into the sea. I wish I could communicate with
one. The sailors say they are stacked spoon fashion, one
slave propped against the knees of another, the men in
the bilge, the women and children in the upper hold; if I
knew their language I would try to convince them to stay
as motionless as scarecrows, for the slightest shift will vibrate
through a dozen bodies, and it does no good making many
suffer one man's discomfort. *Suffer silently,* that was always
my mother's advice. Suffer silently because if you think this
is the worst pain you will feel in your lifetime, you should
be grateful.

Though a firm bulkhead separates my half deck from
the dormitories, I had hoped to sleep beneath a lean-to on
deck, but the chief mate ordered me to return to my berth;
he said that since I've been a first-class passenger on this
Guineaman, with separate quarters, I shall continue to sleep
alone. I am being punished for the privileges I have enjoyed.

I do not consider my private berth an honor anymore,
though it is directly across from the stateroom, a prime
location before the blacks were brought aboard. And with
our carpenter navigating by memory, even the captain has
put off descending to his mutilated charts, his plundered
wardrobe, and Peter Gray.

At least we are permitted candlelight again. My only other
comfort is the wind's momentum, pushing us west, home,
Mother, riding in the harpy's carriage, home, so I will close
my eyes and try to forget where I am. The sound is enough
to drive a boy insane. I know what it is to be a faltering
moth inside the messboy's jar, with wings silky as fur on a
cat's throat. Today I watched the moth battering against
the glass again and again, greedy for the air outside, until
it was too weak to fly, and then it stumbled drunkenly across
the bottom of the jar, and then it collapsed, its wings flapped,
feeble bellows, puffing in silence, absolute silence.

The notable contrast between the captain and the missionary
man is evidence of the failure of intractable faith: the captain
attends to the demands of water and wind, he won't retire
for a night's sleep until we've put hundreds of miles between
this slaver and the coast. A professional smuggler, alert to
dangers, trusting only the carpenter, he's been as single-
minded as the sharks following in our wake, as if he were
named Charles Beauchamp himself, with a surreptitious purpose and an appetite for gold. The missionary seems to
think the name of God sufficient food for our cargo and
crew, but though his damnations are fierce they cannot bruise
a man's skin. Now he's decided that we need to build a
bridge between our ship and the Windward Coast, he insists
a crude bridge could be readily constructed from the material
on board, and he struts about the deck shouting his own
commands: "Children of Eden, hear me: by the strength of

your hands save your fellow men, commit yourselves to the welfare of the human race. I tell you to devote yourself to the mission, give up your base purposes, and build a bridge to Africa."

He is suggesting mutiny, nothing less, encouraging the men to head eastward again, but with such an impractical proposal he has won no followers, no one obeys when he directs: "You, sailor, drive a forked post into the sea, make sure it is secure, and you, drop two planks across the post, and you, man, straddle the planks and secure them with vines, lay poles across and then do the same again, drive a post into the sea, lay the boards, the posts, the same again, until you reach the edge of the lagoon. And finally, weight a bucket, drop it overboard, and when it has filled with sand and gravel haul the bucket and pour the sand upon your bridge, that's right, sinners, bury the planks. Then I will walk back to Africa, and you will follow me."

If the preacher was more reasonable I would explain to him what my father explained to me: first we must eat the things that grow by themselves, and then we must sow, reap, and eat the fruits. The second phase divides mankind. Some claim the upper hand and some defer. We cannot undo the logic that determines us.

I watch as the men distribute bowls of rice and clap hands to make the Africans dance, I watch the lovely women lean side to side, the potato sacks that they wear as skirts snapping like starched sheets on a clothesline. I watch Yellow Will dump the contents of the latrine pails over the leeward rail while sailors scour the hold or splash the slaves with water from the head pump, then unlock them from the gunwale chain and march them back to the underworld. I have been forgotten by Pharaoh, I have nothing to do but keep this record and ring the bell when I remember to and watch as the Africans are brought to the deck in gangs again in the afternoon, fed supper, and danced. All day, sailors try to tempt the melancholics with rum. This disease of heart spreads more rapidly than smallpox, or so the mess-boy contends, he says he's heard how slavers have lost hundreds of blacks to fixed melancholia, the surgeon's term for willed suffocation. It seems Africans have the extraordinary ability to stop their breathing, so we are ordered to watch for any slave who refuses to inhale, to identify a wilting black, we are told to encourage him to drink a half cup of rum, and if he refuses we should box his ears, and if he continues to sit with his head drooping between his knees we should have him immediately dragged to the carpet of blankets unrolled on the foredeck. We don't want the other slaves to catch the fixed melancholia or we shall have a mass suicide on our hands, an irreversible rebellion. I suppose the blacks have ultimate power — we may drive them from the lower hold to the upper deck and back again, but whether or not they ever reach Brazil will be their own decision.

Today I dared to mingle among them, offering chunks of biscuits to the children, who are allowed to wander freely about the ship. When they understood I meant no harm they gathered round me, a swarm of mayflies, their quivering lips flecked with dried mucus and vomit, their hands outstretched, their bellies protruding. But not one of the little Africans would touch me, and wherever I walked I was encapsulated in this bubble, the gap between us six inches thick. With the boys and girls surrounding me it seemed I was simply the space separating my body from theirs, an emptiness defined by the wall of children, as if I were the negation — not the children, not the articles on deck, not the crew or officers. Yes, I think I am only the gap remaining, my borders determined by others. Children. I would have preferred them touching me, pinching and nibbling, like the messboy's Lilliputians, and then I would be certain I am more than a vacuum and a voice.

"What do you want with me?"

"I want," he said, "your infested soul. Admit you are a refuge for darkness. Do you hear me? You're harboring the demon, child, you're a sanctuary for evil, and if you don't purge him from you soon he'll hatch beneath your skin."

The missionary man, like Peter Gray or Brian Piper, thinks he is intimate enough with me to enter my berth in the middle of the night without knocking. I shall never have an adequate rest, not with this crusader intruding at all hours, vowing to separate me from my soul. He has located the top knob of my spine as the place of refuge, he thinks I'm incubating an evil egg at the base of my neck; soon the egg will hatch and the missionary's demon will be born inside me. The only indication of my progeny's growth over the years will be the expanding hump between my shoulder blades.

Reverend Theodore uses my youth to tease or torment me, telling me I have already been damaged by the mulatto king. Doesn't he know that Quince is even now being tugged by the current along the sloping shelf of the ocean while sharks nibble at his stout calves? The man merchant and I will have no contact, so I need not fear the missionary's threats.

"I've done nothing wrong," I growled, belly down on my pallet, my arms arced above my head, my eyes fixed on the portal that was opaque with steamy mist, as if Neptune himself had puffed his hot breath against the glass. With the missionary's hand stroking my neck, tracing the mold of my spine, I was reluctant to push him from me. "Let me sleep," I said, though I would have been satisfied to have him remain beside me, the edge of his fingernails shaving the pimples on my back, if only he wouldn't insult me. For a few moments he was silent, and I drowsily enjoyed the sensation, I think I had nearly fallen asleep when I felt a sixth finger stroking me, an icy, metallic digit gently indenting my skin, a steel-edged finger, a blade.

"Here you are, monster, inhabiting a child . . ."

I knew enough to stay motionless — the captain had advised me to remain stock still when my head is inside the mouth of the wolf. Best not to startle a fanatic from his passion. "A child . . ." Best to participate in the ritual, to put the missionary off guard. As soon as I felt the pressure ease, the blade rising to strike, I would turn. Watch out, Missionary Man, watch out for my viper's tooth, the venom drooling into the puncture, Missionary Man, I'll bite you. But with a final rumbling, "I will drive you from your lair . . . ," he suddenly withdrew.

Once he had gone I waited for my glands to secrete a new casing. From the dormitory I heard only one woman-slave weeping softly, from the sea nothing at all. We were stalled in the doldrums again, the wind had abandoned us, time was a dozen hungry children pressing in, trapping us. I could endure it no longer. I pulled on my trousers, rushed across the passage to the stateroom, expecting to find Peter Gray alone, flung open the door, and burst into the room.

A dense, ecclesiastic incense cloud hung in the air, a lamp with a sputtering wick glowed like a phosphorescent stingray, and the captain himself was a beached fish carcass, his arms spread across the table, the chalice overturned, the brandy puddling around his cheek, clotting his whiskers, the epaulet wings of his uniform fluttering slightly with each deep exhalation. And crouching in the corner of the pallet was Peter Gray, a blanket wrapped around her, drawn in a hood over her hair, her arms clasped about her knees so she resembled a bewildered, captivated monk. Indeed, the sight of our steadfast captain so filthy, so contemptible, seemed to belong to an illustration accompanying a gothic tale.

Perhaps his filth is a contrived disguise; with his mangy, wrinkled old man's hide, his stained lips, his matted hair, no one would recognize him as the commander of the *Charles Beauchamp*. Or maybe Peter Gray has used witchcraft to spur his collapse — she may be surprised at her own powers, but I think only witchcraft could produce the transformation. Or, more likely, I am the one responsible, yes, the blue monkey threw the captain's precious relic out the water closet portal. I thought I was acting honorably when, in fact, I was crippling the ship. If only I could return his secret treasure, or at least replace it.

Well, I suppose it's simple enough to declare my guilt and to use ignorance as a defense, but I'm finding an unruly sentiment bothers me of late. Ever since the night the slaves boarded, my imagination won't stay inside the perimeters of childhood, and I confess I am compelled to treat myself as if I were composed of two, with a voice in my throat belonging to a robust brute — he's inside me, waiting to hatch, just as the preacher insisted. I do my best to contain him, I try to have respectable thoughts, but at night he stirs, taps against his shell, and takes control.

Between sunrise and sunset I am a child, gentle and curious. I need only climb to the main crosstree, where I may pretend the scene below me is the interior of a willow log, the inhabitants ants, an imperfect society, divided not only by language and race but by their purposes. Most insect communities are guided by a single end — propagation of the species or mutual defense — but the insects below don't share a common function. Some work to ensure their survival while others strive to extinguish themselves. This fundamental difference has already proved irreconcilable, and when another languishing slave is pulled from the pits and passages, the captain will dash his cap to the deck, furious at what he can't control.

The captain himself leads a double life — during the day he remains an implacable dictator, but at night he turns into a drunkard. The plague of fixed melancholia spreads among the Africans and the disease of conscience infects the whites; we have been divided from ourselves. So in daylight I am young Tom, stunted, I refuse to grow up. And if anyone tags me with my actual surname, if anyone says that I am the vicarious possessor, the owner temporarily in charge of the slaves, I'll say, What slaves? I see only ants. It's a make-believe voyage and I'm just an indulgent youth playing truant from school, nesting on a tree branch, surveying the activity below.

But at the end of the day I belong to Peter Gray, my body inflated with her breath. And when my seed spurts I can't continue to pretend that she lies beside me. I detest her even more than I desire her, for she has given me an indecent memory, I can't purge her from me. I know what damage she can inflict — she need merely gaze at a man and he withers. The captain will suffer a slow deterioration. After using up ladies as if they were paraffin and always wanting more, he has finally met his equal. Now that we travel the reverse course, heading west again, Peter Gray no longer depends upon an officer's protection. She is only one among many females on board, the men can't blame her for misfortune, and since there's no possibility that she'll be reunited with her kin, she has no use for the captain. I suppose he wants simply to be welcomed in her bed.

Perhaps the captain and I are not so different. Last night as I chafed my hands, murmuring Peter Gray's name, the door to my berth opened and I heard the captain's slurred voice. I feared he had come to accuse me, but he said only, "Tom, what are you doing?" He leaned heavily against the doorframe. Though he held no lamp the faint glow of night revealed his brow glazed with sweat, his gnarled hair, his unbuttoned collar. I clasped my hands together beneath the blanket.

"Only praying, sir," I replied.

He hesitated, as if slowly inhaling my excuse, and then said, "That's a good boy, Tom," and backed away, quietly pressing the door closed.

Education. My purpose here. Above me the sailors tell anecdotes of slave trading. A novice eavesdropper, often I can't make sense of the fragments I catch, but I have understood a few facts: I have found out that a farmer who purchases a slave must check all apertures to make certain the last owner hasn't stuffed his anus with oakum in an effort to hide a bout of dysentery. I have learned that a captain who poisons his slaves because of food shortage won't collect on insurance — better to jettison the excess, sink the unwanted cargo. And I have learned that the worth of each woman-slave has already been determined. The sailors debated the ranking and agreed upon the prize winner — Mad Sable Eve, they've named her, for she was the first African to board the *Charles Beauchamp,* and despite her beauty the surgeon has diagnosed her as insane. I've heard her myself, cackling and weeping, her voice seeping through the pores in the wood.

Inadvertently I've gained knowledge about the dangers and trophies, useless information once I am installed behind an office desk. I don't know how Papa expected me to benefit from the experience. Some contests will thoroughly educate a boy — war, for example, or chess. The game of chess was invented by a Brahmin to teach a cruel prince the limits of his power. But slave trading has no place in my ordinary world, I won't be purchasing a slave to bring home with me, I'm not the one who must consider insurance requirements. This voyage might as well never have been. The sailors' voices travel not between my ears but through my intestines, I strain to listen to the men when they speak of slave scrambles and goddesses, but I expect I'll suffer my own attack of flux and no one will plug me with oakum; I'll excrete my Guineaman education, vent all the information and experiences, and though my sea chest may soon be full of gold, young Tom will be hollow.

"Another tale of woe, Blue Monkey? You say you want to hear about the captain's favorite lady? Well, mine is a very arduous and difficult occupation, and I can't be reciting and cooking both at once. I've got coffee to boil, slabs of pork to dice, yams to peel, so if I'm not preparing a meal, then I'm scrubbing the pots, no time to climb the shroud and chew a plug in the mizzentop, contemplating the perspective, no time to enjoy the satisfaction that only a man whose view is unobstructed can know. You might spend a lifetime traveling from country to country, but you'll never find another phenomenon to equal this: look to starboard, to port, and you can see the shape of the globe, from the pedestal of this ship you can observe the curve. The surface is always falling away from us, we're rising on the bulge of a sphere, so whatever our location we're at the summit. This is the marvel of the world: no level ground, no surface without a slope. Most men forget the glory of the round shape beneath, they think a movement forward is a gradual ascent, not realizing they've attained the apex with every step they take. But Brian Piper knows he's at the top of the mound, he doesn't need to reach a higher point. The surface bends away, so you won't find him contriving short cuts to rise above his neighbor, instead he takes his pleasure in motion itself, in a change of place, he wants to survey the sphere from a variety of points, to sidle back and forth across the shell.

" 'Where have you been before this?' That's the question he'll pose to assess you — 'Where have you been?' Since there's no point higher than another, he directs his ambition to diversity, he wants to arrive at every possible position, tarry a minute, then move on. He won't be called a traveler, for the destination is less important than the roving to and fro. He's a vagabond, Tom, and takes pride in his unsettled state.

"Now I'd prefer to be enjoying the scenery myself instead of tending to these buckets of mush, but I can't stand to hear an empty stomach rumbling, I'll feed these niggers a pound cut from my own thigh before I let a single one go hungry, and with this responsibility do you think I have time to entertain a fledgling? Well, then keep out of my way and maybe Brian Piper will find a spare moment while the stock simmers and the lard melts in the frying pan to tell you how the captain ended up with nothing. Tom, pick up that slotted spoon, stir the soup, and I'll try to pick up where we left off. But first you've got to tell me how many wives we've been through so far because I've lost track, too many items to count these days, and you know I've never attempted so elaborate a history as this before."

"Five," I said matter-of-factly, then quickly corrected myself: "Six."

"Well, which is it, Monkey?" he demanded, and I repeated, "Six, six."

He nodded, apparently satisfied, but he remained silent for a good minute or more. "That leaves us with two," he finally continued, "and we'll take care of both of them this time round. You've got an unsullied nature, Tom, and I'm sorry Brian Piper has been your corruptor, I'll relate the minimum and then you forget what I've told you. So don't try to imagine the scene in the kitchen where the captain's finest trophy was discovered, her forehead not only dented like the whale I once hammered but split entirely open, bone gristle and flesh flapping from her cheek, the vital artery snipped, the bones in her neck exposed, and a single arrow shaft stuck between her ribs like a stripped branch sprouting from a felled trunk.

"But here, Piper's gone ahead of himself again, there's too much to do, too many distractions to tell a story straight. You wanted to hear the truth of the captain's past, and I've been trying to tell you, but I haven't been thinking in sequence today, too many obligations, and now the soup won't thicken, the stove flame sputters, and I've begun with the end.

"Let me try to start again: we're down to the last of the crop, Tom, with six deceased and one still drifting and the eighth wife in Scotland, living in an isolated bungalow in a valley where everything was green as your eyes and growing thrifty. The captain thought no harm could come to his sweetest bride there. Local peasants who brought her goat's milk and eels insisted that she was the most beautiful woman in the world, though I'm told that she hadn't soaped her hair for years, and her fingernails were as long as the prongs of a fork.

"You asked me if the captain kept likenesses of his ladies, and all I know about that is this: he wanted a picture of his most precious wife to hang on his stateroom wall, so he hired a local sign painter to do the job. Though the sign painter worked on the portrait for nearly a year, he finished only one dangling hand. She sat for him six mornings a week, until the day he found her mauled in the kitchen. Surely you've got a sense of it by now: a wife with an arrow in her breast. Tom, you're a veteran blue monkey, and I don't need to describe the ways of men, you've been afloat for a fraction of a year, certainly you've acquired a knowledge of the tumults we can raise. And I don't blame you for your curiosity, every sailor has an interest in his captain, and to prohibit gossip during a sea voyage would be as futile as ordering a man not to dream when he sleeps. So Brian Piper shares his information though he's got six dozen mouths to feed besides his regular crew. I'm a simple fellow and I'd be content to stay an apprentice, second to the galley chef, peeling lemons and trapping butterflies. But I've reconciled myself because I love a long sea voyage — a steady change of location keeps me vigorous, eager for tomorrow, so I do what I can to make my work tolerable.

"Tom, have you solved the mystery yet? A wife bludgeoned, an arrow in her breast. I suppose I'm dangling you unfairly — do you recall the flashy red-haired missus, the troublemaker of the group? A conniver, Tom, no doubt she meant to discourage the other wives so she could have the captain to herself. When she discovered the address of this hermitage she visited not the sweet lady but the village sign painter, a sorry specimen who wanted only to improve his situation, to earn enough to pay his way to a city, any city, where he could set up his easel along a wide boulevard and sketch pigeons and tourists. How she heard about this painter's job and what exactly she said to him we'll never know for certain. Maybe the pitch of her voice drove him mad — they say a woman can do that to a man, so watch out, Tom, watch out for the pretty bird who sits on a gray rock and whistles to you. Turn your back and walk away from her, which is what that sign painter should have done when the young wife paid him a visit. But he was seen tramping the path leading through the hills the next morning, brooding so intently that when he tripped over a clump of grass he didn't stop to retrieve his cap.

"Blue Monkey, don't tell me you're still confused about the whys and hows after I've provided all the necessary information. Ask yourself, what better position for a portrait of a devoted wife is there than the head bent backward, the arms raised, the eyes wide in rapture? And what better model of rapture than Saint What's-her-name, the nun who caught a spear in her breast? Do you catch what I'm after? You probably think Piper's logic has stopped adhering, he's relating the history piecemeal and you wanted to hear a direct account, you're eager to reach the conclusion, Tom, that's your nature, and you miss the minor diversions, the curves and bumps. Well, I challenge you to solve this mystery from the clues provided. Obvious stuff. You don't need Brian Piper spelling out the massacre, telling you how the bludgeoning was necessary to subdue the lady in order to plant the arrow. Only afterward did the artist realize that he'd made a bloody mess of beauty.

"Here, I've deprived you, I've revealed the end so you can't enjoy the effort of solution, I've linked cause to consequence and there's nothing left for you to do. But I ask you to consider it, Tom: what could the young tattler have said to convince the painter that a portrait of rapture, pure rapture, would guarantee his quick success? She inspired him, that's the fact of the matter. She must have described the portrait that would please the captain, and the sign painter tried to execute it, just so. The missus had found a ready assassin in this fool Scot. They say that on the morning the most beautiful woman in the world was found dead, the young peacock stopped chattering for good — she set off to claim her husband, she bought herself a passage on a merchant ship, but before the ship even set sail a fire broke out on board, and the captain's last surviving spouse perished with the crew. A quick end to the history, Tom, I admit, but not as quick as death.

"So now you know all that you need to know, and don't you dare rat on me, it's a grand favor Piper's done for you, and you can't even attend to the easiest job. You've let the meat stick to the pot, I can smell singed pork, and all I asked was that you merely drag the spoon round. I admit I'd have done the same today — you've seen how I lose track of my course, though I'm better with a stove than with words. And just as you've burnt the pork Piper has spoiled the story, he posed the riddle and answered it himself. Monkey, we're two of a kind, and I mean to prove I've grown fond of you. If you wait for me here I'll fetch that uncommon lemon and we'll peel both fruits, the kernel and the pod, we'll squeeze the juice into each other's mouths, we'll chew the shreds, and please don't beg to refuse, for the lemon, even such a rare monster, will rot if we ignore it."

Puffs of wind, feeble swells, but at least the harpy drags her stuffed carcass west, away from the crossroads of zero and zero, so the water rations have been increased to a full cup per day. The men do what they can to keep the dormitories clean — besides daily fumigations they scrub the lower decks with vinegar three times a week, and during this time the blacks are allowed to remain in open air. There's the sailor Mr. Benjamin tickling a girl's chin, here's Pharaoh helping a squatting maiden to her feet, hugging her close to him longer than is necessary. But these rough courtiers are obliged to restrain themselves; my papa never agreed to sponsor rape, and the captain, despite his own record, has forbidden the men to pursue desire to its usual end.

Because of the danger of suicide even the children are fettered about the ankles now, and the twice-daily dance involves merely a slight pendulum sway. The women have taken to singing, and though I don't understand the sense of their gibberish I know that their voices, so terrible and strange, are full of the keenest hate. The one called Mad Sable Eve has a voice as glossy and obscene as a saloon singer's, and while the others chant the chorus she sings a string of low, grinding syllables. Mad Sable Eve seems to have a perfectly adequate grip on sanity when she leads the choir.

An immense native woman, her flesh as inviting as the skin on a ripe plum, her gnarled toes curled under, she looms as solid as the masts, her eyes provocative beacons, warning the men to stay away. She refuses her rations of water and rice. A sacred totem, yet a temptress, too, like the blackbird that plagued Saint Benedict, luring him with its lustful song, driving him into a briar nest, where he took refuge to defend himself against the bird's seduction. And though the sailors fondle the other maidens indiscreetly, they won't touch Mad Sable Eve. I have positioned myself in various places along the rail in order to have a better glimpse of her — from one perspective she seems a charcoal etching, a volcanic peak copied on the bulkhead, and from another perspective, when the white humidity of the tropics is at its noon height, she seems a Venus effigy carved in marble, and I can hardly believe that even as I watch her she diminishes, her huge breasts shrink, her blood thins, even as I look upon her she dissolves, those angry, incantatory melodies dripping from her. When she sings she hardly moves her lips, and I am reminded of my sister's puppets, their voices rising from beneath the table, where my sister would be hiding. The men say Eve is indeed the one whose cries blend with whinnying laughter below, yet it doesn't seem possible that this same beauty could make such horrible sounds. It would be a shame to lose her. I would like to convince her to suffer through the middle passage, for she deserves to emerge alive from this pastry coffin, this wretched blackbird pie.

"Monkey . . . I say, Monkey! The captain has sent for you, he's waiting in his cabin."

I had taken my bowl of slabber and was squatting out of sight behind the bell. With the ship ploughing evenly, the breeze puckering the canvas, and the slaves generally resigned to the passage, I could nearly forget my circumstances. I didn't try to conjure memories of home — my past seems now only a preparation for this journey, and it's the journey I meant to ignore. And I didn't daydream about foreign lands — I've seen enough of the unfamiliar. Instead I let sensations attenuate. I felt but was not conscious of the motion, an uneven rolling, I felt the hazy light drench my eyelids, I felt the cries of sea birds thread into my ears, the men calling for more coffee, the muted groaning of the cargo, and I was liberated not only from this Guineaman but from myself, I slipped out of time, and if only I could resist picking up this pen, then I think I could shed the present entirely, I would be as permeable as water itself, the images passing through me, leaving no trace. But I can't help marking the day's events. Eventually I have to partition my senses, block my ears so I might think, close my eyes so I might dream, sooner or later I have to recall the hundred lives, my father's dollars, an ocean to cross. The only possible alternative would be to reverse the direction, and that, of course, would depend upon rebellion, and mutiny would mean my death, since I'm woven into the fabric of command. But I write this for posterity: *no one ever asked for my consent.* I'm a trafficking hostage, not a volunteer. I do what I'm told.

So though I had eaten no breakfast this morning and my bowl of stew was small, I handed my half-eaten meal to the chief mate, who had come to fetch me, and I quickly put on my shoes. As I walked aft I tried to predict my treatment. I am a thief, and I have seen how cruel the captain can be.

When I knocked, anticipating the usual "Enter!" the door opened of its own accord, and inadvertently I found myself shielding my face against the blows. Immediately a hand grabbed my elbow and yanked me into the smoky stateroom, and upon opening my eyes I saw that my accoster was the missionary, not the captain, who had remained enthroned behind his table, his thick maroon lips curled in a hypocrite's grin — the captain had invited me to his quarters so he could extract a confession, I had no doubt. I only wondered why he had waited so long to confront me. It seemed another world in there, a sacred, clandestine place, so far removed from the crowded dormitory on the other side of the wall and from the camp above. Peter Gray sat cross-legged on the pallet beside the wardrobe, chewing on the tip of an unlit cigar, and though I knew a female hid inside those togs she appeared such a swarthy, mocking fellow I wanted to lunge at her as Yellow Will had sprung upon the black. I wanted to sink my teeth into her jugular and draw blood, I wanted to destroy the contradictions: the woman who had power over me, and the sailor, my equal.

Then, as I struggled to shake loose from the missionary man, I caught sight of a wide-mouthed jar set prominently in the middle of the table, a jar harboring no gray moth but some large, curious variety of salamander, a horned, cream-colored reptile, immobile but vitally alive. As I squirmed I saw the reptile's magnificent tongue flicker. The preacher released me and I bent across the table to study this novel specimen, marveling not only at its strange beauty but at its pupils, cavities sunk in the middle of shining, lidless membranes, like the slits of a papier-mâché mask, so it seemed that with adequate light I would be able to see into its brain. But I knew it wasn't blind — one listless eye focused on nothing while the other strayed independently, scanning the ceiling, the shelves, the tabletop, a dislocated orb swinging in circles, surveying the world outside and finally settling upon a single object: me. The reptile's left eye fixed upon me, measuring my stature, my salt hide, considering the possibilities. Was I tender, vulnerable, digestible, would I taste like worm or leaf, would I be easily dismembered? Not even the sailors have looked at me with such hostility and such desire. The glass partition didn't help reduce the threat, for the danger was in the gaze itself, the hollow eye, and if a dead man has no image, then I must be dead, for the punctured membrane didn't hold my reflection. Why had the reptile selected me?

Because I was the obvious delicacy in the stateroom. The shriveled, wasted missionary man would have made a paltry meal; the captain, veteran of the trade, wouldn't tempt a lizard; and Peter Gray seemed only the bulk of her togs, only the cloth casing. But I have been raised on roasted pheasant and tender, mint-glazed lamb, there's no denying I'm a fair item with my blond lashes and cherub curls, not yet ruined by ambition, disappointment, or sea travel, and even if I have a frail constitution my features are attractive. I do not boast to say my mother thinks me more handsome than my brother, I am sure of this, for once I demanded to hear her estimate, and after she swore me to secrecy she admitted I've got no equal. The living specimen in the jar wasn't the first to show an interest in me.

"Would you like him for your own? Tom, I asked you, would you like him for your own?" the captain chided, interrupting the hypnotic spell, and with a start I remembered my guilt.

I took a few steps backward and faced the court — the missionary man was judge, Peter Gray my accuser. They seemed to have already reached a consensus, they had decided upon my punishment: they meant to watch me devour the lizard, just as Pharaoh had forced Peter Gray to swallow the roach. The captain would secure me to the chair, he would hold me by a shock of hair while the missionary man placed the reptile's foot on my tongue. I gulped a pint of air to give volume to my scream, but the single word I managed to utter, "No," came out a feeble jingle.

"Why not?" the captain asked. How could I reply? "He'd make a fine pet for a boy," he persisted, spinning the jar, and though the glass hobbled across the table the lizard, suctioned to the bottom, remained immobile, basking, as if the trembling glass were a dome of sunlight, and only his left eye, his lidless, probing eye, indicated his attention.

"Do you know what it is? Preacher, tell young Tom what you've brought us." That mild coercion suggested that the missionary man was not willingly participating. And I hadn't been called to the stateroom to face charges for throwing a gold ring into the sea. Rather, the captain had thrust me into his vaudeville, expecting me to act without a script —

today Reverend Theodore would play the fool. "What do you call it, Preacher?" teased the captain. "Does it have a name? A chameleon — isn't that what you told me? And you don't mind if we trust young Tom with the chameleon's care?"

"It's yours now, you do what you please." The embittered missionary didn't try to champion his causes in such close quarters — the voice he has used to curse the captain needs room to expand, open air, so Africa can hear him.

"Will you tell young Tom what you told me, Preacher? About the chameleon's natural states? Tell him how when you found it, it was green, and it turned yellow in your hand . . ." I realized that I could take the lizard with me when I left the stateroom. I would have traded all my possessions in exchange for this pet, and the captain had presented it to me as a gift, though I don't deserve it. The messboy's gray moth seems a pebble to this pearl.

I picked up the jar and examined the jaundiced skin, the roving eye, the horny protuberance growing from its forehead.

"At night it is black," the captain joshed. And then, in a sudden change of tone, "You be sure to teach the boy how to maintain him."

I said eagerly, "Yes, yes," for I wouldn't want to neglect my chameleon. But the missionary man said gloomily, "You need do nothing."

I nearly kicked him in the shin, so desperately did I want the necessary facts — how to feed my chameleon and water it, how much sun it requires, how much sleep. I was its keeper and the missionary man refused to disclose to me how to tend it. *Do nothing*, he maintained, so I would suffer its death, I would lose my prize.

"What does it eat?" I demanded, and the reverend said, "It exists upon air."

"But what does it drink?" I cried, wishing I had a sharp blade in my hand, for then I would have dissected this stubborn missionary man and extracted the information. Facts, I needed, not a dim fable. "And how do I persuade it to change colors for me?" Facts, like those contained in the captain's library, descriptions of physiology, habit, susceptibility to disease, data relating to reptiles instead of to insects.

"You need do nothing," repeated the reverend, a trace of smugness in his voice.

I shall have to carry out my own experiments in order to determine how to sustain my chameleon. Tomorrow I shall feed it boiled rice mixed with diced pork, I shall cover the glass to shield my lizard from the noon heat, I shall flood the jar with a few inches of sea water and let the lizard romp in the puddle. Perhaps I shall teach it to walk on a leash.

The missionary man refused to offer any assistance, the captain lost interest, and Peter Gray remained as silent as my pet. So I asked the captain to dismiss me, and he shrugged, his smile an uneven fissure as he swished a mouthful of brandy. Hugging the container tightly against my chest, I left the mismatched trio.

I returned directly to my berth, placed the jar on a corner of the pallet, and guarded the chameleon through the afternoon, hoping for some clue to the care required, watching the wandering eye, waiting for its skin to darken, but it refused to transform or even to walk for me, its clumped, prehistoric toes positioned resolutely, its tail a curled tendril. I am not convinced it will survive the night; I do not want to sleep, for now I fear I might find it dead in the morning.

Mother, I have a chameleon in a glass jar. It will not eat boiled rice, pork, millet, souse, molasses; it will not sip fresh water. It breathes deeply, cautiously, its hide distending with air, deflating, its sides collapsing around the empty interior, its head drooping beneath the weight of the tiny gnarled tusk.

In the middle of the night, when sleep finally hushed the population of this ship, when the only complaint came from the sea splitting beneath our keel, when the moon retreated behind the cloudbank that glowed a molten brown, I heard a shallow whisper, a voice I couldn't identify — coming from the bilge, I thought at first — a strangled, faint wheezing, rising not from below, I soon realized, but from inside my half deck.

"Who's here?" I demanded, and received for an answer a stubborn silence.

The panting had ceased, and I waited tensely until it began again, such a slight swish of air but distinct enough so that I could judge its proximity to me. I must have stayed awake for an hour straining to hear, finally concluding that this was the voice of the dead, the voice of a drowned man.

Quince. Had his body been wedged inside a narrow grotto in the ocean floor, trapped in a coral net, picked clean by sharks? Had the corpse of the wounded man merchant been washed ashore? I wondered what memories returned to him as his calves leaked that oily red ink, his strength failed, and the murky sky fell away from him. I wondered if in that moment before he lost consciousness he saw hundreds of fish, mottled colors gathering around him, attracted by the blood. I wondered if he could hear them breathing. Perhaps the voice I heard belonged to a fish. No rasping dead man had come to haunt me — instead my ears had grown so acute that I could listen to the fish panting below the *Charles Beauchamp*, their gills fluttering. I was glad to have decided upon the source, to have slowed the propulsion of wonderment; I lose control of my direction when I begin to consider answers to questions I should never ask.

But I didn't remain convinced for long, I couldn't pretend such impossible perception. I struggled to keep from imagining fantastic causes, and I remembered my chameleon. Although in the darkness I could hardly distinguish the outline of the bottled reptile I recalled the missionary's claim —

it exists upon air — and abruptly I stopped wondering.

Of course: my chameleon was breathing. I have a chameleon in a glass jar, and last night I listened to it breathe. It isn't interested in boiled rice, but I suspect it needs more than air to survive. So now that I am a practiced thief I had no trouble stealing the gray moth from the makeshift cache where Piper had hidden it. I dropped the moth into the jar and have only to wait. I don't suppose my pet will be able to resist this treat forever.

Our national fête day. After the slaves were fed second mess and sent below the captain gave permission to break open a cask of New England rum; all afternoon in the sour drizzle men have been shouting, singing, groping up shrouds and backstays, swinging from footropes, dangling from the yardarms, and Piper prepared a loaf of chicken and lillipeas that tasted as bad as any piece of his sea pie. I kept close watch over my chameleon, for I wouldn't have a sailor craving minced lizard for dessert. I didn't even bother to attend the athletic contests, since it makes no difference to me that the sailor called Chowder climbs the ratline fastest or that Pharaoh can lift so many marlinespikes, and if the men want to bloody their lips and bruise their faces I have no sympathy. I heard the missionary protesting from the pulpit, warning the sailors of perdition, I heard the captain call out, "There she blows, three points off the bow!" which provoked the sailors to shout and applaud, stamping their feet in joy at the turn of events; instead of chasing sperm oil monsters around the world they have made themselves rich in a matter of weeks, thanks to some huckster back in America who financed the affair — my papa, the sponsor. My papa, who might this moment be raising his stein to make a patriotic toast in honor of his nation's birthday.

When I finally went above to fetch my meal I saw half a dozen men had greased their chests with palm oil and were trying to wrestle each other to the deck, pouncing, wriggling like beached eels, slithering across the wet planks while the carpenter sat on top a deckhouse and pumped cheerless tunes from his bagpipe. I quickly retired below again. Even with the Negresses complaining on the opposite side of the bulkhead I have come to prefer my private berth to the riot above.

I think I would be as mad as Sable Eve if the captain hadn't named me caretaker, but now I do not have time to indulge myself, I must stay attentive to my charge. The animal is a captivating mystery, and I must deduce its habits from observation and experiment so that when we arrive in New London I will know my pet intimately. Young Tom will be renowned not as a slave smuggler's son but as a transporter of exotic creatures. Won't my sister be disgusted when I sneak up behind her and drop my chameleon upon her lap, won't my mother be amazed when she sees the lizard turn a vibrant green, and my brother, he will try to purchase the beast from me but I'll refuse his terms.

After admiring the chameleon for so many hours I decided I must thank the captain, so after the dogwatch, when the ruckus had finally ceased, I crept to the deck, found the lean-tos collapsed, the men strewn like gnawed cobs from port to starboard, using their bent arms as pillows, senseless drunkards, even Brian Piper lay mounded against the fire-hearth and the helmsman sagged over the wheel so I couldn't determine whether he was awake. The captain, a spent Silenus, napped against the binnacle case, his head lolling on his knees, a parched rattling escaping from his mouth. I did not care to disturb him. Only the tireless preacher had survived the fête, and since he stood in the pulpit, lost in meditation, worshiping his love, his Africa, he took no notice of me. I hurried back to the hatchway without waiting for the missionary man to renew the exorcism. I can't say why he presented the chameleon to the captain, but surely he regrets the offering now that I have been appointed keeper.

Today, all at once, the slaves stopped trumpeting their daily complaints and now the dormitory is unnaturally quiet, the silence a more insistent reminder than any audible protest. It seems the sailors, rumpled, irritable, still inebriated, won't give Mad Eve permission to starve — again she refused to eat her gruel, and though Piper tried to tempt her with a portion of souse she remained as indifferent as my chameleon, which still has no appetite for gray moths.

The surgeon presented the men with an instrument designed to open a reluctant mouth; a speculum unis, based on the leverage principle, consists of two metal spokes attached to a thumbscrew. I didn't intend to watch but I am no better than the crew, imbibing cruelty instead of rum, I keep returning to be a spectator to the next horror. Yellow Will dragged the African woman up the companionway, and once he had her on deck he gripped her elbows behind her back with one clawed hand and with the other hand he steadied her chin. I hauled myself halfway up a shroud so I could see into the circle of men. One sailor positioned the speculum, knocking the instrument with the heel of his hand until the spokes were lodged between the woman's leathery lips, another sailor twisted the thumbscrew, prying her jaws apart, then Pharaoh spooned gruel into her mouth.

I didn't interfere. It was as though the woman had become our figurehead, detached from the prow, an oak harpy with a round pine-cushion belly, enormous breasts, mouth gaping, and the corrugations of her forehead intricately carved — yes, the Eve I saw today was merely another version of the wooden monster, I have replaced the figurehead with a woman-slave because I wanted to make the harpy suffer.

You may blame me for this vision, you may blame me

for every event reported in these pages. Without me there would be no slaves, no Pharaoh, no Peter Gray, no Jack Carvee. I am the one who has taken the common items of a ship — a figurehead, a stateroom library — and made up this entire middle passage. I've turned the original facts into a blurry waste, and today, as I watched the men trying to restore Mad Eve, I realized my imagination has run amuck, like a plague carried by stowaway insects. Blame me, but I cannot help it if my dreams intensify, I cannot keep the harpy from appearing in one shape or another, I cannot forget what I have learned in the captain's stateroom.

But how do I explain the existence of my chameleon? I would surely know how to sustain the lizard if I had invented it, yet I can do nothing but watch it deteriorate. And then there is the discomforting silence below — a thin, far-reaching silence. I am not capable of imagining such a thorough quiescence. *Blame me?* A weak appeal from an unconfident witness.

Today Brian Piper told me about a famous vagabond slaver that has been wandering for thirty years, a slave ship stricken by the disease of ophthalmia during its voyage from Africa to Guadeloupe. According to the messboy, the crew and cargo are all stone-blind, except for a single man, and with this one spared sailor at the helm the vessel overtakes other illegal slavers and begs for provisions and extra hands. Of course no commander would consider assigning his boys to a ship infected with ophthalmia, so for thirty years slavers have spurned the pariah, sailing away as soon as the ship's navigator declares the sorry condition. There couldn't be more than a dozen survivors, not after three decades of living on rain water collected in hammocks and on mullet caught in nets cast by blind men. No one knows how many whites and how many slaves remain, no one cares.

"When you see Calvary's crosses," the messboy warned,

gesturing, as if the trio of sails were on the horizon, "heave short and be off!" A remarkable story, but Piper has won my trust, and if he says that blind men, sea beggars, have been adrift for thirty years, I'll believe him.

But I want nothing more to do with the outside world. I have a chameleon and I must find out what it prefers for its diet by identifying what it refuses, and then I shall theorize about its past in Africa, its years of liberty.

Already I have learned enough about the density and volume of sea water to understand why a passenger must leave his past behind: an immigrant, pilgrim, or slave cannot include his memory among his luggage or he'll sink the ship, a vessel with a capacity of two hundred tons' burden isn't capable of accommodating the recollections of one hundred passengers — even the privileged crew must pack lightly — so on a Guineaman names have no more meaning than numbers and tell little about a person's breeding. I already know how difficult it is to determine the facts — about the captain, about Peter Gray, about the mulatto Quince. What are rumors? An indistinct noise, like the droning chord pressed from a bagpipe bellows. What are rumors? Embellished lies. I demand *facts*, which can be tested, facts, evidence of a thing done.

Fact: my chameleon has not swallowed the gray moth, implying that my chameleon is ill or that chameleons do not ordinarily dine on gray moths. To investigate the past we must move backward carefully, guided by the process of inference, hop-skipping from one fact to another, and since the supply of facts is limited at sea a scientist had best devote himself selectively, no use trying to research an entire cargo's origins. Unless, of course, maintenance can be improved, an unlikely possibility, since supplies, like facts, are limited. So I won't try to trace the Negroes to their source. I'll keep fixed upon a single object — my chameleon — I'll adhere to the scientific method and trust only what I may observe.

The messboy is a notable exception. There is nothing at all scientific about his methods, but these days I am inclined to accept his reports, even though proof may be lacking. This morning he led me to the tryworks, glanced warily from side to side, then crouched before the bread barge, motioning me to do the same; he dragged the box away from the hearthbrick and asked me what I saw nestled in the corner.

"Why, I don't see anything," I said cautiously, knowing that Piper had hidden the bottle with his gray moth here, the moth I had stolen and fed to my reptile.

He shook his head, squeezing my kneecap anxiously. "Do you know what it means, Monkey? I'll tell you what it means: the blind pirates have ransacked us." He spoke in a kind of trance, not with a feverish compulsion, rather with the somber, quiet persistence of a man who has gained wisdom after suffering an irreplaceable loss. Though I had stolen Piper's moth, I believed him when he said with deep conviction, "Now we're all infected."

We had been invaded by blind men. The sailors on watch, rum-saturated sponges since the holiday, wouldn't have woken in the fiercest typhoon; they follow the example of the captain, who doesn't bother to be discreet about his debauching anymore — he has his flask in hand day and night now, and without his turban his hair seems the image of his mind's delirium, wiry bramble dripping gray, as if old age had been spilled over his head. So it's no surprise that the vagabond ship caught up with us in the middle of the night and a group of beggars climbed over the rail.

"What did they take?" I asked, and he said solemnly, "Piper's personal item is enough. Any treasure can be used as a charm against us."

Of course I knew he was mistaken about the moth, but his excitement was infectious. "What will they do next?" I wondered aloud.

"I say they've done enough. We've been infected by the Dutchman slaver, there's no way to ward off the disease. So value your eyes, Tom, enjoy the scenery while you can, for it will seem a dismal emptiness when the darkness comes to stay."

I spent the rest of the afternoon observing my pet, the jar propped between my legs, Piper's moth a wafer of bark at the chameleon's feet. Toward dusk I thought I perceived my vision blurring, and my berth seemed illuminated not by my candle but by the sun filtering through water, a distant light muted by the fathoms. I have tried to imagine life on board an infected slaver, but even when I close my eyes, imitating blindness, I cannot help but blink involuntarily. My chameleon never blinks. Perhaps it longs to be temporarily stricken or to retire to a burrow where no light penetrates, a permanent darkness — perhaps this is what my chameleon needs, not delicacies or water, not simply shade but a refuge from even the faintest light. Left to its liberty, the reptile would crawl beneath a rock. So I have decided I must find a small sepulcher, I will entomb the lizard, relieve it from the pressure of light, and after its seclusion my chameleon will appreciate the variety outside my portal, the whitecap tufts clinging to the bald heads of waves, the boundary of the moon half submerged in night, and the barely perceptible change in the sky as daybreak approaches. I shall put my chameleon in a grave, and when I retrieve the jar I expect the gray moth will be gone, for surely darkness will spur my chameleon's appetite.

Blind, rolling on a syrupy ocean. I placed the glass jar inside a cabinet in the water closet, and this morning when I returned the cabinet door was open, the chameleon gone.

So I know I am blind, for if I could see I would find the jar in this foul-smelling corner where I had left it. We have been infected with ophthalmia, just as the messboy predicted. I stagger about, dazed by the loss. The expanse of water, the fanned sails, the sailors and cargo — these images are half memory, half conjecture. I try to revive familiar scenes to comfort myself, but since I lost my chameleon I can see nothing.

What will Papa think? He puts me in the captain's charge, the captain gives me the simplest responsibility, and I fail. I'm just a wisp of a boy, there's no substance to me, and when I try to hold a jar my hands cannot grip the glass, for I am vapor, fog, I can mold myself around an object but as keeper I'm no better than the wind. The Guineaman's own monkey. Though names are assigned haphazardly at sea, without regard to the past, we cannot help but become what we are called. Ever since I straddled the yard I have cultivated the nature of that fabled animal, I have evolved into a blue monkey, and now I belong to no category, I am neither ape nor man since I've been designated blue.

I have read about the origin of monkeys — how they were God's first creation and would have remained the favored species if they hadn't been given to self-conceit, but because they were boastful and lazy God impaired their tongues. I have read about the flocks of tree demons that waste the hours cursing unintelligibly. Like a monkey I cannot speak the language of man. And like vapor I am an indistinct blue, wafting, spiraling through the shafts and hatchways on this contaminated ship, blindly searching for the jar, the chameleon, the gray moth. Vapor has no home, no fixed place. And monkeys are ridiculous caricatures of men. Papa, you assigned me to this slaver so I might learn the elements of trade, but I have begun to learn about the qualities of ownership as well, and I have discovered that I am an unworthy heir, so please, Papa, do not bequeath your possessions to me, for I shall lose them, I shall lose everything.

"Let me come in!"

"What do you want?"

"Let me come in," I repeated, hissing through clenched teeth. She opened the door reluctantly, and I stumbled toward the table where I had first cast eyes on my chameleon. In my confusion I saw the reptile etched upon the inside of my eyelid — so vivid was the image, the malt skin, the prehensile tail.

"I've lost it," I muttered, trusting Peter Gray with the confession, rubbing the hallucination from my eyes. Who else could I use as my confidante? "The captain's lizard, I can't find it anywhere." I don't know what I expected from her, but now I've given her an even greater advantage. She could destroy me with my secrets as I destroyed her, revealing her purpose to the captain in order to keep her from deserting us.

It seems she intends to forget the mulatto, as well she should. But now that she's given up her purpose she doesn't need my influence, and I doubt she'll go to any trouble to injure me as long as I don't disturb her. She's the captain's tamed beast, her claws retracted, her eyes blinking lazily, though at any moment she could overpower me, and I, a scrawny gladiator, have no weapon to defend myself. I wish I wasn't compelled to visit Peter Gray, but she is one of this Guineaman's magnetic horrors and I return again and again, I cannot help myself.

I don't understand what she signifies. I have seen how men are dominated by misguided passions — love of women, love of drink — that only cause them harm. And now I have my own private obsession. Though I know she'll hurry me toward my collapse I've come to depend on her. Since we sailed out of New London I have spanned a lifetime and accumulated a list of crimes that would take another man decades to collect. I should never have agreed to accept the captain's gift.

Peter Gray took no interest in my distress — she stepped past me and slid her bare foot over the plank between the table and the wardrobe, as if to test a thin sheet of ice. I noticed then that a number of the captain's volumes had been removed from the case, scattered about the chamber, and a few lay open, the striated print like the design on huge butterfly wings. The room seemed a scholar's den and Peter Gray a great thinker. How could my troubles compare to this struggle of intellect? I assumed she must have been considering something as mysterious as the metamorphosis of an arthropod, so when she finally addressed me, challenging me not to describe the process of slow secretion, the skeleton mold, but to defend my papa's trade, I was caught by surprise.

"What gives your father the right, Tom?" she demanded, and I stared dumbly. I had come for help and she wanted only to insult me. Again, I felt as though I had located the lizard, this time I mistook my tongue for the reptile, a log of dead flesh in my mouth.

But though I was shaken I still noticed between her cap and crumpled collar the blush spilling across her cheeks, her knife-blade pupils, her ripe lips, and if she hadn't confronted me so hostilely I think I would have wanted to taste her, yes, I would have licked and savored this luxurious sweet. Finally I managed to say, "All is only show in the world, Peter Gray. We serve God and it doesn't much matter what we do with our bodies."

"But why must the Africans suffer?"

I hesitated. "Maybe it is the curse of Canaan, maybe not," I said, faltering, "but I think it is natural."

"Natural?" She held me accountable, as if my weak reasoning had anything to do with the reality of this middle passage.

"It is in the nature of the African. I mean, it is natural that they, that we . . ." I stopped. "It is — the law, the law of nature. The Creator's design. The Great Architect."

"And how does nature reveal this law?"

"We just know. We know what we are by instinct, no, by observation."

In place of the mulatto Peter Gray has adopted a common cause: abolition. I wanted to tell her that I didn't care why my father invests in slavers or why we collect our cargo from the Guinea Coast. But she looked at me with such contempt that I was forced to defend myself with frantic logic, a hastily contrived logic, a weak foundation. If I was standing on my father's land in knee-high scrub on the hillock's summit, gazing east, I think I would insist on the equality of the races, but a boy on his papa's slaver cannot simply defer to the judgment of an abolitionist, no, I wouldn't have Peter Gray condemning me, and if secretly I indulge in doubt, when challenged I will defend my father, for at heart I am a patriot and a devoted son, I will protect my family from the attacks of fanatics.

I suggested to her that transferred Africans benefit from change, the southern climate will cultivate them, they'll root in the plantation soil alongside the hardy cotton plants, they'll grow to perfection, and if bondage isn't "natural," then neither is marriage or religion. The state of nature may constitute the origin but not the condition of mankind, we must submit ourselves to laws derived from inquiry and experiment, the scientific method; although at any given moment the laws may be inadequate, we cannot abandon the system — a ship is designed to traverse an ocean, a man to sink, so we must resign ourselves to our destiny.

But even as I spoke I knew I would never persuade Peter Gray to accept her place in history, she wouldn't consider the worth of my reasoning, and when I pointed out that the crew makes an admirable effort to keep the dormitories sanitary she interrupted: "Evidence, Tom. You're wanting evidence." A legitimate criticism. Yes, I lack evidence, but I compensate by pondering the issues at length, I have tried

to argue slowly, with conviction; if Peter Gray were not
such a recalcitrant abolitionist she might have been moved
by my defense.

"You could descend to the lower decks, Tom, and decide
for yourself whether or not the conditions are acceptable.
You could spend a night with the blacks."

"But Africans are made from tougher grain," I stammered,
"they don't mind . . . ," though I knew that my words were
meaningless, my logic based on nothing but pride. I wanted
to tell her that it does no good lamenting the discomfort,
we must accept what cannot be altered. Piper thinks a land-
locked man hasn't liberty to equal a sailor's, but in my opinion
the emptiness on every side of a ship might as well be filled
with bricks — there is no way out. A woman intent on refor-
mation should devote herself to the ports and plantations
and leave slavers alone, for an upheaval at sea will cost
lives. Maybe blindness is a blessing on a Guineaman.

"How do you know what they mind?"

If my father were aboard he would have been able to
explain, but I couldn't accurately recall Papa's description
of the benefits enjoyed by transported Africans. I chewed
my lip and tried to remember our conversation the day we
went shooting, but the spray against the portal glass cackled,
laughing at me, the floor tipped beneath my feet, my head
swam with irrelevant memories. One memory in particular
rose to the surface: I thought of the ancient elm Papa and
I had discovered, its split trunk growing like Siamese brothers
bonded at the pelvis. The leaves of both halves of the elm
were a waxy pea green, the trunk's base below the juncture
was riveted with tiny holes, and broad strips of bark had
warped and bubbled. Disease had spread through the roots
and trunk, but the branches didn't know it. I used to believe
that this tree harbored broken dreams, like the elm beside
the River Styx, the core dead, the branches thriving igno-
rantly.

Then I remembered one undeniable advantage: a master

provides his slaves with a cemetery, and the land initially foreign to an African will be for the next generation the land of ancestors. So I said, "We give them coffin plates and nails, a shovel and a patch of earth, so the dead will be ready to rise." She laughed, and I insisted sullenly, "I don't think anything is more important to a man than his place of rest."

"Is that what you think?"

I should have left the stateroom then, but her scorn incited me. "I think the man merchant dumped overboard won't be invited to paradise. Or to hell. I think, Peter Gray, if you were planning on meeting him in the next world you'll be disappointed. The unburied dead drift aimlessly, alone, not even sharks for company once the flesh is gone. Think of it. Whether the lonely shade is buffeted about by wind currents or dragged by the tide, he's got no home."

Until today, I didn't have an estimate of how capable I am, how cruel. For the third time I played the role of the mythical Quince. "The ocean must be crowded with the spirits of the drowned. Let's try to imagine," I said. "You've admitted that Quince was a profiteer, exploiting his own continent. And though I haven't asked for your direct confession, I know the truth: he was your kin, and you meant to join him in Africa, that's what you've been trying to tell me, and I've pretended not to understand. You came all this way only to see him slaughtered before your eyes. If I were a drowned man merchant and had all eternity to do nothing but contemplate my brief life, I think I would regret having forfeited a proper burial. Remember, I'm not a barbarian, I have been baptized, and I know the importance of a grave. I've realized too late that I'd rather be a citizen; a man needs a flag, a nationality, a home to welcome him or he'll go mad, nothing to do but slosh against ships' hulls and islands, nothing to do, and it's no comfort to consider the invisible multitudes surrounding me, all the other souls who did not survive the middle passage."

I had worked myself into a frenzy dramatizing that shade. I panted, on the verge of the insanity I'd only meant to imitate. "So you see, then, the disposal of the dead — it's a crucial matter," I stammered, gulping for words as the African must have gulped for air, "and a plantation slave earns his plot of land, along with a notched wooden cross."

I wanted Peter Gray to evince a dribble of sorrow or even fury, I needed to see the effect I had upon her, but her face was as lifeless as my sister's bald, almond-eyed potato men, her lips curled at the tips like a wax bean, indicating nothing, while I was wandering through the purgatory of her deceased mulatto, trying to flaunt his sufferings. I wanted to injure Peter Gray, I wanted to hear her breathe with a parched throat, to watch her blink bruised, swollen lids, I wanted her to feel the pain of an ultimate loss, but she remained a mask, and it was I whose eyes clouded. Though I vigorously rubbed my chin in an attempt to stall the emotion, I couldn't keep my voice from quavering when I blurted, "Why are you here?" Why? I wasn't certain I knew anymore. I thought I had solved her, but she eluded me, as if all along Peter Gray had been only an empty container, a coffin without a corpse.

"Why?" creaked the beams and planking of the chamber. "Why? Because of you." Of course. She was here because I willed her to be here, she existed for my sake alone. *Because of me.* I jerked forward, intending to embrace her, I would use my icy doll maiden as I saw fit, for a powerful desire had overtaken me, a surging green wave of desire, and I understood how the intricate paraphernalia of my Guinea-man dream converged in the impostor Peter Gray.

But as I approached her she backed away. Hadn't she acknowledged that I was her purpose? "Why?" I asked again, then whispered the more precise "Why not?" I wanted to tell her to pretend, as she had suggested once to me — it seemed decades behind — *Tom, let's pretend we've just met.*

I raised one foot, she took another step backward, and

with a shrug she said, "Just as you say: you've got no grave. You are invisible to me."

Fool, Blue Monkey. I had mistaken her for my own. When she said, "Because of you," I assumed she meant young Tom, but in truth she meant the other, the one she has lost, the one I so deftly play-acted. Quince. I had succeeded in transforming myself, now a drowned man stood in my stead. *Because of me.*

I slunk toward the door and did not turn when I heard her say, "Tom, have you searched the dormitories?" A mocking, insidious proposition. "I think you might find it in the lower decks," she offered, reminding me why I had come to her for help.

Vertebrata: Pisces, Order One. Now we've got our own Selachii on board, our own silver fox nearly six feet long, caught with a spear and a bowline. One of the sailors with the simple name Bill is responsible for harpooning the phantom, so now the fellow has a new title — Thresher, he's called, after the fish's powerful tail, a fleshy, sharp appendage, as dangerous a weapon as a cutlass in the hands of Yellow Will.

When I heard the boisterous shouts from the stern this morning I assumed the men were abusing the slaves so I resisted the impulse to hurry aft and watch the unruly sport, but when the entire crew had gathered by the rail I decided the spectacle must be worth a glimpse. I found Piper in the rear of the huddle. He couldn't see above the heads of the other men, so he lifted me upon his shoulders and said I must serve as his eyes. I curled my legs beneath his arms and tried to cap his slippery brow with my hands, for Piper was unsteady, lurching as the ship pitched.

"What have they got, Tom?" demanded my mount, and I said, "They've got a rope." What were they using the rope to catch? he wanted to know. Three sailors struggled with the bowline while Bill tugged on the cord attached to the harpoon; from my angle I couldn't see the eddy water directly below us, I couldn't tell what the men were dragging from our wake, but I thought there could be only one attraction warranting such excitement. "They must be hauling up a body," I said, and Piper staggered, made a weak attempt to charge through the thorny hedge of men, and whispered shrilly, "Jack Carvee, Tom? Have they retrieved our cook?"

Indeed, we must have been near the location where we had dropped the bundle of Jack Carvee overboard. I realized my mistake and tried to placate the messboy, assuring him, "It's someone else, Piper, they've snagged an African," though I still couldn't see the object impaled by the iron.

My mount bucked restlessly until one sailor muttered, "They've caught a shark, that's all."

Piper sagged in disappointment, and I felt a similar dejection, for I had nearly convinced myself that the sailors had found the body of an African king. But as soon as the scourge tumbled onto the deck I knew I was witnessing a more marvelous event. The fish, as long as Pharaoh, as slick as a greased pig, writhed in the tangled lines, twisted in extraordinary convulsions as if in the next instant it would burst from its own skin, and with that saber tail flailing, a dozen men would have had their own Achilles tendons sliced if they hadn't drawn back in a stampede. Piper collapsed beneath me, sailors tripped and fell upon us, and the pile of men nearly broke my ribs.

The sailors unpeeled rapidly, scrambling to their feet, leaving me with a bloody nose and Piper with a throbbing groin, but I'm sorry to say I deserted the messboy, left him to clutch his knees and curse whoever had jabbed him. I plunged into the swarm, prodding and kicking my way to the front, but now the fish was as lifeless as a huge, muddy, cast-off boot, bludgeoned by Yellow Will, who stood with the hammer still raised in case the shark revived. The harpoon had pierced the corner of the mouth and I could see the armory of teeth, the pink gums — a contorted death grin, a schoolboy's cartoon.

Bill was handed a blade and given the honor of butchering the shark, and as I watched the decapitation my own nose leaked — the blood I swallowed was the blood of the fish, I mingled secretly with that dusky Selachii — and when Thresher slit open the belly I nearly retched. The contents of the fish's gut slopped across the deck, and for a moment my vision returned with dazzling clarity as I discovered what I had lost: my chameleon. Not merely one, but eight, eight chameleons, ripped from the shark's womb, squirming, alive and vigorous. My chameleon, multiplied many times over. I wouldn't have enough jars to contain them all. But when Pharaoh dangled one by its tail I realized this creature with its black ink hide was merely a miniature replica of the mutilated shark: a litter of eight fish had spilled from the punctured sack. Pharaoh swung the offspring over his head in triumph and the sailors hooted a cheer, "Hurrah for hard times!" in celebration of this rude birth and of our next bountiful meal.

Sometimes I imagine a ship on the horizon, an ophthalmic slaver tagging behind us, a persistent follower. I have heard of a form of torture where a solitary man is confined in a room and observed through a glass panel, watched incessantly as he sleeps, eats, and defecates, the guard replaced every four hours, so the prisoner is always alone and never alone. A man is bound to give way, for what else can the burden of an unrelenting gaze do for a fellow but humiliate him? It makes no difference if our predators are blind, for their vision doesn't depend upon the eyes — the pirates know us intimately by their instinct, through their fingertips, and from our stench, the ineradicable trace of our crime.

Another hogshead of rum was opened today and the men feasted on shark steak and shark chowder, but I preferred to draw my dinner from the buckets of porridge prepared for the slaves, and instead of joining the crew on deck I retired to my berth, where I am alone and never alone, no one for company and no place to hide from God and the ophthalmic pirates. I would give myself up if this were an option, but I have nothing to surrender, nothing, no chameleon, no gold, no Bill of Rights, so what else can I do but resign myself?

Peter Gray has suggested that I should investigate the dormitories. But I should have to borrow courage from another man if I intended to pass the bulkhead, I would have to ask for the loan of a swarthy voice so I could sing loudly, "Hurrah for hard times!" while I pressed into the lightless belly of the *Charles Beauchamp.* No — I renounce my chameleon. Peter Gray wants to trap me, all along she has been trying to replace Tom with her mulatto and she almost succeeded, I nearly drowned in imitation. But I won't mingle with the crew or with the blacks, I won't be dyed or bleached, I'll stay a blue monkey, cover my portal with my mother's handkerchief, and I shall surge ahead, relishing speed more than motion; I prefer to rush toward the finish rather than to limp as an ancient, peg-legged vestige. I have lost my prize possession.

But how can I be certain that Peter Gray didn't find my chameleon and stash it in the hold with the women or in the bilge with the men? I know well enough that I won't be sure of anything until I investigate. If I want to uncover the truth of the matter I must enter the night lit with clusters of eyes, constellations of eyes. I shall have to crawl across their legs, using my hands to search the valleys and crevices, probing the festering craters along the surface, groping until I find the dry, jagged blister on this carpet of skin: my chameleon. Maybe I will have to remain in this windowless dormitory, a blue monkey glued to their lap. Maybe, once I find what I am after, I won't be able to return from below.

We plough through the sludge of a windless cesspool where weeds torn from bordering continents collect and waves crest and deflate without breaking, like the membrane of jellyfish puffing on a rock. My dream of a cornmeal sea has begun to come true, and the chance of ever seeing my family again grows more and more unlikely. The sailors grudgingly attend to chores, and when the slaves have been aired and sent below again the men drink, belch, and sing, before sunset they retire into their tarpaulin shelters, and nothing can rouse them. The ship might as well be deserted. The sailors' legs protrude like legs of a turtle from its shell, and I must wind carefully across the quarterdeck. I envy the men their secure carapaces and their intoxication — they do not smell the sea, they do not fear the weather or ophthalmic slave ships, they forget the blackfish oil, they forget our crimes. But lately my own memory is quicker than ever, with thoughts colliding like waves of the legendary maelstrom in the North Sea, and I hear the splash, I watch with my mind's eye as a crate, a duffel, and a black man are heaved into the sea. Memory bullies me, drags me to the rail, and repeats the scenes: a blood-paved road leading toward the shore or a creamy patch of foam lacing the surface, momentary traces above sinking treasures, like smoke rising from a funeral pyre. Of course the bubbles have long since disappeared, the blood dissolved — but it seems everything thrown off this Guineaman has converged, opposing currents have forced the refuse to the center, and a layer of leaves, feathers, nail shavings, American flags, biscuit crumbs, tobacco ash, and hair steeps beneath the sun.

We roll forward, dependent upon the wind, an unreliable accomplice. I do not trust even the slightest flippant breeze, for I can tell from the grating whistle of air that the wind despises men who place barriers of canvas across its path, men who even now visit bordellos and saloons in their dreams, oblivious to the potential for disaster: the wind need only spit, and we'd soon be flailing in this putrid bath, this southern Sargasso. Having spent so many weeks at sea I can read the weather as deftly as the next man can, and I am certain the swill on the surface spells out doom.

This morning two sailors argued over a pannikin full of rum, each claiming rights to the beverage, and when one decided that spite would satisfy more than quenching his thirst he tossed the pannikin overboard. The cheated sailor grabbed a length of brittle rope and began to beat the other man, lashing his chest and face, and when the captain appeared and quietly demanded that he hand over the rope, the sailor ignored him, whipping randomly now so no one could approach or even pull the fallen man to safety. But the captain said with the grace of one gentleman asking another for the time, "And why not?"

"Because I'm using it!" the sailor replied.

Still the captain persisted with his tame request, the sailor turned a deaf ear to him, and the captain repeated, "But why not?"

With each repetition the sailor became increasingly uncertain, and by the fourth demand the sailor had forgotten why. His arm dropped limply to his side, the rope falling in a coil on the deck. The fellow who had been receiving the blows managed to crawl away, and with a finger crooked the captain signaled to the chief mate, the mate motioned to the sailors, and the crazed man was seized, immobilized by Pharaoh and his henchman, Yellow Will. I waited to hear the punishment decreed. But the captain had already grown bored with the incident, he didn't probe the motives, he didn't call for witnesses — he merely asked for the sailor's word. "Promise me you won't raise your hand against a man again," the captain said, and the sailor, strung between our Guineaman's fiercest marshals, had enough sense to reply, "I promise, sir." The surgeon helped the injured man to his feet, but the captain paid no attention to the welts and the lump already the size of a horse chestnut below his eye. I suppose the captain has resigned himself to a state of lawlessness, he knows now that punishment will achieve nothing. I wish he had realized as much before he sent Jack Carvee to his death.

According to the reverend, civilization has already passed its peak; with paradise behind us we have entered the season of discord and the population has been divided, brother against brother. He says fallen men have only one purpose: to locate the serpent and to expel it — an impossible task if the serpent, as the preacher maintains, has wound around our bones, wrapped our hearts in a dull golden band, poisoned us. I don't know what the missionary man hopes to achieve. He urges us to rally, yet he believes our defeat is inevitable. He has selected the messboy to be his disciple, and while Piper works in the galley, whistling through the gap in his front teeth, Reverend Theodore counsels him on divine will, attempts to indoctrinate him. I am sure he will have as much luck converting Brian Piper as we would have persuading the blacks to be grateful. As far as I'm concerned, I'd rather be host to the enemy than submit to the reverend's blade. What he calls faith in God is nothing but the wild ambition of an alchemist.

I have it, an answer! Mother, your son has turned his berth into a laboratory, his portal into a microscope, he has withdrawn from the sports of daily life and sequestered himself. I have gone an entire day without food, so absorbed in my science I don't have time to eat, and now I feel as vaporous as the heavy mist exhaled from the surface of the sea. Through my portal I have been watching as droplets leap from the crest of a wave and grab hold a hovering partner — accomplished acrobats, they dangle in the air, then slowly rise, coupling, mingling so each single drop accumulates, each particle of fog grows nearly as plump as a bullet. Most sailors despise a pea soup fog but young Tom has found this intermediary state instructive, he has discovered that the ocean keeps scrupulous account, retrieving whatever it loans. Tomorrow this cloud will lift, by nightfall we will have rain, and the ocean will absorb each wayward evaporated nymph. So upheaval is only temporary.

Someday I will have my own vials, beakers, and stoves, I will decompose water, dissect toads, investigate the throat of a morning glory, and count the number of cells on a dragonfly's wing. I didn't yet understand natural law when I tried to define it for Peter Gray, but after spending so many hours pondering the mysteries of the sea, I have learned that there is only one reliable law: the law of destruction. I agree with the missionary — civilization must accept the law of destruction. A chemist knows that only by destroying can a substance be reconstructed, transformed from one shape into another. Birth commences with decay.

Papa, you tried to explain this law to me, tried to diagram the process, but I was too young to understand. Well, I have finally comprehended what you meant when you explained your reasons for investing in a slaver. You have a vision of the future. *We commence by destroying* — every businessman and every chemist should understand that this process is essential to success. And if destruction is the rule, the turbulence of rivers has no more significance than a blush rising upon a young girl's cheek, for water circulates as regularly as blood, and if cliffs crumble and islands sink the changes should not be attributed to extraordinary causes. The land is always modifying — here's the reason for our discontent. We're soil bred and we know by instinct that the ground beneath will crumble or erupt, we know that the earth has been stocked with fire, the heat penetrates our soles, so we might as well each build a reliable craft and escape to the sea, congregate in this porridge and sail toward the middle of nowhere. As we evolve we will regress, we will become the invertebrates we once were. Let's take charge of our destiny, let's stop lamenting the changes and apply ourselves to chemistry. In no time we'll be able to plot our course, and since the points of start and finish are bound to be identical we might as well turn about now and sail toward zero-zero, the center of the matrix.

Slaves, women, old sea dogs — beware of young Tom the scientist, he's eager to dissect you, he wants to chart the differences, trace the branches to the trunk; in order to align a blue monkey with a particular species I've got to prove my oddities are common, which means I must pin a specimen to the board, incise its soft belly, and search until I find myself inside, a silky, short-tailed, blue-rumped monkey. Beware, for Tom is a ruthless, methodical investigator and has learned to ignore cries of outrage. My papa will be proud of me — this sea journey has made me muscular and confident, just as he hoped. But while he is concerned with material profit I have devoted myself to inquiry, my goal being not to increase the production of cotton and sugar but to hasten the slow process of evolution. We'll all converge eventually, why not tomorrow?

How could it be possible? Piper on his knees, a rapt believer? Piper dishing out salt pork and pickled onion, ordering us to rejoice and be glad, as the chief mate might issue the command to take in the royals? Piper telling us to be alert to the dispensation of spirit? Piper, the missionary's convert? Perhaps it is only a temporary affliction.

"Tom," said Piper, "I want that notebook from you," and I said, "Why, what do you want with it?" and he said, "We want to read it," which of course I wouldn't allow, since among other things I've referred to the messboy's disgusting habits. But he maintained that I had a confession to make. "A confession?" I demanded, fearing he had finally discovered that I'm the burglar of the *Charles Beauchamp* — I owe him a gray moth. "Hand it over or I'll add your thumbs to this evening's slabber," he insisted, motioning with his butcher blade, so I puffed my chest and said, "Go ahead and take my heart, but you won't have my secrets."

Just then the wind blew a fleck of sea foam in my eye. Piper took advantage of the distraction and leaped upon me, twining his fingers in my hair, tearing a fistful of honey locks, he sank his teeth into my shoulder and I pounded the cavity of his swayed back, but I might as well have been hammering a nail into a sponge. Inspired by a perverted sense of justice, he would have murdered me if murder was necessary. He has been reborn with a radical conviction, and since size and rank make me an easy prey he came straightforward to attack, he gobbled and ripped until I was too weak to do anything but weep. I sobbed indulgently, howling not because of the pain but because of the betrayal. I had come to love Piper as a brother, and here he was pulping me in order to disclose my sins, trying to string me up like the missionary's guinea fowl and make me an icon of evil.

I could hear the chief mate laughing. "Boys, boys," he said, and I was sure the entire crew, the captain, and maybe even the Africans had surrounded us. But when Pharaoh hauled the messboy off there were only a few men gathered, and even they dispersed as soon as the fight had been interrupted, only Pharaoh and the chief mate lingered, and since no one ventured to inquire about the provocation I burst out, "He tried to kill me!"

"There's slop to boil," the mate grunted, and Pharaoh prodded Piper toward the stove.

"He wants my book." I hiccoughed, and the mate, in a rare show of sympathy, said gently, "And don't you let him have it."

He took my elbow and escorted me to the rail. I leaned over, letting the cool spray rinse away Piper's filth. "You've got a record to keep," the mate said, "you've got to sing the wonders of this voyage. Prove to the world that we've treated the cargo fairly, tell them how we purify their quarters with tar smoke and add shredded pork to their rice. You're keeping an honest account, I trust, not jotting any foolhardy notions, distorting the truth."

"No need to worry, sir. I report only what I see," I assured him, and the chief mate combed his fingers over my stinging scalp, returned to the sight of the battle, and picked up my book and Company hat. Propping my cap awry upon my head, he said, "You're a decent lad," and he handed my book to me without even flipping it open to scan a passage — his complete trust shames me. I shouldn't want him to read what I've written. I've been a traitor to my father's enterprise on occasions too numerous to count, but I shall make up for my disloyalty, and while Piper has registered as the missionary's crony and will do whatever he can to reverse our direction, I will mount the harpy and apply both crop and spurs. We've got no time to lose.

Who am I? A blue monkey, slight as a bullrush stalk, but what I lack in substance I make up for in purpose, so tonight I will explore the piece of Africa stored in our hold, I will study the blacks, I will make a category in my notebook and fill it with a list of their habits, patterns of sleep, language, physiology, feeding, urination, courtship rites, I will come to know this tribe intimately, and you may be sure I'll document my findings with scrupulous care. Peter Gray will see I'm no coward. In the end I will reclaim my chameleon.

So, Papa, will you wait for me while I explore the catacombs? Mother, will you prepare a feast for my homecoming? I shall want a dozen shucked clams, mashed potatoes, a boiled lobster, and a cup of melted butter all to myself — my lips will gleam in the firelight, my lashes will be clotted from the steam. Little sister, will you keep watch and shout, "He's back, our Tom has returned!" when you see me kicking pebbles, jouncing casually along the road, biding time, and my brother, if I haven't appeared by midnight tomorrow, will you come after me?

I think if I traced the Nile to its source I wouldn't have more thoroughly plumbed mystery than I had tonight when I took my lamp and passed into the dormitory. Admittedly my scientific curiosity waned as I stood beside the bulkhead dividing us. But I didn't return to my berth — I remained at the opening while my body entered the tunnel, I watched the boy, my father's son, stepping carefully around the huddled forms, his lamp dangling from his fingers, the light a snappy macaw inside a cage.

Monkey, tell me what you've seen: I've seen how a woman-slave can discourage her enemy from attacking by assuming a grotesque shape, chewing her tongue, letting spittle collect in the corner of her lips like foam of insect larvae glued to rotting wood. I've seen a small child slung like a sack of grain across a Negress's outstretched knee, others disguise themselves as roots, as clumps of moss, pebbles, leaves plastered to the planks. There are girl-slaves oddly shaped, with gawky, cracked elbows, swollen knees, gaunt bodies bulging with snags and knobs, and there are women who have perfected the art of mimicry, sitting absolutely still, not even a perceptible suction of their cheek, so I doubt if a shard of mirror held above their lips would mist. I have seen buffed flesh wink the lamplight back at me, the skin an impermeable casing that could not be pierced with an ice pick. But the common defense is vitality, the determination to endure, and if I were to compare these Africans to a particular species I would say that though they shall soon be sold as milch cattle, and though, at liberty, they might work as industriously as humble bees, at present they are most like maggots that can survive for months inside a sealed barrel of wine.

Each body is as distinct as a flake of snow, as silent as waterweeds. The Davy Jones devil might have planted them himself, and I have been strolling through his garden at the bottom of the sea. It was an extraordinary feat merely to breathe, for the darkness was so thick, so rancid, the viscous air nearly suffocated me. I watched a boy named Tom shuffle along the narrow aisles, I heard the leather of his shoes creak, I felt his pulse race. I realized that the miracle of life is not the physiology that makes life possible but the will to live.

If a hunter stands immobile for a length of time, he will hear the sounds of the forest gradually increase as the wild creatures mate, court, flit about, hide, and devour one another. When I hesitated in the aisle and listened closely, I heard at first the sounds I made and then the sound of life around me — blood pumping, eyelashes crunching gently as the women blinked. After a moment these soft noises were subsumed by a growing racket, the humming and clatter of thoughts, and like the chants the women would sing, these unspoken words made no sense to me, no sense at all.

But I was drawn, like a compass needle to a magnet, to the leader of the choir — Mad Sable Eve has been shackled to the bottom hatchway stair so the sailors can easily fetch her at messtime. I approached her, straining to hear the secrets cascading inside her head, pleased simply to be near her. As I listened to the phrases of these strange, silent melodies, it occurred to me that I must have come for a distinct purpose, I must have been assigned to repeat to this Negress some dire communication. But Mad Eve's potent fury disconcerted me, I couldn't remember what I had meant to tell her. As the woman-slave stained with the light of my lantern stared impudently at me, I felt as vulnerable as Cleopatra's vassal, responsible for the content of the message. What message? I wrenched away, scrambled out of the dormitory before she could demand, *What do you want here? Why have you come?*

Here, Papa, my version of a famous political confrontation.

An Englishman calls, "Order, please!" There is a scuffle in the back row, something to do with the uncertain proprietorship of a cigar. The speaker clears his throat and waits for the disturbance to subside. "Gentlemen, Lord Palmerston solicits your sympathy, he intends to discourse upon the topic of African trade, the results of Parliament's embargo and the ineffectiveness of our navy's efforts to impede transportation. Sir, the podium is yours."

Lord Palmerston begins. "My friends, I cannot overemphasize the importance of this matter, our moral duty as Christians is . . ." (The obligatory silence is interrupted only by the nasal rattlings from a sleeper in the pit, until Lord Palmerston turns to the matter at hand, the traffic of human souls.) ". . . and how many we cannot count. Estimates of one hundred and fifty thousand slaves per year probably constitute but a third of the number of Africans imported to America — fellow men who deserve . . ." (A citizen in the balcony shouts, "Up the daily wages of indentured servants, abolish slavery at home!" causing indignant mutterings as he is stifled by an anonymous hand while Lord Palmerston continues.) ". . . our protection from smugglers, and I maintain, good sirs, I maintain that the responsibility must be accepted by other nations, through correct diplomatic channels we must convince governments to organize patrols, we must end the genocide of the Africans." ("Animals!" someone insists.) Lord Palmerston objects: "But haven't you heard, sir, how innocent peoples of the grass are driven from their tents, how they flee to the hills and the kidnappers pursue them? Haven't you heard how entire tribes will take refuge in a cavern hardly more spacious than the coal furnace below our feet, how kidnappers leisurely build bonfires outside the entrance and the peoples of the grass must choose between slavery and incinera-

tion? Who are the criminals? Have you forgotten Collingwood?"

Next, Mother, I call to the stand the octogenarian slave-
woman named Happiness, whose extraordinary case was
publicized by abolitionists.

"Collingwood? Captain Collingwood? Do you think I will
ever forget? True, I was a small child when I found myself
marching in a cafila, my neck fixed between the prongs of
a wooden pitchfork, one hundred and fifty miles in ten
days, but though it's nearly seventy years behind me, I still
have a sharp recollection of the wicked shepherds, my thirst
and broken blisters. And the fact is I'm here, on the wrong
side of the sea, and not a day goes by when I'm not remember-
ing the cafila, the long walk to the coast, there to be tied
to an iron stake in the barracoons and branded with a *C*
for Collingwood, examined by a French doctor, and mated
temporarily with a Bristol boy, which is why my first words
in English were obscenities. My Bristol husband secured
me a space on the infirmary floor, there to work through
the illness of the waves, and when I fell asleep in a puddle
of my own vomit my Bristol husband washed me, perfumed
me, fed me spoonfuls of lime juice, for in good health I
would bring a fair price. So when the drought threatened
and the ship languished in the ocean desert, my Bristol
husband shared his water rations with me, and when Captain
Collingwood selected the first twenty slaves to be thrown
overboard, my Bristol husband hid me under a tarpaulin —
I remember how the cover stank of dead fish, and I decided
this must be what the eye jelly feels beneath a closed lid, a
dank, stifling darkness, protected by nothing but the thinnest
membrane. Later, with our destination in sight, my husband
kissed me farewell, gave me my name, and had me chained
with my people on the deck. I learned soon enough that
our numbers had been reduced by one hundred and thirty-

two, in increments of twenty, over a period of five days, which is why years later I was found in an abandoned chicken coop, a flap of my skin with the letter *C* inscribed stuck to the paring knife I'd used to carve the square from my shoulder, a neat job I'd done, and I remember thinking as I bled to death how we might sell our excised brands to our white mistresses, they could make alphabet quilts with the patches, swaddle their babies in our skin: a piece of Happiness, a piece of Charity, we'll keep your children warm."

I am sure, my dear mother, you would put an end to my indulgent fancies, you would order me to remain at the table until I had committed to memory an entire psalm, and when I tired of my studies you would have me spend an hour matching plants my sister had collected to illustrations in my botany text. I would cock my head while you twisted a washcloth in my ear, then I would lunch on spiced sausage. You would ask me to recite the psalm, next the Pythagorean theorem, you would not allow a pause between the topics of concentration — the mind's effort must be continually focused, inquiry directed, for a boy should acquire intimate knowledge of a variety of subjects before he decides upon his specialty, which he should do early in life or he'll end a dabbler, which is what the captain seems intent on becoming, leaving navigation in the hands of the chief mate and the carpenter, leaving discipline to Pharaoh, as if he had forgotten his contract. Hedonism is his philosophy and he has accumulated plenty of diversions — Peter Gray, the missionary man, a dozen pints of brandy still sealed, and, most recently, a wheel that he unpacked from his trunk, a small wheel with a diameter the length of my forearm, propped between two poles, a wheel that turns without the aid of wind or steam, a perpetual motion machine. He sits hour after hour watching the spokes revolve, delighted by the contraption, entertained by its mystery.

"Tom, what keeps the wheel spinning?" he asked as I entered his cabin.

I carried a jug of water and a loaf of bread, having received orders from Pharaoh to deliver these items to the captain. A faint, grainy dusk drained in through the water closet portal, and the single candle seemed to inhale the natural illumination, drawing the light into its own smoky yellow dome. At first the only discernible form was the wheel with its heavy stubbed spokes and double rim revolving lazily upon the table in place of the chameleon, the charts, the paperweights.

"Tom, what keeps the wheel spinning?" the captain repeated.

I clutched the loaf like an unwanted book I meant to toss upon the flame, I probed the gloom and found greasy red crescents shadowed by the captain's side-whiskers, the silver mica shards of his eyes, black lines separating each segment, so his face seemed a portrait rent apart and reglued haphazardly.

I felt faint sympathy revive for this commander, who cared to do nothing but stare at his perpetual motion machine, one hundred lives entrusted to him and he wanted only to watch a wheel revolve, replenishing himself with hard bread and water and of course his brandy, the captain needs his brandy to remain interested in life. I wanted to humor him, so I pretended to marvel at the mystery of the wheel though I knew there must be a trick, a hidden device propelling it, no wheel will turn continuously without an external force. But still I pretended to be awed, as if the machine were the captain's own invention.

"How is it possible?" I wondered aloud, and the captain shifted eagerly in his chair, gripping the brace of the wheel without disturbing the motion.

But the voice that responded did not belong to the captain, the words "By divine permission" emanated instead from the corner, and I saw then that the captain and I were not alone. The missionary man stepped from the shadows of the night cabin, after him slouched Peter Gray and the missionary's new consort, Brian Piper. An unlikely team, united by the passion of their convictions, all three dedicated to disrupting the middle passage. I don't know why the captain prefers their company to mine these days, unless they have won him over to their cause. What would I do if the captain himself denounced the *Charles Beauchamp*, both the ship and my father? This Guineaman grows increasingly churlish, with its rebels fomenting disturbances, like rancid meat in the bowels. Maybe it is up to me, the blue monkey, to keep this untrustworthy captain sane and purposeful.

I tipped the candle toward the wheel, and after a brief investigation I thought I had discovered the trick of the machine. So I set the bread upon the table and announced, "You've hidden metal plates between the edges of the rim, sir — I'm no fool — each metal piece right side up is shaped like a nine, upside down a six, and Captain, we all know that a nine is top-heavy, a six weighted at the bottom, so when the number nine reaches the summit it turns over, drags the wheel, and then the next nine teeters, dives, pulls the wheel a quarter round, so as long as you've got a nine at the top, a six falling to the bottom, the wheel will spin forever."

I remembered my earlier determination to humor the captain, to play along with him. But why should I try to promote illusion for such a man, with his history, his reputation? If he can discard his guilt as readily as he can order a lame man heaved over the rail, then I should have no misgivings about puncturing his belief in miracles. Reasoning thus, I came full circle, the weight of logic exceeding the weight of sympathy, so my explanation for the perpetual motion machine seemed again a fair solution.

The missionary man grumbled, the captain continued to stare with drunken fascination. I had entered a den of fanatics, and nothing could shake their irrational beliefs or distract them from their urgent ambitions. Belief, not the poles of good and evil, is the catalyst, the force behind perpetual motion.

I thought I had decoded the cipher of their behavior and could mark the point on a chart where their dreams intersect: Africa. Everyone in the stateroom had a special interest in the continent. Their beliefs could be charted like trade routes, each arcing course distinct from the others, and the sphere made up of the circles would be the globe itself. Such a neat, geometrical diagram I could have drawn right then to explain the contradictory versions of reality. I thought I had human nature figured out, or at least the motivation of these four, I thought I was an acute observer and had determined exactly how the captain, Peter Gray, the missionary man, and Brian Piper were using one another to achieve their private ends. So shrewd I felt, but my confidence was pierced by their laughter. Crackling hiccoughs began first with Piper, my former friend, the newly inducted member of this society, and the humiliating laughter proved infectious. Soon the missionary man emitted high-pitched yelps, I heard Peter Gray's titter, even the captain surrendered to mirth. They had found another method of abuse, one much more effective than a beating or seduction — their gasps were ragged, pinching me, scratching, raking across my face, they laughed at me as the world had laughed at Newton.

Suddenly it seemed that all the sermons, the tales, and the histories had been designed to torment me. My education has consisted of nothing but calculated insults. According to them, my destiny has already been determined, I'm bound to fall. They have portioned out my identity, fracturing me into separate Toms. To the missionary I'm the dwelling place of evil, to the captain I represent his lost youth, to Peter Gray I have served as a poor but useful replica of her African brother, and to Piper I'm an unbeliever. The blue monkey can do nothing but feel guilty and doomed, while these manipulators guffaw at their victim: *see how he trembles, quavers, buckling beneath the load of shame, staggering ahead through his father's labyrinth, look how he shivers at the sound of the minotaur's growl, watch him careening against the walls; Tom, we recommend that you avoid that dark corridor, and don't try to retreat, and don't, God forbid, stand still, for the monster can track your scent — here, strap on this pair of wax wings, boy, now watch him rise, the fool.*

Don't blame me for this hysteria. A boy on his father's slaver has to contend with so many uncertainties. My mind is nothing but an arena, the antics directed by adults, applauded by adults, and what a jolly time they have had watching a boy trip over his own feet. All along I have been trying to determine whom to trust, but now I know to trust only myself. A snide, cynical, suspicious blue monkey — this is my new identity.

I had no purpose here so I haughtily withdrew from center stage, I left the captain's stateroom without asking to be excused, and though I heard his laughter curdle into an indignant call, though I heard him repeat my name twice, demanding that I return and stand at attention, I continued to climb the companionway into the open air.

But there are some things a boy can't forget. Today I feel the presence of the blind pirates as I might feel the burden of a debt. Secretly I search the water with the leather-bound scope, but I might as well be scanning the sun for fleas — the magnifying lens doesn't produce an ophthalmic slaver. Out of sight, out of reach, they force me to consider the limits of my father's power: not every man in the middle of the Atlantic is bound by contract or title to the *Charles Beauchamp*.

And then the sea shudders, the sky curses, the song "They Call Me Hanging Johnny" trails to silence, and I am re-

minded that I have no importance in the larger scheme. A
boy may pound his chest and declare his worth, but direct
a blustering squall his way and the same resentful chap
will seek shelter in the folds of his captain's cloak.

This morning, because of the heat, the slaves were allowed
to remain above, and the sailors took turns hauling buckets
and spilling sea water in an attempt to harden the pitch
melting in the planks' seams. Black tarry medallions stuck
to the bottom of my shoes as I tried out my new persona —
I strutted importantly among the slaves, thumbs hooked
under my armpits, heels clicking, pretending a discerning
eye, letting my glance roam from body to body though of
course I'm no judge of capability, I can't estimate a man's
lifespan by examining his teeth. The missionary also walked
from slave to slave, dipping his fingers into a bowl of molasses
and marking foreheads with a cross, but predictably the
Africans smeared the molasses, licking it from their palms
as soon as the reverend had moved on.

Even Peter Gray prefers the upper deck to the oppressive
atmosphere in the captain's stateroom; she wanders aimlessly, her pea jacket like a canvas sheet wrapped around
an old clock tower. The sailors squint in welcome, coupling
their nod with a malevolent grin — they assume that they
have interpreted this aloof stranger correctly, I've even heard
them call her "missus," thinking this an appropriately rude
epithet for the lad who has been kept below for the captain's
pleasure, entertaining no glimmer of suspicion that "missus"
is entirely accurate. Such fools, these cocky, deep-water
smugglers, insulting a woman for being a woman; they find
Peter Gray more provocative, more amusing than the sev-
enty-odd blacks, they have taken to jeering at her instead
for the same reason that they ignore the ragged chickens
in the coop but will risk falling overboard in an effort to
catch an albatross alive, though everyone knows an albatross
hosts legions of fleas and can't be kept as a pet and can't
be eaten, the only parts of an albatross worth saving are

the wing bones, which the sailors say make the sweetest
stems for pipes when properly scraped and fit to the bowl.

So I spent half the day dabbing my moist face with my
mother's handkerchief, assuming an aristocrat's manner so
convincingly that by noon word had spread: young Tom
was acting grand. Yellow Will confronted me and demanded
to know if I considered him common, and I said, "Worse
than that," which won for me cheers from men standing
near and wrath from Yellow Will. He started to reach for
my throat, then had a second thought; he retreated and I
continued my promenade, proud that I had stood up to
Yellow Will, until he returned with the sailor who serves
as the ship's barber. Yellow Will seized me, announcing
that Squire Tom had an appointment. He proceeded to
tackle me right there on the quarterdeck, he straddled my
chest, and at first I thought I would be a victim of buggery
for all to see, but he had another method for abusing me —
he held me supine while the barber, his hands wrapped in
white cotton cloth, lathered my beardless chin with . . .

Mother, read no further! You don't want to know how
your son was befouled with muck, pig excrement, Mother,
spread round his lips and cheeks, beneath his nose, and
he couldn't struggle, couldn't toss his head back and forth
because the barber immediately applied the razor and Yellow
Will warned me that my jugular would be sliced if I tried
to resist, so I have endured the first shave of my manhood,
Papa, I have held my chin steady for the barber. I admit
my eyes watered, and after a half-dozen strokes Will released
me and I rolled onto my belly, spitting cotton, and then I
crawled to the barrel of wash water and plunged my head
in up to my neck, following Jack Carvee's example; perhaps
I shall drag myself to the hog sty tonight and suck the dew
from the iron grating, relishing the tangy, rust-flavored nectar, and by morning, if I am lucky, my bones will be picked
clean.

When I surfaced I expected to see the entire crew collected, laughing at me, but eight bells had already signaled dinner for the Africans and I had been forgotten. I staggered across the deck. The barber had dealt a mortal blow, beheading me, I could feel nothing above my shoulders, and the sailors quickly turned their eyes away when I passed, unwilling to look at the bleeding trunk of an executed boy. Where was the captain? Why hadn't he come to my aid? Or has he appointed Pharaoh and Yellow Will as this Guineaman's dragoons and authorized them to hound slaves, women, and boys for the sake of a spectacle? On a pirate slaver the order of the day is not law but lawlessness, with the captain presiding over chaos. I've joined ranks with the other victims — Jack Carvee, Quince, the African madwoman — and I've lost faith in evolution. I say this not simply out of sympathy for the weak but out of anger, too: Dragoons, beware — even if you dump an injured man into the sea you can't extinguish his passionate hate, you ignite a man's rage and you'll pay, dragoons, he'll rise against you, as he did today in a furious twister, reminding us that we have no more power or significance than a butt of driftwood floating in a trough between waves.

One minute the sun's rays shone like organ pipes through the layer of clouds, the next they were velvety with drizzle, and behind us, in place of the distant masts, we saw the front curtain of a squall, rain falling vertically, the sea lying flatter than drenched fur on a dog. The squall passed within a half mile of our starboard rail, and the sailors who had paused to watch the storm resumed their work of dishing boiled rice to the slaves. But I climbed into the pulpit and alone saw the horizon throw up a looking glass, so the squall that had sidled by us approached its formidable mirror image, twin storms clattered toward each other and collided, twin charcoal clouds met and blended, sinking lower, the water foamed as the squalls embraced, and now a single storm cloud fought against the ocean, rearing backward, straining to snap the threads of rain. All at once the crest of a wave erupted and water spiraled upward, twisting into the center of the funnel-shaped cloud, and then this spout began to dance across the surface, hurtling back toward our ship. I tried to shout for the captain but I couldn't find my voice, though it didn't matter, for by now he and everyone else, including the slaves, were crowded along the rail, and except for the distant rattling rain a tense silence hung, heavy as the suctioning cloud that would soon be upon us. Retribution. The waterspout was retribution, we would all suffer for the crimes of such men as Yellow Will.

At first the waterspout moved in a direct path, then, mocking our impotence, it wheeled in a loop, retreated a short distance, and surged ahead again. In those moments before the impact I found myself pleading silently not with God but with the captain, as if he could have inhibited the wind. Such wind, curling, whipping around us, smelling of exotic lands, stinging our cheeks with grit from the past. This air had gone round the world through the centuries, and I feared that we would be sucked out of time into the ballooning cloud — we'd disappear without a trace, and we'd be nothing but a legend. Maybe that is enough, I thought grimly, to survive as a legend, to be invoked, retold, as immortal as wind. I would never have to suffer a shave again. Dumbly, impassively, we watched death advance, and I tried to convince myself of the advantages: it would mean the end of confusion, the end of pain. But suddenly, without warning, the cloud vomited the foaming column of water into the sea, and after depositing its insult, slid toward the horizon, gray billows trembling from the exertion.

The sailors didn't linger to watch the storm retreat or to contemplate our last-minute gift of luck — they were already shepherding the slaves, organizing them in rows on the quarterdeck again, preparing them for exercise. I spotted the captain just as he had thrown his head back and tipped a flagon of brandy to his lips, I saw the missionary man thumbing through his Bible while Piper set out biscuits to be consecrated, I saw Peter Gray standing by the rail, shifting her weight from one foot to the other, tilting her chin so coyly I would think any sailor who had been watching her would grow suspicious. But the men were absorbed with the slaves, and such things as Peter Gray and storms had been forgotten.

Not by me. I still feel dizzy from this confrontation, and I think if a waterspout comes again I will take charge, order the sails reefed or the ship brought about; I cannot bear to do nothing. Defense won't immortalize a man but it will keep him occupied, distract him from terror. Never again, Mother, shall I try to convince myself that death is preferable, never again shall I stand helplessly by.

On the other hand, what compares with a graceful surrender, with a Sabine girl parting her legs, with Priam on his knees or a dolphin panting on the deck of a Guineaman? The fleeting squall left behind a swill of vegetation, so the water, sluggish and lifeless at first glance, has turned into a metropolis teeming with schools of mackerel, mullet, snapper, and shark. The men drag trolling lines from the stern, and today a sailor snagged a dolphin. I perched atop the rail, balancing precariously so I could watch the fish die, and a glorious finale it proved, with the dolphin melting into a multicolored puddle, a pastel stain upon the deck, its hide transforming from solid silver-white to stripes as the body arced against the weight of gravity, flopping feebly as if to catch its tail in its mouth. When my end is finally imminent, I hope I too will sport all the colors of the rainbow.

A command. A requisition. A bidding. The captain has invited me to dine with him — "Six bells prompt, in your best regalia," the chief mate directed. I don't have the courage to decline.

· · ·

Grilled dolphin steak in a mustard sauce, yam glazed with blackstrap, beans in vinegar, pickled onion, a fine claret; how silly to think I had anything to fear from the captain, who is, after all, my father's employee. He doesn't suspect that I am a thief and a prodigal. At the start of the evening he appeared gentler than ever — the horizontal brow wrinkles were like a dozen supple lips, such expressive lines, I think I would know him intimately if I were allowed to examine his forehead at length. But I kept my eyes respectfully low, though from time to time I did steal a glance, watched his wrinkles purse and yawn, watched his dextrous eyebrows bounce as he spoke passionately about the quality of the cargo and how pleased my father will be. I think if the captain's sentiment were to reach a slightly higher pitch those eyebrows would begin to flap and alight from his head.

Inexplicably, I have regained the captain's affection, and now he treats me not as a cabin boy but as an equal. He poured my wine, toasted my health, and though his wheel contraption, his perpetual motion machine, sat upon a chair like a silent third dinner guest, spinning endlessly, the captain did not challenge me to solve the mystery of the machine and made no direct reference to his toy.

During the course of the evening, however, we found ourselves speaking about the French colonies, and he told me about a Caribbean rebel named Vincent Ogé, who was broken on the wheel. The French Assembly had failed to include his people in the Declaration of Rights, so Vincent Ogé incited the island natives, riots erupted, and white children were killed. Here the captain paused, and then, addressing not me but the motion machine, he described how the wheel dislocated every joint in Ogé's body and not once did the man cry out. I wanted to ask him if he had witnessed the torture himself, but with a sigh he remarked upon the unusual tenderness of this dolphin flesh. I complimented the feast, the wine, even the comfort of the stateroom though tiny wafers of soot from the lampwick hung in the air and the heat was oppressive.

I was grateful to be alone with him — Peter Gray was gone, and the door to her closet swung ajar, banging open and closed with the motion of the ship. As we sipped our cognac the captain must have noticed me looking toward the empty berth, for he murmured, "A saucy treat, eh, Tom?" and I knew he wasn't referring to the brandy. "An unexpected pleasure," he added with a fraternal wink.

I began to wonder if the dinner had been designed to trap me, the liquor to enhance his advantage, but the captain continued to speak in a friendly manner, his voice so casual that I was sure he meant me no harm. "I've never been so fortunate in my career," he said jocularly, and to himself, "She's a lucky addition," and then, with sudden animosity, "Don't you trust her, Tom, don't believe anything she tells you." It seemed as though I were hearing my private ambivalences spoken aloud: the captain, too, is tossed about by fluctuating emotions — one moment he lusts for her, the next he condemns her. We have not only shared Peter Gray, we have shared this disorienting motion, careening from desire to disgust and back again, and with this glimpse of the captain's torment I felt the bond between us renewed.

"Sir, she's not worth the worry." A feeble attempt to comfort him, but I think I did some good, for he offered a wan smile, reached across the table to clink my glass, and I perceived the extent of his loneliness. In whom may he confide? Certainly not in the missionary, and he must keep his distance from the other officers and crew, for confession is sure to diminish authority. I am all he has left. And I, better than anyone else, know how women have wound around the captain's heart, like those demons the missionary keeps challenging. "Sir," I said with wine-induced bravado, "let's renounce her, let's renounce all women!"

He raised his glass to toast the suggestion, and I heard

myself say with thoughtless audacity, "You don't have to hide it from me — your past, I mean. I know about you and the ladies."

"And what exactly do you know about me, lad?" inquired the captain, amiably enough, though perhaps if I had been attentive I would have noticed his eyebrows bristling.

"Oh, about the wives you've had — the one who went up in the balloon, and the handful who slipped arsenic into their wine —"

"Arsenic, Tom? What have you heard?"

"You don't have to pretend, Captain, you have a reputation — don't try to deny it," I said, motioning toward the wardrobe.

He laughed again, a wet, nasal snort, and asked, "A reputation, Tom?" as if I knew better than he.

"A reputation for opening a bottle, taking a sip, then throwing the rest away," I joked. "You always want more than you have, you never finish what you begin." But the captain's features puckered as if his face were attached to a drawstring, and I let my voice trail off.

No sooner had I fallen silent than the captain sprang up, grabbed my throat, and cried, "Who profits by slandering me?" With his fingers nearly crushing my esophagus I could only gasp the name, I coughed out, "Piper, Brian Piper," but the captain kept throttling me, demanding, "Who insults me? Who?" and only when I had nearly blacked out from suffocation did he release me.

"The steward, you say? He's the chatterer?" As I rubbed my neck I thought to myself, *I must warn him, I must protect Piper,* for even if he has turned against me I don't want to see him lashed to the mast and flogged.

"Captain," I pleaded hoarsely, "don't blame Piper, I'm the one who demanded the truth." Truth indeed — clearly the captain was enraged not by slander but by truth. The ring hidden in his wardrobe was all that remained of everything he ever loved, and this trip has been nothing more than the slow procession home from a funeral. "If you care at all for me, sir," I said, "don't punish Brian Piper."

Well, it became apparent soon enough that the captain's anger was a mere passing fit, and with another swallow of brandy he absent-mindedly placed a finger on a wooden spoke of the wheel to speed the rotations, whispering, "Tom, I might as well admit it."

"Sir?"

"When I was half your age I was already a veteran on the sea," he began, and I wondered what this had to do with the messboy. "I shipped out regularly from New Orleans to Africa. By my sixteenth year I'd helped import nearly six hundred slaves, I had gained a reputation in the trade, established myself as a reliable hand. Invariably, the officers of the brigs came to depend on me — as I depend on you, Tom — for every man likes to keep the image of his own spirited youth in view, he wants to be reminded of a time when the ocean was a marvel to him, the water gleaming with potential adventure. Experience makes a sailor dull, it will happen to you. And someday you will want to survey the sea with fresh eyes, so you will hire a boy to accompany you. One captain in particular took an interest in me, he invited me to join him at his table two meals a day, every day we were at sea.

"During the course of the middle passage a revolt broke out among the slaves. They had procured a few machetes and galley knives — who knows how the devils armed themselves? They seemed to do nothing but invoke a blade and instantly they were holding it in their hands. But we quickly crushed the rebellion, and we lost only two sailors, three, perhaps. The captain ordered nine slaves executed. So nine men were selected, shot in front of the other Africans, and at the captain's direction the corpses were beheaded. You see, he wanted to deliver a warning to the mutineers, and since he didn't speak their language he organized a panto-mime, he had the nine bleeding heads stacked in a tub and he assigned me the task of distributing them. He wanted the Africans to kiss the mutilated lips of their dead brothers, and in order to show them what was expected we had to demonstrate. The captain assigned me to the post of instructor: I had to kiss each bloody mouth before passing the head down the row. The captain thought this job the highest honor. But in the eyes of every head I saw my own fate."

Surely this ugly job would leave an impression on a boy, but I thought the captain wrong to connect this one episode with his destiny, and I told him so.

"Like a cat, Tom, I'm like a cat, allowed to live eight lives, to die eight deaths, and to be reborn as many times," he said quietly, studying his knuckles, "but nine is the limit, everyone knows."

"I didn't think you were given to superstition," I said, trying to cheer him.

"Eight bloody heads . . . the ninth will be my own."

"Please don't speak to me that way, sir!" How unfair, I thought, for a captain to be flirting with his own death in front of a boy. I did not want his confidence anymore, I would rather he kept his grim presentiments to himself rather than burden me. If my papa had ever conceived that the captain would appear so morose he would have selected a different model for me, but since the captain is my educator I must try to benefit from him. Did I learn anything tonight? I learned that romance is a sickness and a man's immunities grow ineffective with time, I discovered that even a gentleman as godless as the captain has a strain of mysticism in his heart, and I've decided never to fall into the same mire. The captain is a pessimist through and through. I know what he was telling me: he assumes when Peter Gray is done with him she will deposit him in his coffin. She is his ninth love, and the number nine is the captain's doom.

I gave up the futile effort of dissuading him, I sat in silence while the old man lamented his fate, cursed the vagaries of life. Eventually his speech grew thick, his lids heavy, and his chin dropped to his chest. I heard the long inhalation as he drew sleep into his lungs, and instead of immediately exiting I strode around the table and placed my hand upon his shoulder, upon the gold epaulet cord. I don't know why I felt compelled to touch him this way; I cannot say how long I remained by his side.

If: If I were Brian Piper I would have thought twice about gossiping with the Guineaman's blue monkey, I would have considered the captain's temperament, his inclination to rage at the slightest provocation. I would have already devised an avenue of escape, collected a month's worth of provisions, been prepared to flee in a whaleboat at any moment, for when the captain discovered I had been publicizing his humiliating story he would demand my life, nothing less.

If I were the captain I would try to forget my past, to forget the horrors I had witnessed and the ladies I had known, and I would fight the attraction to Peter Gray. But given such a scarcity of females on board I might, with great reluctance, allow myself a few indulgences. Eventually I'd have to admit that I was implicated, bound inextricably, I would fall for her. And given my history of misfortune I would expect only tragedy ahead, having long ago been convinced that the ninth round in love would destroy me — unless I destroyed her first.

If I were Peter Gray and had seen my purpose slashed and drowned by pirates, I would wonder if my life was worth the trouble, but I would survive for pride's sake, I'd make this slaver suffer. I would have to tolerate the captain's advances, for his protection was essential — alone I stood no chance against the men.

But since I am not Peter Gray I have a perspective denied to her, and I think I should tell her about the captain's forecast. Having concluded that the ninth alliance with a woman will prove fatal, he'll try to crush Peter Gray in a desperate effort to protect himself.

A poor job butchering the pig. While two sailors held the animal flat against the planks Piper slit its windpipe, a ribbon of blood squirted across the faces of the sailors, and the pig scrambled up, trotted wildly over the deck with the men stumbling in pursuit. I would have laughed aloud at the sight of a wounded pig and famished sailors if I hadn't so recently been at the wrong end of the butcher's blade. I pressed my fists against my ears to smother the cries after the pig had been recaptured, I closed my eyes so I couldn't see Piper plunging the knife into its throat again and again, long after the animal lay inert.

The chief mate must have noticed me wincing; spitefully, he ordered me to fill a bucket with soapy water, and I spent the afternoon scrubbing blood from the deck and puttying gouges in the wood. The knife thrusts were so powerful that the messboy had stabbed the shape of a letter in the planks beneath the slaughtered hog — his initial, a crude *P* perhaps, but a capital *P* nonetheless.

"Peter Gray," I whispered, having found her a few rungs up the shroud, glowing like a clump of zoophytes floating in the moonlit sea. "I need to talk with you."

At first I thought the sudden shattering behind me was a rifle shot but it proved to be only a clumsy watchman who had dropped a lantern in the helm, where the night watch lounged and the steerer hung on the wheel. Rough curses followed the crash, a call for water to put out the sparks, and then darkness enveloped the voices again.

"What do you want?" she asked, gazing down at me, her legs curled around a ratline, her arms braided with the shroud ropes.

"I've come to warn you."

"To warn you," she echoed, as if she were a hollow chamber.

I asked her why she sat tangled in the shroud when it was nearly midnight, she sneezed a delicate child's puff for reply. I thought it better than to press her for a reason, so I continued. "I think you are in danger," and she sighed, "Danger . . ." I realized she was making fun of me again, ridiculing my kindness. "I think the captain means to . . . ," I faltered. She completed my sentence with, "To bury me at sea?" With a swift motion she descended a few feet, caught my chin, and cupped her hand tightly to pucker my lips.

"Tom, didn't anyone inform you that a citizen engaging in traffic can be adjudged a pirate and on conviction thereof suffer death? You're taking a risk, participating in the trade of blood."

Abolition again, always a cause. Women have nothing better to do than to muster support for causes they don't understand, and if it's not slavery, then it's vivisection or intemperance they're protesting. She released me, and as I rubbed my chin I wondered whether she had watched the barber shaving me, whether she had seen the men frosting me with the brown miasma. I shrank from her, withdrew a few paces into the night because I couldn't stand the thought of Peter Gray observing my humiliation or humiliating me further. From the beginning of this voyage I have felt the weight of her morality, as if her judgment were fair and legitimate, which it certainly is not, for though she may condemn trafficking she thinks nothing of spreading her legs for the captain in order to keep him dependent on her, without qualms she will untie a schoolboy's drawstring so he will give up the key to her compartment. I don't understand how she manages to inspire guilt in me when I have been nothing all along but an innocent passenger while she has exchanged virtue for a few meager benefits. She raises the banner of abolition, as if this could excuse her. Peter Gray would like to serve as the conscience of this ship, but in reality she is corrupt and does not deserve to wield such power over me.

I wish I had the strength to resist her. Like the captain I am addicted, like the captain I am fully aware of the problem, yet still I return for more. I admit I didn't seek her out tonight solely to pass her a warning, I admit I was hoping to revive her interest. But she has a cause to champion, and just as the missionary accuses me of harboring a demon, Peter Gray blames me for being the son of my father; because of my size and my inexperience I serve as a ready locus of evil, because of my youth I am prime material for preachers and militants, they think they can turn me against myself. Well, they should know that because I am a child I am innocent. Papa would never have permitted me to board this slaver if he thought I'd be in danger with the law.

"I suggest you find another guardian, Peter Gray," I muttered from the shadows. I would have liked to remind her of the futility of her righteousness — no sailor would take the time to hear her defend the dignity of the human soul; they want merely to collect their wages and hurry to saloons.

"On conviction thereof suffer death," she repeated, resting her hand upon my shoulder just as I had touched the captain. Even the blessed darkness wouldn't hide such a provocative gesture from an inquisitive eye; luckily, the men were circulating the whiskey and keeping the steerer company, so no one saw when Peter Gray extracted herself from the rope web and gently pushed me to my knees, no one watched as she began to unbutton her jacket, peeled back the coarse wool from the linen shirt, shook her arms free. If Brian Piper could have seen me he'd wonder why I had been privileged to take part in this magnificent vision. With one hand I struggled to loosen my drawstring, the other hand slid inside the chemise and cupped over her breast, as Cupid fondled Venus. I sensed our time was short, I would wake either from this dream of love or from the dream of the middle passage, and whether I found myself in my own bedroom or in my half-deck berth I would be alone. Here was the only pertinent fact: soon I would be alone again. So before I lost her I wanted to consummate with haste, but of course I couldn't unknot my drawstring, and I couldn't locate the interior of Peter Gray, for she had already evaporated, like everything else I have valued, she had disappeared completely.

I don't know how she managed to slip from my arms. Before I could sit up she gathered the bundle of her jacket, and with a derisive laugh she was gone. I groaned softly, stretching my hand skyward in an effort to catch the Dog Star so I could squeeze the yellow light from it and extinguish it forever.

Why pretend any longer, Mother? Though in my confusion I have insisted otherwise, in truth I have been traveling through channels and canyons inside my skull, and now I have grown tired of the trip, I would like to send everybody home so I may have my world to myself again. Why have I indulged in such fantasies of oppression? I think I have been trying to call an end to this journey by invoking all sorts of impediments — storms, hostile Africans, phantom slavers. I have mistreated others inadvertently, mistreated myself in retaliation, but I cannot sink this ship or stop the middle passage; until now I have had no more control over my inventions than a man has over his heartbeat. Still, it is comforting to admit that one day I shall sit again at the kitchen table and listen to my little sister playing in the yard, and I'll laugh to myself at the thought of this difficult voyage to Africa that I never took, the impostor Peter Gray who never existed, the dolphins and flying fish that I have never seen and probably never will. Yes, it is reassuring to know that someday this unreal experience will be only a memory. I should like it to end at the earliest convenience.

If I have learned anything since I embarked I have learned to immerse myself in other lives, I have participated with great interest in Piper's gossip, in Peter Gray's obscure secrets, in the captain's confessions, at times I have intentionally filled the gaps with my own presumptuous inventions, I have even imagined what it means to drown and have very nearly experienced the separation of body and soul at the instant of death. So I should think myself capable by now of finally taking control.

How can I collapse the whole construction? Why, how else but with mutiny, of course, mutiny, the only possible solution. Clearly, Peter Gray means to incite the slaves, she won't waste the opportunity for revenge now that the Africans are on board, and with the sailors drowning in rum they will be easily subdued. The missionary man will prove a useful aid, for though he still makes overtures to gain the captain's favor I am certain he continues to despise him. And Brian Piper is already the missionary's disciple. But what about me? What shall become of the Guineaman's vulnerable blue monkey? Maybe it is time to align myself with the opposition, to give up hopes of ever becoming an honorable gentleman — I'll let others take the necessary steps, I'll let them perform the mutiny, which I trust shall be rapid and bloodless, and I shall try to keep out of the way.

Or have I fooled myself? Have I wrongly assumed sovereignty over this voyage when in fact I am no more than a journalist, my words inspired by events that will occur whether or not I am present? Perhaps this chronicle could be kept by someone else. I had thought my decision to introduce mutiny into my notebook would determine the general state of affairs, but it might be that I have no more effect upon this Guineaman than a gull has on a sperm whale swimming just below the surface.

·   ·   ·

Or do I simply have a remarkable ability to read a man's face for hidden passion, enabling me to predict an impending riot as accurately as the carpenter can describe the contours of the ocean floor? I saw it in Peter Gray's eyes, I felt it in her touch, and I can say without hesitation that before the week is through the ratio of master to slave will be inverted. There might as well be a prophecy inscribed in the soft surface of the moon, so convinced am I that revolution is almost upon us. Someone will be sacrificed. Yet nothing has changed. The *Charles Beauchamp* glides evenly — the ship has learned to handle itself and the steerer is a mere token piece, as useless as a flag.

At least we adhere to routine, thank God for routine. I try to remember to ring the bell at every half hour during my watch, I look forward to coffee in the morning, despite the unnatural circumstances on board I depend on the carpenter's bagpipes to soothe me in the evening; the quarter-deck still stinks of rum, the lower deck of naphtha, the ivory crescents of my fingernails lengthen, my bladder fills and I empty it, my chalky tongue cleaves to the roof of my mouth, and fresh water seems the most valuable treasure in the world. And when I grow weary I douse my lamp, pull the covers over my head, and with the ocean hissing sweet dreams to me I try to sleep. No. I can no longer depend on sleep. Not with fear coiled inside me, not with the certainty that tomorrow or the next day all order will be sundered.

Yet what if I wait for nothing? What if the change I anticipate is merely a gradual change inside myself? I must decide: do I mean to control this ship or to be controlled? Of course I would choose the former first, I would rather dictate the outcome. But just as I know that the ocean never alters, that the land continually revises its shape, that a conical island may be a flat plateau in the next millennium, I know

that time is the constant factor, and I, the variable. I am
continually and unwillingly transforming, I can't predict
what my condition will be tomorrow. Will I kneel before a
potentate? Will I grow a beard or cultivate a dandy's mus-
tache? I cannot remain as I am.

But what does this conclusion matter? What good is any
kind of insight if the insight doesn't make a man stronger?
I may prove to myself that I have an existence independent
from the world, I may decide to follow the migratory route
from birth to death without anyone's company, but my decision won't have an iota of influence. I will grow up regardless
of my inclinations, I will grow old and sick and die. Time
itself might as well have its own personality — it could feel
dejected at the summer solstice, mourn the shrinking days,
but little good consciousness would do, winter will arrive
and the faculty of reason only increases the misery. How
absurd these inventions, calendars and clocks — they are
the root of all sorts of complications.

If only I could simply pass: like time, like an abandoned
ship, like a molecule of water in a river. But no, I waste
the night sliding back and forth between worry and hope,
I spoil my few hours allotted for sleep because I can't help
but devote myself to this obsessive speculation: will I ever
see my home again?

Papa would say, "Always something to learn. Always an
unknown. A door to open. A foreign land." So there's no
use stifling curiosity, Papa would agree that I should inspect
the goods. I will go below to the crawl space where the
men-slaves are stashed, and I will study them as I've intended
to do, and later, when Peter Gray rallies the Africans, when
the cry of mutiny resounds, perhaps I'll even have a friend
among the mob.

·   ·   ·

"Where are you going?"

"Sir?"

"Where are you going, Tom?"

I don't know why I felt inclined to hide my purpose from the captain, I could have told him I meant to visit the lower dormitory, and he would have had no reason to hinder me; but suddenly I felt responsible for the burden of my secret: *mutiny*, I have heard the winds whispering, a shrill whisper that the captain had not discerned.

We met in the passageway outside the stateroom. Three brass buttons were missing from his uniform, and as he stumbled against me I smelled not only the stench from the hold but a peculiar, sickly sweet odor clinging to his whiskers that reminded me of geraniums rotting in a bowl. So I postponed my expedition, and supporting two thirds of the captain's weight I helped him back into the stateroom, lowering him onto the narrow daybed. As I struggled to loosen his collar I tried to picture the stalwart commander, the firm, inspiring man, I tried to contrast the sorry sight before me with a memory, but no matter what scene I invoked the captain of the past remained a shadow and this sorry loafer was the only skipper I had ever known. I wanted the other so desperately that I found myself stroking his beard, which only served to provoke his mirth, drawing his mouth into a wide, pale-lipped grin.

Disgust trailed close behind my sympathy. When I released him he flopped back against the pallet, looking not anything like an officer but like a dolphin dehydrating on the planks of a Guineaman. How could I shake dignity back into him? Without considering the harm I might cause I snatched the word from the still air, placed it like a wafer upon my tongue, and instead of swallowing it I spit it at the captain. "Mutiny, sir," I said. "You had best beware."

I doubt I shall wield such a powerful weapon ever again. I doubt I shall provoke a passion to equal the captain's outrage today. The dead dog before me leaped to his feet, lashed out his arm, and boxed my ear so forcefully that I careened backward, and the wardrobe rose up to meet me. Mother, I've still got a lump on my forehead as large as a peach pit to show for it.

But the captain instantly regretted the violence — in a moment my head was resting on his lap and his fingers were combing the locks from my eyes, which, to my regret, had begun to well with tears. But the captain took no notice — he was impersonating a grieving Madonna, lamenting softly, as if I were already halfway to the netherworld. I tried to push myself up but the captain insisted on holding me, and his fingers started a tentative journey away from my throbbing skull, crawling gently down my collarbone. Suddenly my clothes seemed made of ice and the captain's fingers were warm as a stovepipe, so comforting, so kind. I wanted to wrap myself up in his heat, to feel his hands melt into a puddle on my chest.

Then I remembered the captain's own comparison between fingers and insects — *devouring slowly, steadily* — I remembered the evening the captain had taken my hand in his. I recalled the gifts he has offered me. As his fingers continued along their serpentine course I began to struggle wildly, and in my panic I sunk my teeth into the captain's arm, just above the elbow.

The coarse cotton of his sleeve offered adequate protection against a young boy's nip, but the captain didn't bother to continue his caresses. Instead his face hardened, like a monarch's profile embossed on a coin he had a severe, unyielding expression, and I wanted to apologize though he was the one who had knocked me nearly senseless, he was the one who had tried to take liberties. Yet I could judge from the captain's frown that his attention had already shifted from me back to the word I had spoken.

If the devil is a missionary's worst fear, then mutiny is a cavalry of devils to a captain, and by now I have a fair idea of what it means to be at sea, alone, with no one to

trust. *Trust.* Maybe this has been my greatest loss, not innocence but trust. I am obliged to suspect everyone of hidden
motives. What would it matter to me if they tarred and
feathered the captain? It would mean one less pair of scalding
eyes, one less pair of cloying, lecherous hands. With the
officers and crew of the ship engaged in riot I would be
free to wander aimlessly — the men would have no spare
time to treat me rudely, I could come and go as I pleased.

The captain didn't demand more information — he was
not interested in details, and I didn't care to linger in the
stateroom. Though but a quarter of his age I have ushered
in an unwanted future, and now the captain won't be able
to see his dreams of triumph come true. I've tainted his
possibilities, ignited his fears. Where shall he hide? Certainly
not in a boy's groin.

I had a conversation with myself today. I asked, "Tom, do
you think the captain merely wanted to comfort you?" and
I replied, "I know what he wanted!"

"But Tom," I pressed, "he could have done what he
wanted, if buggering you was his desire."

"Desire!" I scoffed. "Don't tell me about desire. I've seen
enough since we left the shores of America behind to understand desire. A man has to depend upon the supply available,
and when the supply is limited to the passengers of a Guineaman a sailor must sort through all the scoundrels and dere-
licts to find a suitable object. Of course a man covets what
another man possesses. The captain has borrowed me from
my papa, he has marked me as his own property, off limits
to the crew. I can't help it if I am a rare item — young,
slight, soft-spoken, with sensitive skin and taffeta hair. And
I can't help it if the captain has lost sight of decency."

"But Tom, could it be that you are your own most passionate admirer?"

"I don't know what you mean."

"Could it be, Tom, that you are simply enamored of yourself? Why do you blame the captain for touching you so tenderly? Jealousy, Tom — you're afraid of losing yourself."

"Maybe that's so. And maybe I blame Peter Gray for putting my emotions in a tumult."

"And Piper — he came to you for comfort."

"And the missionary — he has been trying to divide me in half." I couldn't dismiss the argument. Whenever I've been stroked, kissed, fondled, embraced, I have assumed a disreputable intent. "Then I confess: I don't trust love. I don't trust love in any form. I've got myself to look after and I won't belong to anyone." I thought this was a sufficiently honest response.

"But Tom," I nagged, "could it be that we have grown tired of each other? Could it be that as much as you want to divert the advances of courtiers, you might prefer others to me?"

"You think I'm fickle, do you? Well, I am Tom, my father's son, and I intend to keep to myself."

In this realm between the continents there is no possibility for an ordinary marriage, no chance of a normal engagement between a man and a woman. Union on board a Guineaman requires a displacement, and I shall not be committed to any substituted love.

Mother, you prepared me for peace and prosperity. You did not prepare me for this. And Papa, you praise gentility above all virtues, yet you never taught me about the mind's transforming powers: we may become whatever we want.

I have discovered that a man may use more than his wealth and influence for defense; the strongest patriot is not a magnate but a jester. From the women-slaves I learned passive methods, from the men I have learned active defense — such uncommon gymnastics, marvelous feats. But the performers followed no script and were indifferent to their audience. Indeed, as I stood looking at their improvisations I felt as though I were witnessing that extraordinary moment of second birth, each body struggling to break out of its cocoon.

Come Papa, it is your turn now: descend the ladder and turn toward the rear of the ship. Your lantern will illuminate first a crumpled leather hide that is an African, next to him a gigantic worm who has tucked his arms against his side and chews his tongue as if he were preparing to gnaw his way through the bottom of this Guineaman, to scuttle the ship, leaving us to drown while he slithers through the hole and swims home, evading fishing nets and eel traps, not daring to surface for air until he reaches a coastal lagoon.

And look, there are others who inflate their cheeks, puffing angrily, some who crouch, their bare rumps elevated, some who keep their hands waving, as if they were trying to carve a hollow in the air. And there are slaves whose eyes and nostrils dispense a thick, colorless sap, slaves whose toenails are as treacherous as the pincers of a fiddler crab hidden just below the sand, slaves so emaciated they dissolve into the dark. But more remarkable than any single man — have you noticed, Papa? — is the perpetual motion, the bodies straining against the pressure of gravity, barrel chests heaving, some men squirming as though gunpowder had been rubbed into raw wounds on their backs. One man rotates his wrists, another trembles from head to foot, as though overcome with laughter.

In theory, such exercise achieves nothing at all, but now that you have examined the cargo you must have some understanding of a man's possibilities for freedom — the dance in this crawl space has no beginning or end, and spectators who chance to glimpse the scene can feel nothing but terror, for it will seem to them, as it seemed to me today, that the entire population of the world is absorbed in a trance from which it will never wake.

·　　·　　·

But of course to an incurious observer the *Charles Beauchamp* appears quite civilized, quite proper. The *Charles Beauchamp* seems to have time for everyone, welcoming preachers and carousers, musicians and Negroes, captains and stowaways. The *Charles Beauchamp,* dependable and wise, needs no one's counsel. I doubt this ship has an equal. Oh, there may be clippers that ride low in the water, their long, elegant hulls designed for lightning speed. And there may be schooners that can carry a cargo twice as large as ours. But the *Charles Beauchamp* is so dignified, so reliable. Like Papa. With a clear purpose. A definite direction.

I wonder if my father has as many secrets as the *Charles Beauchamp.* I wonder if the thoughts stored in my father's head are as numerous as the bodies stored on this ship. My father has lived for nearly half a century, he must contain a great stock of memories. But he has always remained silent upon the subject of his past, though some nights I have heard him groan in his sleep, a groan similar to that made by the masts of the *Charles Beauchamp* buckling beneath the fierce winds off the coast.

After probing the recesses of this ship I have come to realize that complexity is determined not by the structure of the organism but by the scientist himself. While one man may divide his specimen into spirit and matter and leave it at that, another man will explore with a microscope, he will carve up the whole, dissect the parts, slice the arteries, puncture the atoms, he will keep finding a smaller parcel contained in the larger, and this endless process of investigation will unnerve him, he will slide into a delirium of possibility: what will he uncover next?

I wish I had been content to watch the *Charles Beauchamp* lumbering across the ocean, to admire the ship and to respect its privacy. Instead I must pry into its closets and corners, I must locate its gaps, I must listen to gossip, oracles, histories, until I make the many secrets my own. I may never know the absolute truth. It is enough to penetrate the dreams.

The *Charles Beauchamp* sails with confidence, but I've glimpsed the visions, I've heard the cries, I know what one *Charles Beauchamp* hides beneath the veneer of white canvas and sturdy planks, and what the other hides beneath his surtout.

Papa, did you expect me to discover the secrets, or did you place me on board this vessel to try my faith, my loyalty, as Bluebeard tested his wife by leaving her with his keys? I am ashamed of the man who has made this journey possible, yes, I am ashamed to find such disparity between the handsome appearance of a ship and its debased work. I shan't ask for your autobiography, but I wish you had told me a little more, I wish you had warned me that Charles Beauchamp has no pity, no compassion. Your only advice was to stay true to my class. Now I have absorbed not only your forbearance, not only your pride and gentleman's sobriety, I have been obliged to accept your shame as well. Not the facts of your past, not the suicides, forced matrimony, professional disgraces that gloss any random family history — the facts don't matter anymore. Instead, I have discovered that you are haunted by unnatural ambitions, and now I am haunted too.

But we shall keep the world from discovering us — at the end of the voyage I shall discard this notebook and forget what I have witnessed. You may be sure I shall keep my sea chest locked. And if my friends demand to see what I have brought home from Africa, I will show them only the money we have earned. I won't give them reason to doubt us.

The captain has the men lashing every movable object on board in preparation for the hurricane that is sure to strike when we reach the other side of the horizon, or so the captain believes, though the barometer remains steady and the sky spattered with clots of frothy white, the mildest of clouds; I don't think we have any cause to worry. But the captain has spent the afternoon in a tirade, calling the men a set of worthless loafers who might as well abandon ship, and I heard the sailors muttering that they would be pleased to do just that, to leave this cursed Guineaman behind, but of course if they did begin to pack a whaleboat with supplies the captain would aim his pistol and peg them one by one.

Only I know why he despises his own crew. When I ignited the fear of mutiny in him he must have assumed his own boys were the rebels, and I am not compelled to tell him otherwise, in truth I don't mind if he abuses the men. They will benefit from a tighter rule after these many days of carnival. So I stood out of the way while they collected buckets and sponges and cursed the idiocy of the labor. With the glassy water and the dry, temperate winds, they say we'll be welcoming a sea serpent aboard before we are visited by a hurricane.

The captain remained by the wheel, giving orders through the chief mate. I have done a thorough job on him, convinced him that we are on the brink of chaos — he's suffering the panic of an insane duke, one who thinks himself surrounded by traitors. I have infected the captain with fear and the men must endure his tyranny until we reach our home port.

For two days the captain has kept all hands on watch, though there is nothing to see but a barren sky and an unbroken horizon. While the carpenter keeps our hearts beating in time with his bagpipes, the sailors pass the hours in lazy conversation, trading boasts about sorties with famous Singapore whores, cargoes of shark tails and opium, unforgettable acts of darkness accomplished — a foot-long sword swallowed, a white-hot coal held in the palm of a hand.

But I've got no interest in the common seaman's adventures or in the clouds or the seascape; instead I choose to watch a pantomine that has no meaning to me. I am not sure why I prefer the dormitories. Perhaps I find it easier, if I'm to be excluded from conversation, to be excluded from all communication. So I stumble along the aisles, the narrow passageways, and though occasionally I catch my toe on their chains, their outstretched feet, though I may share the cramped, fetid drawer with dozens of unwashed bodies, there is really only one dancer occupying the dormitory, one dancer and me. Here is a difference between the upper and the lower decks: above, voices bounce from one fellow to the others, and I don't have the courage to join in, but in the bilge I can pretend that I belong, I don't have to ask for anyone's permission. I belong.

Watch, and watch again. Nothing new. The captain, not the sky, is dark, glowering, nearly bursting from the storm inside him. And young Tom is his provocation.

Are you fast married, Captain? What, sir? Do you want to hear my thoughts? It's a vicious guess, and I apologize beforehand. Now listen: a contented beggar has all he needs, but a rich man who fears he shall be poor one day already lives in absolute poverty. And the beloved husband who suspects himself a cuckold has already lost his wife. And a captain who punishes his crew for a mutiny not yet committed has already condemned himself.

But is it my duty to advise the captain? Must I tell him whom he should accuse? The captain naturally assumes that the strongest men are the ones who mean to overthrow him, so he points his telescope toward the quarterdeck, he focuses on Pharaoh, Will, Thresher, on any pirate with iron hands and a wolfish disposition. I suppose he thinks such loners as Peter Gray or the missionary man aren't capable of violence.

If I were inclined I would advise the captain to trace mutiny back to its source, to locate the impetus, to ask himself who would have cause to conspire against him. He should heed what the Romans used to say: so many slaves, so many enemies.

Among our own slaves there is sure to be one Spartacus who, with the help of a few sympathizers, will wage an attack and free his people. But which of the feeble, afflicted blacks is the captain's equal? Who is strong enough to challenge this Guineaman, as Spartacus challenged the army of Rome? Certainly no African below would be able to rally — the slaves have been kept on the verge of starvation, and I think a band of marionettes would make fiercer rebels.

True, hunger can inspire a man to amazing deeds, yet there is an even greater rage than hunger, and there is someone who will seek to revenge the ultimate loss — the loss of his own life. A drowned man will stop at nothing. I used to think water washes away all traces of a crime, but I know better now.

The same. Nothing particular transpired today, nothing unusual. The missionary praised God from his pulpit or crusaded on the upper deck, Peter Gray rode in the crosstree, the captain remained a nervous tyrant, and the messboy spent the day boiling vats of bean soup. Oh — we breakfasted on fresh pork, that was unusual.

Woken by the ship's bell, summons for all hands, not yet dawn but the sky had a greenish tint, no cause for worry, hardly more than a belch and it was over, over too went the carpenter, headfirst over the lee rail, yanking on a halyard and he lost his grip, only a slight splash, then the shout, "Man overboard!" Lines tossed but our beloved carpenter had sunk into the billows. Captain remained at the helm, crew frantic now. "Man overboard!" Some clambering over the rail as if they meant to join the carpenter but the ship didn't turn about as might be expected, steered a steady course through the curtain of rain, and as we mounted the next swell I saw a gray bundle floating on the crest of a wave. Or was that a stormy petrel? Captain asked, "Who is overboard?" a quarter of an hour later. Chief mate's answer: "The carpenter, sir." And the captain's reply: "Well, he's gone now, the best of the lot." Proves the truth of the superstition: death prefers the good to the bad. What will be missed? Accurate soundings, sturdy repairs, a lemur's instinct for the route. And music. We will have no music. Meant to ask our carpenter for instruction upon the bagpipes, too late now. Already requested from the captain and granted rights to the carpenter's instrument, which I have hidden in my sea chest. I will find someone at home to teach me. Or maybe I should give these pipes a proper sea burial out of respect for the deceased.

The same: hastening at twelve knots, though we've lost our favorite man. The sailors move about like defeated troops, mute, stunned. I would not have believed that a pirate slaver with a full load could advance so quietly. Mutiny is certainly the common thought — if the sailors hadn't entertained the notion before they surely have by now, since our only carpenter, our bagpiper, was left behind. I can hardly endure the wait, hour upon hour of pregnant calm. The captain has turned the men into his assassins, and I suppose he has already imagined the battle in intricate detail, the weapons that will be used against him, the spurt of maroon blood. Soon his fitful visions will destroy him. Better to be among the drowned, I should think, than to be tortured by such expectation.

In reality, we are all just numbered players on the field, easily replaced, and only two men determine the outcome. Two absent opponents — one in his office and one beneath the surface of the sea, the African born in the American's greed, like bacteria thriving in mulch, fighting for control of a slaver, recognizing no limits, no prohibitions, a ruthless, lackluster contest with a single rule: winner takes all.

I wonder if there are as many bones in the human body as there are stays, halyards, and braces on a ship. Papa may lose his Guineaman because of me. If the blue monkey hadn't interfered I expect the middle passage would have been completed without major incident: the cargo would have been landed safely, the blacks dispersed, the sailors paid, the captain thanked, and my father satisfied with the profits. I would receive his generous praise, my salary would be his commending words, along with admiration from my brother and sister and my mother's tender, appreciative touch as she trimmed my hair. I should have plenty to do advising prospective seamen on navigation and slave trading, transcribing my observations on the habits of Africans, entertaining my schoolmates with an account of my adventures.

Instead we will return as fugitives — if we return at all — only to be scorned by slaveholders, reviled by philanthropists. I should like to promote peace and undo the effects of my actions, I should like to put my papa at ease again. What have I done to hinder him? Why, I have been a squealer, I have passed secrets among various members of this assembly — I might as well unlock the slaves' fetters and be done with it.

I didn't intend to provoke such animosity. If I were given a second chance I would know better than to warn anyone about a hidden plot. Now I can only take cover in the thicket of rigging line and watch the hardwood planks of this ship warp and swell from the tension as the incompatible elements inside my father's head prepare for riot. I don't mean to compare Papa to a distant Jove who watches his warriors battle for rights to the land — Papa is more like Virgil, who had to imagine a Camilla and an Arruns before he could set them against each other. The man who provides for us has created us. Then why should I blame myself for the hostilities if I am just another aspect of my father's ambition? Because I have disrupted the balance — a difficult task, considering the poise of the *Charles Beauchamp*, but I have done it — I have introduced the possibility of mutiny on board this slaver, which is like whispering "suicide" to an abject man.

Mother, don't bother to counsel me on my duty, don't try to instill courtesy in me any longer. In order to survive on this Guineaman I will no longer act the little gentleman, instead I will be as brutal as the famous pirate De Soto and as unforgiving as the judge who ordered his execution.

I only ask, Papa, that you point your gun toward the sky instead of at me when I begin to howl, aim at the full moon, fire, and put out that lascivious eye that drives men insane. And do not despair if your son has returned to you without his agreeable disposition, do not regret your decision to send me to Africa, for wicked Tom will prove useful. He will drown kittens and hang a dog by its neck, he will beat the neighbor's spoiled child, he will clench a dagger between his teeth and climb into your enemy's bedroom and stab a sleeping man, he will do your bloody business because Tom has acquired a terrible disease and there's only one possible cure — to pass on the affliction. I am the villain of this story. I shall strike down anyone who stands in my way, and if any fellow dares to raise his hand against me I shall seize that hand, hold it flat upon the tabletop, and pound it to pulp with a rifle butt, so disown me if you prefer, I've learned how to survive without anyone's help. If I must I'll join a mercenary troop, I'll contract myself to a foreign war, and I'll fight for pleasure, not for any principle.

Go ahead, condemn me, but listen first: I have found my chameleon.

Before I explain further I want someone to tell me whether an animal without a voice is capable of feeling pain. In a book I've borrowed from the captain's stateroom, the author contends that an insect does not have the capacity to suffer, and he offered these examples: a longlegs spider will continue to jaunt about after a boy has plucked off half of its whiskery limbs, and a horsefly shorn of a wing will hop impishly across the sand. A bee without an abdomen will sip from a honeysuckle blossom. And a disemboweled ant will march in a file with its comrades.

I am not sure I should believe everything I read, but the author makes a convincing case that insects feel no pain. If it is true, then they are lucky hellions. I would like to sleep soundly tonight and wake up tomorrow in the form of a tough cockchafer. For pain is a fellow's weakness, and fear of pain turns a man into a coward, and though we may be more refined than the bug we are also more vulnerable. As soon as a species inherits a voice it inherits agony.

Yet we cannot know for certain whether the humble bee or termite feels anything from its wounds. I would like to think that as long as there is silence, there is peace, but I cannot be sure. I would like proof that my chameleon did not suffer — I do not mind so much that it is dead, but I want to be assured that it expired painlessly. I have no clues. No witnesses. I did not see the blade fall, I did not hear the crush of vertebrae, I did not see blood spurt from the stem. I saw only the remains.

The captain himself escorted me to his stateroom, and I glanced immediately down upon the table, where there is usually one surprise or another awaiting me. Today the surprise was my chameleon — it resembled a water-color lizard, illusory, lifeless, and without thinking I reached for it, ran my index finger along the dry, corrugated skin. When I lifted it by the tail the head remained upon the tabletop. I had found my chameleon, yes, but in two pieces, and

the captain had meant to tease me by positioning the parts
so the reptile looked intact.

I wanted to hide from the captain, for I had been assigned
as the keeper of his rare possession. And I wanted to kill
whoever had mauled the lizard. But I couldn't act upon
either impulse. The captain had ushered me from the upper
deck in order to humiliate me, and I could only clutch the
reptile's tail and try to blink back my tears.

Of course we weren't alone — the captain had invited the
fanatics and charlatans of this brig to watch me as I grieved.
The missionary, the messboy, and Peter Gray were crowded
around the table when I arrived. The captain doesn't understand that because of him, these three have lost what they
valued most, he doesn't understand that they despise him,
and since they are the only ones on board incapable of mutiny — or so the captain thinks — he likes to keep them near.

"Tom?"

"Sir?" I placed the body back upon the table, aligned
the head to the torso with a taxidermist's care so that the
chameleon appeared whole again.

"Have you, or have you not, been making frequent trips
to the hold?"

I mumbled yes, he ordered me to speak up. "I have, sir!"

"And did I, or did I not, charge you to look after the
specimen, the reverend's generous gift?"

"You did."

"I see no need for further deliberation. The chameleon
was found below, Tom, as you see it now. What got into
your head, boy? God knows how a saintly woman like your
mother could have harbored such a monster in her womb."

Would it have done any good to protest the accusation?
I could have cited only my affection for the creature as
defense, and even if I insisted that I loved the chameleon
too much ever to hurt it I had no proof of that love. The
only proof was laid out upon the table, like a strip of bacon
ready to be fried.

I responded with a futile, knavish outburst — instead of denying the crime I attempted to accuse the jurors, I pointed my finger, the finger still tingling from the texture of the reptile's coat, at the three heath witches, and said, "Here are your traitors, Captain. They hate you with a passion. They think of nothing but how to destroy you."

I fell abruptly silent, and the only sound was the captain's even breathing, so much like a chameleon trapped inside a jar. I expected violence to follow my announcement, a pistol to explode, a knife to plunge between ribs, but no one moved. It was as if I had struck a porcelain doll with a hatchet, and the blade, not the doll, had shattered. I was astonished by my own attempt to betray these three with whom, in various degrees, I had been intimate. I was the one who had turned my father's commercial scheme into a travesty. I have wanted to muddle the order on board this ship ever since I lost sight of America, and if mutiny will be the culmination, then I should be considered not only a witness but the inspiration. I am the enemy, a Janus looking behind and ahead.

The captain had already decided whom to distrust. A reasonable, taciturn magistrate today, he asked, "But why should they want to turn against me?"

"Sir, throw them into the bilge!" I said shrilly, keeping my gaze fixed on the body of the chameleon, which seemed like an unfinished model that would spring magically to life as soon as its maker breathed on it.

"But what would they gain?" prompted the captain, pouring a brandy, offering the cup to me.

I refused it with a frantic gesture. "They'd gain the satisfaction of revenge, Captain, revenge, sir, for you have a debt to pay, or so they think, you've deprived them of their dreams. Isn't that so, Piper? Wouldn't you have preferred to remain Jack Carvee's second? And you, Reverend, every day you leave your mission farther behind, now you've lost your function, Reverend, you won't be baptizing a continent in the near future. And you, Peter Gray — but do you all know what is hiding beneath that cap and pea jacket? May I tell Piper and the reverend the truth, sir?" Without waiting for permission I burst out, "Peter Gray isn't what you think! Someday this same sailor will be giving suck to a babe, Reverend, that's right, Peter Gray isn't what you think!" I pressed on, my hands clenched into white-knuckled mallets. "Piper, the spirit you saw on board was flesh and blood, not a ghost but a conniver, not a dead wife but a girl as real as you and me." I did not wait for a response, or perhaps I had an intuition that there would be no response, that the secret of Peter Gray was commonly known, at least among this tribunal. So I turned, finally, to the instigator herself, I met the eyes I thought would be red with anger but were, instead, impassive.

I knew right away that nothing I said would make an impression. The audience in the stateroom was deaf to me, as we, perhaps, are deaf to the moth beating its wings inside a bottle. Perhaps the moth rails at its captors, curses us, though we hear only the soft thumping of its wings striking the glass. And perhaps the old woman — the one who told my sister that if she stood in a meadow at dawn and listened closely, she would hear the dew evaporating and the flowers sighing — perhaps that beggar woman wasn't insane after all. The author of this study of entomology proposes that God has spared the insect from pain, but I wonder if in fact God has simply spared man from the annoying sound of suffering. So many miniature lives, so many deaths.

"You, Peter Gray, have lost your man merchant. The captain ordered him tossed overboard and now you would like to do the same to the captain. Sir, believe what I am saying," I implored. "You knew that she meant to join the mulatto in Africa, and you made sure she had no opportunity to desert during the loading. But she stole the key from me, she escaped the night we brought the slaves aboard, and she was watching from the crosstree when the men attacked Quince. I wonder, Captain, if you had intended all along to have him shredded, if you had commissioned Yellow Will beforehand to leap without provocation. And maybe you only feigned indignation, maybe you were glad to see the poor brute die. Not that I care what you intended, sir, I am sure you keep the welfare of the crew in mind, but consider how she must hate you now. She has crossed an ocean to watch you murder her kinsman, the mulatto named Quince; she means to return the favor and do to you what you did to him."

I staggered as the floor tipped slightly. I was intoxicated with a strange thrill from the triple denouncement, though it was obvious I had succeeded in convincing no one. Then, along with the incessant noise of water splitting to let our Guineaman through, I heard a new sound — the tick-tock of a watch that was strung upon a nail. The watch must have been hanging against the beam since I entered the stateroom, but I heard it now for the first time. I waited like a man condemned to hang — no, like a condemned man who has tried to save himself by trading secrets to the enemy.

What do you mean to do with me? I wanted to ask, but the words were strangled in my throat.

"Tom," said the captain quietly, "explain to me why anyone would want to revenge a man who never existed."

Let me sleep, Papa, or prod me awake, but do not leave me in between. I don't know what to believe, whom to mimic or to ignore. "Please, sir, what did you say?"

"A man who never existed, Tom."

"But Quince — ?"

"Was just a word, Tom, nothing more than the sound of the letters."

"You said he would devour me! You said he was the most powerful man merchant of all, and that our success depended on him!"

"We had you spellbound, my young friend. A jest, Tom, but a purposeful jest. I wanted you to know the terms at stake in this business, I wanted you to be aware of the dangers."

"What about you, Peter Gray?" I demanded. "Quince was your reason for boarding this Guineaman, you've spent years in pursuit. Don't try to deny that you had a relative who made himself rich selling human souls. You meant to join him in Africa, maybe you thought you could convert him from his criminal life, or maybe you wanted simply to be near him. Quince — he was the only one who mattered to you."

Her reply was merely a dull, flat, perjuring gaze.

"Reverend, you must admit you spoke of him with terror in your voice. Your chief desire was to destroy him, you couldn't have lied yourself into such a passionate state. And Captain, you assured me that you had been an eyewitness to the ceremony, hundreds and hundreds sacrificed."

But no matter how zealously I begged them to confirm my recollections they remained silent, all of them maintaining that Quince was simply a cleverly devised myth, and a myth could not inspire a man or a woman to mutiny. But neither could a myth leave a stain of blood upon the water.

"Why, Captain, why did you want to keep Peter Gray locked below when the Africans were taken aboard?"

"Tom," the captain said, laughing and mussing my hair indulgently, "don't you see? You're the pride of this ship, it's my job to keep you safe, to entertain you, and to shape you into a man according to your father's wishes."

"And you, Reverend? Is it true? Your devil doesn't exist?"

He stared severely, implacably.

"What about you, Piper? You haven't forgotten Jack Carvee's fate?" I said boldly, my last attempt to salvage the accusation I had made, provoking only a grunt from Piper and a condescending chuckle from the corner of the captain's mouth. The captain has nothing to fear from a stowaway and two fanatics — they are bothersome but harmless, and as loyal as dogs, or so he thinks, a fatal misjudgment. He would be better off distrusting everyone.

"You see, Tom, now you've proven to me that I may count on these three as completely as I count on myself — for they've played their parts convincingly, they've been attending to your upbringing while I've been distracted with other matters, and I am sorry to say that it is you, Tom, who have disappointed me. You don't seem to have followed our example or profited from the lessons."

As he talked my head filled with fragments: hot-air balloons and lakes of blood, barrels of witch hazel, palm wine, fetish ceremonies, arsenic, painters and dressmakers — he wanted me to believe that all had been constructed for the sole purpose of my education, he wanted to assure me that nothing I have heard is true, nothing accurate, to convince me that the entire effort of the Guineaman voyage has been for my interest alone, that I am here to be educated, and all the suffering I have witnessed and the stories told to me were designed to improve my character.

"And the ring hidden in your wardrobe — it was for my benefit?" He nodded with popish solemnity, clasped his hands, rubbed the tips of his forefingers together.

"Tom, I've had enough time to think this matter through," he said at last, plucking a strand of his beard and winding it around the tip of his thumb, "and I still don't understand your motive. You've been keen on provoking me lately. I've always known boys are wicked characters, but I thought you were different, I thought you would treasure the gift."

I felt as though I were looking out from the mirror, trapped in my reflection, unable to speak until the other spoke, unable to move. I have known since I spread my bedding in my own half-deck berth that I was a privileged passenger. I have never denied that education was my reason for riding this slaver, but I have learned to play the game wholeheartedly, I have believed the unbelievable — and nothing else matters — *I have believed.* Now the captain would like to enlighten me, he wants to say, "Lower the curtains, put out the lights," as if a simple command could extinguish us.

"What is it you want, Tom? A book? You showed an interest in my library. Go ahead, choose a title, here, I'll select one for you, this will do as fine as any other." He folded my arms around the volume. "What else can I do for you? Why, I can try to show you right from wrong, I can try to teach you decency." His even, benefactor's façade was finally giving way not to outright fury but to restrained anger; he took a step toward me and I backed away, bumping into the door, clutching the book as a feeble shield now, expecting to be kicked and cuffed, expecting blows.

But the captain devised a more memorable punishment. With one hand he grabbed the head of the reptile, with the other hand he twisted my collar. "Don't make me touch it again," I pleaded, but he held the snout close to my own and said, "Kiss the chameleon, Tom."

No one will steal my experiences from me. I know what I felt. I felt a sharp pain tear through me and I did not cry out, I did not allow a sob to rise from my throat. You would have been proud, Papa, to see your son remain so dignified, you would have been pleased to see how stoically I endured the punishment while the spectators enjoyed my humiliation. I have grown so much wiser, I've reached a pinnacle, and from these heights I can still see faint stains like an oil slick on the water. No one will deny I've made rapid progress, so I tip my cap and thank you, Papa, for submitting me to the trials of a sea voyage, I thank you for forcing me to improve, and Mother, to you I beg softly as I've begged before: *I want to go home, please come and take me home.*

Now my life is unnatural to me, and I must luff the sails, come about, I must rehash the voyage and find another name for myself. I'll be a man of the times, dishonest and skeptical, and when Piper tries to entertain me with lies I will grab his forelock, bring his face close to mine, and say, *I've got better things to do,* and I'll saunter away, past the captain's deserted berth, up through the rear companion-way, and when the missionary man tries to convince me of my guilt I shall tell him I have no interest in the hereafter, and when I see Peter Gray keeping watch from the crosstree I will pelt her with handfuls of sea biscuit, then climb atop the deckhouse roof and watch as Yellow Will and Pharaoh put a rope round the captain's neck and draw him up to the yardarm, and while he is choking Pharaoh will grab his swinging leg and Thresher will chop it off at the knee, then they will shoot him in the breast, cut the rope, and throw him over the starboard rail. I'll watch the blotch of red widen and fade until I see it no more.

Then I will steal a lance and dodge the grasping hands of the lecherous men and leap from the stern into an eggshell tub, paddling furiously with my hands toward the horizon until I have reached the blind slaver. The few survivors still on board will pull me up between the davits, and the ship's navigator will throw his arms around me, praising God for sending an able man. With a spyglass I'll scan the water for the *Charles Beauchamp,* but the metallic surface will be empty, no speck of sail, not even the tip of a mast; the *Charles Beauchamp* will disappear entirely, never to be heard from again.

After the navigator prepares a supper of marrow broth and rice he will lead me to my private berth, identical to my half-deck quarters here except that the tiny portal window will be shattered, still intact but with intricate cobweb fissures obscuring the view. But I will be content to feel the cold, pocked surface of the glass and listen to the sound of the water. The next morning when the navigator asks for my assistance I'll shrug, offer some sort of gentleman's apology to let him know he will have to pilot and dead-reckon by himself. I should think he will have no trouble hoving to; he must be as accustomed to his solitary job as a lighthouse keeper who has tended the lanterns for seventy years.

But I have not been forgotten. Piper brings me dandy funk, which is nearly as good as duff, baked instead of boiled. The missionary brings a copy of the liturgy, Peter Gray brings the companion volume to the book the captain loaned me. They leave their gifts just inside my door and then they scamper off, like children who have come to glimpse a prisoner sentenced to the block.

I need time to recuperate, so I remain in this berth, waiting for the day when my little sister will climb the attic stairs and open the closet door, finding me as she has once before, buried beneath overcoats, curled on the closet floor, where I came to escape my father's wrath.

As soon as the light splashed in I turned over and mumbled drowsily, "Square the main," or a similar nautical command. My sister clapped her hand across her mouth to squelch her shriek, then she seized my arm, yanked me roughly, and said, "Tom, you are dreaming!" with a spatter of laughter, as if sleep and inadvertent fantasy were a hilarious joke.

Fully awake by then, I shooed her away, told her to leave me alone, but I couldn't resist her chocolate button eyes, her pouting lip. So I added, "Don't come back, unless you have come to bring me a holy water sprinkler, and in case you didn't know, a holy water sprinkler is the same as a morning star." She scampered off to fish the heavens for the prize, thinking that I had requested a rare jewel instead of a spiked ball on a chain.

These, then, are my options: to desert by way of the sea and find refuge on a pirate slaver, or to desert by way of my mind and return home. I am not sure which I prefer.

I shall have to delay the decision, though, for even now I hear the captain shouting for a reliable crew to replace the bunglers in his charge. I nibble my sweet dandy funk, prop a hard splinter of dried apple between my teeth, and chew sluggishly, thinking ahead not to my next meal but to the captain's fate. I should like to see his face just before the slaves beat his brains to pulp with their wooden spoons.

He tried to forget the threat of mutiny by humiliating me but the prospect has already wedged itself deep in his thoughts, he continues to insult the men and to keep them scurrying from one duty to another. If a sailor attempts to lean against the rail and daydream about the life he would be leading if he had been born under different circumstances, the captain immediately orders the loiterer up to the yard, assigns him to some grueling and unnecessary task. I suppose once a commander has become convinced that treachery is being plotted behind his back he can't let go of the notion, just as some men can't forget that winter stars are passing overhead during a summer afternoon.

Blank, blank, blank — this is the content of the scenery. The captain believes any unauthorized activity to be merely a camouflage for ingrates and freethinkers, and to ensure his own safety he won't permit the Africans on the upper deck. By depriving them of fresh air and a view of the sky, he is taking away the little reason they have to hope.

I should know about hopelessness, for it has been pressed against my lips, I have suffered a sensation from which I will never recover; even now I feel the chameleon's poison dissolving the ventricles in my heart, and as long as I remain on board this ship my contaminated blood will continue to pulse in a loop from my head to my feet, back to my head, around again, and unless the surgeon has a strong antidote there shall be nothing left of me when we reach New London but a steaming puddle upon my bed.

Meanwhile, the men grouse as men will. All night and all day they wait upon the Guineaman's Caesar while I try different methods of inducing sleep — first I count backward from one thousand, then forward, then for hours I lie like a tamarack board, and then I try to exercise my muscles, wiggling my fingers, my toes, making my thigh muscle taut, I try to exhaust myself with perpetual motion — but still I cannot sleep. It seems I will never sleep again, at least not until the captain finally has his nightmare and the pressure of suspense is relieved. If I could hasten the outcome I would, for it is a terrible thing not to sleep.

Nothing but a cat's paw of wind, nothing but an ordinary day, topsails set, yards braced, nothing unusual.

"Tom?"

"Go away!"

"Tom, listen: meet me at midnight tonight, by the bell."

"I want nothing to do with you and your wretched companions. You are dirty, rude, and unkind, and I shan't soon forgive you for what you've done."

"At midnight, Tom. Goodbye for now."

I don't dream of Neptune like other boys would. I don't have a vision of the sea king standing in my berth, with a toasted shark impaled on the prongs of his trident. Instead I dream of Peter Gray. I am sure if I went up at the designated hour I would find only sea birds, drunken watchmen, and a sleeping crew.

All the while I thought I had been spying on her she had been the more thorough traitor, pretending to confide in me when actually everything she had said, every intimation of love, every gesture and embrace, had been prescribed for my improvement. My father had hoped to make me both clever and virile, so he assigned the captain to tutor me, and the captain enlisted Peter Gray as his assistant.

Papa wasn't satisfied with parables to teach his son right from wrong — he had to finance the fables and cast me in the leading role. But now that this expedition has begun to disintegrate I have nothing to lose, I will orate and flaunt with a green actor's bravado. My lady has asked me to attend her. Well, then, I shall be prompt.

Of course when I found her on deck she was not alone. She and her two conspirators were gathered around an oil lamp, meditating upon the caged flame, and since the rest of the crew had bedded down aft of the tryworks they were blocked from my view, and I from theirs. When Peter Gray motioned me to sit beside her I obliged, squatting with regal indifference, pressing my knuckles into a groove worn in the planks.

She said, "Tom, we're going to give you the honor . . . ," and I looked up at her in confusion. I thought these three cared about me as much as they would value a mongrel dog thrusting its nose in the ashes on the outskirts of Sodom.

"We're going to let you be the one," Peter Gray continued, "to acquire the deckhouse keys. You will steal the keys to the lockers, and we will destroy the instruments."

So she wanted the son of Charles Beauchamp as an accomplice after all. Was this, too, another lesson in gentility, part of my father's scheme? Clearly not — I am no better than a terra cotta figure, hollow and mute, cast off by the captain, who foolishly has come to prefer Peter Gray to me.

I studied her broad, flat nose, then I turned to the wizened missionary. "Reverend, tell me how one man may give freedom to others who are already servants to God," I demanded, and of course he had no reply. So I said to the messboy, "Piper, how many law-abiding seamen have become merciless buccaneers because of the embargo?" I paused, then scoffed, "You probably can't count that high. And you, Peter Gray, I will remind you that the tobacco in your cigars was planted, cultivated, and picked by slaves. But I'm sure you won't admit to hypocrisy." I could have seized the clapper and clanged it hard against the side of the bell and still I wouldn't have shaken these three from their fixed convictions. And though in the stateroom I had tried to implicate them, today they wanted my assistance.

"Why do you think I would agree to help you?"

"Because you're fond of us, Tom, in your own way," said the messboy, old Piper, my shipmate and friend, the gentlest, homeliest messboy I'll ever meet, without the fear of God making his voice an octave higher, here was Piper, as harmless as a goat.

"Piper," I said with nascent hope, "those stories you told me concerning the captain and his wives — they were a lively enough distraction and I'm grateful to you for the entertainment. Useful tales, Piper, I thank you for your time. You've given me insight, and now I understand the mysteries of this Guineaman better than I know myself."

I stopped. With the vessel ploughing so evenly I felt as though I were perched not on the spine of a sea creature but on the outstretched wing of a bird gliding just above the surface of the water. We are lucky to have such easy weather for our middle passage. If I were prone to superstition I might read a portent in the constellations — a promise of good health and prosperity — but I do not think the stars indicate anything but the importance of luck. And luck will change. I would be content to divide my time between floating and scavenging like a stormy petrel rather than to select one of the inane occupations a man must find for himself — medicine or farming or banking or the industry of selling plots, digging graves, building vaults. I have heard about pious Christians who demand not only that the coffins of the deceased be placed so the corpse's feet point east, toward the Mount of Olives, but also that the corpse be smoke-dried, eviscerated, and treated with mineral preservative or some other embalming formula. Indeed, "preservation" is a title that could describe nearly all kinds of employment. Except for mutiny, which has the opposite intention, as the captain knows.

I must decide whether to protect my father's business or to sabotage it. Peter Gray's strength lies in her clever timing. She might have asked earlier for my support, and I would have refused, but since I have no obligation to the captain anymore she stands a chance of enlisting me. On the other hand, she has revealed herself to be a slippery, unreliable friend. Sometimes I feel that I should like to turn my back on the other sex forever. But here, I've digressed from my main concern, so I must pick up where I left off, my address to Piper, who seemed the old Piper revived, yet even as I spoke he cocked his head to glance sideways at me, his lips pursed with a sucking sound, his grin returned.

"Tom," he said, "I only repeat what I've been told."

I snapped, "You don't have to point out that you are just like the others, contracted to shape me into a gentleman. But though you've taken the available ingredients and hashed, sifted, stewed, steeped, boiled, fried, and mangled them, I can still taste what went into the pot. I can sort the facts from your embellishments, if I was keen on doing so. You see, you've never had me fooled. And you," I said, turning to Peter Gray, "the Great Pretender — not for a moment did I mistake your guile for affection." How gratifying it was to assume a superior position. I could have ranted on and proved myself a skeptic, I could have separated the real captain from the false one or Quince from the make-believe character as easily as yolks from their whites. Instead, I cleared my throat, spit a sour clot of mucus into the sea, and told them I would consider their request.

But my indifference was only a paper mask — I know that the ship won't stay intact much longer. The glue my papa stocked is thin, the boards begin to splinter. I shall have to take apart the *Charles Beauchamp* and rebuild it with my own tools. Yes, I have decided: tomorrow I will offer my assistance to Peter Gray, but not because I am devoted to the cause of abolition. My own freedom is my sole concern, and by impeding the middle passage I shall escape from the future my papa has arranged for me. We will retrace our eastward course, and I'll be educated not by his agents but by the cargo of slaves, I will learn their language by listening to tales of crocodiles, warriors, and two-headed birds, and I shan't care whether the facts can be verified, for they won't be constructed for my behalf. I will be a mere visitor, a genuine foreigner, and someday I'll set foot on the continent that you denied me, Papa, I will continue to oblige you and devote myself to my education, but this time round, instead of training to take your place, instead of learning about who I must become, I shall discover all that I am not.

What is sleep, anyway, but death's cousin? I am not the first to point out that there will be plenty of time for sleep in the grave — the poets have said it before me.

There are others who forfeit sleep. These last days Peter Gray has hovered on deck or in the crosstrees, floating like the sluggish wisps of smoke from her cigars, unwilling to keep the captain company at night, unwilling to share his gimbaled bed. So she is not such a steadfast pretender after all and cannot be the mistress of the man she intends to overthrow. I found her above, as I had expected I would. I meant to shrug my promise of allegiance and hurry back to my berth and fall into a deep, contented slumber.

My father has wanted to hear me describe to him man-to-man how a woman's thighs are as soft as damask and how her heart pumps a warm, salty cream. Well, I have tasted woman on my fingertip and even now, with the red

clay strata of dawn visible on the horizon, I can still smell
her. I don't think the fragrance will ever wash away.

I do not think I love her. No, I am certain I do not love
her. But she seems my other half, and I have wanted her
as badly as Narcissus wanted his reflection. When I found
her alone by the bell tonight I immediately began to calculate
how to use her dependency to my advantage. I said, my
voice quaking slightly, "Peter Gray, I will do whatever you
ask if you —" and stopped abruptly, for I couldn't bring
myself to beg a vulgar act from her.

She only laughed, chucked me across the chin, and drew
a plump Havana from her breast pocket; when she touched
a flame to the tip it seemed to me that she raised an eyelid,
revealing her single, glowing Cyclops eye, the same eye that
had trapped me, perused me, scorned me weeks ago, when
I was still unused to the sea.

"The trouble with these is," she said, holding the cigar
as though it were the fragile stem of a champagne glass,
"that it takes half the day to finish one."

She tossed the cigar over the rail, took a step toward
me, and right there on the open deck we began to wrestle
while the iron mast rings clanked and the bald-headed moon
grazed the deck with a lewd light. She ripped open my
shirt, buttons popping like drops of sizzling oil, and I felt
her palms against my bare chest. But now I found myself struggling against her, I resisted the advance as I have
resisted the captain, the missionary, and Brian Piper.
Peter Gray laughed aloud, twisted her wrists free from my
grasp, and reached for my crotch. She pressed her pelvis
against me, licked my earlobe, but even as my breath grew
short my shame increased, for the intimacy was unnatural, she meant to secure my commitment to her cause
once and for all, to assume complete control over my desire.
I heard myself exclaim, "Leave off or I'll scream. Leave
off!"

As long as I ride my father's slaver I refuse to grow up,

that's right, I refuse to take my place along the line, I refuse to be called a man. Let the sailors boast of exploiting the voluptuous Hottentots or the Angolan maidens who have labia down to their knees, let them collect their semen in jars and compare the volume, let them frequent whorehouses from Liverpool to Singapore — I'll have none of it.

This time I was the one who disappeared. With my shirt flapping open I slunk across the deck, ducked through the damp black companionway into my half-deck hole, and hid myself beneath the blanket. I have been trying to peel the skin from my bones ever since.

The mother said softly, "Have a bit of supper, and you'll feel better." The child replied with remarkable courage, "Mother, I will have to wait for the sea to give up her dead before I can drink a cup of your beef tea."

He asked her to shut the door behind her, and when he was alone with his toys again he heard the tumbling sea and felt the stern beneath his feet lift up and up and up; he traced the wrinkles on the face of the miniature wooden figurehead, he saw the scrimshaw sailors pivot and come to life, he saw an officer in the mizzentop point the spyglass west, the sharks and albacores leaped from the throw rug, the petrels, terns, and gulls fluttered out of the wallpaper, the parasitic feather flies hopped off the sea birds and landed on deck. And though it is a fine thing to ride a lively swell the boy could not devote himself wholeheartedly, for the muffled ticking of a clock nearby reminded him that this was only a game. He wondered if the sound was a pendulum knocking, or, more likely, the clang of a hammer and chisel carving a name, dates, and an aphorism in stone. He hoped it would be a witty, unusual summary, pertinent but succinct, for the clap of metal against metal and the cough of the spike chipping the stone was unpleasant. He hoped he would not have to listen forever. He hoped the sound was not, in fact, made by graveyard tools, nor by a pendulum clock, nor even by a nursemaid clicking her tongue against the side of her cheek. He wished the ticking would cease.

Today the captain gave strict orders not to be disturbed. He must have decided that the best medicine for fear is brandy and means to drink himself to safety. If I am lucky he will not wake when I enter the cabin or begin my speech or lift the keys from his coat pocket. The captain, after remaining in exhausting suspense, waiting for mutiny, won't soon be kicking up his heels and frolicking on deck. I think if I stuck my mother's knitting needle between his ribs he would feel nothing. And he won't hear me when I whisper:

Captain, I haven't come to defend myself, and I don't mean to take up your time with my concerns, but I did want you to know, sir, that your effort hasn't been wasted, despite what you think, and though I may have advanced only a fraction I want to tell you how much I appreciate your help. Without your advice I would know nothing about the study of entomology or the law of evolution or the statistics of trade. What I've gained, Captain, is a sense of the world. I have seen how harmony arises from the conflict between opposing powers, I understand why increased returns do not promote higher wages, I know that we are all inclined toward idleness, and I am convinced now that mankind has slid from the crest and is on a downhill spin that can be reversed only by the strongest individuals, men like you, sir, who take responsibility for shifting the continents, remaking cultures, and though one generation must suffer through a middle passage I am certain that the next generation will benefit from the transfer, and though I would like to celebrate the human spirit I have to admit that the sad facts of history attest to our decline.

That's all I wanted to say, and if you will excuse me, sir, I won't disturb you any longer, just let me plump the pillow and pull the sheet to your chin, then I will leave, I will creep backward through the door but first I will slip your keys from the pocket of your coat, please don't bother to wake up, you need your rest, I shan't intrude again.

The tasks that seem most grueling to contemplate inevitably surprise us with their ease. Last night I slipped into the stateroom, stole the keys, and delivered them to Peter Gray, all before the bubble of a three-minute glass could have emptied. But I suffered afterward — the difficulty was not in the theft itself but in the hours of remorse. I returned to my thin mattress and pressed my fists against my eyes to plug my tears, and it was only a matter of minutes before the harpy came for me.

She sank her claws into my shoulders, flapped her heavy wings, rising unsteadily. A strong current caught us, buoyed us through the layer of clouds, and at high altitude she sped forward gracefully. For hours, for days I hung limply thousands of feet above the sea. I do not know when her claws retracted, but at some point in the journey she let go of me and I had to grip the spike legs to keep from plunging, I held on until my fingers went numb. But I did not fall. One moment I was above the clouds, the next I was on board the Guineaman again, everything arranged exactly as it had been when I left, so that the man climbing the shroud was still halfway to the crosstree, the smoke ring from a sailor's pipe hovered an inch above the bowl. Nothing had moved. And still, nothing moved. I was on a model ship inside a bottle.

As I tried to regain my balance I heard the hard, impatient rap of an open hand against the outside of the glass. I looked up and saw my mother looming over me, but instead of a tea tray she held a dead gull by its feet. Suddenly the beak opened and a huge silver eel burst from the bird's mouth, followed by another one, and another, like a string of handkerchiefs pulled from a magician's sleeve.

Now you may be sure this was as discomforting a dream as I have ever had, but the terror came not during the harpy's flight nor with the vision of the eels dripping from the gull — I've seen comparable horrors since I left home. These sights were disturbing, but much worse was the knowledge that I was inventing the scene even as I stood helplessly by.

I hear the Seven Sisters whispering in the sky. Can anyone tell me the hour and the minute of sunset tonight and sunrise tomorrow? What is the position of the sun in the zodiac? What phase will the moon be in on the first of next month? But there is always more to calculate: the date, the day, the month, the length of the orbits of Saturn, Jupiter, Mars, Venus, and the moon.

I have heard of a clock built over a century ago that keeps track of all this information and more. I expect someday a gentleman will be able to carry such a clock in his pocket, a gilded, copper-backed world, a microcosm hooked on a gold chain. Men will adorn themselves not simply with precious stones and metals but with a wealth of information, and the most powerful magnate will be able to answer any question put to him.

The way to incapacitate such a man is not to bind him with hemp but to deprive him of his instruments and then to blindfold him and spin him three times round. Try to locate the donkey's rump now, sir. We have stolen your sense of direction, and when you go above you will find yourself hopelessly lost.

A *Flying Dutchman*, a runaway, my father's pride, a derelict, chimerical ship.

· · ·

The compasses have been dismantled, the charts, sextants, octants, and telescopes have been removed from the deck-houses. We are lost at sea. But no one dares deliver the news to the captain. The men agree: Let him enjoy his last minutes of bliss, let him sleep. It's understood that the sailor who wakes the captain to tell him that the *Charles Beauchamp* has been vandalized will be the first man blamed. Already they suspect each other, as well they should, for they share responsibility. Who has crippled the *Charles Beauchamp?* We all have.

I am glad that the captain continues to sleep and that my father remains thousands of miles away, so neither of them can watch the men lowering the whaleboats from the davits as quietly as wood lice drop from the gill of a toadstool to the ground. The sailors swiftly sort out supplies, tie knives to lanyards strung around their necks, load demijohns of water and sacks of farina, working with mechanical urgency. The men know that when the captain discovers his ship has been handicapped he will wield the cutlass without discretion, and even the most agile of the crew will be hard pressed to escape him. The men assume that a commander intent on murder has the support of God, and it makes no difference that the crew outnumbers him thirty to one. What else to do but desert?

I sit cross-legged on the deckhouse roof and watch as Pharaoh oversees the distribution of the goods, making sure each boat has equal ballast. We are not far from the coast of South America, and I have heard Yellow Will promise the men that they will reach Rio de Janeiro within three days. Well, good luck to them. I shall miss their bawdy songs and crass manners, I shall miss their muscles, their contented belches, their greasy faces. When the canvas isn't bulging with wind a sailor's diaphragm expands with anticipation, so whether or not we have moved forward a few kilometers, a sailor's spirit brings a ship closer to its destination. Without able men busy at the mastheads or at the wheel, the *Charles Beauchamp* will be tossed about by chance winds and currents. Without instruments we cannot dead-reckon, and without the carpenter we won't be able to plot our course by observation, log lines, and estimates.

Though she pretends otherwise, Peter Gray is no different from the rest of her sex — she has taken it upon herself to change our destiny, she has plotted a mutiny but has not planned past the initial upheaval. She can only hang back and watch helplessly as the men make off with our commodities, leaving us with nothing but crumbs, rice, and a few barrels of fresh water. I wish now that I was a man among men, abandoning a doomed slaver, finding pleasure in the simplest things — a pannikin of rum, a shark-meat steak, a woman's plump buttocks, a rude joke. But it is too late, I have committed myself to mutiny and like a fetus in a bottle I shall never be more than my potential.

Who am I? Copper-bolted, lined with white pine, belted with oak, crowned with spruce, with three courses, four sails to a mast, an elliptical stern and rounded bow, stocked with blackfish oil and no biscuits, a captain and no crew, furnished with wooden pallets, one gimbaled bed, two water closets and a dozen buckets, a traveling wheel and no compass, lanterns and a few spoonfuls of oil, outfitted with a starboard gangway and a cutting platform where sailors would have divided the whale carcasses. I am an entrepreneur, built in New London, named after the man who financed me but anonymous during the middle passage, sailing without a national flag, made for one purpose, serving another, I am a devil but a necessary devil, contributing to history, I am a gentleman and a pirate, a statistic, a receptacle, an envelope addressed to America containing a message no one can decipher. I have been left to starve. I am unreal,

an experiment, a foolhardy and failed attempt, I am a farce,
a mistake, a treasured possession. But above all I am a coincidence.

I agreed to take this passage to Africa for the sake of adventure, but now, as the men slide over the horizon's dip, I
must face the fact that adventure has been impossible. Thrill
depends on danger, and though I have been knocked about,
insulted, mistreated, I have been protected, my success en-
sured as long as I remained within the boundaries of my
papa's influence. I went to sea thinking myself the bravest
of fellows, but in truth my comfort and my safety had been
purchased long before I climbed the gangway. My father
must have hoped that this smuggling enterprise would be
just difficult enough so that once I had come halfway I
would not want to retrace my course, and simple enough
so that I would not be easily discouraged.

But now the whaleboats are sailing off and the men shout
from the safe distance, calling goodbye to their very own
Desdemona, goodbye to Fantasy Sue, goodbye forever to
Sable Eve and to all the other black wenches they have
forsaken, farewell to Tom, to Piper, to Reverend T., *adios*
to pretty Peter Gray. With the *Charles Beauchamp* drifting
aimlessly and the first of the Africans emerging from the
forward companionway like rats squeezing through a crevice
in a crumbling wall, I have begun to realize the extent of
my new isolation. Throughout this middle passage I have
been my papa's primary concern; but with the crew sup-
planted by slaves, I am just an unwanted, malignant germ.
Still, I must continue to report, for this is my job, to tell of
fantastic events, to describe for you, Mother, how one woman
has already untied her waistband and plunged the cotton
cloth into a bucket, wringing fresh water over the face of
a child who stands like a fledgling, his mouth open to catch
the drops. Skeletal men squat on their haunches or lean

precariously over the rail or splash themselves with the few inches of brackish water left in the washing tubs, girls massage each other's shoulders, and children with swollen bellies and spidery fingers stare contemptuously at me. I have staked out a refuge in the crosstree, and when I see a boy thrust a bullying fist toward my nest I say a last-minute prayer, asking God to bless my family and forgive me my sins. I shan't be spared for long. I don't know why I haven't yet suffered the usual fate of a white man among hungry savages.

I diminish with the *Charles Beauchamp* — our strength and reason deteriorate, leaving us with parched lips, a smoking firehearth, and blurred hallucinations. I hardly recognize the rigging, the deck and davits and hatchcombs; soon everything will appear entirely new to me, I will reach that highest pitch of delirium when even my hands will seem to belong to someone else.

I may try to treat myself with the medicines left behind by the surgeon — linseed, chamomile, gum arabic, Epsom salts, emetic, bark wine, manna, mustard, and camphor — but I cannot be cured. What's done is done. Now the ship is crowded with images that spring from a sickly mind, and I am surrounded by a language that makes no sense to me, no sense at all. Except for the reverend's sermon, floating on top of the babble like a colorful splotch of grease on water: "Lo, I am with you," he hails in English. "I am with you always, even unto the end of the world," as if the Africans could understand. As if they bothered to listen. As if they needed him.

There are many ways to talk: a poor man extends his open hand, a bride ties a string round her forehead, a guard raises a flag to announce a public execution, a woman washes the feet of her guest, a mourner dresses in black, a landowner builds a stone wall, a queen points her scepter, a horse perks its ears forward, an officer wears gold epaulets, a sailor sends a coin to a woman he met in Mozambique, a dying man will groan, shudder, and fall silent, a doctor will pull a sheet over the corpse's face, a prisoner uses stones to gouge his initials in a dungeon wall. Surely I will find a way to communicate.

The missionary man has already succeeded: though our supply of water won't last a fortnight, our dry beans and rice not much longer, though the women do not have strength enough to lift the children and the men cannot climb a shroud, though we drift aimlessly, without chart or compass, our sails luffing while Peter Gray holds the wheel and Piper tries to show the Africans how to tie a bowline knot but they with their jungle mentality twist the rope into a tangle, though chaos is our condition and we have little reason to hope for improvement, still the reverend pushes through the bracken of wasted human bodies so he may reach the foredeck and ring the bell at every half hour, punctually.

And throughout this day of judgment the captain sleeps greedily, as if rest were the gold he had hoped to acquire. Perhaps he has already decided to take no action at all when he wakes, or perhaps he simply doesn't want to wake. I shouldn't like to see the captain paralyzed; he is troubled enough, and if he cannot stamp and shout his irritation he will soon be gyrating as wildly as a waterspout. Maybe I should prepare him, hint at the changes that have occurred while he was sleeping. Who knows? I might renew his faith in me and convince him that we could benefit from some alternations; he might participate willingly, enjoying the simple luxury of travel, forgetting his contract, his responsibilities, forgetting above all that he has been betrayed by the son of Charles Beauchamp.

"Excuse me, sir, but I've brought your coffee — syrupy, the way you like it — along with biscuits and a slab of fresh pork, the last pound of the last sow, grilled especially for you by Piper. I hope this will revive you, Captain, I thought you would want to splash yourself with sunlight before another night sets in, for though I know how precious rest is to an industrious man like you, I also know that the extra hours lost in sleep can never be recovered, so I thought I'd be the one to wake you, sir, and welcome you into the day."

I spoke in a voice too low to rouse him. I bent closer and studied the curve of his beard, the black threads sewn into his skin. As I watched, another intruder, bolder than me, climbed along the precipice of the captain's ear, struggled through the side-whiskers toward his eye, paused, felt the ridge of the brow with its antennae, then scurried on, and only with this renewed momentum did I think to flick the roach off the captain's forehead, tapping the captain back to consciousness as well.

He grunted, cleared mucus from his throat, and sat upright with a roar. Likely he had been dreaming that hordes of children were descending upon him, their mouths wide, their little eyeteeth filed to sharp fangs. I had come here to wake him, to try to bolster him before he discovered the fact of mutiny, but now I wished I was miles away, huddling in the prow of a whaleboat. His chest heaved, he pressed his fists against his temples, and his knuckles seemed stripped of skin.

"You were dreaming, sir," I said to reassure him, hoping he would be relieved to find himself in the stateroom of the *Charles Beauchamp* rather than chained to a palm tree. "But you're awake now. I've brought your coffee — syrupy, the way . . . ," I recited, only to be silenced by the captain, who pressed his finger to my lips so that I, too, was locked in a sarcophagus. I could not move my legs, I dared not speak. Above us the cacophony of African voices announced the fact, as clear as a written declaration: *Make no mistake, Captain. You are no longer in control.* I felt the blood pulsing in his fingertip, I felt his breath against my neck, I saw my face distorted in the side of the metal cup.

I became the captain. Like him, I slept soundly through half a century, waking into an unfamiliar world where only heirlooms, log books, and legends remained to prove that I ever existed. I had no place here, I did not belong. Crippled. Useless. Nothing to do but wait. Nothing to do but remember the days when healthy men brought fifty-two pounds in Brazil, women forty-one pounds, pirates still ruled the waters off the island of Ascension, every registered sailor could set the mainsail in contrary winds with his eyes closed, and no one complained about the salt beef and biscuits, we were grateful for a spoonful of blackstrap boiled with our coffee, if we were lucky we had a barrel of New England rum, and the Africans were glad to leave their wattled walls, their droughts, their tribal feuds behind.

But, like the captain, I had no wish to find that steaming hot spring which provides a man with a second youth, I would just as soon drink hemlock sap to speed my deterioration, for it was not my stamina I missed but a younger world and the opportunities available, when nothing could stop a man who had strength, wit, and ambition. Now I was no more relevant to history than a garden slug, my element was mud.

Then the moment passed, I belonged to myself again, and instead of bringing the captain useful equipment — the leather-bound telescope or the octant with an ebony frame and ivory scale — I had brought him breakfast. Breakfast in bed. An indulgence, to be sure, but the captain deserves a final luxury, and I wanted to regain his affection. He picked a crumb from his tear duct, wiped his lips with the back of his hand, and swung his feet onto the planks. He shook his head as if to drain his ears of water, then suddenly he pivoted and reclined again, drawing the sheet over his chest.

"I think I shall rest a few minutes longer. You're a good boy, Tom. Bring me a drink and go."

As soon as he had emptied half of the contents of the flask into his mouth, he closed his eyes and by the count of ten had fallen back into a deep slumber, an enviable state. I watched him sleep. He seemed just another instrument, a wooden appendage of the *Charles Beauchamp*, built with augers, pitch ladles, and caulking mallets, designed for a single purpose, and now that he has lost that purpose he has lost all interest in life.

When I grabbed the handle to leave, the door resisted me; I tried to yank it ajar but someone had locked the door from the opposite side with the very set of keys I had stolen from the captain. I tugged and kicked, I shouted at the witch who had done this to me, I damned her, but I was trapped, alone but not alone, buried alive, sharing a coffin with a man who was as good as dead. I hammered my fists against the door until my knuckles cracked and bled.

A grown sea, a furious sea. Our masts strain and crack, the captain's coffee splashes over the brim of the cup, and the tidewater in my veins churns angrily. But at least I have found a pen, a felt blotter, and ink, and I am well enough to write.

It is quiet above. Perhaps the Purrow Bush has called a meeting. I have read about these secret African societies in the book my brother gave me. A Purrow Bush diviner can decide where his tribe should wage war by watching vegetables boil in an iron pot. He will collect odd trinkets — padlocks, gun rods, crucifixes, tea strainers, paper collars,

Belfast cord, and wooden nails — to ward off evil spirits. A Purrow Bush doctor conducts autopsies to see if the body's internal organs have been mutilated by demons, and he will find out whether or not a woman has committed adultery by forcing her to drink a poisonous concoction made from sassy wood bark. A Purrow Bush trumpeter announces a meeting by blowing into a bottle with a hole drilled in the neck. A girl who accidentally intrudes upon a Purrow Bush meeting is put to death. A boy who stumbles upon the forbidden haven is inducted into the society.

I trust that as long as I remain locked inside the captain's suite, they cannot force me to recite their secret oath.

"Tom!"

"Captain, you're awake."

"Of course I am awake. You might as well throw a bucketful of live coals across my face. Now put out that light!"

Obediently, I blew against my cupped hand. The flame folded into itself and died, leaving us in a dim, watery world. There was just enough light seeping in through the water closet portal to outline the captain's profile, with his Medici nose and tightly curled beard, just enough light to give substance to the narrow wedge of table, the bookcase, wardrobe, and sea chest — but not enough to give surfaces distinct colors; even now the interior remains only varying shades of gray, ash-gray, mud-gray, a glossy pewter.

The captain murmurs softly in his sleep, like a mourning dove hidden inside a hedgerow. I stand in the water closet to look out through the salt-crusted window. If it was a clear afternoon and I had access to the navigation locker and could measure the angle of the sun I would be able to calculate the hour. If I had a flat piece of wood, a log line, and a half-minute glass I would be able to determine our speed. If I had a sextant I would obtain our current latitude. But I am no longer interested in current drifts or the swell of the sea. As night sets in it is enough of a task to determine where I end and the air begins.

Hardly enough oxygen in the captain's quarters to fuel both a boy and an officer. By inverting the order of this slaver, by stealing the captain's keys, I have imprisoned myself. I cannot ask, What will become of me? because I have stopped becoming.

But I can continue to pretend, at any rate, and this is the most precious freedom left to me. I pretend that I am in a passenger car on a train, the window blinds drawn, sleet pelting the glass. Or I pretend that I am a woman, black, indomitable, a West African woman standing on the deck of a Guineaman. Or I pretend that I am a sailor, broad-shouldered and tan. I sit on the narrow table and swing my legs, knocking my heels against the wall to mimic a pendulum's tick.

But I cannot forget the captain. I study him hungrily, obsessively, I bend close to him so I can see the curve of his nostrils and feel his breath against my cheek. When he stirs I quickly back away — I do not want to disturb him again. There is no defense against an assassinated man who has come back to life.

I build my own slaver, using the captain's possessions. I fold three of his clean white handkerchiefs in triangles and tie them to pipe stems. I position these in the wooden tub that the captain uses to soak his feet. I sharpen a razor and carefully shear a handful of hair from the captain's scalp. I wind the long strands together and stretch the cords from masts to bulwarks. I set his wheel — which long ago stopped revolving — in the helm, I notch the top spoke so a steerer will be able to determine the position of the rudder in the dead of night. The incense burner serves as the try-works, a paperweight as a glass binnacle case, and the guinea coins inside are needle compasses. I use chips of melted wax as hatchcombs, a cowhide book marker as the gangway, and I construct a cutting platform with matchsticks. I don't need to hang davits or to build a storage room below, for my ship will have no sailors and no cargo.

The last article to be positioned is the chameleon's head, my talisman, an inspiring figurehead pinned to the front rim of the tub. Although the ship is misproportioned — the traveling wheel is taller than the mizzenmast — the sails flutter, droop, and tighten, and when I spin the wheel the tub turns about.

Papa, listen closely: do you hear the women husking the rice? The slow, steady pounding is the sound of your heart. Do you hear the low gabble? The slaves have called a palaver to decide upon our fate. Do you feel the resistance of the water, the force of the wind? Did you ever think that your hired smugglers would desert, the expedition would fail, and your son would turn against you?

I have learned that the man who tends his secrets carefully, disguising his true allegiance, will always have the upper hand. And the man without any loyalty is the most powerful of all. The captain's door will never be unlocked, for Peter Gray must know that despite my size and frailty I am dangerous. As dangerous as any sea-bound flea.

At least there is plenty to do. I inhale, exhale, sip the captain's brandy, visit the water closet, watch daylight grow and fade, watch the captain sleep, yes, I have plenty to do, I drag my model ship across the planks, I read about aphids and carpenter ants, I put on the captain's jacket and admire the square-shouldered bulk of my looking-glass reflection. From time to time the captain groans, grasps wildly at the air, and I rush to him, help him mount the bedpan, and afterward I whistle softly to lull him back to sleep.

Twice he has woken and demanded his brandy, I hold the flask steady while he tips it against his lips and gulps.

I do not know what to tell him when he calls for a drink and the flask is empty.

Once upon a time, my father said, a boy playing truant from school spent the morning dawdling on a rope bridge strung over a sluggish creek. I asked if he had gone to fish or to wade, and Papa said no, he only went to watch the creek flow beneath his feet. I said he was a foolish boy, he would never learn to read, and Papa said that was probably so. But on the particular morning that the young truant sat on the bridge, a strange phenomenon occurred: the invisible thread holding his shadow to him broke, and the dark image drifted downstream among the branches and dead leaves. I asked my father what became of his shadow, and he said, "Why, it was swept out to sea."

Papa, maybe the boy on the rope bridge was you, maybe I am not the first to break off from you and float away. You wanted to make me into your purest reflection, you wanted to impress me with your prowess, so you filled the hold with Africans and claimed them as our property. But you never considered that the connection between a father and his son is as fragile as that between a man and his shadow. If you block the available light you will lose your shadow. I cannot imagine what a man must feel when he looks down, expecting to see himself, and he sees only water.

"Tom, untie me!"

But I remained seated upon the blotter, knocking my heels against the legs of the table. While he was sleeping I tied the man-mountain's feet to the bedpost with a shirt, bound his hands together with boot laces, and strapped a belt across his chest.

"Not until you tell me your plans, sir." I kept my eyes averted for I did not want to meet his furious glare.

"Let me loose!" he insisted, and I said, "No, sir."

When he had struggled against the bonds long enough to realize that his freedom depended upon my consent, he quieted and said gently, "What do you want from me, Tom? Is it a book? You may have any of my books."

"I want to know, Captain, what you mean to do with yourself."

"Why, come here and pinch me, or better yet, untie my hands and I'll pinch you, I'll box your ears, boy, I'll show you what I mean to do!"

I waited until his anger had subsided again. "Sir, now that you've lost command —"

"Lost command, you say? But there's no cause to worry, lad. I've decided to give the blacks free run of the ship, exercise will strengthen them and they will fetch us a better price in Brazil. Now be a decent fellow and untie me."

"I want to know what you've got left, not an unreasonable request, Captain, and if you would deign to tell me . . ."

As I gained courage I glanced up at him. He seemed shrunken now, his lips quivering, his eyelashes sticking when he blinked. A harmless and isolated monster, Beauty's dying beast, and I was handling him as if he were a bull to be castrated and branded.

"What do you want from me, Tom?"

I rushed to him, fell on my knees beside the bed. "Captain, you were in charge of my father's ship, you signed the register and are bound by law to the *Charles Beauchamp*. But there must be a point where Papa ends and we begin. Now they've locked us up together, as though I am as guilty as you, but I am only added ballast and have nothing to do with the trade. Or I have everything to do with it, if you spoke the truth when you told me that this hell has been contrived for my benefit, my benefit alone. But there must be some aspects of the *Charles Beauchamp* that are not my fault, and if you'll admit this, if you'll assure me that a few of my experiences have been authentic, then I'll untie you, sir."

I had reached a hysterical pitch, and now the captain looked up at me with a false, fawning sympathy, gazed past me, and said drowsily, "I see you've built your own little ship, Tom. What a clever boy you are."

Sleep, sir, sleep, while magenta clouds slide west and the new crescent moon hangs just above the horizon and planets appear in the darkening sky. Sleep swaddled in secrecy, Captain, while I dismantle my Guineaman piece by piece, pipe stem by pipe stem. Take back your handkerchiefs, your buttons, take your dead chameleon if you want it, sir, take the candle wax, the paperweights, take your wooden tub — I've got no use for it — take your tacks and thread, take your books, your uniform, take whatever is rightfully yours. No need to move, Captain, I will heap your belongings beside the bed, don't worry, I will return everything, and when I am through I will beat my hands against the wall and cry for help.

"Monkey, be still!"
  "Piper, is that you? Piper, let me out, I beg you."
  "I'm not allowed to do that."
  "Then bring me water and a loaf of bread. I will see that my father rewards you generously," which was not entirely accurate, of course. I will see that Papa rewards him, yes, with a hangman's noose, though given the state of affairs Piper was not in any pressing danger. I will probably be examining the mollusks on the ocean floor before I am looking at my own home, the slate walk, the large white petals from the tulip tree scattered like severed tongues around the yard.
  "Better than that, Tom. I've brought you and the old man a Sabbath banquet, so say your grace, move away from the door, and don't try to exit without permission, Monkey.

I am bringing you your dinner, not your liberty, so stand aside."

"All right, I'm behind the table. I promise I won't try to bolt," a promise I intended to keep, for though I longed to saturate myself with the salt air, to ride aloft in the mizzen-top, to face leeward, to cavort, to twist in the air like a touch-me-not pod bursting at the light pressure of a finger, though I wished terribly to celebrate my youth, to kick and cartwheel and throw biscuit crumbs to the mutton birds, I didn't have the courage to face the Africans. I wondered if they had built thatched huts on deck or if they were busy collecting the scant supplies left behind by the crew. Perhaps they had broken apart the poultry coop and devoured the last hen, raw. Or maybe they had woven fishing nets from stays and halyards and were dining on fresh albacore.

"Piper," I said urgently, as he curled his arm around the door, balancing the tray on his fingertips, "who is handling the ship?"

"You shouldn't need to ask," he said angrily, sliding the tray onto the table. "Trust Him."

"Who?"

"Him! Him!" He jerked his thumb toward the ceiling, snapped his arm out and pulled the door shut.

Trust Him, they tell me, trust the man in charge, trust God, trust an officer, a shipowner, a navigator, a man merchant, it doesn't matter whom you trust, just *trust*, this is the essential rule. And I have refused. I trust no one, not even myself anymore. I surveyed the meager fare — farina, coffee, a glass jar filled with water. It occurred to me that they might very well intend to fatten me, and at the end of the fortnight Piper will plunge a kitchen knife in my gullet and they will bind me to the spit. Well, I will not give them the pleasure of a succulent hock, I will decline their food.

But a guzzle of water, fresh water, now this would be a benign pleasure. I reached for the jar, but as I raised it to

my lips I saw what appeared to be a torn piece of paper
floating on the surface. A smuggled note from Peter Gray,
I thought, too hastily; a closer look revealed the paper to
be nothing but a moth, Piper's moth. With its wings outstretched on the surface of the water, its furry head sloshing
against the glass, the dark leaf veins forming concentric
arcs across the wings, it seemed an extraordinary ornament,
a tiny bat made of wire and silk. Piper's gray moth.

I am trapped in a world where nothing is forgiven, ever.

Somewhere there is an island where flocks of golden plovers
flash like a purseful of coins dumped from the sun, fish
spill out of the waves, turtles drag themselves as slowly as
the shadows grow, robber gulls strut and preen at the edge
of the surf, huge white butterflies with eyes imprinted on
each wing are dashed about by wind currents, and just above
the tide mark a single line of footprints leads toward an
outcropping of rocks. Somewhere there is an island where
a man hobbles around the circumference, searching for
crabs, berries, turtle eggs. A man with a poultice wrapped
around one leg, a poultice made of huge leaves shaped
like goat's hooves. Perhaps the man has already perfected
his magic arts, perhaps he has the power to stir the ocean
and send our ship tumbling against the rocks — the hour
will soon be upon us when the ship will founder and time
will cease.

Mother, if you made a list of commendable attributes and
nailed it to my wall as a reminder, I think I could cultivate
the gentleman inside me. I want to please you, nothing
else. But now I am without direction, without guidance,
no one whispers advice in my ears, no one threatens to
whip me with a lanyard if I disobey. It seems it was another
boy who once wandered the decks of a Guineaman as silently

and audaciously as a cockroach, another boy who listened in amazement to stories of broken-hearted women and who played the part of a mythical giant — a man merchant, an African king and cannibal — another boy who watched instinct propel men to abhorrent acts, another boy labeled Blue Monkey. It seems impossible that I ever wandered freely among the Africans, handing out biscuits and marveling at their disguises. No, I never was that boy. All along I have been a clay figurine, made by a Dahoman potter during his spare time, stored on a shelf in the pantry, just another piece of property gathering dust, without opinions, inanimate, entirely unchanged since the day I was pulled from the kiln. To whom do I belong? I do not know.

But if it is the same to you, Captain, I shall sample the gruel after all, I will let you hover inside your dream, and I might as well eat your portion as well, if you don't mind, for a boy needs nourishment, and what would it matter to me if the Africans grind me to powder and use me to spice their soup, since I feel nothing, know nothing, remember nothing? A tripart blue monkey locked in a cabinet, somebody's embarrassment, a misbegotten purchase.

And a cold, gluey porridge this, Piper's Sabbath feast — leftovers from a middle passage that was never completed. I will finish the brandy, Captain, and tomorrow I will uncork the last bottle you have hidden inside your sea chest, and if you wake I will share the brandy with you, and the water, too. In fact, you may have the moth water all to yourself, and the next day, well, we shall hope that the messboy prepares another banquet to sustain us while the ship revolves in ever smaller circles, canting to starboard, approaching the center of the funnel, Neptune's mouth.

My brother used to have a passion for trapping wild animals, teasing them with a pole, and then releasing them. One day in early spring, when there were still patches of snow

on the ground, I found a trap he had set months earlier
and forgotten. The snare was nestled in a swampy groove
between grass clumps, and a thin membrane of ice covered
the wooden jaws, which had long ago snapped closed around
the front paw of a raccoon. The raccoon was gone, but
the paw, nothing but two twig bones, broken claws, and
tufts of frozen fur, remained. I wondered if the trapped
animal had been some lucky fox's feast. But there were no
traces of the carcass left so I concluded that the raccoon
must have bitten off its own limb and escaped alive. As I
bent down to examine the rotted paw, my breath misting
in the damp, silent cold, my fingers stiffening, I found myself
listening with a raccoon's ears. I could not conceive of the
pain, but I could listen, and I heard the sound of cartilage
ripping, fangs sawing through bone, a steady, relentless
chewing, the tongue clicking, the low, chirping cry, I heard
the raccoon biting through the tiny ligaments, the calcium
casing, into the marrow.

I listened to a similar sound in these quarters today —
the sound of a man dreaming. I heard the captain's nightmare as clearly as I once heard a raccoon chewing off its
paw.

In the woods I could leap up and run away, stamping
through the crust of ice covering shallow pools, drowning
out the noise. Here, there is no way out. Except, perhaps,
through the shuttered skylight. This morning I pulled the
sea chest to the center of the floor, climbed up, and pounded
my bruised knuckles against a slat. The two nails securing
the narrow board gave easily, and with another thrust I
forced the end up and moved it aside, creating a large trian-
gular opening. I pushed my head into the gabled interior
of the skylight, where before the mutiny our compasses
had been installed, illuminated day and night by sperm oil
lamps. Now the wooden stand was empty, the instruments
gone.

From this position I could see only the awning between

the deckhouses and just a splinter of sky. I could not see
the wheel, the helmsman, or anyone else. It seemed that I
had entered a void, a barren place, I had broken out of
my sepulcher into a deserted churchyard. I had long since
been assumed deceased. And now I had peeled off my cere-
cloth, opened my grave, and reached the surface of the
land of ancestors, the land of the dead.

But then I heard, with abrupt clarity, the sounds of children coughing, sails fluttering, and the reverend preaching,
instructing his congregation to keep themselves in the love
of God, to snatch their brethren from the fire, to resist
corruption. A futile speech, his English meant nothing to
the Africans. And why did the reverend think he could
convert them when they were busy preparing offerings for
their own gods in thanks for their liberation? Likely I would
be the first sacrifice — a blue monkey slaughtered on the
altar.

The missionary man needs less messianic zeal and a more
persuasive voice, like the New England preacher who travels
from town to town with his own circus caravan, igniting
the faith, replacing the people's general apathy with an urgent desire to serve the Lord. I remember that on the day
my father took my brother and me to hear the preacher
there were crab apples spilled across the road, and I enjoyed
rolling toe to heel, splitting the pea-sized fruits beneath
my shoes. Though we arrived ten minutes prior to the posted
starting time, a large crowd had already assembled around
the canopied bandstand, where, my brother reported, a jug-
gler was throwing flaming batons in the air. I asked Papa
to lift me onto his shoulders but he said no, it wouldn't be
proper, so I had to stare at the rear pockets of trousers,
the flounces attached *à disposition* to dresses, the printed
cotton, moiré silk, white muslin, I had to remain in this
forest of Sunday vestments while the preacher mounted
the platform to tell us how he had come to know God.

"Sir, I was once like you, with a modest fortune, a parcel

of fertile land," he began, and I imagined he was pointing directly at Papa. "I thought I had everything I wanted, I thought I was content, until a voice came to me and said, 'Webster Ross, you won't be content until you get rid of your money.' And I said, 'Lord, I worked hard and now I mean to enjoy my wealth,' and the voice said, 'Don't deceive yourself.' I asked the Lord to give me time to cogitate upon the matter, and the Lord commanded me to paint all the windows of my house black and to put out the lamps and sit in the dark until I had made a decision. I could have stayed there a day or a year and a day, I don't know how long it took before I changed my mind but you see me now before you, you see for yourself that I have changed my mind and changed my life. Indigent in material goods, yes, but I am the richest man among you, and I have come to ask you to give up your miserly hoards, to wake to everlasting life, to free yourself from contempt as I have done, save yourself now and you shall be rewarded on Judgment Day. Paint your windows black, ladies and gentlemen, remain in the eternal night until you decide whether your gold is enough to make you happy."

He continued in this manner, warning the populace, presenting himself as the ideal, and though I couldn't see him I took his message to heart. I decided I would renounce my inheritance; I hoped Papa would distribute his money among the poor.

But Papa did not even wait to drop a coin in the top hat the clowns were passing. As we walked away from the gathering I kept my eyes downcast, and Papa asked me why I was so sullen.

"Because," I said, "I am ashamed to be seen as your son in public."

Instead of slapping me, Papa told me to perk up, and he led us toward the riverbank where the roaming preacher's caravan was parked. Though the performers were still at the service on the green, the horses tethered in a nearby grove, Papa entered Webster Ross's carriage without permission, and he ordered my brother and me to do the same. We obeyed, my brother more eagerly, and I heard him exclaim in wonder as I raised my foot to the iron grill step. I poked my head in to find not the grim, Spartan interior of an apostle's carriage but a lavish salon, with red velvet walls, moose antlers made into candelabras, silver tea trays, and china vases — the aristocratic refuge of a fraud. How my father laughed at me, I shall never forget.

You would have laughed today, Papa, if you had seen me in such an awkward position, like a cat with its head stuck inside an empty fishbowl. As I struggled to pull myself down again I caught sight of a child leaning against the case, a naked toddler pinching the tip of her tongue between her fingers. She stared with a blank, uncomprehending expression, her eyelids and cheeks piebald from dried salt, while I pleaded silently, begged the little sprite to help me.

The ancient Greeks called it the divine. In Provence it is *lou Prègo-Diéu*. The English know it as the praying mantis.

Mother, if you ever chance upon her perched on a rock, her green linen wings spread out in a long train, her sawtoothed forelegs raised toward heaven, her head erect, like a scepter's diamond, do not stop to examine her. If you are ever wandering the countryside and you find her with her arms lifted in supplication, do not stop to marvel at the lime-green, slender creature, do not approach her because she will trap you with her Medusa eyes, she will cling motionless to the rock summit as you amble toward her, and when you are near enough to reach out and stroke her wings with your finger, she will convulse and rear up on her hind legs. And though you will be fully aware that you are standing face to face with your own death, you will not back away while there is time, nor run, nor turn, nor cover your head with your arms; instead, you will step through the grass toward the shale throne because the mantis is your destiny, you cannot escape, the mantis has been waiting just for you.

And Papa, never throw yourself into the arms of the queen, for during the long embrace she will suddenly plunge her snout into your neck, she will tear off pieces of your flesh, she will suck the marrow from your bones, she will gorge upon you, devour your limbs, your head, your abdomen, every part of you except for your wings, at least she will spare your wings. And there you have it: the closest possible union, a conjugal feast. When she has rested sufficiently she will gather sprigs of thyme and secrete a spongy cradle with her eggs inside, proof that the strongest love is a begetting love. Please don't dismiss this warning as a boy's indulgent fancy — once the mantis locks you with her eyes you will be unable to resist. She appears so delicate, so pure, an emblem of piety, but her legs are in truth the implements of death, an executioner's blades, Papa, so do not let yourself be seduced. A mantis has indefatigable power. We don't stand a chance against her.

I should know, for I have witnessed a victim plodding straight toward her mandibles, I have watched a man confront her face to face and give himself up without a struggle. The captain has disappeared into the belly of the mantis: no one will ever hear from him again.

So many species, so many peculiar traits, but the mantis is by far the most spectacular of all, glorious and monstrous at once, with a grip so resolute, such arms, such granite arms. I shall never forgive my father for trusting me to the captain, who has provided a thorough education in the most essential subjects: jealousy, bombast, ruthlessness, lechery. Papa thought him a fine example of an officer and hoped I would acquire his courage and pride, but he must have realized that the commander of the *Charles Beauchamp* had only one objective — to forget. The captain was a fugi-

tive, haunted by his own ignoble past, a man who had destroyed everything he ever loved.

No one warned me that as soon as I untied him the captain
would guzzle an entire pint without stopping for air, then
throw the bottle to the floor, his deep, labored respiration
would slow and stop altogether, his face would turn the
color of swamp water. Fixed melancholia. No one said that
I would blot his brow with a damp rag and climb onto the
pallet and let him hold me because this was all he wanted —
to clutch a forgiving lover — that I would try to coddle him,
to urge him to breathe for me, but he would refuse. As
his stiffened body relaxed and his pulse grew faint I, too,
would feel languid, entirely safe.

The captain helped to end the spell of my insomnia and
I finally slept, Mother, in the captain's arms, for how long
I do not know, long enough for my hair and fingernails to
grow, for beads of mold to collect on the wings of the moth,
for the captain's blood to freeze in his veins, so that when
I finally did wake I was not able to escape from the tireless
embrace, I was trapped, Papa, pressed between the captain
and his dream bride, the only woman he ever desired, a
woman who did not exist, a deadly, imaginary beauty who
alone had the power to free the captain from himself.

He has been traveling in one direction. Perhaps my father
appointed him commander for this reason: a man driven
by impossible love is capable of unspeakable cruelty.

I thought I would have to remain in his clasp until my
own death released me. But when I raised my eyes I saw
in the gap left by the loosened slat the same tot who had
spied me in the skylight case — she was pressing her face
against the glass, flattening her nose, staring down without
curiosity or interest, as if she had been waiting for me to
act, to transform, to rip open the captain's arms, as if she
had grown bored and was about to turn away and go off
in search of a more enthralling exhibit, so I drew in a lungful

of oxygen and bellowed with all my might, an incoherent wail, a cry to rouse the dead.

No, not loud enough.

Stern all, bury your dart to the hitches, search for the artery, kill, cut in, try the blubber, bail the case, clean up, and stow. As simple as that.

Life. Life everywhere, propped on the rail, in the crosstrees and tops, life dozing, life scratching its crotch, life beating slowly on an overturned wooden tub, life inside the nostrils of children, life in the voices carried by the wind, life crowded on deck and wandering below, searching for hidden jugs of water and spilled grains of rice, life trembling with hunger, life venting into wash basins, life spitting blood, dull-eyed life, persistent life, life sharpening hatchet blades and tugging a line, life wedged between drooping stalks of bodies, life searching the horizon for help, life blessed and blessing, life longing, life waiting, life wasting away.

It was Peter Gray who finally entered the stateroom and released me from the coil of the captain's arms. Now I may wander where I please. I am a bystander, a spectator to life's little scenes, to this festival of sorts. The Africans have found meat, an ample amount — everyone, even the children, will have at least a minced spoonful. They gather around the tryworks and take turns stirring the broth in the iron pots while the messboy examines the carcass, traces the course with a cutting spade, complaining because the blade isn't sharp enough and it will be a bloody business.

I push myself to the front of the crowd, and though they must shift to make room for me, no one pays me any attention — they have food and I am just another hungry mouth, a child nobody wants, left to my own devices. I position myself by the stove so I can see the head, his blue-veined eyelids like tarnished coppers placed discreetly to hide his soul from view, his crooked teeth forcing his lips open into a mocking grin. I watch as one man slides the iron bar across the door, another man stuffs the oven cavity with kindling — brittle rope, straw hats, linen rags, whatever other paraphernalia they have collected. The flame licks out and I find myself thinking of the old woman who tried to convince my sister that the body is a servant to the mind and persuaded her to put her hand in the fire. My sister returned home, sobbing, her skin blistered and charred; of course Papa showed no mercy and ordered the hag to be exiled from the neighborhood, I don't know where she went. My sister sleeps with one white glove on, but her skin remains discolored, and she insists on washing her damaged hand every hour during the day, as if she believed that she could scrub off the outer crust and uncover tender, pearly-white, unscarred flesh.

As I look upon the flame I understand why my sister was so easily fooled — the fire seems as harmless as a rainbow inside a cascade's mist, as inviting, as miraculous, and I wish I could throw myself into it and feel instead of searing pain a tepid, soothing warmth, I wish I could swim in the colors and escape uninjured, but I can do no more than scrape the grooves between the bricks with my nails, loop my fingers through the ring riveted to the side of the hearth, and rock on my heels, throwing my head backward, exposing my throat, staring up at these cannibals, who chatter peacefully among themselves as if today's fare were no different from the usual. I make believe that I am already inside the flame, drenched, rollicking in the fire. I swing back and forth around the iron ring, and my eyes focus on one woman's face.

With a wild animal's glistening hunger she studies the carcass on the block. I recall that she is the one the sailors named Mad Sable Eve, the one strapped daily to the speculum unis. Her skin parched and loose, the whites of her eyes streaked with red, still she vigorously circles the stiff thigh with her palm, rubbing vegetable butter into the flesh. For a few hours hunger has been waylaid — though the wind blows us aimlessly about and the fresh water is fast being depleted, Brian Piper and the Africans prepare a feast, a barbarous feast.

I turn to watch the messboy as he outlines the path where the incisions will be made — across the abdomen, up each side of the torso to the collarbone, then across the waist, dividing the body horizontally. What will he do with the head? If it were the head of a sperm whale we could use the precious white brain liquid as fuel for our lamps — the profit from pure spermaceti contained inside a whale's skull has been known to pay the entire cost of a voyage. But not this time, the yield would be small, the expenses have been high.

Piper might as well have sewn another face over his own, so expressionless he remains as he prepares to carve, only a vague furrow along the bridge of his nose to indicate his unease as he gets ready to dice the flesh into choice pieces. The captain has provided us with the means to survive at least another week, another week to wait for help, another week of sunrises, days to spend lounging on the mizzentop and nights to spend dreaming of home.

I would rather die. I cannot stand to take part in the butchery, I could never swallow the broth. What with life so tenuous and I at the height of my youth, I must not waste a moment, no need to rest with the end pressing in. I will find Peter Gray and beg her to save the captain from this humiliation, I will offer myself, my own entrails and flesh, they may quarter me, wrap the parts in palm leaves, and roast me at their leisure, for I am still a child and haven't yet earned a monument, while the captain deserves the high-

est honors, if not for his qualities, then for the losses he
has suffered and the pain he has endured throughout his
career.

I call out her name as I push my way through the thin,
perspiring stalks. She does not answer. Perhaps she refused
to wait for the journey to end and hurried on ahead of us,
brave soul, to test the route. But how shall I manage without
her? Who will comfort me?

"Peter Gray!" I cry joyfully when I finally discover her
sitting against the steering gear barrel. She does not glance
up. She is too busy admiring the shape of her instep, coddling
her bare foot. As I approach I can see she is trying to take
out a splinter buried in her heel, pinching folds of skin
together, so absorbed in the operation that she seems to
think herself completely alone.

I squat in front of her, wordlessly I push her fingers away
and with my own I massage the calloused skin, press my
thumbnail against the embedded sliver. I do not glance up
at her, I do not care what she thinks of me. With my other
thumb I work the needle toward the surface, catch the exposed tip between my nails, and slide it out. I do not bother
to display the trophy. I flick the splinter over my shoulder
and squeeze her heel to make sure the extraction is complete.
A bead of blood oozes from the puncture, a tiny scarlet
bubble, like a spark blown from the stove, a drop of pastel
color. As it begins to dribble toward her heel I raise her
foot, I do not know what I intend, but I lift her foot and
press my lips against the wound, I do not understand why,
I draw my tongue across the toughened skin, I do not know
what I want, but I taste the brine, the deck varnish and
tar. She remains motionless — nothing else matters but
this — she does not pull away. She permits me to lower
her foot and examine it again. The wound is moist, licked
clean, only a red welt to show where the splinter had been
embedded, and when I finally look up at her I see not the

expression of contempt I expect, nor disgust, nor impatience,
I see only my confusion mirrored in her dark eyes. We
cannot believe that our games have led to this.

Voices, old tales, a tick-tock of syllables, a newly invented
world, not mine, I've got no right to it, not anymore, I am
a minor figure, here to wander among the ruins and gather
souvenirs. I cannot see with their eyes, I cannot imagine
so thoroughly, but I can listen to the conversations, I understand nothing but I can watch them sprinkle salt into the
tryworks pot and chant their harvest hymns. If they could
shake the captain awake and thank him for his sacrifice, I
suppose they would. They delay the act with their prepara-
tory rituals, their songs, prayers, mimicry, and dances —
only the drummer indicates that the broth will soon be ready
for the meat, his palms slapping faster and faster against
the bottom of the wooden tub.

I must keep reminding myself that I am no more responsible for this middle passage than I am for the yellow fever
that in 1830 nearly turned the H.M.S. *Eden* into a ghost
ship or for the executions on board the brig *Kentucky* or
for the slaves suffocated in the *Progresso*'s hold in 1842. I
am no more responsible for the condition of this ship than
I am for any other Guinea voyage. I have been a passenger,
a mere witness recording a historical event, now I am baggage
left behind, surviving on small kindnesses — a sip of water,
a scrap of biscuit, and soon a cup of thin, well-seasoned
broth, which I will accept gratefully, for I have reached
that point where nothing, absolutely nothing, matters more
than survival.

Peter Gray, the only able sailor on this vessel, steers us
about and tries to snag the wind inside the canvas, to no
avail. We are broken, the damage is irreparable, and when
the men tug weakly on the rigging lines the halyards snap,
the hemp has become brittle as hair, and the masts, frail

as bamboo pipes, begin to crack, as if the ship were designed to do exactly this — to disintegrate between two continents, like the island of Atlantis. Unless we are rescued soon we have no chance.

The missionary man orates from his pulpit, reminding us that life is everlasting, the women handle the meat with infinite tenderness while Piper sharpens his cutting spade, and I close my eyes, wishing that a shoreline would appear in the distance. I blink, squinting hopefully across the empty, rumpled surface.

There is no help in sight. If I had a spyglass I could survey the universe with more confidence, but even without any lens I remind myself that emptiness is an illusion, life thrives continually in miniature and far away, and if only we had the eyes of a falcon and a jackal's ears we wouldn't be afraid of solitude, for there would be no expanse so wide that we couldn't see to the opposite side, no pure silence, and a man would not have to hold conversations with himself. We would have evidence enough that we are never alone, a fine thing to have evidence. But what does it matter to the rest of the population whether or not we have passed by? The wake dissolves, nothing to show, the thread attached to the yards is pulled, the masts collapse, and the square-rigged model sailing ship slides out through the neck of the bottle.

Another trick, another secret, and an empty bottle to smash upon a flat rock, Papa, which has been your reserve plan if the original failed, you mean to let us disappear without a trace, no reason to hold an inquiry if no ship named *Charles Beauchamp* ever sailed from New London to the Gulf of Guinea, no need to file a claim for the loss if the authorities ask you about the nature of your cargo, the quantities, the value. Let the *Charles Beauchamp* capsize in the next squall, and explain to the neighbors that your son Tom ran away from home last March, you haven't heard from him since, and Mother, for the sake of the family's reputation, forget the truth, tell my brother and sister to do the same. The world must not know that the *Charles Beauchamp* is adrift, without captain and crew, with a woman at the helm, seventy fugitive slaves, a zealot, a messboy, and a blue monkey — Papa's rampant ambition, and now his most closely guarded secret, his shame.

But we cannot disappear. One way or another we will draw attention to ourselves and Papa will have to confess that he, Charles Beauchamp, did equip and finance a Guineaman, did appoint a captain, did assign his son to a private berth, did authorize the illegal shipment, did give permission to cut, to mutilate, to drown any insubordinates, did stand helplessly by while his vision went off course and spun out of control, did order the ship to be built with rags, thread, and tobacco pipes, did mean to disown the *Charles Beauchamp* if it ever foundered, did mean to disown his son as well, to shrug off the dream, to forget the middle passage as he would forget last Sunday's game of croquet, to erase us, to deny us, to pretend that we were nothing more than an intention.

But we will shout, *Long live the Charles Beauchamp!* until my father admits that we belong to him. So I warn you, Papa, to prepare for our return, don't try to block out the pandemonium by burying your head in the duck down pillow, for we will make ourselves heard, first with a distant clatter, like the sound of thousands of gypsy moths gorging upon the leaves, then as a rumbling applause. We will gather our strength with the help of a potent bullion, and Piper has indicated that he will save the delicacy for last, an excellent cordial indeed; he will roast the heart, glaze it with blackstrap, then slice paper-thin tournedos. I will eat piously, reverently, paying the highest honors to the dead and replenishing myself, for the most important thing is to survive, and though you will try to convince yourself that we never existed I promise we will survive until the end of time. You, the embarrassed sponsor, would want to exterminate us by forgetting us, would want to insist that the *Charles Beauchamp* has remained inside a bottle all along. But though this might well be true I still maintain that we have sailed west to east, east to west, west to the center of nowhere. It makes little difference to us whether or not the journey can be measured in real nautical miles — we have suffered, this is adequate proof, we have suffered because of one man's ambition, borne his suspicions, his rages, his fears.

But now, at last, we are propelled by our own need to return to West Africa, where the women can plait their hair again and dress in muslin, the men can hunt civet cats and antelope, they will rebuild their thatched huts and drive stakes into the ground to mark the boundaries of their land.

Until then, we must keep the *Charles Beauchamp* afloat and learn to use the wind to our best advantage; our common aspiration to endure must compensate for the lack of skill, and while the Africans sanctify the meat I place my foot upon a ratline and climb to a crosstree platform and scout the horizon ahead, *nothing*, behind, *nothing*. Below me, black-fish oil, spilled across the deck.

Someday the land to the east will rise like Piper's giant fish, slap its tail upon the surface of the water, and swim slowly toward us. And while we wait for it we will bask in the fading sunlight, comforted by the gentle listing of the ship, the breeze, the water gurgling around the hull. How grateful I would be if the sun never set, the earth stopped revolving, the heat continued to drench our eyelids, and by and by a few seeds started to bounce against the canvas, stray seeds tossed about by the air currents, soon a whirlwind of seeds brushing softly against my skin, filling my mouth with cottony flakes when I yawn. I would not care if the cloud was soon dense enough to obscure the sun, and though in this blizzard I would not be able to see the deck or the ocean below, I would scrape the sticky floss from my tongue and announce, *Land!* as if I could already see the sheen of

dew coating cattail stems, smell the fragrance of fruit moldering in the grass, taste sour rose-hip tea. Even though the
top of the masts would be hidden I would call out again,
Land! as though this were the name of a friend I had found
wandering in the storm, and I would swing onto the shroud
while the bouyant seeds swirled as weightlessly as vapor,
clotting my throat, stinging my eyes, I would descend reck-
lessly, because even if the ship careened and my foot slipped
off the tarred ratline I would fall into the feathery drifts
already blanketing the people crowded on deck, I would
sink ever so slowly, until I was completely submerged.